on a
SOMEDAY

**Center Point
Large Print**

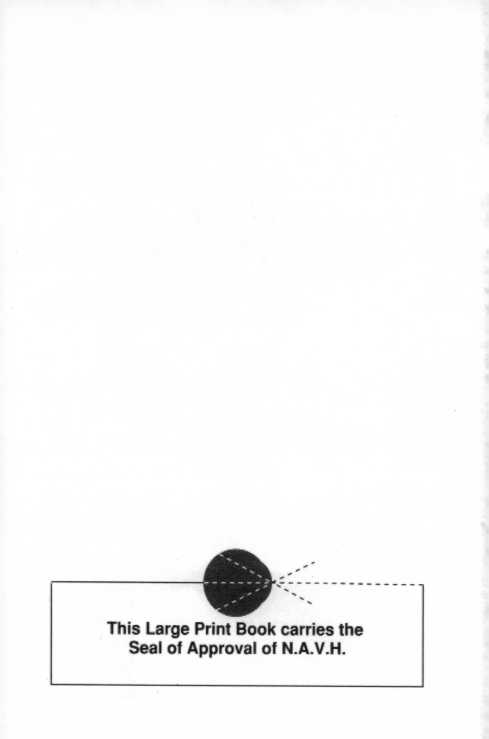

**This Large Print Book carries the
Seal of Approval of N.A.V.H.**

on a SOMEDAY

ROXANNE HENKE

CENTER POINT PUBLISHING
THORNDIKE, MAINE

ISBN: 978-1-60285-524-3

Library of Congress Cataloging-in-Publication Data

Henke, Roxanne, 1953-
  On a someday / Roxanne Henke.
      p. cm.
  ISBN 978-1-60285-524-3 (library binding : alk. paper)
  1. Women authors--Fiction. 2. Large type books. I. Title.

PS3608.E55O5 2009b
813'.6--dc22

2009010664

Grow old along with me! The best is yet to be, the last of life, for which the first was made. Our times are in his hand who saith, "A whole I planned, youth shows but half; Trust God: See all, nor be afraid!"

ROBERT BROWNING

He gives strength to the weary and increases the power of the weak. Even youths grow tired and weary, and young men stumble and fall; but those who hope in the Lord will renew their strength. They will soar on wings like eagles; they will run and not grow weary, they will walk and not be faint.

ISAIAH 40:29-31

For Lorren

Dreams . . .

I turned onto my side and smiled across the pillow at my new husband.

He smiled back and reached for my hand.

"Someday we're going to go to Paris," he said.

"And Switzerland."

"London?"

I nodded. "There too."

Still holding hands, we both rolled onto our backs and spoke our dreams into the moonlight slipping into our bedroom.

"Someday," he said, "I'm going to restore an old car. The one I didn't get to have in high school."

"And someday," I said, "I'm going to teach at a college and maybe write a book. I don't know what it will be about, but . . ."

"I'll read it," he said, squeezing my hand.

"And I'll ride in your car."

PROLOGUE

Claire

A low hum rose from the women sitting in the rows and rows of chairs as I paced at the back of the large hotel ballroom. It was time for the program to begin, and all I could think about was how far away I was from where I *should* be.

"I'm so honored to once again be introducing our keynote speaker for tonight." The woman who had picked me up from the airport looked up from the microphone and smiled at me in the back of the room.

I gave her a little wave to let her know I'd heard. What was her name? Out of habit, I rubbed my fingers across my heavy necklace, fingered my earrings, and glanced at the thick, gold bracelet on my wrist. Everything was in place . . . except my train of thought.

My eyes flicked to my purse tucked under a corner of my book table. My cell phone was in there, a potential time bomb waiting in my message in-box.

An hour. In one hour I'll be done. Then I can check the rest of my messages.

The woman at the podium hardly looked at her notes. "Ms. Westin's first book, *The Friendship Factor*, quickly rose to the top of the bestseller

11

lists across the country. She has appeared on the *Today* show and *Good Morning America* and has been invited to share her message to women's groups around the country. Her Friendship Factor workshops are sold out almost before the tickets go on sale."

Miss Speaker looked down at her notes and gave a chuckle into the microphone. "Let's put it this way," she went on, "if I stood here and told you all of our presenter's accomplishments, we'd be here all night. You know her name as well as I do. So please join me in giving a warm welcome tooooo . . ."

There was an orchestrated pause as I began striding toward the front of the ballroom.

"Here she is, ladies, everyone's best friend, the Friendship Doctor . . . Claire Westin!"

"Goodness," I said, stepping behind the podium and arranging the notes I'd already placed there. "Linda made it sound like I know what I'm doing."

Right on cue they laughed.

I pressed a smile onto my lips and slowly turned my head from one side of the auditorium to the other, pretending I could actually *see* the people in front of me.

What was I doing here? I should be back in Carlton. Of course, I was supposed to be here, too. Two places at the same time. Impossible. I looked at the notes in front of me. I knew what they said.

I'd repeated the words hundreds of times, and yet right now I couldn't remember even the first one.

Focus. I closed my eyes for one, brief second. *Oh, Lord. Help me.*

Okay. There. I remembered. For the next sixty minutes I would be the person they thought I was. *Claire Westin, Friendship Doctor.* And then . . . ? I'd have to figure that out later.

My amplified voice carried through the large room. "Ladies, are you living the life you want?"

The laughter quieted as my audience took in the question. Words I knew would make them think. Start examining their lives. Their relationships. Were they living the life they imagined? Only they could know.

As for my answer to that question?

The only answer I could come up with was . . . *no.*

THREE YEARS EARLIER: WHAT A DIFFERENCE A DAY MAKES . . .

Claire

"So, you see, class . . ." I turned from the diagram I'd made on the whiteboard at the front of the classroom and pointed at my scribbling. "Social interactions—connections—have been vital to the development of society in all cultures throughout time."

"Professor Westin?"

13

My eyes scanned the large classroom to find the voice. There were a lot of familiar faces in this sophomore level class, students who'd taken Contemporary Social Problems 101 and followed it up with Contemporary Sociology 201. I couldn't help but feel I'd done something right by having so many returning students. The downside was the familiarity they felt with each other, and with me, their instructor. Some nights I had to scramble to squeeze my lecture in between all their chatter. Now, where was that question coming from? Ah, Sadie, her hand in the air. She walked the fine line between inquisitive student and brownnoser. I could always count on her for a response. "Yes?"

"Then you're saying it's not *what* you know, it's *who* you know?"

"Good observation."

Before I could follow up, Mark Jonas jumped right in. "What she's saying is that frat parties are a symbol of upper-level society in action."

The class burst out laughing. I couldn't help myself; I did, too. Leave it to Mark to extrapolate my caveman-like diagram into a justification for partying half the week. And since this was a Thursday night class I had a good guess where he'd be headed as soon as I wrapped up this lecture. I looked at the large clock on the classroom wall. Time to call it a night and get everyone home . . . including me.

Still smiling, I pointed my black felt-tip marker at Mark. "You're a genius, Mr. Jonas. Let's hope you apply that upper-level thinking to your term paper." There was a collective groan throughout the classroom. "Yes, this is your reminder. The final will be in two weeks. Your end-of-term paper will be due by the end of next week's Thursday night class." I put my marker onto the top of the long, island counter that served as a desk for this lecture hall and rubbed my hands together as if I'd been using chalk. "See you Tuesday night."

Notebooks closed. Feet scraped and shuffled. A low buzz of conversation followed the students out of the auditorium. I stifled a yawn. This was one of the larger lecture classes I taught, and not my favorite simply because it was a night class. Maybe I was getting too old for this. Spending two nights a week, not to mention my several weekday sessions, with a bunch of eighteen-, nineteen-, and twenty-year-olds put me in my place. Middle-aged. Upper-middle aged. At fifty-one there were other ways I'd rather spend my evenings, although I knew if I'd spent this night at home my role wouldn't be all that different. Jim and I were empty-nesters, but that didn't mean I was completely done with parenting, yet. Our two older boys were out of the house and far from home, but the phone rang often enough that it sometimes seemed the boys lived right next door. Drew had flown the farthest from our nest,

15

elbowing his way to New York and a job as a loan officer at a bank in New York City. Reed, two years younger than his brother at twenty-eight, was busy drawing commercial buildings at an architecture firm in Minneapolis. My guys weren't twins, but being barely two years apart in age and looking like a matched set of brown-haired, brown-eyed bookends, they were often mistaken for each other when they lived in Carlton. Back in their college days, they would've been prime study subjects if I ever wanted to write a paper on the dynamics of female attention regarding the young, male species. I had no doubt both of my young men were still gaining their fair share of female attention in their new home territories.

I smiled to myself as I tamped a stack of class notes into a neat pile, remembering how our daughter, Kaylee, couldn't quite fathom what all those young women saw in her two older brothers. Back then her brothers were nothing more than teasing tormentors, but she did grasp the fact that some of their guy friends were pretty darn cute. In fact, Kaylee had married one of them last year. Brad Keller. She'd turned twenty-four a month ago, old enough to give me hope I might have a grandchild one of these days, but between her job in Social Services and being back in grad school to get her master's degree, I wasn't holding my breath for a baby announcement anytime soon.

If Kaylee was going to announce anything, it would be that she'd finished the draft of her thesis and was counting on me to proof it for her. Which reminded me—not only would I have her paper to critique, I'd also have a mega-stack of end-of-term papers to grade in a week's time. She and I had developed a tag-team sort of approach when it came to her grad school writing. She wrote. I critiqued. She rewrote, while I worked on my own creative-writing project.

Which was another reason I would have rather spent the evening at home. I'd made some good progress on my personal-writing assignment. Maybe when I got home I'd have a little mental energy left to add a page or two to my manuscript. With a final tap of my notes on the countertop, I slipped them into a file folder and then turned to erase my diagram from the whiteboard. I wasn't the only professor who used this classroom. I glanced again at the clock on the wall. The book I'd been working on for the past two years . . . well, make that three . . . four . . . could it really be *five* years since I'd started on my grand idea? . . . was always at the edge of my to-do list. I made a pact with myself—if Kaylee hadn't e-mailed me her thesis to look over, I'd get to work on my writing. No more procrastinating.

Publish or perish, the academic threat that hung over all professors, kept me constantly on my toes when it came to my work for the university, but this project I was working on in my spare time had nothing to do with scholarship and everything to do with my heart. The scant amount of attention I'd given my dream idea these past busy years didn't mean I'd given up pursuing it. I wasn't a mathematician, but I didn't have to be a whiz to know three kids, a dog, a husband with a career as busy—busier—than mine, and me teaching full time as an adjunct professor added up to a hectic life. Instead of beating myself up for not making any progress on my book, I should be—

"Professor Westin?"

I about jumped out of my skin at the unexpected voice. I'd thought I was alone in the lecture hall with my thoughts. I clapped a hand over my heart, trying to keep it inside. "Oh! You scared me."

"Sorry." Sadie ducked her head in apology. "I didn't mean to . . ."

"That's okay. It's good to get my heart rate up. Now I won't have to go jogging." I smiled. "What's up?"

"Uh . . ." She pulled a small sheaf of papers from the backpack hanging off her arm. "I, uh, was wondering if you'd have time to look over my final paper? I just want to make sure I'm on the right track?" She talked in questions. The kind of unsure, lack-of-confidence manner that plagued so many students I saw. If only there were a way to teach these young people more than sociology. A way to let them know there was a whole social network around them, ready to support them if they'd only reach out.

Well, it seemed Sadie was reaching out to me right now. The time clock that had been ticking off the remaining minutes of my evening came to a stop. My project was going to have to wait. Again. After all, the book I was working on was nothing but pie-in-the-sky. A pipe dream I had no way of knowing would ever turn into something more. I was a professor first. Dreams came . . . ? Well, not *now,* anyway.

I reached for the papers Sadie was holding. "Let me take a look."

She breathed a small sigh of relief. "Thank you?"

Call me magnanimous. I certainly didn't have time to preview all my students' term papers. But considering Sadie was the only one who'd asked, I was willing to oblige. Besides, if I was honest with myself, I'd admit the idea of heading home and diving into my side project at this time of night wasn't all that motivating. I'd put things off this long; another night . . . or two . . . or three . . . wouldn't make an iota of difference. I'd get to it . . . someday.

I skimmed the first two pages of Sadie's paper. There were no obvious typos or grammar problems. Her subject was interesting and one of the many I'd recommended in the class syllabus. To gauge the content of the paper, I'd have to read the whole thing without Sadie's watchful eye monitoring my every blink or frown. And I'd do that *next* week, when the paper was due. "This looks fine." I held the paper her way.

"I can leave it with you?"

It was a good thing Sadie didn't write the way she spoke. Reading a term paper of nothing but questions would be almost as annoying as listening to a conversation peppered with them.

"That won't be necessary." I placed the term paper on the counter in front of her and blinked my dry eyes. Going home and climbing into bed was the more-likely next step of my night. "It looks to me as if you've got a good grasp of the material. I'll look forward to reading your paper when you turn it in next week."

"I could leave it with you now?"

That's all I'd need, one lone term paper floating around with my class notes and papers. A recipe for misplacing it, for sure. I preferred tackling my students' papers in one grand marathon of grading. Of course, I couldn't get through more than sixty term papers in a night. But in a week of focused concentration, I could easily separate the good from the not-so-great, as well as point my finger to the papers that more than likely came right off the Internet. From what I'd seen of Sadie's paper and her past performance in my class, she didn't need to worry. Her paper would be near the top of the grading scale.

I held back a tired sigh as I nudged Sadie's paper her way. "Next week will be soon enough. Here's a trick I've learned about writing papers . . ."

Sadie's eyebrows lifted. She was all ears. Make that all eyebrows. If only all my students were so eager.

"I've learned that if I write something and then let it sit for a few days, when I get back to it I see the words in a whole new light."

Don't you mean if you let the words sit for weeks . . . months . . . we're talking years here . . . ?

If only my brain was as inspired when I tried to work on my project, as when it came to chastising myself for *not* working on it. What was that old saying? Those who can't *do* . . . teach. Something like that. Whatever. It was only a reminder that I wasn't making any progress in what I was attempting to do. Well then, I'd better *teach.*

I pushed the chiding aside and concentrated on the student in front of me. "Sadie, if you wait until Monday and then sit down with this paper and reread it, I think you'll be able to be your own judge of how good it is, or where it might need a little work."

"Really?" For once an appropriate question.

"Really. You're a good student. Learn to trust your instincts."

Sadie smiled. "Thanks."

I cocked my ear. Had she really ended a sentence with a plain-old *period?* I decided to take this small victory and run with it. I tucked my class notes into the crook of my arm, ready to head home. "See you Tuesday."

"Tuesday?" She was back at it. Fingernails on the chalkboard of my inner critic.

Just possibly I was getting too old to do this job. Or maybe I was just too tired. Either way, I needed to get home and get my head on a pillow. So much for my good intentions of working on my project. I started up the aisle of the classroom, Sadie at my side. We were about to push through the double doors that led to the sidewalk and then the vast parking lot, when I remembered, "My purse!"

I twirled on my heel. My car keys were in my purse. My purse was on the floor behind the lecture counter.

"Go on," I urged Sadie as she paused politely in the doorway. More brownnose points, no doubt.

"You don't mind?"

I had a wild idea of pairing Sadie up with Mark Jonas. She really could use a small dose of his charisma, and I really needed a break from her non-question-questions. "No, no. Go." I was already halfway back down the sloped aisle.

"Okay, bye?"

My back was to her. I gave in to the urge and bit my tongue in a way that didn't hurt but made me feel childish . . . and better. "Bye." I hoped she couldn't tell my teeth were clenched.

As the door clunked closed behind Sadie I hurried down the aisle to the lecture counter. Sure enough, there was my overflowing purse on the floor. I bent down to get it. At the same time I heard the noisy classroom door clank open. Don't tell me Sadie had returned with more questions. I was tempted to duck behind the counter and stay there. Night classes were long enough without students who thought nothing of staying up until the wee hours biding their time with a professor who needed twice as much sleep as they did. I might as well get this over with.

I stood up. "Sadie? Was there—"

"Claire?" My husband, Jim, stood at the top of the slanted aisle.

"Jim? What are you . . ." I took a step toward him and then stopped. In all the years I'd been teaching at the university never once had Jim come to my classroom. He'd been in my office in the Humanities building only a handful of times. There was no reason for him to be here.

"Claire." Jim was walking my way, his face an unreadable worry. "Oh, Claire." He reached for me and pulled me into his arms.

"Jim. What?" My voice was muffled as he held me tightly against his chest. Confused, I let him hug me for a long moment, then my pounding heart took over and I pushed my way out of his arms. "What?" I asked again.

Jim rubbed a hand across his face. "It's your mom."

"My mom?" The only image I could conjure up was of her sitting in her favorite chair with a ball of yarn at her side and a set of knitting needles in her hands.

"Your mom . . . She—" Jim pulled in a long breath and then blew it out. "She . . . died."

"Died?" It was as if I'd never heard the word. Didn't know its meaning.

Jim nodded. "Your dad called. She had a heart attack while they were watching TV. One second she was laughing at something on the program they were watching, the next, he said, she slumped over and was . . . gone."

"When? Where are they? She? Him?" I didn't know what I was saying. My mom and dad lived in the house I'd grown up in, in a grand old section of Carlton. Well, as grand and old as it could get in North Dakota. They'd talked of downsizing for years, but my brother, sister, and I had talked them out of it. The only place I could imagine my mom was at their house.

Jim pulled me close once more and cupped his warm hand around the back of my head. As he filled me in on the details, he rocked gently, as if the motion would comfort both of us. "Your dad called from the hospital. The ambulance took her there, but he said he already knew she was gone. The funeral home is coming to pick up her—" There was a catch in Jim's throat. He cleared it. "To pick up *her.*"

Body. That was the word he didn't say. My heart did a misstep as it tried to do what my mom's couldn't anymore.

Jim released his hold on me and stood with his hands on my shoulders. "I told your dad I would come get you and we'd meet him at the hospital. He rode with the ambulance."

"Has anyone called Kathy or Gary?" Neither of my siblings lived in Carlton. It would take Kathy several hours to drive here from Minneapolis, and Gary would more than likely fly in from Denver. How could my brain so quickly wrap itself around this news and logically plan what came next, when my feet felt as though a thick carpet had been yanked from beneath me?

My husband scrubbed his fingers against the slight stubble lining his jaw. "I don't know. Your dad called and asked for you and then told me what happened. I didn't think to ask about Kathy and Gary. We'd better get to the hospital. This could be a long night."

It *had* been a long night. A longer week. A blur of hours and days. A haze of activity that seemed to blunt emotions waiting for release. Picking up Gary from the airport. Trying to follow Kathy's instructions as she arrived and took over . . . once the bossy older sister, always the bossy older sister.

As the "baby" of my siblings, I'd learned to take a backseat when it came to the opinions of my older brother and sister. I sat silently holding dad's hand as they made arrangements at the funeral home and church. I politely accepted casseroles, Jell-O salads, and banana bread from well-meaning friends and neighbors as they stopped by Mom and Dad's house to offer condolences. Make that *Dad's* house. Through it all my dad managed to walk through the days with hardly a tear. My fearless dad was no different faced with this tragedy than when his own mother died twenty years ago. Stoic was the word that came to mind. Maybe his age, seventy-seven, gave him perspective. He'd certainly seen more loss in his life than I had in my fifty-one years.

I tried to be as strong, but I cried when I called my teaching assistant to fill in for my Tuesday night class. My voice clogged when I called the head of the Humanities Department and asked to cancel my 101 class that met on Monday and Wednesday. I said I'd be able to make it for the Thursday night session—after all, my personal life didn't mean much to my students. They were counting on next Thursday as review time for the final test the next week. If there was such a thing as a good time to die, my mother had picked it. The spring semester would be over in another week. I could stumble my way through a handful of classes. Grading end-of-term papers would be a good diversion. As a lawyer, Gary would take care of the legal matters. And then, once Kathy returned to Minneapolis to tie up some loose ends, she would return to Carlton and we would help my dad sort through Mom's things.

Mom's funeral held a combination of grief and the celebration of a life well-lived. Drew, Reed, and Kaylee found time to write up a list of favorite memories of their grandmother that they delivered as a threesome. They had the congregation laughing one second, wiping tears the next. My mom would have been proud.

In the midst of our sadness, Gary managed to tip his lawyer's hat, mentioning Mom's will, which understandably left everything to Dad, and dropping the hint that we might want to think about helping Dad downsize. "Maybe he'd like to move to an apartment," Gary suggested as if he had no ties whatsoever to the home where we'd all grown up.

His suggestion came much too soon and for once I was glad when Kathy spoke up and informed Gary that she and I would see to it that Dad had all the help he'd need. If there was an apartment in Dad's future, it wouldn't happen during Kathy's watch.

"See you in a couple weeks." Kathy's eyes filled with tears as she gave me a quick hug. The task that lay ahead of us, sorting through our mother's belongings, might be almost as difficult as the days we'd just been through.

• • •

"This part won't be so hard." Kathy stood in front of the open doors on Mom's side of the closet with her hands on her hips. "I'm thinking we can give all of Mom's clothes to a thrift store."

All of them? To a thrift store? "Don't you want—"

Kathy held up a hand. "Don't start, Claire. If we start going through each of these pieces one by one, we'll never get through this."

"But some of her things have hardly been worn."

"Are you going to wear them?"

She had a point. But her sureness grated. I reached around Kathy and pulled an almost-new brown sweater from a hanger. "Maybe," I said, slipping into the cozy cardigan. It was a poor substitute for my mother's arms, but I wouldn't tell that to Kathy.

"Grab one of those bags and let's get started." She pointed to the bright yellow box of trash bags she'd found beneath the kitchen sink.

I couldn't help but think Mom had no idea when she'd bought the box of garbage bags that in a few short weeks they would hold almost every item of clothing she owned. Well, except for this sweater. I pulled one of the black bags from the thick roll and fumbled at the compressed end until it opened. "The least we can do is fold them nicely."

Kathy shot me one of her *looks*. "Of course,

what did you think? That I'd just throw her things in there as if they were—"

Now it was my turn to hold up a hand. "Don't start."

I blinked back the tears in my eyes as I pulled a handful of hangers from the closet and began folding blouses. *Busy* was better than arguing. Or crying. I'd done enough of that these past couple weeks.

Taking things out of the closet a couple items at a time wasn't getting us anywhere. I grabbed an armful of clothes and made my way to the other side of the queen-sized bed my mom and dad had shared for fifty-seven years. The mattress had probably been changed a few times over the years, but from the looks of it, it was due for replacement again. Knowing Mom, she'd make do with it as long as possible. Or, I corrected myself, she *would* have. I could almost see her waving a hand at Dad. *"It's still perfectly good, Ronald."* How long would it take before I quit thinking my mom was still here?

I dropped the bundle of clothes onto the bed and listened to the inner voice I'd inherited from my mother. *This is a perfectly good dress. And look at this blouse. I wore it for Claire's birthday dinner. Someone will get a lot of wear out of this.*

I had no doubt they would, but I prayed I wouldn't bump into whoever happened to buy it off the thrift store rack. Seeing someone else walking around in these all-too-familiar clothes would be more than I could bear.

"Look at this." Kathy held up a maroon, shirt-waist dress. Her wrinkled nose told me what she thought about it. "Did you ever tell her this went out of style thirty years ago?" She laughed as she loosely folded the dress and tossed it into the bag.

Me . . . Mom's clothes police. Right. I bit my tongue and turned to my stack of clothes. Kathy wasn't the daughter who'd lived in the same town as her parents all these years. She wasn't the one who often accompanied Mom on a shopping trip to the mall. I'd learned a long time ago our mother had her own taste in clothes and it was best if I, for the most part, kept my opinions to myself. We got along a lot better that way. It would be too easy to lash out at Kathy. To tell her about the times her strong opinions came right through the phone line and left our mother near tears. Now wasn't the time to say things I might regret. Things my mother would never bring up herself.

It's okay, Claire. You know Kathy. It was as if Mom were still here, trying to smooth things between my older sister and me. I watched as Kathy hurriedly folded a sweater, a pair of pants, another blouse and tossed them aside as if they belonged to a stranger . . . not our mother. I opened my mouth. There were some things that *had* to be said. Before I could speak I stopped myself. The job we were doing was weighted with emotion. Who was I to judge Kathy's method of getting through this trying time?

I concentrated on my pile of clothes. Went back for more. The only sound in the room was an occasional sigh from Kathy. She left no secret how she felt about our mother's out-of-date wardrobe. A rattle from a hanger tossed into the middle of the bed served as punctuation for her sighs.

"How are you girls coming along?" Dad stood in the doorway of the bedroom. Was it my eyes, or did he not stand quite as tall as he had a month ago?

"Almost done," Kathy said, sounding as satisfied as if we'd cleaned out a moldy corner of the basement instead of our mother's clothes closet.

I crossed the room and wrapped my arms around my dad. "This is hard," I said.

His breath caught in his chest as he held me close. He cleared his throat. "Well, it had to be done." Dad released his hold on me and stepped into the room. His bedroom . . . a room without Mom. Who was I to complain about things being hard?

Kathy tossed the last of the garments into a bag and tied the top tightly. "Done." She stood straight, her hands on her hips. "What's next?"

Like this was some sort of clean-'em-up, move-'em-out assembly line.

Dad stood in the room, surveying the bags of clothes on the floor, the empty hangers on the bed, and the one side of his closet that was completely bare. "I don't—I didn't—"

There was nothing to say. Blinking back my own tears, I pretended to look at my watch. "It's almost lunch time. We should think about getting something to eat."

"Great idea," Kathy chimed in as if she was starving. "I'm so tired of funeral food. Let's run out for something. Let me go wash my hands and then we'll go."

As usual, Kathy left no room for debate.

Behind my closed lids I rolled my eyes at Kathy's dramatics. It had been not quite a month since Mom's funeral. True, Dad still had a couple well-meaning casseroles in the freezer, but it wasn't as if we'd been eating stale cookies the whole week Kathy had been here. I'd been doing most of the cooking, at my house, for my sister and Dad. I was an expert with my trusty slow-cooker, a skill I'd learned from Mom. Jim brought home the ingredients from the store and I popped-in-and-plugged-in so a hot meal would be waiting at the end of a day of teaching . . . or sorting through Mom's belongings.

"Claire?" Dad waited until Kathy left the room, then put his hand on my sleeve and pointed to a plastic tub tucked into a corner on the far side of the dresser. He kept his voice low as if he were talking about a secret treasure. "I was wondering if you could take a look at that stuff in there."

"What is it?"

Dad walked to the tub and tugged it out of the corner. "This is—*was* your mother's stuff. Her *projects* she called them." He pulled the lid from the top and held up a ball of yarn that was attached to a partially finished *something,* knitting needles included. With his other hand he reached in and pulled out what looked to be a very wrinkled pillowcase . . . half-embroidered, a needle with a thick strand of green floss was woven into the fabric. His brows furrowed together as he fumbled through the bin. "You know your mother. She was always starting something or other. I know I won't know what's what."

What-was-what looked to be wrinkled and tangled, half-finished handwork that completely filled the plastic tub.

"Oh, goodness, I—" I was about to say something that would sound exactly like my sister, Kathy. *I think we should throw them out.* The look on my dad's face stopped me. "Sure I'll look at them."

"Let's go." Kathy was back. Her eyes locked onto the ball of yarn in my dad's hand, followed the yarn right into the tub of clutter. "What in the heck is all *that* stuff? It looks like it should go straight to—"

"It's Mom's projects," I interrupted, sounding as if I knew exactly what Kathy was looking at. "I'm going to sort through them. I think it'll be fun."

That last sentence was for my dad. A white lie I hoped God would overlook.

"Lucky you." Kathy lifted her eyebrows at me.

A flame of anger swatted at my breastbone, tears threatened to close my throat. Kathy's calloused attitude might be her way of coping, but it wasn't mine. I felt like lashing out at her, but that would be stooping to her level. Instead I plopped down on the floor beside the bin and spouted off my own set of instructions Kathy-style. "You two go eat. I'm going to stay here."

"Claire—"

I wasn't about to let Kathy talk me into tagging along and listening to more of her loud opinions. "Kathy," I said, hoping I sounded a bit like I was talking down my nose at her, "you'll be leaving in the morning. Dad can see me alone anytime. You two go and have lunch together. I'll be here when you get back."

"But what will you eat?"

"Funeral food," I said, stooping to her level after all.

With a huff loud enough to let me know what she thought of my revision of her plans, Kathy led Dad out of the room.

I waited until I heard the side door close and Dad's car start, then I reached for the phone on the nightstand. Punching in the number of my best friend, I pressed my back against the side of the bed and prayed Julie would pick up.

"Hello-oh." Julie's familiar greeting was all it took to get me started.

I growled into the receiver. "Arrrrggghhh! She's driving me nuts!" I tilted my chin toward the ceiling as if I was howling at the moon. "Help me."

There was a low chuckle on the other end of the line. "Kathy, I take it." Julie knew exactly who I was complaining about.

"You got that right." Already I felt better. Julie and I had been best friends since junior high. She understood perfectly the love-hate relationship I had with my older sister. There was no need to explain that even though at some level I adored my sibling, Kathy knew exactly how to punch my buttons.

"Take a deep breath."

I did as Julie ordered.

"Now, repeat after me . . . only one more day . . . only one more day."

Now it was my turn to laugh. "Yes, Doctor Freud." The famous psychologist had nothing on my friend Julie. As easily as Kathy wound me up, Julie knew how to diffuse the pent-up tension.

"So, how's it going? Are you sure you don't want me to come help?"

I ignored her offer, as I had the multiple times she'd volunteered. "We're almost done," I said as I surveyed the empty closet and the jewelry chest Kathy and I had gone through. I'd had this notion going through our mother's things together would be a job Kathy and I would, in some odd way, enjoy. Not the fact that we were disposing of Mom's belongings, but that we'd be able to share our memories of Mom as we sorted. It hadn't taken more than an hour that first day for me to discover Kathy had no inclination to turn sentimental over our task. She was her usual, bossy self. And Julie was my sounding board.

"How can two people from the same parents be so different?" It wasn't the first time I'd posed the question.

"Maybe they took the wrong baby home from the hospital." One thing I loved about my friend, she didn't let me wallow in my irritation. She was always quick to help me see humor in even the most exasperating situations. "So . . ." There was a hint of amusement in Julie's voice. ". . . who do you suppose was the wrong baby? You or Kathy?"

I burst out laughing. "Thanks, I needed that."

"What time will Kathy leave? Do you want to get a walk in tomorrow?"

I answered in a millisecond. "Yes." Already I was imaging how good it would feel to stride out. To take deep breaths of fresh air. To vent to Julie in person about all the tiny annoyances a visit with my sister unearthed.

"Who do you suppose Kathy will walk with?"

"What?" Julie's question made no sense.

"Claire." Julie sighed into the phone. "You're a

sociologist. Certainly you know you don't have the market cornered on an irritating sibling. I was wondering who Kathy vents to?"

Her question stopped me. "Ha-ha," I said into the phone, but I wasn't laughing. It had honestly never occurred to me I might be just as infuriating to Kathy as she was to me. Duh. Once again, I had to hand it to Julie. She never pulled punches. Never tried to sugarcoat my complaints. Instead she made me look at both sides, even while she made me feel better. No wonder she was my best friend.

"Only one more day." I repeated Julie's mantra. "Only one more day."

"Call me as soon as she leaves tomorrow. I'll have my walking shoes on." No "goodbye." Julie and I both knew when it was time to hang up.

Ah, I felt much better. In the quiet of the empty house I scooted close to the bin of yarn and cotton my dad had asked me to go through. Digging my hands into the jumble, I pulled out the top layer of . . . stuff. Oh, my. Even though almost every image I conjured up of my mother pictured her with some kind of project on her lap, looking at what was now in mine, all her work seemed to have been for . . . nothing. I smoothed my hands over the wrinkled cotton pillowcase. The flowered design was only a third complete. It would be a beautiful and useful piece of bedding . . . but not like this. I rummaged further into the bin and drew out a stiff piece of canvas, a needlepoint project that might have been lovely . . . if it had been done.

I knew better than to suggest to Kathy that *she* might like to finish them. Even the thought of Kathy's reaction made me smile. Kathy had no patience for that sort of thing . . . not even *watching* our mother do the work. *What are you going to* do *with that?* As if all Mom's effort was nothing but a waste of time.

Surveying what Mom had left behind, for once I was ready to admit maybe Kathy had a point. What *would* we do with all this? I fingered through the bin, adding up all the time my mom had devoted to . . . what? Nothing, it seemed.

I'd thought cleaning Mom's closet, folding her clothes and putting them into trash bags, had been hard, but that work hadn't prepared me for this. A tangle of yarn and thread as complicated as the tears I held back. Kaylee had defended her thesis in the midst of the funeral aftermath, ending with a well-deserved, "Job well done." Jim and I had been as joyful as possible considering what had just happened. I'd always thought I would be teary-eyed as I watched Kaylee, my youngest, walk across the college stage and receive her master's diploma, but Mom's death had put things in perspective. Kaylee had worlds ahead of her to conquer. There was no need for tears . . . only smiles. So, then why did the thought of my mother leaving behind all this work, all these dreams unfinished, push me to tears?

I swiped at my eyes with the wrinkled pillow-case. There was nothing to do but throw all this out. I started pushing the remnants of Mom's projects back into the plastic tub. If I hurried I could carry the whole bin out to the alley and dump the contents in a trash can before Kathy and Dad returned. Dad would never have to know what happened to Mom's projects. If he asked, I'd be vague and say I'd *taken care* of it. I scooped the rest of the partially finished items into my arms and topped off the tub. In a few minutes I'd be done. I reached for one last project that had eluded my grasp as the thought occurred.

What about your *unfinished project?*

My hand paused in the air as I looked down at one of my mother's uncompleted knitting projects. *Mine?*

Yes. Yours.

My knack for handcrafts had never materialized, but I knew exactly what project that soft voice was suggesting. The book I'd been dabbling at writing for the past five years. If something were to happen to me, what would Jim, or my kids, or *Kathy* for that matter, think about those two-hundred-some pages of a story with no end? Funny, Julie hadn't kicked me in the *bee-hind* for all the talking I'd done about my book project with nothing to show for my gabbing. My efforts so far had amounted to nothing more than this tub of old yarn.

Suddenly, I knew what to do with this bin of discarded dreams. All Mom's work wouldn't be in vain. I pushed the pillowcase and needlepoint canvas back into the bin. The ends of yarn that hung over the sides, I tipped back in. I had the perfect place for this conglomeration of odds and ends. I knew exactly what to do with it. I got onto my knees and snapped the heavy, blue plastic lid into place.

There. I brushed my hands together as if my project were already almost done. *Oh no,* I wasn't going to turn into some saint and make sure every undone stitch my mother hadn't made was filled in by me. What I was going to do was take this container and set it right beside my computer desk. Every time I had to vacuum around it, or sidestep to my office chair, it would serve as a reminder. There was no one . . . *no one* . . . who could finish my undone project but me.

There would be no more wasted time *wishing* my project complete. No more half-hearted stabs at progress. I pushed myself off the floor and lifted the heavy tub to my waist. Balancing it against my hip I angled my way out of the bedroom, down the hall, and out the door to my car. Steadying the tub against the side of the car, I opened the back door and placed the oversized container on the backseat. This was my reminder.

My awkward, too-big, inconvenient reminder. My mother's efforts would not be in vain. Every day they would prod me on. I would do what she didn't. I would finish my project—my book—and dedicate it to my mother.

Jim

"Here's to winters in Arizona and golfing every day." I lifted a clear plastic punch cup in the direction of Arnie Matthews and tried to look enthused for my burly friend. We'd served together on the Carlton Chamber of Commerce board for the past three years. He'd been talking about selling his vacuum cleaner store and retiring since the day I'd first shook his thick hand. Now that the day had finally arrived, he looked about as happy as a kid with mumps eating a dill pickle.

"Humph." Arnie drained his glass and looked around the store that was set to change hands on Monday. Then he looked into his empty punch cup. "After all these years you'd think they could come up with something better than this."

Arnie's staff had done the expected. A bowl of red punch. A half-eaten white cake with "Happy Retir—" written in blue frosting. And a dish of nuts Arnie was picking the cashews out of as intently as if that were his new career.

From another part of the store a vacuum cleaner hummed. "Think you'll miss that sound?" I asked.

41

"Not really. Maybe. Who knows." Arnie popped another nut into his mouth.

I took a sip of the too-sweet punch and tried to dredge up some conversation. This all-day open house for Arnie was winding down along with topics of conversation. Now that Arnie had sold his business and resigned from the Chamber board, there didn't seem to be much left to talk about. I should have gotten here earlier when there were more people to visit with, but Fridays were always busy at the grocery store as people geared up for the weekend. I'd been lucky to get away at all. "So . . ." I asked a little too loudly even for a vacuum cleaner store, "how does it feel to not have to get up and go to work?"

"Ask me tomorrow." Arnie sure wasn't helping any.

"Hey, there." I clapped him on the back. "Think of all the beauty sleep you'll get to catch up on."

"Beauty sleep. Right." Arnie tossed a handful of nuts into his mouth. "I should have never sold the place."

What to say to that? Arnie had gotten everything he'd wished for. A buyer for his business. Freedom from the work that had occupied him for forty years. Wasn't this what everyone looked forward to?

As I took a gulp of punch an unexpected space opened somewhere inside my stomach. Questions about the future seemed to drop in and tumble about. At age fifty-four I'd certainly tossed the "R" word around in the back of my mind on more than one occasion. Most of my colleagues were approaching the age when, instead of constant talk about business, more and more the conversation included retirement plans, IRAs, Social Security checks, and Medicare cards. Stock portfolios, winter homes, and golf scores were as likely topics as the future of the business climate in Carlton, North Dakota. And, I had to admit, whenever there was a glitch at the store these days, instead of spending hours and days stewing over the problem, I'd escape in my mind to all sorts of possibilities that didn't include the daily grind of owning and operating the largest grocery store in Carlton. Make that *two* stores. Westin Foods North . . . and South.

Speaking of which . . . Arnie might be done working, but I wasn't. I threw the last small sip of warm punch into the nearby garbage can and reached to shake the guest of honor's hand. "Good luck to you, Arnie."

"You need a bagger down at the store? A stock boy? Stock *man?*"

I wasn't sure if Arnie was pulling my leg or dead serious. I decided to play along. "I'm always looking for help. Turnover is the name of the game these days. In fact—"

"I don't know what I'm going to do."

Oh man, why hadn't I come—and left—earlier?

Arnie ran a hand along the back of his neck and cast a glance around the vacuum cleaner store. "All I did was aim for the day I'd be done, and now that I am . . ." He looked at the floor, then at me. As if *I* had his answer.

Oh, boy. I jingled the change in my pocket. "Call me. We'll go golfing." Or something. I had a hunch Arnie's schedule wasn't going to jive with mine anymore. "Speaking of turnover, one of my checkers decided to backpack through Europe for the month of August. She told me yesterday and she's leaving on Monday." I made a show of glancing at my watch. "I've really got to get going. I have someone coming in for an interview." Actually she wasn't coming in for another forty-five minutes, but I wasn't about to stay here and help Arnie plan his future. I wouldn't have one to look forward to myself if I didn't keep my business running. "Congratulations," I said, pumping Arnie's hand again.

"For what?" he asked.

I hoped Arnie didn't expect an answer.

Climbing into my car, I couldn't help but hear Arnie's last words echo through my mind. *For what?*

Arnie was already questioning his decision to retire and he hadn't actually *not* worked for even a *day.* I didn't understand what he was grumbling about. Wasn't this what we all worked for . . .

retirement? The goal was to *work* in order to *not* work . . . eventually. Wasn't it?

The wheels of my car crunched against the small stones on the asphalt of the parking lot as I backed out of my spot. I pushed at my turn signal and headed south toward the store. My *work.*

As I maneuvered through the streets of Carlton, I rolled down the car window and rested an elbow on the edge. Hot end-of-July air felt good against my air-conditioned skin. All too soon I'd be back at the store, back inside. Lucky Arnie, he could spend the rest of the summer outside if he wanted. *If he wanted,* that was the key. He could do anything in the days ahead. I couldn't help but imagine what tomorrow would be like for Arnie. Sleep in. Read the paper as long as he felt like it. And then . . . what? Even in my imagination I couldn't quite fill in that blank. Oh, well, that was a bridge I wasn't planning to cross for a while, and I knew Arnie—his middle name was *Grumble.* His wife was going to have her ears full now that Arnie wouldn't be heading to the shop every day.

Maybe Arnie's not grumbling. Maybe he's afraid.

Afraid? Of what? Freedom?

Purpose.

As I pulled around to the back of the grocery store, jumped out of my car, and made a beeline for my office, the odd thought thumped like a double-beat on a bass drum. *Pur—pose.* Purpose.

Now there was a concept I had no time to contemplate. Who had time to think about lofty things such as that when every day was laid out like a Monopoly game? Get up. Wash up. Kiss Claire. Head to the store. Do not pass Go. Collect two hundred dollars . . . and, hopefully, more. From the time I felt the cold blast of air-conditioning coming from inside the store each morning, my only purpose was to stay on top of things.

I tugged open the back door of the store and was greeted by icy air. That meant the cooling system was working exactly as it should. One less thing to worry about. I walked the short hallway, and then bounded up the three steps leading to my office. Over the loudspeaker system of the grocery store I could hear one of the front-end people calling for a price check. I smiled to myself. So, things hadn't fallen apart during my hour at Arnie's party, which had felt more like a wake. I was so used to the constant white-noise of paging baggers and price checks it was surprising I even noticed the request. Same-old, same-old was a good thing when the boss was away.

I slipped into my office. With any luck, during the hour I'd been gone the paperwork on my desk wouldn't have multiplied mysteriously. It was a minor miracle to find my desktop exactly as I'd left it—all except for two sticky notes stuck to the center of my computer screen.

A phone number was scrawled below. Ted Driver? Ted Driver? The name tumbled through my brain, searching for a face to go with it. There was something familiar enough about the name that made me feel I should know him, but dang if I could come up with any info. The phone number meant nothing other than it had a North Dakota area code and a prefix that wasn't from Carlton. The only way to put my brain out of its misery was to give the guy a call.

Then again, I might as well take care of the second note first. A name and number I recognized. Bob Marsden from the bank where Westin Foods did all its business. Before I reached for the phone, I tapped at the computer keyboard. If there was a problem with my account, I wanted to know about it before I talked to Bob. Nope. The balances in my several accounts were healthy. I'd paid off the store loan four years ago and only recently had begun to think about doing some updating to my two stores. A malfunctioning meat cooler had sidelined that plan temporarily. Who knew why the bank president was calling? The only way to find out was to call him back.

I glanced at my watch. Almost 4:30. I knew the phrase "banker's hours" was a shortcut way of saying the top dogs could duck out early and play golf, especially on a beautiful summer Friday afternoon. But, I also knew my banker. Bob Marsden was as hardworking as they came. If he was out playing golf it would only be because the guy he was playing with had some business to discuss in between driving and putting. Since he'd left this message during the hour I'd been at Arnie's party, chances were good I'd still find Bob behind his desk.

As I reached for the phone, there was a soft knock on my open office door. "Jim?" Donna Bitz, my produce manager and all-around right hand, poked her head in. "The gal you were going to interview for the open checker position is here."

Fifteen minutes early. If her punctuality was any indication of her work ethic I couldn't afford to keep someone like her waiting. My phone calls would have to wait. "Send her in."

The young woman stopped just inside the doorframe and gave me a little wave. "Hello. I'm here."

"Yes, you are." I bit back a smile and walked around my desk to shake her damp hand. The girl didn't look a day over sixteen, but then I was a terrible judge of age. Anyone under thirty was beginning to look juvenile to my work-weary eyes. I'd been at this too long. Gone through more employees than I cared to count. This gal already had one point going for her . . . she was early. I was tempted to tell her "you're hired" on that basis alone. "Have a seat."

Donna handed me the application the young woman had filled out and scooted out the door. Scanning the form, I walked back behind my desk. There weren't many qualifications that would eliminate someone from this job. As long as they could stand behind the counter, scan groceries, and punch in a code now and then, that was good enough for me. A pleasant personality was a plus, but not a necessity, sad to say. The big-box stores springing up all over Carlton were taking a bite out of the employee pool all over town. I wasn't the only mom-and-pop operation begging for workers.

"Kara, is it?" I looked over the top of the form to the young woman sitting across from me.

"Yup. Ah . . ." She cleared her throat. "Yes."

With her straight blonde hair bobbing on either side of her face, she nodded. "Nelson."

"Kara Nelson. Let's see . . . you're a high school graduate. Honor student." I lifted my eyes over the top of the form and took another look at my applicant. "I'm impressed."

She looked at her lap. "Thanks."

If she was that smart she'd soon be looking for a job that offered more challenges. Already I was afraid she wouldn't last long.

Which means you've already decided to hire her.

Yes, I probably had. But a guy had to make it look like there was some sort of screening process besides "here and breathing."

49

I tapped the form with one finger. "I see you're a college student."

"Uh-huh. Well, not so much in the summer. I'm only taking one class. I really need—" Kara stared at her fingers before lifting her eyes. They briefly met mine, then focused somewhere against the wall over my shoulder. "I'm just going to tell you and then if you don't want to hire me, that's okay." She paused. "I have a little boy. Mason. He's one." Her eyes flicked to mine, then away. "Don't worry, I won't miss work. We live with my mom. I'm not—" She stopped again and swatted at the air with one of her hands as if pushing the rest of her sentence away. "I suppose you can fill in the blanks."

Actually, Kara was talking so fast I hadn't had much time to do anything but listen. Before I could think of anything to say she went on.

"I really want to make a good life for Mason. But everything is so expensive and day care is nuts. My mom works, too." Kara's eyes met mine for a brief second, a hint of spunk, as if to say they weren't living off the system. "I was hoping I could work at night. That way I can study and be with Mason during the day, and my mom can watch him when I work. I've got a student loan for school but that doesn't cover everything. And . . . well—" Her hands raised a little bit off her lap and then fell back as if all the strength had suddenly left them. "I'd really like this job."

Ah, the magic words. *I want this job.* It occurred to me that Kara didn't really know a thing about the job she was applying for. If I was going to make this interview seem real, I should ask her about her math skills, how she was at making change, or small talk. What she thought might be the most difficult part of the job, her honesty, and if she liked working with the public.

Then again, anyone in my position these days knew the only *real* qualification was that she was willing to work. "Can you start on Monday?"

"That's it? Aren't you—" Kara looked as if she was doing her darnedest to keep her jaw from dropping open. "Sure," she stammered.

"Talk to Donna on your way out," I said, walking Kara to the door. "She'll give you the details. What shift you'll be working. Where to pick up your apron and name badge. And . . ." I realized I was out of instructions. It had been a long time since I'd personally trained anyone. My job was hands-off when it came to my employees. While their jobs were the *face* of the store, I ended up in the back office doing the paperwork that kept the store running.

"Glad to have you on board. See you Monday," I said, shaking Kara's hand.

I did a one-eighty and beelined back to my desk. Actually, I probably wouldn't see Kara on Monday, or most any day. My days were spent juggling time between Westin Foods' north and

51

south locations, meeting with the store manager of my north-side location, paddling to stay on top of the targeted gross for each store, studying SKU rationalizations, and keeping the front-end system software up-to-date. Not to mention returning phone calls that came in when I was out congratulating Arnie on retiring.

I reached for the phone, punched the button that read "speaker," and keyed in the numbers for Bob Marsden, my banker.

"Bob," I said after my short wait on hold. "Jim Westin here."

"Hey, Jim. What are you still doing in the store on a beautiful summer Friday like today?"

I could hear paper shuffling in the background. I chuckled and projected my voice so the hardware in the base of the phone could amplify my words. "Same thing you are. Work."

"Ah," Bob said, a touch of wry amusement in his tone, "that old four-letter word . . . work."

My eyes landed on the payroll checks waiting for my signature. "What would we do without it?" An image of Arnie, scratching his head at what tomorrow would bring, floated in my mind's eye. "What's up?"

"Got a question for you." Bob's tone grew serious.

I reached for the phone receiver, cancelled the speaker feature, and held it to my ear. I didn't want whatever Bob was going to say projected for anyone passing by my office to hear. "Shoot," I said.

"We're looking for an outside director to serve on our bank board and your name came up." Bob gave me a second for his words to sink in. "Think you might be interested?"

My eyes did a quick scan of my office. The four walls and my messy desk pretty much made up my day-to-day world. Claire taught night classes two evenings a week, hours I often spent back at the store trying to tie up loose ends left frayed from the day. A change of venue and bank business challenges would be stimulating in a way the food business wasn't. And, I had to admit, Bob's offer was flattering. I'd started in this business as a stock boy for my dad when I was old enough to reach the middle shelves. At age fifty-four I had a lot of years and blades on my box cutter. My whole life had been spent in the grocery business. Never, in all those years I'd spent grumbling about being Dad's carry-out boy, did I ever think I'd end up owning the store . . . much less *two*. I'd also never imagined myself on the local bank board. I might not have time, but I was interested. "What's involved?"

"A once-a-month meeting that might take a couple hours. We have examiners show up yearly and the board meets with them for an exit review." He drew in a breath as if buying time to think if there was anything he was forgetting.

I might as well jump in and maybe nix my chances. "I have no idea what a bank board does."

Bob laughed. "Neither do I. *Kidding,*" he added quickly. "Actually, Jim, I think you'd enjoy the challenge. There're a lot of routine things . . . policies to approve, regulations to keep up with. But much of what we do directly affects the community. We review new loans. Talk to new businesses looking to come to town. It's challenging, interesting, and rewarding. Speaking of which, there is a small stipend that comes with the position."

The money didn't entice me, but the inside scoop on the Carlton business community did. I'd always valued being part of our growing community, and this was a way to give something back.

"Oh," Bob said before I could speak, "and you can come to our yearly Christmas party . . . rubber chicken and free drinks."

I laughed. "You drive a hard bargain."

"Actually . . ." his voice was tinged with warmth, "we have a very nice holiday get-together. Thick steaks. Bonuses for the staff. Time to reflect on the past year. Party aside, I think you'd enjoy the position."

My mind was made up. "I think I would, too."

"You're saying 'yes'?"

Thinking fast, I rolled a pen between my fingers. I should maybe run the idea past Claire before agreeing, but after all our years of marriage I

54

knew she'd tell me to go for it. I tossed the pen onto my desktop. "Yes."

After I hung up the phone, I wrote the date of my first bank board meeting on my calendar. Funny how a new challenge could change the outlook on a day. Arnie might be done with his years of work, but I felt as if I still had rungs of my career ladder to climb.

I picked up the second sticky note on my desk. *Call Ted Driver.* I didn't know a Ted. Unless he was the potato chip guy, but I thought his name was Fred. Maybe someone wrote it down wrong. I punched in the unfamiliar number and hoped I wasn't calling some telemarketer.

A pleasant voice. "Driver Family Foods."

I pulled the receiver away from my ear and gave it a *look.* I was calling a *grocery* store? "Uh, is Ted Driver in?"

"Sure is." There was a slight rustle, then, "Ted! It's for you."

"Got it," a man's voice responded further away. Another line picked up while the woman hung up on her end. "Ted here. What can I do for you?"

"Jim. Jim Westin. Westin Foods," I said, feeling a bit flustered. It wasn't often I was on a phone with no idea why I was calling. "I had a message on my desk to call—"

"Jim!" Ted said, as if we were old friends. "How you doing?"

"Fine," I said to this perfect stranger. "You?"

"Great. Just great. How's business?"

I'd keep my answer short and vague. I wasn't about to trade war stories with someone I'd never met. "Good."

"That's great."

I looked at my watch. Late afternoon on a Friday wasn't the time for a social call from a guy I'd never heard of. If Ted didn't get to the point soon I was going to do it for him. With the receiver pressed to my ear, I stood and looked out the window of my office that overlooked the store selling floor. There was a backup of customers waiting to get checked out. Typical for a summer Friday, everyone wanted to get home and get on with their weekend. Including me. Was I going to have to light a match under this *Ted* fellow? "What did—"

"I suppose you're wondering why I called?"

"Yes, I am."

His voice took on a different tone. "You interested in buying a grocery store?"

All of a sudden he wasn't beating around the bush anymore. His question came at me from left field. I plopped back down into my chair, a thrum of excitement tickling my ears. *Interested in buying a grocery store?* Was I? I already had two and they kept me running full time. I said the first thing that came to mind. "If you can manufacture more hours in a day."

Ted laughed. "I hear you. This business keeps a

guy hopping, doesn't it?" He didn't wait for an answer. "I can't keep up. The kids don't want it. So I thought of you."

Me? If I were going to offer up my stores for sale, I certainly wouldn't call a perfect stranger. "Who *are* you?" I asked. "Why me?"

Once again there was a low rumble of laughter from Ted. "Took you by surprise, huh?"

I laughed, too. "To be perfectly honest with you . . . yeah. I thought I was returning the call of the potato chip salesman."

"Well," Ted replied, "I'm looking to sell a little more than 'chips.' "

"Guess so," I answered, pulling a pad of paper toward me. "Why don't we start over. Why are you calling me?"

Over the next few minutes Ted Driver gave me the short version of his life in the grocery business. It more or less matched my story . . . a dad in the same line of work. A son who took over the store. The only difference was that Ted had fifteen years on me. He was sixty-nine and more than ready to call it quits.

"I don't want to sell out to a chain," he explained. "Not if I can help it. I did a little research," he went on. "I'd like to see another guy in here who has a heart for small towns. Not that Carlton is small," he hurried to add. "But my shop isn't that far from Carlton and I thought it might fit in well with your stores. Family run, you know."

Oh, I knew all about family run. So did my kids. They never had to play "store" with the other kids. They had the real-life version at their disposal from day one. Stocking shelves and sweeping the sidewalk had kept them occupied before they were old enough to make change, then each of the three had taken their turns at front-end jobs. Kaylee had worked as a cashier until she got her undergrad degree, Drew and Reed had moved on to other jobs more in line with their college majors. Drew was putting his business finance degree to good use at a bank. Reed had his sights set on architecture since he'd gotten his first Lego set. I nursed a secret hope that one of my kids would be interested in keeping the family business going, but right now none of them seemed to have an ounce of interest in choosing the grocery business as a career.

But I didn't need to worry about that at the moment. Ted was rattling off details. He had done his research . . . he was giving me answers to questions before I could even ask. I clicked a pen and started jotting. Square footage. Gross sales and net. The size of his customer base. His store was seventy miles from Carlton. Far enough to not compete with me. Close enough that once I had a local manager in place I could drop in often enough to keep an eye on things.

"So . . ." Ted said, "You interested?"

I drummed the tip of my pen against Ted's net

sales for the last three years. Not bad. Not bad at all for a store his size.

My mind was tumbling around more than numbers. Arnie had retired as of today. "Ted," on the other end of the line, wanted out, too. I had a few years to go before I'd even consider selling or turning the store over to one of my kids. And, if I took Ted up on his offer, I'd only be digging in deeper. Did I really want to go that route?

I did some quick-figuring in my mind. If things went well I could have Ted's store paid off in no time. His square footage would fit into one of my stores three times over, and his revenues were pretty darn good for a store his size. But did I need another headache? Another store to worry about? Things were going well just the way they were.

You're coasting. You could sit back and ride right into retirement in a few years.

Coasting. Man, I didn't like that thought. The one thing I'd vowed never to do. I had a *thing,* a not-a-good-thing, for people who were complacent in their work. What was the point if you weren't challenged by what you did?

I tossed my pen onto the notes I'd taken and leaned back in my chair, tucking the phone receiver into my shoulder. "I'll be honest with you, Ted. When I got up this morning I sure wasn't thinking about adding a new store to my business, but you've got me thinking."

"That's what I wanted to do . . . get you thinking. You want the weekend?"

Once Ted got going the man didn't waste time.

I scratched at the back of my neck. "Tell you what. I'm going to need to run some numbers. Talk to my banker. And my wife. I—"

"Speaking of wives . . ." Ted drew the word out. "Mine's giving me the evil eye right now. Been on the phone too long for her taste. And there's a lineup at the checkout counter. She's as anxious to get out of this business as I am. We're getting too old to work this many hours. She wants a motor home and a map. The further she can get from that cash register, the better." Ted cleared his throat. For the first time in this conversation he sounded nervous. "Okay, so maybe I shouldn't be telling you all this stuff. Might talk you right out of the deal."

"Don't worry," I said, sitting up. On the paper in front of me I drew an arrow pointing to the price Ted had named and underlined it. "I know exactly what I'm getting myself into. Give me until Wednesday to get back to you."

"You got it."

Thoughtfully, I hung up the phone. Who knew my afternoon would turn out like this? A retirement open house. A spot on the board of a local bank. And maybe a new store to add to Westin Foods North and South. What would Ted's store be called? I drew a quick map in my mind and laughed to myself. Westin Foods Further North didn't have much of a ring to it. But the possibilities suddenly lining my plate were enticing.

Like a little kid with a whole dollar to spend, I rubbed my hands together. Wow. What an afternoon. I glanced at my watch. After six o'clock on a late-July Friday. Even climbers had to call it a day . . . or a week. Those steaks Bob Marsden had mentioned during my first phone conversation sounded like just the ticket. I'd have my butcher wrap up a few on my way out of the store, then get home and fire up the grill. Claire and I could relax on the deck. Maybe Kaylee and Brad would stop by. And then, later, when we were all fat and happy, I'd tell them Westin Foods was expanding.

Something scratched at my stomach . . . hunger? Worry? Was taking on another store at this point in my life too much?

Nah. I'd never been one to back down from a challenge. That nagging sensation must be hunger.

Drew

"Excuse me. Excuse me," I repeated for what had to be the dozenth time. People bumped my shoulders from one side, then the other, as if I were a human pinball. There was no way to walk through this mass of humanity without touching someone. And yet, no one else seemed to be compelled to apologize. Except me. I was going to have to get

61

rid of the North Dakota–nice persona if I was ever going to get to work. "Oops . . . excuse me."

Mom had trained me too well. I lifted my brief-case and put it against me like a leather shield. If I made myself take up less space, maybe I'd make better headway getting out of the New York subway system.

Along with what seemed like a thousand other faceless people, I climbed the stairs to street level. Fresh air greeted me. If you could call it *fresh*. Bus fumes and car exhaust mingled with the humid August air. I dropped my briefcase to my side and shouldered my way down the sidewalk. Despite the early hour, taxi horns were sounding off. Delivery trucks blocked a speedy sprint down a crowded street. This wasn't Carlton, North Dakota, that was for sure.

As I waited for a stoplight to signal the "walk" sign, I tilted my head and gazed upward. Skyscrapers soared into the sky all around me. I joined the mass of people crossing the street. Two more blocks and I'd be at work. Even after two years in New York I sometimes still marveled that this small-town kid from the Plains was living and working in the Big Apple.

"Watch where you're going, Mister." A stocking-capped kid made an elaborate side-step around me, as if *I* was the one going in the oppo-site direction of almost everyone on the sidewalk.

I could feel my brows furrow as I tossed him an

annoyed look. I had half a notion to turn around and ask him why he was wearing a stocking cap in August. Didn't he know how ridiculous he looked? Okay, so maybe my North Dakota nice was wearing off after all.

Keeping my eyes to myself I stayed in the stream of foot traffic, bearing left when I came to the building where I worked. It would be a relief to get inside where the congestion was less, and where there would be familiar faces instead of only strangers.

I swung open the door to the bank and nodded at the security guard standing inside. "Hey, Frank."

"How are you today, Mr. Westin?"

Mr. Westin. I chuckled to myself, wondering if Frank knew I had just turned thirty. That whole Mister-thing made me feel as if I was creeping up on middle-age.

I paused beside my favorite guard. "I'm doing well, Frank. You?"

"Can't complain. Big news is my granddaughter lost her first tooth last night." He grinned.

Frank had to know our bank dealt in million-dollar deals every day. Having the tooth fairy drop by more than likely wouldn't interest too many of the bank employees streaming in behind me. But, I'd noticed, not too many of them even glanced Frank's way. They might not even know he had grandkids. Or that his granddaughter had been diagnosed with asthma last year. Call me a hick from the sticks, but where I came from, it was normal operating procedure to get to know the people you worked with, even security guards.

"Wow," I said, remembering the time the tooth fairy had left me a whole dollar, "what's the going rate for teeth these days?"

Frank shook his head and smiled. "You don't want to know."

I shifted my briefcase to my other hand. "Well, if you need a loan, you know who to talk to."

"That I do. Have a good one." He lifted his hand in a friendly wave as I turned to head to my office.

Nodding at Sharon, the receptionist, I stepped into the elevator and rode it one floor up. "Morning." I greeted Kelly and June, a couple of the administrative assistants lining the path to my office. Turning left I headed past the corridor of small offices lining the outside wall of the building. My space was small, but it did boast a window. Not something every junior loan officer could hope for in the high-rent district. I opened my briefcase on my desktop and pulled out a couple files. The minute or so I spent talking to Frank each day made this city seem a little less impersonal and a little more like home, but now it was time to get to work.

As I moved my briefcase to the floor, my eyes landed on the framed photo on the credenza beside my desk. There we were, all six of us. Mom, Dad, Reed, Kaylee, her husband, Brad, and me. Last year's Christmas card photo. The only time I'd been home since then had been in April for Grandma's funeral, and no one had felt like taking a family photo then. But Mom was going to have another opportunity to get an annual family photo in six weeks . . . not that I was counting, or anything. Dad and I had a standing date for the opening of pheasant season in October. Reed, too. No doubt Mom would be close by, camera in hand, ready to snap this year's holiday photo.

The thought of going home sent a deep breath into my lungs, as if I was already smelling the crisp, clear, North Dakota air. *Home.* There was no way New York was ever going to feel like Carlton, but then I wasn't sure I wanted it to.

I swiveled my chair away from the photo and back to the business of the day. Working in New York had been a goal of mine since high school, but lately, I couldn't quite remember *why* living here had seemed so important. Oh, sure, New York City was the business capital of the world, but when you got right down to it, business was *business* no matter where you sat behind a desk. There were days I looked out my window and instead of seeing concrete, bricks, and glass, I noticed the birds swooping through the corridor of buildings. Where in the world did they call home in this cityscape? What did they eat? Where did they find water? It had to be my Midwest roots kicking in. Only someone who'd grown up watching birds nest in trees, seen them rooting around in grain fields for kernels of wheat, and drinking from prairie potholes would worry about city birds. Most of the people I knew here thought of birds as a nuisance.

I punched the "start" button on my computer and gazed out the window while it booted up. I'd better quit thinking about home. If I kept it up, I'd do exactly what my dad wanted me to do . . . move back to North Dakota and join him in the stores.

What would be so bad about that?

Number one was the fact that I had my own career. Number two was . . . I ran a hand along my jawline. Funny, it seemed I'd forgotten the automatic objections that had rested at the tip of my tongue every time Dad brought up the subject. Come to think of it, he hadn't mentioned it at all the last time I'd been home. Or when we'd talked on the phone since. Maybe he'd finally believed me when I told him "no way."

A weird, empty feeling weighed in my stomach. In spite of all my protests, there'd been something flattering about Dad wanting me to join him in the stores. Had he—

"Drew?"

A familiar voice zapped me from my faraway thoughts back to reality. A smile crept onto my face even before I turned my eyes. Now there, right there in my doorway, stood the number-one reason I wanted to stay in New York. Trisha

Collins. Internal Marketing Liaison for the bank. My girlfriend of seven months.

"Hey there." I couldn't help but grin at her as I tilted my head and motioned her to the empty chair across from my desk. "Come on in."

"You're not busy?"

Actually, I had a loan committee meeting to prepare for, but that could wait a few minutes. "Not for you."

Trisha slid into the chair, tossed a quick glance over her shoulder to make sure no one was near, then leaned forward and whispered, "I'm looking forward to dinner tomorrow night." She quickly sat up straight, her professional posture intact.

"Me, too." I did my best to wipe the smile off my face and shuffled the papers in front of me, trying to make our little ruse look authentic. If anyone walked by my office it would be *my* face they'd see. While there was no outright *rule* against bank employees dating, we both agreed it would be best to keep our relationship on the down-low.

I dared a glance at my doorway. Empty. "How's my South Dakota sweetheart?" Sheesh, if any of my buddies heard me they'd know I was a goner.

"She's great," Trisha answered, her eyes crinkling at the corners. She turned serious. "I want to talk to you about something tomorrow night."

It was the fact that Trisha was practically a North Dakota neighbor, coming from just south of the border of my home state, that had formed an instant connection between us when we'd met at the company Christmas party in December. Trisha's story was similar to mine. Small-town kid makes it in New York. Okay, so neither of us were "kids" any longer. At thirty-two, Trisha was two years older than me, and had been in New York since she'd graduated from college with a degree in Business Communication.

I had a hunch *communication* was exactly what my South Dakota girl wanted to talk about tomorrow night. Communicating about our *relationship*. Where it was going seemed to be the topic of the day lately.

Wasn't it the guy's job to drag his feet? I played along. "That so?"

Trisha looked down at her hands in her lap. I knew the fact there was no ring on her left hand was becoming an issue with her. But she knew we'd only been dating seven months. Hardly enough time to expect a proposal . . . even from a good old trustworthy guy from North Dakota.

I had a surprise for her tomorrow night. A question I couldn't wait to ask. Or maybe it was Trisha's answer I couldn't wait to hear.

"So . . ." I pretended to be fascinated by the few drops of Cabernet left in my glass as the waiter lifted Trisha's and my dinner plates from the table. I waited until he left then asked, "What was it you wanted to talk about?"

We'd already dissected our projects at work. I listened patiently while Trisha talked about the baby shower she was planning for her best friend. She indulged me as I analyzed the pros and cons of training for a marathon . . . a new goal now that I'd hit the big 3-0. But all of that was small talk compared to what I really had to say . . . it was time to get the show on the road. "You wanted to talk about something?"

Trisha didn't speak. She lifted her hand and pushed her hair behind one ear, then the other. The pause was growing uncomfortably long. Her nervous gesture threw me. Suddenly I felt nervous, too, but not because of what I'd been prepared to ask. What if, instead of Trisha asking where our relationship was heading, she was going to head me off at the pass and sideline me altogether? The small box in my sport coat pocket felt like a piece of lead. A piece of shrapnel that might be headed straight for my heart.

Trisha folded her hands and rested them on the white tablecloth between us. She drew in a deep breath, then looked me in the eyes. It occurred to me that if her day job didn't work out, Trisha would make a great poker player. I had no idea what she was planning to say. I wiped my palm against the napkin on my lap.

"We've been dating seven months now, Drew. You know I'm thirty-two. I don't have the luxury of—"

"Dessert?" The waiter's timing couldn't have been worse.

Or better.

Who knew what the rest of Trisha's sentence would have been. With a clarity I hadn't seen until just this second, I realized whatever Trisha was going to say didn't matter. What I had come here tonight to say was all that counted.

I turned to the waiter. "Could you come back in about three minutes?" I already had my hand in my pocket, my fingers wrapped around the ring box.

The waiter caught my look of quiet desperation. "Certainly, sir."

Trisha took his leaving as her cue to continue. Once again she tucked her hair behind her ears. "What I was going to say—"

"Will you marry me?" The words fell out of my mouth unaccompanied by the semiromantic speech I'd planned.

"What?" Trisha seemed to be suddenly at a loss for words. But when I just grinned, she finally said, "Did you just ask me to . . . ?"

"Marry me? Yes. Yes, I did." I fumbled in my pocket. Somehow the ring box had fallen out of my grip. "I, uh, this isn't going at all like I thought it would. I was going to get down on one knee, and then I was going to tell you a whole bunch of, well . . . stuff . . . and then I was going to give you . . . *this*." Finally I managed to get the small velvet box out of my pocket and onto the table. I flipped open the lid and found myself staring down at the diamond solitaire I'd picked out. Turning the box so Trisha could see I'd given this some thought, I repeated my question, "Will you marry me, Trisha Collins?"

"Are you serious?" Trisha's mouth dropped open. Her eyes darted from me to the ring and back again. "We've only dated—"

"Seven months. I know." Now I was really getting nervous. I'd hoped for an immediate "yes," not an analysis of this slightly speedy proposal.

"You haven't even met my parents."

"You haven't met mine, but I'd still like to marry you."

She sat back in her chair. "I wasn't expecting this."

When she put it that way, I wasn't expecting the way things were going, either. I felt my Adam's apple bounce as I swallowed against the nervous cough nudging the back of my throat. Okay, so maybe this was a dumb idea. What had I been thinking? Obviously, I hadn't. Who proposed to someone after only dating seven months? I should have given this more thought. More time. I was an idiot. A first class Dumbo. If I could do this over—

"Yes."

"What?"

Trisha was grinning at me. "Yes!"

71

"Really?" As if I didn't believe her.

"It's crazy . . . but, yes, I'll marry you." She'd cupped the velvet box in her hands.

I pushed myself away from the table and took two big steps toward Trisha. She stood and threw her arms around me. "Yes! Yes!"

It was a word that didn't get old. I bent to kiss her as the people near us in the restaurant somehow figured out what was happening and started clapping. I slipped the ring on Trisha's finger. It was too big, but her grin told me she didn't mind.

Wrapped in Trisha's embrace, I almost didn't feel the small rustle behind me. I stepped out of our hug to see that our server had placed a large slice of chocolate cake in the center of our table . . . with two forks. "Compliments of the management," he said.

Trisha and I looked at each other. "Yes," we said together, sitting down to dig in.

There was nothing but our silly smiles and crumbs of chocolate cake left on the plate when I put down my fork, leaned forward, and asked Trisha, "By the way, what was it you were planning to talk about tonight?"

"Oh, gosh." Trisha put her palm over her heart. "I can't believe I forgot all about that. Well, considering *this* . . ." She wiggled her left hand, causing her new diamond to catch the candlelight. "I guess I can believe it. I was going to tell you that I'm . . . I *was* . . . thinking about moving back to South Dakota."

"You are? *Were?*"

She nodded. "I'm kind of *done* with the whole New York thing." With her index finger she dabbed at the crumbs of cake on the plate between us, scooping up a few and putting them in her mouth. She lifted an eyebrow my way. "Except for *you,* of course." Once again, she poked at the bits of chocolate, then looked straight across the table at me. Her eyes held something . . . a request? A challenge? "I'd really like to get back home."

Home. That word seemed to be the word of the week. I picked up my water glass and gulped the icy liquid. My home was here. In New York. There was no way I was moving back to the Midwest.

No way.

Claire

It was a beautiful late-August morning. Not a cloud in the sky. The perfect day for a walk and for sharing all the news I had to tell Julie. As I turned my car into the parking lot I spotted Julie already waiting. Jogging in place. Stretching tall and then touching her toes. She took our couple-times-a-week walks more seriously than I did. Not that I didn't appreciate the exercise, but the number one reason I walked with Julie was for *therapy*. Talking with Julie always made me feel better. *Troubles halved, joys doubled* is what happened when I talked with my best friend. Today was going to be nothing but joy.

I pulled in beside Julie's vehicle, tucked my purse under the seat, and then swung my legs out of the car.

Julie waved and jogged over to meet me. "What?" she asked before I could even stand up and say good morning.

I bit back a smile and bent over to retie my tennis shoe. How in the world did Julie know I had news? "I didn't say anything."

Julie put her hands on her hips and twisted left, then right. "You don't have to. I can tell just by looking at you that you're dying to tell me something. Spill . . ."

"How do you do that?" I asked, standing and then touching my toes.

"Do what?"

"Read my mind like that?"

Julie grinned. "See, I told you that you had something to tell me." She grabbed my arm and pulled me onto the walking path that wound through the park. We fell into stride, side by side.

It was what the weatherman called a "Goldilocks" day—not too hot, not too cool. The early morning air was just right. The sun dappled through the trees that lined the walking path.

"Well . . . ?" Leave it to Julie to make sure I told my news first. She was the kind of friend who was more interested in hearing *my* struggles and victories than in sharing hers. Over the years I'd learned friends like Julie were few and far between. Most people I knew were much more interested in doing the talking, rather than the listening. Julie was one of the few people in my life who knew most everything about me. And, with a nudge of her shoulder against mine, she let me know she was waiting to hear what I had to say. "Talk."

I shook my head slightly, as if I still couldn't believe what I was going to say. "Well, here it is: I'm going to be a mother-in-law!"

"You already are," Julie reminded me. She knew my daughter, Kaylee, and Brad had been married almost two years.

"I mean, *again.*"

Julie stopped in her tracks, in the middle of the path. A runner behind us veered around to the left with a "Whoa!" and kept running.

Julie stood still with her jaw dropped open. "Who's getting married? Drew? Reed? Oh my gosh, neither one of them has been dating anyone . . . like . . . seriously. Have they?"

"I didn't think so, but apparently I'm a bit behind the dating curve." With my head I motioned to Julie that we should keep walking. College would be starting up next week and after our walk and a shower, I needed to spend the rest of today getting organized for my classes. "That's what I get for having two sons. Kaylee can't keep a thing from me, but both my boys would rather have their eyelashes plucked out before telling me anything about their personal lives."

Julie skipped ahead of me, turned around and walked backward while she asked, "So *who?* What? When? Where?" She spun on a foot and fell in beside me again.

"Drew."

"Drew's getting married?" She clapped her hands. "Yay." She paused. "Are you excited?"

I nodded. "I think so. When he called he sounded so . . . so . . . I don't know . . . soft. Tender. I've never heard him like that before. It was really kind of sweet. I have to trust Drew's judgment. He's got a good head on his shoulders. If he loves Trisha, she must be someone special."

"Trisha?"

"Yup. Trisha Collins. She's from South Dakota, but lives in New York, of course. She works in the bank with Drew and that's all I know. Oh, and she's thirty-two."

"Her clock must be ticking." Leave it to Julie to cut right to the chase.

"Yeah," I said, picking up the pace, "I thought about that, too. But then Drew's thirty, and if young men have 'clocks' I suppose his is beginning to sound loud and clear, too."

"Have they set a date?"

I nodded. "They want to get married soon. Like . . . over Thanksgiving."

"Is she pregnant?"

Now it was my turn to stop in my tracks. "Julie!"

She squeezed her eyes tightly shut and scrunched up her face. "Sorry. My big mouth wants to apologize right this second."

One thing I usually appreciated about Julie was that she never danced around anything. Not even potentially sensitive subjects. I always knew right where I stood with Julie. However, that didn't mean I always *liked* what she had to say.

I started walking again, leaving Julie stewing in her apology a few steps behind me.

She ran to catch up. "Really, Claire, I'm sorry."

"I know." We walked in silence for a while. After a few minutes I was ready to talk again. "You know," I said slowly, "it never occurred to me until you said it that she might be . . . could be . . . pregnant. Now what am I supposed to do?"

Julie didn't miss a beat. "I say you celebrate their engagement. Drew and this *Trisha* are certainly old enough to deal with the situation if that's what it is . . . and I hope it's *not*. At least not yet. But you have to admit that having your first grandchild would be kind of exciting."

Even though Julie was right beside me, I knew she could tell I was rolling my eyes. "Talk about putting the cart before the horse. Here I was, getting enthused about telling you Drew was getting married and you have me waiting for my first grandchild."

"Slap me," Julie said as she swatted at her cheek with her hand. "But, you have to admit, being a grandma could be kind of fun."

"Julie!" I bumped her shoulder with the heel of my hand. This was a subject Julie and I had tossed about more than once. Her two daughters were close to Kaylee's age, in their early twenties, with no intention of getting married anytime soon. And Kaylee had recently informed me that she didn't know if she *ever* wanted to have kids. Her job in the county Social Services Department had her working with too many dysfunctional families and their kids. According to Kaylee, she wasn't so sure it was possible to raise a kid who wasn't mixed up. I pointed out that *she* seemed pretty put together, but Kaylee discounted my comments with a wry, *of course my mother thinks I'm perfect,* comment. Our girls were so far from the mindset Julie and I had when we were their ages. If we hadn't been married and had babies by our midtwenties we would have thought we were has-beens.

Julie and I rounded the halfway point on the loop around the park. Halfway through our walk and I hadn't even begun to tell Julie all I had to say. But first I wanted to finish up this rabbit-trail of our conversation. "Being a grandma is on my 'someday' list. I'd rather have my kids be good and ready for that stage in their lives. I don't want pressure from me to be the reason they decide to have a child."

"Oh, I know." Julie waved a hand through the air. "But it's fun to dream about."

"There are lots of fun things to dream about."

We walked in step, each of us in our own dream world. We had the kind of friendship where silence was okay. But it never lasted for long.

"So," Julie asked, "what do you dream about these days?"

"Besides a wedding in three months?" I bent over and tossed aside a small branch that had fallen on the walking trail. "Oh . . . sometimes I dream about what Jim and I will do when we retire. I think it might be fun to get an RV and trav—"

"An RV? You've *got* to be kidding." Julie walked sideways while she laughed in my direction. "When did you go from fifty-one to eighty-one?"

"What's wrong with an RV? I think it would be a great way to see the country. Think of all the packing and unpacking you'd save. Not to mention not having to stop and go to the bathroom."

Julie lifted one finger. "Now there's a point."

Lately, we often found ourselves discussing the downsides of getting older. Our reading glasses and unreliable bladders were only two of a whole list of grumbles. But, more and more, I found myself noticing some advantages about this thing called "aging." For one, I was much more confident than I'd ever been when I was younger. If I didn't feel like doing something, I said so . . . and then didn't stew all night afraid I might be missing out on some fun. And there was something strangely appealing about wondering what life held in the years beyond my teaching at the university.

"I dream about . . ." Julie's voice was dreamy and wistful as she paused, then held an edge along with a giggle, ". . . ditching my job. Not having to get up every morning at the crack of dawn. No more putting on makeup everyday. No more *having* to exercise. And I could do without ever having to cook again, too."

I laughed. "It sounds like you plan to turn into a chubby little plain-Jane, sitting on a couch eating your meals out of a bag of chips. Retirement doesn't mean quitting *life*."

"I know. That's my fantasy retirement. In reality Bill and I will probably work until we drop from sheer exhaustion. Have you looked at those retirement charts? The ones that show you how much money you should have saved before you think about quitting work? Man, I wish I'd seen that when I was twenty."

I took a giant step over an anthill in my path. "Would you have paid attention?"

"Probably not. But claiming ignorance makes me feel better." Julie veered off the path and toward our cars. We were at the end of the long loop around the park. "Have time for coffee?"

I looked at my watch. "I'd better get cleaned up and then head over to campus. I'm teaching an extra section this semester and I need to get the syllabus copied."

"Call me later." Julie pulled open the door of her car.

I reached for the door handle of my car and then remembered. "Julie! Wait!"

"Claire." Julie was laughing. "Shhh . . ." She put a finger to her lips. "We may be getting older but I'm not deaf, yet. I'm right here."

"Oh, my gosh," I said, hurrying around the back of her car to stand near her. "I can't believe I almost forgot to tell you my other news. I finished my book."

"The one for book club? That hardly seems worth screaming about. I thought it was kind of bor—"

"Not *that* book." I swatted at Julie's arm, then poked an index finger at my chest. "*My* book. The one I've been working on since my mom died."

Julie's eyes widened. "You *finished* it? Really?" I nodded.

Julie opened her arms and wrapped me in a warm hug. "That is *so* cool. I've never known an *author* before. But I can't say that anymore. Hey there . . . *author."* She released me from the hug and gave me a high five. "Way to go."

Besides my husband, Jim, Julie was the only other person who knew how diligently I'd been pursuing this project. Even if the book never got published, at least I wouldn't have the regret of an unfinished dream hanging over my head the rest of my life.

"What's next?" Julie knew writing a book was only one step of the journey.

With the tip of my tennis shoe I scrubbed at the gravel in the parking lot. Completing the manuscript had been hard enough, but I knew the next step, trying to get it published, might be even harder.

I bit at my lip and looked at Julie. "One of my faculty friends in the Sociology Department has a brother who owns a small publishing company. They don't do many books a year, but she said he might be willing to take a look at it and offer some advice." I brushed imaginary dust off my sleeve. "Of course she said it almost a year ago, when I didn't actually have anything written to show anyone."

"You do now." Leave it to Julie to give me a shot of much-needed confidence.

I pressed my lips into a wry smile. "It's easy to make an offer when there's nothing on the other end. I just want him to *look* at it. Maybe her brother can tell me if my words have any merit.

Any *chance* of getting published." A small gust of wind pushed my hair across my face. I turned my face into the breeze and swept my hair back. "Really, I know the odds of having anything happen with this book are so small. I don't have my hopes up at all."

"I'm going to pray, anyway," Julie countered. "When are you going to give the book to him?" There was my friend, again, not letting me rest, not letting me put things off until it was too late to do anything about it.

"I don't know. I really hadn't thought that far."

"Do it tomorrow."

A burst of nervous laughter pushed past my throat. "I can't do it tomorrow."

"Why not?"

"Well, for one, I need to print out a clean copy."

"You can do that today after you get your syllabus copied. Right . . . ?"

"I suppose . . ." This was going way too fast. Part of me wanted to sit for awhile in my dream world, imagining the day, sometime in the future, when I had a book published. If I didn't *try* I could always imagine it *could* happen. Once I handed that manuscript over it was yea- or nay-time.

"Okay," Julie said, pointing a finger at me, "your assignment is to get that book printed out this afternoon."

"Hey," I countered, "I'm the teacher. I'm the

one who's supposed to be handing out assignments . . . not you."

Julie put her hands on her hips. "I'm your friend. Your pushy, I-want-to-see-this-happen-for-you friend. Are you going to get that book printed out this afternoon?"

I rolled my eyes. "Okay, okay. If for no other reason than to get you off my case." I gave Julie a cheesy grin. *Satisfied?* Then I turned and walked back to my car.

"Call me when you get it printed out." Julie wasn't going to let this die.

"Julie." A couple steps brought me to the passenger side of her car. I spoke over the roof. "I told you . . . nothing might come of this. Don't get your hopes up, because I don't have any. Hopes that is. The odds are slim to none."

"Well, I'm voting for *slim.*"

As I turned back to my car I couldn't help but shake my head at her persistence.

"Call me."

I patted my hand in the air as if to quiet her. "I will."

I climbed into my car and started it up, giving Julie a quick wave as I backed out of my parking space. Part of me wished I'd never opened my mouth about this project. Julie would hound me until the manuscript had died a natural death . . . as I was almost certain it would. The best thing might be to do exactly as Julie had told me. Print it out, hand it over, and then . . . then . . . ?

I pushed at my turn signal and took a left out of the park. In a few short minutes I'd be home, and in an hour I would be on my way to campus. A couple hours after that my syllabus would be done, and I'd have no more excuses to keep me from printing out my book. A hot flush seemed to zing through my chest and move quickly outward, engulfing me.

Oh, Lord, why am I scared?

There was no answer, just the heavy thump of my heart and my two sweaty palms gripping the steering wheel. I drew in a deep breath and tried to stifle the hum of the unknown. The buzz of all the possibilities that could be.

There was one thing I didn't dare tell Julie. One thing I could hardly admit to myself. Unlike my mother, who'd left a bin of unfulfilled projects behind, I'd completed mine. It would be a lot easier to know what to do with an embroidered pillowcase instead of a manuscript for a book. But, in spite of my fear, and what I'd told Julie, I did have hopes for this book. Big hopes.

But what if they amounted to absolutely nothing?

ONE YEAR LATER:
A SATURDAY IN SEPTEMBER

Jim

"Do I hear a thousand? A thousand? One-zero-zero-zero. Yeah! Yeah!" The auctioneer pointed somewhere vague on the opposite side of the crowd from where I was standing.

"The bid goes your way." Now he was pointing at me. "Do I hear one thousand two? One thousand two?" The guy made it look like he was scanning the small group of car buffs clustered around the '68 Dodge Charger, but I knew he had his eye on me.

I rubbed at the side of my face, doing some quick math in my head. How high was the yokel on the other side of this junker going to bid? He'd already pushed me four hundred higher than I'd planned . . . if there really was another bidder in the crowd. Who knew where the auctioneer was pulling those bids from? Could be from the thin September air.

"One thousand going once." The auctioneer stopped for a long breath, as if it was exhausting wheedling money out of middle-aged guys trying to recapture their youth. "Going once. Going . . . once . . . Tell you what . . ." The auctioneer dropped his mike and then lifted it again. "We're going to take a little break here and let some of our bidders think things over. This car should be bringing a lot more than this." He turned and picked up a can of Pepsi and took a long swig.

A hint of autumn was in the breeze on this September Saturday, but I was feeling hot under the collar all the same. I hadn't planned on attending an old car auction this afternoon. I'd stumbled upon it on my way to keep tabs on Ted Driver's old store in Emerson. The newest addition to Westin Foods.

Well, technically, it maybe wasn't all that new, but it had taken several months to hammer out the deal with Ted. By the time I took over, nearly five months had passed since Ted's unexpected phone call over a year ago. Westin Foods, the Emerson location, had been up-and-running for nine months now. A *baby* I was still getting used to tending.

My idea had been to take the long way to town. The old highway out of Carlton, and then some back roads into Emerson. As long as I had to work on a beautiful Saturday, I thought I'd try and make the best of it.

Curiosity got the better of me when I saw a series of signs announcing: Car Auction Today! I turned in . . . and here I was, standing in front of my adolescent fantasy car. Not counting the dust . . . and rust.

One of the auctioneer's cronies sidled up to me. "It's a great car. Needs a little work."

I looked at him out of the corner of my eye. "A little?"

"Okay, a lot. But you don't find honeys like this on every street corner." He tilted his head toward the rusty, formerly cherry-red vehicle. "You get this baby restored and she'll be worth twenty-five grand."

I knew that. I'd had my eye on a muscle car like this since I'd been sixteen. Of course the car in my imagination was factory perfect. Gleaming paint. Chrome shining like mirrors. Eight cylinders. Four speeds. And if I'd known Claire back then, I would have imagined her in one of the black vinyl bucket seats.

Now those seats were cracked, the chrome that was still there was scratched, and so were the mirrors. The car might still have eight cylinders and four speeds but I doubted any of them worked. But still . . . I wanted it, dings and all.

What will Claire say?

I tugged at the back of my neck. Oh, I knew exactly what my wife would say, "You bought *what?*" And then she'd add, "And just where do you plan to keep it?"

Yeah, there was that, too. Where *would* I keep it? For now I'd haul it to my side of our double-car garage where it would be convenient to work on when I had a little spare time. I'd park my regular car out in the driveway until I got the Dodge restored. Claire was always telling me I needed a hobby. Restoring an old car would be the perfect pastime. Who knew, maybe Brad would help. Tinkering on a fixer-upper would be something I could do with the boys when they were home visiting. A family project. I liked that idea.

I gave the auctioneer's helper a subtle but definite nod.

"Yeah!" He shouted, throwing an arm into the air.

The auctioneer swung the mike to his mouth. "New fire, new blood!" He handed off his Pepsi can to someone standing near him. "Thousand two. Thousand two. Do I hear four? Four? One thousand four?"

I closed my eyes for a second. What had I done? One thousand two hundred dollars for a piece of rust. What had I been thinking? When would I have time to even haul it home, much less work on it? *Please, someone else bid on this.*

"Yeah! Thousand four! That's four on this side." The auctioneer pointed in the opposite direction from me.

Yes! Someone had taken the car off my hands.

"Do I hear six? Six?"

I shaded my eyes with my hand. Where was this yokel who kept bidding me up? Did he know something I didn't? Was this car more than an adolescent fantasy? When you got right down to it, a muscle car like this was really an investment. Heck, I was on the bank board, I knew what interest rates were doing. If this car was in mint condition my return would be sweet. I nodded my head once more.

"Yes-sss-sss! One six! Look at that, folks. There's at least two people here today who know what this baby is worth. One six. Do I hear eight?"

A small trickle of sweat slid down from my hairline, past my ear. I should have my head examined . . . the head that kept nodding every time the auctioneer looked my way. I was *not* bidding again. As soon as that other guy took it off my hands, he could have it. It was enough to know that for a few seconds, in my imagination, the car had been mine. It had been fun while it lasted, but I had my hands full with my three stores, the bank board, the Chamber of Commerce, my spot on—

"Sold!" The auctioneer was pointing my way.

Me? I looked around. Maybe that other guy had moved right beside me. No. The auctioneer was definitely pointing at me. If it was possible to feel slightly sick and elated at the same time . . . I did.

"Congratulations, sir."

I nodded, for what I hoped was the last time today. There was a smattering of applause as I dug in my back pocket to pull out my bidding number.

How in the world was I going to get this piece of rust back to Carlton? And how was I ever going to explain this to Claire? Especially when I could hardly explain it to myself.

"Hi there, Mr. Westin. Uh . . . Jim." My Emerson store manager still stumbled over what to call me. "Ummm . . . just a minute." Janice stared down at the fresh produce a customer had placed on the checkout counter. "What is this?" she asked the shopper.

"Cilantro."

"Oh, uh . . ." She cast a nervous glance my way. "Okay. I'll, uhhh, have to look that up. We didn't used to carry that." Janice paged through a printout she grabbed from under the counter.

I had a feeling Janice would feel a lot more comfortable if I wasn't breathing down her neck. "Talk to you in a minute," I said, and headed to the back of the store where the small meat department lined a portion of the back wall.

As I walked along, my eyes took inventory on both sides of the aisle. Kidney beans, lima beans, black beans on one side of the aisle. Mushroom soup, tomato soup, cream of chicken soup, and more held down the shelves on the other side. Westin Foods had added a host of new products to the inventory in this small store, and the locals were rewarding us with increased patronage.

I stopped to rotate the labels forward on a few turned cans. Brand names facing out was the way I wanted items displayed. There was a can of vegetable soup in with the chicken noodle and I returned it to where it belonged.

Ted Driver had been anxious to sell his little gold mine, but by the time all was said and done, the deal-making had taken almost six months. Driver's Family Foods had turned into Westin Foods midwinter. Not the most convenient time in North Dakota to be making seventy-mile trips several times a week. I thought I'd walked through all the possible scenarios that adding a new store to my lineup might create, but I hadn't anticipated the learning curve that seemed to baffle the checkout clerks when I switched to an automated scanning system. Ted had been doing it the old-fashioned, punch-it-all-in-with-your-fingers way. The computerized system hadn't come cheap, and we were still trying to get some bugs out. From my point of view, the bugs mostly consisted of the old employees who really didn't want to learn a new system—but they were coming around. I hoped.

"Chester, how are you?" I waved at my butcher from across the meat counter and then pushed my way through the swinging doors, walking back to where he was mixing up a batch of the local salami the Emerson store was known for. Lucky for me Ted had included his secret recipe in the store deal. "How's it going?" I asked.

"I was going to call you," he said. "Give me one second here." Chester poured a couple handfuls of spices into the meat mixture, along with a scoop of black pepper. He turned around to the sink and brushed the spices from his hands, gave them a quick wash, and then began drying them on his apron. "Glad you came by. This morning when I came to work the meat cooler seemed to be acting funny."

Funny. The technical term for a potential disaster in the butcher department. In this business a "funny" cooler had nothing to do with ha-ha, and everything to do with spoiled meat and moola . . . not the cow kind of moo . . . the money kind of moola.

"Have you been monitoring the temperature?" I asked.

"Trying to, but it's been kinda busy today, so it's been hard to keep track. Kent called in sick so I've been back here by myself."

Kent, my sometime-when-I-feel-like-working meat department employee. Several employees like Kent had made it tempting to clean house when I first took over. Set in their ways didn't begin to describe the staff I inherited. But, in a small town, I knew better than to let everyone go, at least right away. I'd come to learn my staff was related to three-quarters of the people in Emerson. *Meet my cousin, Mr. Westin. This is my aunt . . . or uncle . . . or grandma.* No, I couldn't afford to offend anyone, not when I had a store and a new computer system to pay off . . . not to mention the possibility of new coolers.

Come to think of it, I couldn't afford a big

equipment breakdown like that, either. I glared at the meat counter as if my eyes could fix the problem. "I'll call a repair service and have them come check out the coolers first thing Monday."

Chester leaned forward and rearranged a few packages of steaks. "Do you want me to call Jerry? That's the guy who always did the fix-it work for Ted. He could probably stop by today."

And he was probably Chester's second cousin once removed. This wasn't how I liked to do things in my Carlton stores. I wanted people working on my expensive equipment who'd been trained specifically for refrigeration work. Then again, Ted's equipment wasn't new. If this Jerry-guy could keep my coolers from breaking down over the weekend that would be good. More than good. "Go ahead," I told Chester, "give Jerry a call. Let me know what he thinks. Anything else?" I asked.

Chester shot a glance over my shoulder across the meat counter. "I think Janice wants to talk to you."

I turned around. Sure enough, there stood my store manager, shifting from foot to foot. If body language could talk, I'd place a bet that what she had to tell me wasn't good news.

I shouldered my way through the swinging doors to Janice's side of the counter. "What can I do for you?"

She cast a quick look at Chester, then stared down at the floor. "You can let me quit."

"Quit?" A string of nerves stretched tight along the side of my neck. "What brought this on?" I turned and motioned for her to follow me to the small office at the back of the store. When we both were settled in chairs I folded my hands on the desktop. "You don't really want to quit." Maybe if I stated it as a fact, I'd change her mind.

Janice nodded. "Yes, I do." There were tears in her voice. "I never wanted to be a manager. I like visiting with people coming through the checkout line. I liked working for the Drivers." She blinked up at me. "Not that I don't like working for you, but all I have is a high school education. I don't understand the new computer system and I'm too old to take this much stress."

I had no idea how old Janice was, but I didn't think she was much older than me at fifty-five. "I understand," I said, putting every ounce of understanding I could muster into my words. Empathy went a long way in dealing with personnel problems. "There's always a learning curve when we're faced with something new. I think if you give it a little more time you'll find the new system easier than the old one."

The words weren't even out of my mouth before Janice started shaking her head. "I've worked here almost twenty-five years and I think that's long enough. I don't like being in charge of the ordering. Or making out the schedule."

I unfolded my hands and placed them on the

desktop. Maybe she didn't understand that we were still transitioning things between the three stores. "I'm doing the ordering from Carlton," I explained. "I'm counting on you to let me know what we're running low on here in Emerson."

She continued moving her head from side to side. "It makes me too nervous. All I wanted was a job where I could pass some time. Not one I had to worry about at night when I went home."

Welcome to my world. I sat back in my chair. Why in the world did everyone think owning your own business was the gold standard? Everyone who *didn't* own a business seemed to think a business owner could take off all the time he wanted, reach into the till and grab money if he needed some spare change, and sit back and count his fortune. *Ha!* The reality was that I often worked seven days a week. Even if I wasn't in the store, I was thinking and worrying about it.

I leaned forward. "Are you sure this is what you want to do?"

Janice pressed her lips together, then spoke. "I am. I'm going to spend more time with my grandkids. If you need me to fill in now and then at the checkout counter, I suppose I could come in sometimes. But I'd like to be done by the end of the month. Is that okay with you?"

"I suppose it has to be." I stood, walked around the desk, and shook her hand. "It was good having you as part of the team."

"Thanks," she murmured as she left.

I turned back to my small desk, pulled in a long, deep breath, and then slowly released it through my puffed cheeks and pursed lips. What did I ever see in all this?

It's all part of this game you call business. What would you do without your stores to run?

What would I do? Oh, that was easy—I'd restore my new old car. I'd play golf five days a week. I'd—

Come on. You can't play that much golf. You need more in your life than old cars and golf.

It never paid to argue with myself . . . one side of me always lost. I bit back a wry smile. The truth was, I did need more than those things, and I found the challenge I needed in my business. As irritating as some of the day-to-day problems were, I couldn't imagine anything I'd love more than running my stores. They were what got me out of bed in the morning. No, I couldn't imagine my life without my work.

Which was a good thing . . . wasn't it? I sat back down at my desk and pulled a piece of paper near. Picking up a pen, I started a list. This Saturday, which had started out rather uneventfully, had morphed into a day filled with challenges. Over the years I'd learned to prioritize. Number one. Maybe Chester would know where I could get a trailer to haul my rusty Charger back to Carlton. Number two. I'd wait to hear what Jerry had to say about the cooling system in the meat display. Number three. I paused, my pen in the air. Janice. What was I going to do about Janice leaving?

I tossed the pen onto the desk top, sat back in my chair, linked my hands behind my head, and stared at the ceiling. Janice had been my only option for store manager when I took over Ted's store. His wife had been his right-hand assistant. None of the other employees had any sort of management experience. Other than Janice, the staff was mostly part-time and fairly young . . . or old. Not that age mattered so much, but training did, and they didn't have anything beyond cash register experience. Chester was a gem, but he had his hands full running the meat department. I'd wanted the transition to be as smooth as possible. Transferring someone in from Carlton would have been like telling the folks in Emerson they didn't hold muster next to the big-city boy who'd taken over their little-town store. Small town politics played a big part in a community of this size. What was I going to do?

Pushing myself out of my chair, I tucked the to-do list into my shirt pocket. I had a week or so to drum up some brilliant idea. Janice had said she'd stick around for a little while longer. In the meantime I'd round up a trailer to haul my new hobby home. With any luck at all, Claire would see how overloaded I was with these new problems that had cropped up in the Emerson store, and she'd chalk up this rusty-car purchase to temporary insanity.

As it was, right now, the only thing keeping me from blowing a gasket was the thought of getting under the hood of that old car and pretending I had no other care in the world but to get that ancient engine running.

The thought of having the luxury of time to tinker caused me to draw in a long, calming breath. Ahh . . . someday soon I would do just that . . . but first I had to get my old jalopy home.

Drew

"Dad? What? I can't hear you. Wait a minute, you're breaking up. Let me get—" I pulled my cell phone away from my ear. Sure enough, I'd lost the call. You'd think living in New York, the center of the business world, someone would have invented a way to keep a cell phone connected. I snapped the cell phone shut. It didn't pay to try to return the call until I got into an area that had clear reception. And right now I was a moving target.

I jogged my way around what appeared to be a large group of tourists gawking at all Central Park had to offer, including runners like me. Trisha hadn't been one bit pleased about me taking most of a Saturday afternoon to get in a long run. Part of my idea to get in shape for a marathon. An idea I was still trying on for size. She was especially unhappy because I'd spent the morning at the office. I had a big loan closing on Monday and the only way the paperwork would be ready for the ten o'clock meeting meant me putting in some overtime on the weekend. Even my offer to take Trisha out for dinner hadn't pushed the frown off her face, but she did agree. Chalk up one point for me. Okay, maybe a half-point.

I wasn't thrilled to spend Saturday morning at work, or go through my run with my cell phone clipped to my running shorts. But I'd promised my boss I'd be available all weekend if any last-minute details needed tending before the loan closing on Monday.

I picked up my pace, focusing on another runner ahead of me. Let him clear a path through the people meandering through the park as if they had nothing on their minds but the beautiful fall day.

Whomp! Out of nowhere a Frisbee bopped me in the chest. I stopped in my tracks and managed to fumble the disk between my hands and not drop it.

"Sorry about that." A young woman came running my way, followed by a large dog. She gave me a sheepish grin. "Rex was supposed to get that."

"It's okay," I said, puffing hard and handing her the toy.

"Good catch," she called over her shoulder as she tossed the Frisbee and sent Rex running.

I bent over, hands on my knees, trying to get my breath. Running a marathon was one thing. Training for it was another story completely. If I'd known it would take this much time to prepare to run twenty-six miles, I might never have attempted it. But now that I'd worked my way up to fifteen miles, I wasn't about to back down. Besides, my coworker, Steve, had put money down on the fact he didn't think I had it in me to run that far. Nothing like a little friendly dig to make me determined.

I glanced at my watch. Another forty-five minutes to run to get my time in. Standing straight, I shook out my legs, working up the gumption to get on pace once more. As if my cell phone knew I'd rather have a break, it chimed. *New message.*

Almost certain the message was from my dad, I didn't bother to listen to it—just hit speed-dial and called him back.

"Drew," said the familiar voice, "you'll never guess what I'm doing."

I paced onto the grass, shaking out the tiredness in my legs. Dad sounded a little breathless himself, as if he'd just finished running a couple miles beside me. "Okay . . . what are you doing?"

"I'm standing in our driveway looking at my dream car."

Dream car? That didn't sound like my dad at all. He was a buy-'em-practical kind of guy. "Dad," I answered, "I can't even imag—Wait! Let me guess, you bought a Corvette." Now *that* would be sweet.

There was a long pause on the other end of the line. A small chuckle. "You know, that might have been a better idea. Wish it had occurred to me a couple hours ago."

I walked over to a bench, lifted my running shoe onto the edge, and leaned into the stretch. "What's going on?"

"Oh-hh . . ." Dad said, "I got caught up in an auction today and I ended up with a car." He sounded tentative.

"What kind of car?"

"Well . . . that's the thing. It sort of needs some work." There was a long pause. Knowing my dad he was pushing his fingers through his hair. "How do you feel about helping me restore a '68 Dodge Charger?"

"A '68 Dodge? You bought a car that was made before I was *born?* What did Mom say?"

Another soft chuckle. "Uh, I haven't exactly told her yet. She's not home right now. Although it'll be hard for her to miss, considering I need to clean out the garage before I have a place to put it."

"Dad?" I felt my brows push into the middle of my forehead. "Are you, like . . . okay?"

There was that nervous laugh. "I hope so." His voice was stronger when he spoke this time. "I was thinking maybe when you come home for the pheasant opener we could do a little fixing on the car. Think you might be able to stay a couple extra days past the weekend? I'd take some time off from the store and we'd—"

"Dad. Wait." How was I going to tell him? "Umm, I'm not sure I'm going to be able to make it for hunting. Things are really busy at work and I'm up for my annual review and I think . . ." Was I ready to share my hunch with my dad? ". . . I think I might be getting a promotion."

There was a long silence on the other end of the line. Then . . . "That's great, son. Really *great.*"

Something in Dad's voice didn't sound right. As if he wanted to say something more, but hesitated.

"I'm proud of you," he said. But still, there was something unsaid.

I sat down on the bench, put my elbows on my knees, and then spoke into the phone. "What is it?"

"Nothing, Drew. I'm proud of you."

"Dad, come on."

"Really, Drew. I'm happy for you. You've got a great job. You're doing well. I'm a little disappointed you might not make it home for hunting. But, a promotion? That's great. What more could I want?"

I glanced up at the big city skyline. What more? What more? I knew exactly what he wanted. He wanted me to come home and help him run the stores. To his credit he didn't say it.

He didn't have to.

. . .

"Happy ten-month anniversary." Trisha smiled at me across the candlelit table and lifted her water glass my way.

"Happy anniversary." I touched my glass to hers, hoping my buddies wouldn't find out about our ten-month celebration. I'd never live down the ribbing. One *year* was mandatory. *Ten months . . .* ah, not so.

We hadn't made a habit of celebrating every month since our small, Thanksgiving wedding, but to my benefit, after a day spent working and running, I was able to get back into Trisha's good graces by taking her to the restaurant where I'd so clumsily proposed. If my guess was right, we had the same waiter, too.

"Have you decided?" He stood by our table, with nothing to record our orders other than his memory.

I looked at Trisha. "Go ahead," I nodded.

"You go first. I'm having trouble deciding."

I addressed the waiter. "I'll have the rib eye, medium rare. Baked potato and the Caesar salad."

"Ummm . . ." Trisha bit at her bottom lip. "I guess I'll have the petite rib eye. Medium." She handed the waiter her menu. "Hash browns with extra butter. And honey mustard on my salad."

"Very good." He didn't blink an eye at Trisha's unusual order as he turned to leave.

My wife was a seafood gal when we ate out.

No butter, and salad dressing on the side. I leaned forward. "You're having *steak?* And extra butter?"

"I'm starving." Once again Trisha picked up her water glass and sipped, then reached for the bread basket. "Want some?"

"Man," I said, reaching for a hot roll, "you'd think *you* ran fifteen miles today." Oh, great, that was *not* a p.c. thing to say. Not on our ten-month anniversary. Or anytime, for that matter. I snuck a glance at my wife.

Instead of shooting me daggers, she was calmly buttering her dinner roll, a serene smile on her face. She took a bite, chewed slowly as if savoring each morsel, and then swallowed. "What would you say if I told you I'm pregnant?"

"You're *what?*" As if I'd never heard of the concept. "You're . . . ?" I coughed, the bite of roll in my mouth suddenly dry and in the way.

"Pregnant." She—there was no other word for it—beamed.

"How did you—Are you sure? I . . . I—" I sounded like a sitcom guy. It wasn't as if I hadn't known this was a possibility. While we hadn't been exactly *trying,* we'd done nothing to try *not* to. After all, both Trisha and I were in our thirties. Time was moving on. But for just this second, time seemed to have stopped. I sat back in my chair, suddenly very warm. I slipped out of the jacket I was wearing. "Wow."

"Wow, indeed." Trisha's eyes . . . yeah, well, they *twinkled.*

I was starting to sound like a sappy kind of first-time dad. But, I realized, I didn't care. I leaned across the table and took Trisha's hand in mine. "Whoo-hoo," I said softly.

Trisha laughed and lifted her chin. "Got any thoughts about being called 'Daddy'?"

My Adam's apple bobbed. *Daddy.* Wow, again. I hadn't thought that far ahead. "When are you due? Uh, *we* due?" I asked.

"I did the home test last night. Maybe I'm a month along. So that would put us at about May."

"May." I sounded like an echo. A very surprised echo.

She leaned forward, excitement in her eyes. "What would you like to name our baby? Any ideas?"

"Caesar?" The waiter's timing was impeccable. He set my salad in front of me as Trisha and I burst out laughing. The waiter looked a bit confused as he set Trisha's salad in front of her. "Is everything all right?" he asked.

"It's perfect," Trisha said, grinning at me. "What's wrong with Caesar?" She laughed as the waiter left.

"Nothing like high hopes for our kid, huh?" The news was starting to settle in around my racing thoughts. A baby. Wow. I picked up my fork and speared some lettuce, suddenly ravenous.

Instead of beginning to eat, Trisha put her hands in her lap and appeared to be praying. I held my fork in mid-air, not sure if I should try to quickly join her or continue to eat. It wasn't that I didn't believe in praying before a meal. Growing up in Carlton, saying grace had been automatic around our dinner table, but somewhere along the line between college and moving to New York, my habit had fallen by the wayside.

In a short minute Trisha picked up her fork. She looked over at me and smiled. "I'm so happy to be pregnant. I had to say 'thanks.'"

Having a baby was already changing things, it seemed.

"That was great." With my thumb I nudged my empty plate toward the center of the table, the smell of sizzling steak lingering in the air.

"It was." Trisha had eaten every bite.

As if on cue, our waiter appeared and lifted our plates. "Dessert?"

"No—"

"We'd love some," Trisha said, changing my mind for me. "Do you have crème brûlée?"

"Excellent choice. I'll bring it right out."

"Two spoons, please," Trisha instructed. She looked my way. "I hope I'm not eating for *three,*" she said.

My heart did a sudden double-thump. *Three?* Trisha, plus baby, plus . . . ? Was she talking twins? There was no way she could know that . . . was there? Not this soon. Not without seeing a doctor. It felt as if the blood was draining from my head to my stomach.

"Drew!" Trisha was giggling. "Don't pass out. It was a joke."

I wiped at my upper lip with my napkin. "Not so funny," I replied. A deep breath was in order. "Now I really want that promotion."

"Yeah." Trisha rearranged the napkin in her lap. She shook her head back, letting her hair move away from her face. "I suppose we should talk about that . . . my working, I mean. I never thought I'd say this, but I think I'd really like to stay home with our baby."

Our baby. The two words sounded surreal. A few hours ago I'd been obsessed with training for a marathon and getting a promotion, now I was going to have a family to provide for.

"Drew?" Tricia was leaning forward, looking at me. "Did you hear me? I said I've kind of been-there-done-that with the career thing."

I hoped I could be forgiven for zoning out for a second. My mind was moving a hundred miles an hour. "Um-hm. Yeah. Okay." Living in New York wasn't cheap, but we'd figure something out. If I got the promotion, there would be a raise to go along with it.

I watched as the waiter put the crème brûlée on the table between us. Did he have any idea what had happened during the meal he'd served us? That Trisha and I had gone from being a simple *couple* to a *family?*

I picked up my spoon and tapped at the brown sugar crust, took a scoop of the creamy pudding below. What did it cost to raise a child? We were definitely going to need to look for a bigger place. Our one-bedroom-with-an-office-nook apartment wouldn't hold a baby for long.

"Tell me what you remember about growing up in Carlton." Trisha's voice drifted into my racing thoughts.

"What I remember?" I gave my head a shake. I'd been a million miles away in my own bubble of plans. I refocused as I reached for another spoonful of the crème brûlée. "What I remember? Well, there was a grove of trees behind our house by the alley. Reed and I used to hang out in there and pretend we were spies." I laughed at the memory. "Actually, now that I think about it, that grove of trees was probably two trees and a couple shrubs, but we could see across the alley and watch the neighbor's two dogs in the kennel they had in their backyard. We'd whisper and make elaborate plans to dash into their yard and free the prisoners." I took a bite of dessert while I retraced the memory. "Of course we never *did* anything, but it sure was fun imagining we might."

Tricia held her spoon above the dessert. "I remember you telling me about the time you and

Reed were trying to stack cans at your dad's store, and instead of putting them in a pyramid like your dad had shown you, you guys decided to see who could build the highest tower."

"Oh, man, yeah." I raised my eyes, as if I was seeing the scene play out on a screen in my mind. "And then Dad walked around the end of the aisle and we knew we'd been caught doing something we weren't supposed to. Reed jumped in front of his tower to try and hide it from Dad, and both of our stacks of cans fell over. Dad was *not* a happy camper." I laughed at the memory. It sure seemed funny in retrospect. And when I thought about it now, I wondered if my dad hadn't ended up having a good laugh about it behind our backs. *After* we'd been scolded for denting the cans and not doing our job.

As much as I'd complained about having to work at the store, the job taught me a lot about working with merchandise and people. Dad instilled a strong work ethic in his kids, something I was seeing pay off in my career now.

There was the slightest catch in my throat, and I coughed against the surprising emotion these thoughts of my childhood triggered. Working alongside my dad was an experience I'd never trade for anything.

Oh.

I looked across the table at Trisha. Her eyes were locked on mine. She didn't say a word as she raised her spoon and put a sweet bite of dessert into her mouth. She didn't have to.

I knew what she was getting at. And, I could tell . . . she knew that I knew. She wanted us to move home.

DECEMBER: PRESENTS COME IN ALL SORTS OF PACKAGES . . .

Claire

How could a house get so dusty in one week? I swiped at the filmy layer of dust covering the surface of the end table at the end of the couch. Well, okay, maybe it had been two weeks since I'd dusted . . . but still. I moved to the coffee table and carefully maneuvered my cloth under and around the ceramic Nativity set on display. Christmas was right around the corner. The tree was up, I planned to bake a couple batches of Christmas cookies this afternoon—a rare day when I didn't have to be on campus—and the kids would be home in three weeks. All the important bases were covered. A childlike sense of anticipation fluttered inside me. Did anyone ever outgrow the thrill of Christmas?

Thrill or not, this house needed a good once-over. I tossed my dust rag on the floor near the front door, then got busy with the noisy job of vacuuming. There. Next on my agenda was to shake out the kitchen throw rugs and my lint-filled dust cloth. Grabbing the two rubber-backed rugs off the floor, I held them over my arm and opened the front door. This was going to have to be a fast job—it was *freezing* out here. Stepping onto the front landing, I almost tripped over a medium-sized box sitting in front of the door.

"Whoops!" I danced a bit on the frosty step, trying to keep my balance. The mailman must have made his rounds while I'd been vacuuming. Our curious dog, Pesto, poked his nose against the package. "What do you think is in there?" I asked, stooping to pick it up. I had a hunch it was the Minnesota Vikings sweatshirt I'd ordered Reed for Christmas. Then again, this box was much too bulky to be a single sweatshirt. I left the rugs outside on the landing and carried the package inside, closing the door behind me.

One glance at the return label sent my heart racing. *West Press.* Wesley's publishing company. Make that *my* publisher. There could only be one thing inside this box. My book. It had actually happened. My dream. My vow. All of that was inside this box.

Heart pounding almost as hard as the day Wesley had called with the news he wanted to publish my book, I tore at the wrapping. If I wanted to keep my fingernails intact I was going to need a knife to slice open the heavy packing tape. Carrying the box, I hurried into the kitchen and quickly cut through the tight seal. Then I stopped. While the flaps were still closed everything remained the way it had been in my imagination. The dream of writing a book about friendship. The vow to use my mother's incomplete projects to spur on my own. Once I opened this covering it would all become real. Was I ready?

Oh, Lord, make me ready for what You have planned.

Ready or not, I opened the box. There wasn't one book inside, there were ten. Ten pristine copies of the slim volume. Oh, my. I spread all ten copies out on my kitchen counter and pressed my warm palms against my cheeks. I knew what to do with one copy. Put it on the shelf I'd just dusted. But nine more? I could wrap up one for each of the kids and put it under the tree. But that seemed a little self-important, didn't it?

I had nine copies of a book I didn't know what to do with. Give one to the local paper? Was it too presumptuous to assume they'd want to review it? I could donate one to our city library, but wasn't the point to have people *buy* my book? I rolled my eyes at my doubts. I had no idea how to act like a writer. I needed to call Julie. She'd know.

Removing the lid from my steaming to-go cup of coffee, I inhaled the enticing aroma, blew across the misty surface, and then took a sip. Carlton's Book Nook had the absolute best brew in town. I replaced the lid, assuring that my coffee would stay steamy as long as possible. *Hot* coffee was my beverage of choice, and a perfect way to warm up on a cold, December Saturday. The icy wind had literally blown Julie and me into the store. After picking up our coffees, we'd gone opposite ways to browse.

Jazzy holiday music played softly in the background as I shifted the cup to my other hand and pulled an interesting-looking book from the shelf. The author was unfamiliar to me, but that didn't matter as long as the story line caught my imagination. I got enough nonfiction reading in my daytime hours at the university. When I wanted to escape, fiction was my drug of choice. I balanced my coffee cup on the edge of the shelf and opened the book to read the inside front flap.

"Claire, come here, I have to show you something." Julie had appeared out of nowhere and was tugging at my arm. Her voice was a whisper, library-low, almost secretive. "Come on." She tilted her head as if urging me to move quickly.

"What? Wait. Let me read this." I took a side-step away, trying to keep my concentration on what looked to be an engaging story.

"No," Julie said, removing the book from my hand and putting it back on the shelf. "You have to come *now*. Seriously, this is worth it."

It wasn't often I felt irritated with Julie, but I did now. We were supposed to be enjoying a Saturday morning of leisurely browsing. We'd started off at a local boutique, moved down the street to the Book Nook, and were planning to have lunch when we were done here. Julie and I had completely different reading tastes. She gravitated to nonfiction, self-help types of books, whereas I wanted nothing but fiction. I was almost sure anything Julie wanted to show me wouldn't be worth all this drama. But then, that was typical Julie.

Grabbing my coffee cup from the shelf, I followed my friend away from my beloved fiction, past the bargain tables of discounted books, and, sure enough, into her preferred self-help section.

I stopped in my tracks. "Julie, you know I—"

"Shhh . . ." Julie turned around to look at me, an impish grin behind the finger she put to her lips. Once again, she tilted her head. *Follow me.*

She might be able to lead a Sociology professor to the self-help section, but she couldn't force her to like it. I stubbornly stayed right where I was, removed the plastic lid from my coffee, and took a long swallow. There, now I'd follow her.

Julie rounded one aisle, did some fancy footwork as she turned around to face me, then stepped aside and pointed to the top row of books on the shelf behind her. One arm swung gracefully outward as if she was a product model on *The Price Is Right.* "Ta-da."

"I don't see—"

But then I did. The shelves around me seemed to fade into the periphery. A strange echo chamber formed around my ears. The soft music in the background receded to almost nothing. Julie had turned nearly invisible at the edge of my line of sight. What I did see—all I *could* see—was . . .

I put a hand over my mouth, whispered behind it. "My book."

At first I felt a chill, almost as if I might pass out, then my heart picked up its rhythm and did double duty, a hot flush rising to my face.

"Claire." Julie now had her face pushed right in front of mine. "Do you believe it? Isn't it cool?"

It would have been *cool* if I wasn't quite so warm. I set my coffee cup on the ledge of the bookshelf and tugged at the neckline of the sweater I was wearing. I needed some air. An odd feeling of embarrassment crept over me. As if now everyone would *know.*

Of course they'd know. I'd written a book, for goodness sake. It had been published, and now, somehow, it had found its way to my local bookstore.

"I don't believe this," I said, reaching out and picking up a copy from the shelf. "I never thought . . ."

"I'm going to buy one," Julie said, taking another copy off the shelf.

"No! You can't."

"What do you mean I *can't* buy your book? Of course I can, and I will." She turned and headed for the cashier counter.

Me? I was rooted to the spot. Holding a copy of my year-ago summer's project between my hands. *The Friendship Factor.* It was one thing to see my book on the kitchen counter. A whole other thing to see it here. How had my book gotten on this shelf without me knowing about it?

I ran my hand over the cover, tracing my name with my finger as if outlining the path my manuscript had taken since it left my computer. The manuscript had traveled a circuitous route from my faculty-friend in the Sociology Department, to her brother, owner of a small press publishing house. He'd been enthusiastic about my first attempt at writing a book.

"This has real potential," he'd said in a phone call. *"I'm thinking you could submit this to one of the big guys."*

The only trouble was, I didn't know any of the big guys. I didn't know the first thing about publishing anything more than an academic article or two in a professional journal. I was content to know that even a "little guy" was interested.

"I'm willing to stick with *you,*" I'd told Wesley, my friend's brother, and now, it seemed, my publisher.

The whole experience seemed surreal. Wesley had kept me abreast of the process through e-mails and an occasional phone call. He'd worked with me on some minor editing, and then said he was going to do all he could to get this book distributed far beyond the regional territory where his products sold reasonably well.

I had no idea what *reasonable* was, but anything beyond the ten free copies he'd sent me, hot off the press, would be more than I expected.

I'd gotten caught up in the new school term. My teaching schedule was full. Semester tests were right around the calendar. For all I knew of the publishing industry, I assumed my job was to let Wesley do his.

And, apparently, he had. Here I stood, in the Book Nook, holding a bonafide copy of *The Friendship Factor* in my hands. *Claire Westin* on the cover for all the world to see.

I felt one eyebrow rise in wry amusement. Ha . . . *all the world.* Yeah, right. I'd be lucky if my little treatise on friendship sold more than a few hundred copies. Make that a few dozen. Wesley didn't pull any punches when he filled me in on the facts of small-press publishing. He was going to take a leap of faith with my book. They rarely did print runs of more than a thousand. He was going to double mine. *Don't get your hopes up,* he'd said, then went on to tell me what he was going to do to try and make my book different. He probably said that to all his writers . . . who knew?

His enthusiasm wasn't catching. Instead it made me nervous. What if the book didn't sell? I didn't want to be responsible for his overconfidence in my writing. Or the hit his business would take if my book bombed.

"Don't worry," he'd said. "I'm willing to take some chances with this one."

It was out of my house . . . and my hands. All I could do was pray. God was the ultimate marketer. I'd been percolating my theories on friendship since I'd done a research paper on it for my master's degree. Writing about friendship from a theoretical view was slightly tedious, but when I started adding tidbits about the friendships I'd had over the years . . . especially my bond with Julie, the text had come alive. I'd been happy with the final product, but not one bit confident about how it might sell. Julie had given me two thumbs-up and a *big* hug when she'd read my final draft. But what else did I expect from my best friend? Either way, whether my book sold well or not, I at least had the knowledge that this was one dream I could put to rest.

I opened the front cover of the book to the dedication page. There it was:

To my mother, with love.

I felt a thickening in my throat and found myself blinking at the sudden stinging in my eyes. This was one project my mother could say she helped complete. I hoped she was telling the angels in heaven right now.

I put the book back on the shelf and couldn't help myself from counting . . . two, three, six copies on the shelf. Face out, which I knew to be a good thing. Well, at least Julie was buying *one* copy. My book wouldn't be a complete skunk.

"Claire, get over here." Julie was waving me over to the checkout counter.

For a quick second I closed my eyes, steeling myself. Knowing Julie she'd already told the clerk that the real-live-author of the book in her hands was standing right over *there.*

Once again, or maybe it had never stopped, a hot flash of emotion washed up from my middle and into my face. *Oh, just doing my beet imitation,* I imagined myself saying as I walked toward the store clerk.

"This is the *manager,*" Julie said, pulling me forward. Apparently Julie had already alerted the woman to my authorial status.

"Hi." A woman, who looked to be about my age, walked around the end of the counter and shook my hand. "It's a pleasure to meet you. I understand you teach at the university. We don't get many authors from right here in Carlton."

What was I supposed to say to that? Put me in front of a classroom and I knew my stuff, but being referred to as an *author* was something altogether different. "Um, thanks for carrying my book." Was that what authors said?

"It's been selling well," the manager said. "We

ordered three copies to begin with and then a local book club decided to use it for their discussion next month. We got in another dozen and I'd guess they're half gone. Would you be interested in doing a book signing?"

"A book signing? Me? I—"

"Of course she would." As if she'd been waiting for an invitation, Julie pulled her planner out of her purse. "Are you thinking before or after Christmas?"

"Let me check our schedule." The manager ducked behind the counter and pulled out a calendar. "It's not much lead time, but we have another author coming in for a signing in two weeks. I should be able to get another shipment of books in by then. It works well to have more than one signing on the same day." She smiled my way. "People who love books love meeting the people who write them."

"I know," said Julie as if I wasn't standing right there.

The store manager held a pen my way. "Could you sign the books we already have in stock?"

"Uh . . ." I cleared my throat. "Sure. I guess."

The store manager rummaged under the counter and pulled out a roll of "Autographed Copy" stickers. "I'll put these on after you've signed the books. Thanks for doing this. We really appreciate it."

"No problem," piped Julie, taking the pen from

the manager and turning me toward the books.

Somewhere along the line my coffee had cooled. As I followed Julie through the aisles, I took a lukewarm sip and wondered just when this morning had gone out of my control.

This book thing was taking on a life of its own . . . whether I wanted it to or not.

"And so . . ." With the side of my fork, I cut a bite of salmon and speared it with the tines ". . . thanks to Julie I'm going to be having a *book signing* at the Book Nook in two weeks."

Jim took a drink of skim milk, then a forkful of rice pilaf. "That's great." He sounded a million miles away.

"Jim." I nudged him under the table with my foot. "I really need you to listen to me. I said I'm going to have a book signing. At the Book Nook."

"I heard you." Jim put a piece of salmon into his mouth and talked around it. "I said, 'that's great.'"

Turning my fork over, I pushed some peas around on my plate. "Yeah, great."

He took another bite of salmon. "You don't sound very excited."

"Well . . . I am." I put my fork down and put my hands in my lap. Looking up at my husband, I added, "Kind of."

"What's wrong?"

Now that I had his attention I wasn't so sure I

wanted it. I shrugged a shoulder and lifted my fork again, poking at the food on my plate. "It's something I never thought about doing. A book signing and . . ." I lifted my hand in the air ". . . whatever. I don't know, I guess I thought I'd get that whole friendship book thing out of my system. Write the book and be done with it. If nothing ever came of it, well, it's not as if I don't have enough to do. I'll be correcting term papers at the end of the month. I've got a full load of classes to teach. The kids will be here for Christmas. I'm not sure this is what I signed on for."

A wry, half-laugh escaped from Jim. "Ha! I'm not sure any of this is what we signed on for. Guess what I heard today?"

"What?" It was just as well the conversation turned away from my wavering self-doubt.

Jim reached for the bowl of rice and scooped another helping onto his plate. "Rumor has it there's a *super* being added onto the Target store at Westwood Mall."

My jaw dropped open. "Where did you hear that?"

"The Chamber meeting today."

I closed my jaw, but couldn't help worrying out loud. "I suppose that means they'll be adding a grocery line?"

"That's what it usually means." I knew he didn't mean to sound short with me. I could see the worry etched between his brows.

It wasn't as if Westin Foods didn't already have competition. There were two other large grocery stores in Carlton. The owners knew and respected each other, a sense of healthy competition among them. But having one of the national chains come to town changed the idea of healthy competition into a possible fight-for-your-lives battle.

Oh, my. No wonder Jim sounded so distracted. Suddenly my book signing sounded like small potatoes next to Jim's worry. The big-box stores were a mixed blessing in a town the size of Carlton. While the national chains offered a large variety of merchandise and low prices, the locally-owned stores had a difficult time competing. Carlton had already seen the demise of a couple mom-and-pop type cafes, along with our downtown drugstore. Would Westin Foods be able to hold its own against a *super*-anything?

"Can you do anything about it?" I asked.

"Other than not like it, you mean?" Jim gave me a thin smile, then resumed eating and talking. "If I put up a fuss, I'll look like I don't want Carlton to grow. But I'd be lying if I didn't say I'm worried. Not only can they offer lower prices because they buy in such volume, but I'm also worried they're going to take my employees. I'm not sure what kind of benefits they offer, but I'm already offering the best we can afford. The thing is, the grass is always greener on the *other side* of the grocery aisle."

Now it was my turn to give him a thin smile. "At least you've still got your sense of humor."

Jim finished off his glass of milk. "We're going to have to compete with customer service. It's the only weapon I've got . . . North Dakota 'nice.'"

He pushed himself away from the table and began clearing the dishes. Pesto took that as his cue to start begging for leftovers.

"Lay down," I reminded, nudging the cream-colored terrier with my foot. Whenever the kids were home, the little pest was used to getting scraps slipped to him under the table. But age was getting the better of him, and a touchy stomach meant leftovers days were over. It was nothing but a vet-recommended diet for him.

"Come here," Jim coaxed. He pulled a small dog treat out of the cupboard and put it in Pesto's dish. "There you go." Pesto snapped up the treat and then trotted into the family room.

Jim picked up some dishes and carried them to the kitchen counter. Ever since the kids left home, Jim had been a real trooper, pitching in with household chores. We both worked full-time and more, and my schedule usually held an evening class two nights a week. We made a point of enjoying our relatively rare evenings at home together.

I stood from the table and held my empty plate in one hand. With the other, I reached out and rubbed a gentle circle on Jim's shoulder. "I'll clean up tonight."

"That's okay, I'll help," Jim said, opening the dishwasher and placing his plate inside. He loaded the dishwasher while I put away the leftover rice and threw away a tablespoon of peas.

Maybe instead of worrying about what the future held, it would help to talk about more practical matters. "When are you going to do something with that old car in the garage?" I asked, running hot water into the sink. I squirted some dishwashing soap into the pan I'd used to steam the salmon and began scrubbing.

"Don't remind me," Jim said. "I'm beginning to think I should look for a storage place to keep it. I had good intentions, but with all the stuff I have going on now . . ." His words trailed off. He grabbed a dishtowel off the oven door and started drying the pan I'd washed. "Believe me, I'd rather have my regular car in the garage. Shoveling snow around a car sitting in the driveway is a pain in the back. I don't know what I was thinking when I bought that old thing. Maybe I should try and sell it."

I knew enough to not say anything. We'd had enough words about that old thing when he'd brought it home in September. I wasn't nuts about sharing the garage with what amounted to rusty parts, but Jim had been as excited as a teenager. He worked hard and certainly deserved to indulge himself in a new hobby, but as far as I could see, he hadn't done much more than stand in the garage and stare at the contraption.

He put down his dish towel and bent to put away the pan he'd just dried. "I'll get at it someday. Maybe when Drew and Trisha are back for Christmas he can help me figure out where to start. Things have been too bus—" The ring of the telephone cut him off. Perfect timing if we were talking about being swamped.

"I'll get it," I said, wiping my hands on a kitchen towel and reaching for the phone. "It's probably Julie notifying me of a Midwest Book Tour she's lined up. Hello?"

"Claire? It's Dad."

"Dad, hi!" I tucked the phone under my chin and motioned Jim that I'd finish up. Sometimes, between my teaching schedule, keeping up the house, grading papers, staying in touch with the kids, Julie, and Jim, I let too much time pass between talks with my dad. If I remembered right, it had been Monday the last time we'd talked. Almost a week ago. "How are you?"

The pause on the other end of the line was too long. "Not so good. I don't want to bother you, but—"

"You're no bother, Dad. What's wrong?"

"Well . . . I had a little fender bender on the way home from the grocery store tonight and I think I might—"

"What were you doing going to the grocery store this time of night? It's slippery out, and freezing." We'd certainly come full circle if I was the one telling my dad he shouldn't be out after dark.

Again a too-long pause. I felt the sting of my words in that silence. My dad had turned seventy-eight, not ancient or feeble. He deserved better than my reprimand. "I'm sorry, Dad. Tell me what happened."

He didn't take long to get to the point. A slippery intersection had done the trick. He'd bumped over a curb and run down a stop sign. The police had come and taken information. Dad waved off a trip to the hospital. He was fine. Except, now he didn't think he was.

"I've got a goose egg on the side of my head, and I'm a little dizzy, too. I would have driven myself to the hospital, but under the circum-stances, I . . ."

Here was where I could make things right again. "I'll be right over, Dad. Get your coat on. I'll come to the door and help you to the car."

I hung up the phone, reached for my car keys on the top of the fridge, and grabbed my coat from the line of hooks near the door. Pushing my arm into the sleeve of my coat, I headed to the family room to let Jim know where I was going. So much for a quiet evening at home enjoying the lights on the Christmas tree with my husband.

I'd barely started explaining the situation to Jim when the phone interrupted. I grabbed up the family room extension. "Dad, I'm on my way."

There was a light laugh on the other end of the line. "I'm sorry, I guess you were expecting another call." The woman's voice was unfamiliar.

"I guess I was," I said, my brain too swamped with other things to laugh along. "I was on my way out the door. My dad—" Oh, goodness, this woman didn't call to hear my litany of woes. "I'm sorry, who did you want to speak to?"

"I'm calling for Claire Westin."

She didn't sound like a telemarketer, but I was still tempted to say "she's not home," but adding a lie to my list of concerns was all I needed. "I'm Claire," I said, tucking the phone between my cheek and shoulder as I started to button my coat. As soon as she started her sales pitch I'd say I wasn't interested. That I didn't donate money over the phone. I'd be out the door in half a second.

"Oh, hi, Claire. You don't know me, but I'm the chairperson of the Carlton Community Club, Ginny Black. I'm calling to . . ."

It would be one thing to blow off a telemarketer from Timbuktu, something else to cut short someone from the town where I lived. Someone who just possibly shopped at Westin Foods. Someone who could very easily switch her shopping to SuperTarget. I sent up a quick prayer that whatever was ailing my dad wouldn't get worse in the next five minutes. *Twenty-five dollars.* If she asked for a donation, that's what I'd give. And then I'd hightail it over to Dad's.

". . . and we thought it would be great if you could be the featured speaker at our next meeting."

What? Somewhere along the line I'd missed a whole paragraph of conversation. I pulled the receiver from my ear and squinted at it as if I could read the part I'd missed. Through the cluster of tiny holes at the base of the receiver I heard, "We'd pay you, of course."

"I'm sorry," I said, tucking the phone back to my ear, a bewildered chuckle escaping from between my lips. "I don't think I heard all that. I was waiting for you to ask for a donation."

"Oh, no." Ginny laughed. "No, not at all. Someone gave me a copy of your book, *The Friendship Factor*, and I had a hard time putting it down. I'm in charge of lining up the speaker for our January meeting and I thought of you."

"Me?"

"Yes . . . ?" Now Ginny was starting to sound bewildered.

"What are you—? I mean, what would—I'm sorry," I went on. "I was on my way out the door and, obviously, my mind is already out there. Could you tell me again why you're calling?"

"Sure." Ginny was probably regretting ever dialing my number, but I had to give her credit for hanging in there. "We're a group of young working women in the community and we meet once a month for networking and support. One thing many of us have talked about is that we don't have time to cultivate friendships like we'd like." She took a breath. "Your book really hit home with me, and I think it will with the rest of the group. Would you come talk to us?"

"I . . . uh . . . I . . ." Teaching sociology to college kids was one thing, but did I really have anything to say to a group of professional women? Hadn't my book said it all? Couldn't they read that and . . . talk about it?

Ginny misinterpreted my hesitation. "We can't pay much, but we do offer an honorarium."

I glanced into the family room at my husband sorting through store printouts on his lap, while a small stack of Christmas gifts I'd planned on wrapping tonight stood sentry on one end of the couch. I thought of my dad more than likely standing on the front step waiting for me. It wasn't as if I had nothing to do, but I did feel a little bit flattered to think that Ginny wanted me to talk to her group. I had over a month to think about what I'd say to the women of the Community Club. The quickest way out the door was to say, "Yes, I guess I could do that."

"Great!" Ginny sounded much more certain about what she was committing to than I did. "I know you're on your way out. Here's my number. Call me and we'll talk about the details. I can't wait to hear you speak. This is so exciting."

I jotted down her number and hurried out the

door to the garage. In spite of my worry about my dad, there was another emotion simmering in my chest. As I started the car and backed out of the garage, I tumbled this new feeling around inside. My students were in my classes because they needed the credits to complete their degrees. The women of the Community Club would be coming to hear me speak because they *wanted* to. And, I had to admit, there was something about that tiny distinction that thrilled me.

Jim

"Let us pray." The minister stood in the center of the elevated section at the front of the church, right behind the casket that held my Chamber buddy, Arnie Matthews. "Lord, we now commit our friend and colleague to Your . . ."

I bowed my head, but my thoughts weren't focused on the words the minister was saying. Out of the corner of my eye I scanned the men in the row where I was sitting. Beside me, a handful of the Carlton Chamber of Commerce members held down the pews. Apparently, it didn't take long for people to forget a formerly active member. I wondered if the men and women surrounding me were as dazed over Arnie's sudden death as I was. He'd retired . . . when? I snuck a peek at the funeral program in my hand and counted on my fingers. The end of July a year ago. Add in August. September.

October. November. And now it was the middle of December. Less than a year-and-a-half ago. I could almost taste the overly-sweet punch I'd drank in honor of his retirement. Certainly Arnie hadn't planned on leaving this earth only seventeen months after he sold his business.

I gave my head a small shake and tried to concentrate on what the pastor was saying. If he was offering comfort, I could use a good dose of it.

"Our days are numbered by You, oh, Lord . . ."

Numbers. Arnie had been only sixty-two. Seven years older than me. Is this what I had to look forward to? Quitting work and then keeling over? If so, maybe I should sell the stores and take my numbered days, and do some relaxing. But who'd be nuts enough to buy my three stores with a SuperTarget coming to town? Now was not the time to look to sell out, but what I could do was take a lesson from Arnie—well, maybe not from him, but from what happened to him. Life was short and the end could come without warning. I should quit thinking about business 24/7. I should get busy, get some heat into my garage, and start fixing up that old Dodge I'd bought this summer. The old car had done nothing but take up space since I'd hauled it home with good intentions. Drew and Trisha would be home for the holidays in a week. Reed would be home, too. And Brad could help. The four of us could at least make some progress taking the engine apart and running interference on the rust, while the gals were inside cooking up Christmas stuff. Arnie's sudden death had pulled the car mat out from under me, but possibly something good could come from his demise. Instead of waiting for *someday* to roll around, I'd make a point of getting more life out of the days I was currently hurrying through. After I stopped by the store.

Even though the pastor was still praying, I found myself tapping my toe, itching to get on with this day. I'd paid my respects, taken a message from Arnie's life, and now I was anxious to practice what the pastor preached. But first, I needed to scan some data for the stores. See what products were moving and what was stalled on the shelves. Even with all the changes technology offered, the grocery business was labor intensive. Trucks needed unloading. Shelves needed to be stocked daily. Produce and meat required monitoring for freshness. All that took people power, and all those employees looked to *me* for their paychecks. Even a funeral couldn't stop the fact that people needed to eat.

As the organist played the opening bars of "Amazing Grace," I discreetly pushed back the cuff of my shirt and looked down at my watch. There were only so many hours in the day, and with a bank board meeting later this afternoon plus the work I had waiting for me at the store, my ambitious plan to start restoring my old dream car suddenly seemed more work than fun. Maybe the kids would get my enthusiasm back where it belonged. After all, I was counting on this project to do more than simply restore an old car. I was hoping it would give me a new hobby, provide a bridge into retirement, and provide an interest I could share with my sons and son-in-law. I'd prove to Claire that my auction money was well spent. And my time.

The pallbearers slowly marched Arnie's casket down the aisle, followed by his dry-eyed but drained-looking wife. What must *she* be thinking? A casket and a funeral were certainly not the retirement activities Arnie had in mind a year ago. Claire and I really needed to sit down one of these days and seriously talk about what we hoped the future held for us. The good news in all this was that I was seven years younger than Arnie, and healthy. My doctor had confirmed that at my annual physical.

Annual?

My eyes semi-rolled into their sockets while I tried to remember exactly when it was I'd gone in for my last checkup. Maybe it had been closer to two years ago, not one, but I'd checked out hale and hearty and I felt fine. In fact, I felt better than fine. I'd better. I didn't have time to be sick.

Bob Marsden, president of the bank board, tapped the tip of his pen against the last item on the agenda for this meeting, then laid down his pen and folded his hands on top of the paper. "I'm sure we all agree the recent growth in assets is encouraging, but along with growth comes growing pains. I've talked the situation over with our lending team and we agree on the need to add at least two loan officers to our slate of lenders. Any discussion?"

"I agree," Tony Johns, one of the senior lenders spoke up. "And the sooner the better. Who knows what kind of business we might bring in if and when we have adequate staff to service our customer base."

As the other board members discussed the budget for hiring two new loan officers, a thrum of an idea sent my fingers tapping against the edge of my chair under the heavy boardroom table. *Drew.* This would be the perfect opportunity to bring him back to Carlton.

The perfect opportunity . . . *if* he wanted to come. But I knew his feelings on that topic.

Then again, maybe I didn't. What I did know was that he didn't want to come back and work in the store. He'd never said a word about not coming back *period.*

You're not thinking about using the old bait-and-switch tactic, are you?

One side of my mouth lifted in a silent smile. Of course I wasn't.

Was I?

"Here you go." I tossed a greasy rag across the top of the engine block to Drew. "Your mom will pitch a fit if we drag old car dirt into the house."

My oldest son wiped his hands on the rag and stared down at the conglomeration of dusty and rusty engine parts. He looked over at me, a smirk on his face. "What were you thinking?"

I couldn't help but laugh. "I know, I know."

"Dad, you are never going to have time to restore this . . . this . . ." He waved one hand in the air, a helpless gesture.

"Junker?" I supplied.

"I'm glad you said it."

It was cold in the garage, so I didn't have much time. This would be the perfect opportunity for me to bring up the subject of Drew moving back to Carlton. *I was hoping to have a little help,* I could say. But, no, that would be too obvious. I'd bide my time. Drew and Tricia had flown into town late last night. Reed would be arriving sometime today. I had four whole days to find the perfect way to let my son know he was needed back home. And not just to work on an old junker.

Reed reached for another piece of the apple-strudel bread on a platter in the middle of the kitchen table. "This is good," he said.

I'd brought the bread home from the store for Claire to try while the kids were home. It was a new item we were featuring for the holidays, and an easy breakfast for our visiting crew. Especially handy since Claire was having her first book signing at the Book Nook later this morning.

"Really," she said now, "none of you have to come."

"Oh, right, Mom." Drew chimed in. "As if."

Claire took a sip of her coffee. "I think having all you guys there will make me nervous. What if no one shows up?"

"All the more reason we should be there," Drew added.

"I can't wait." This from our daughter-in-law, Trisha. "I've never known anyone who's written a book before. I think it's exciting."

"Well," Claire said, smoothing her skirt with her hands, "you are way more optimistic than I am. Someone told me that if you sell between three and seven books at a book signing you're doing better than most."

"There you go," I said, counting the heads at our table, "Drew, Trisha, Reed, and me. Oh, and don't forget, Kaylee and Brad will be there. And knowing Julie she'll beat all of us. That's seven copies right there."

Claire gave a nervous laugh. "You are *not* all buying copies of my book. Talk about a pitiful book signing when the only people who buy a copy are related to me. Except for Julie, and she might as well be." Claire stood from the table and lifted the now-empty pastry platter. "What are you guys going to do the rest of the morning while I'm at my *big gala?*" Her tone of voice let us know exactly what she thought her morning might hold.

"I don't know," Reed said with a shrug of his shoulder. He looked at me and cocked an eyebrow. "Can we come play at the store?"

I pretended to ignore the pointed look Drew sent Reed's way. "Of course," I said, acting as if having my sons at the store was business as usual. "If you still remember how to stock shelves."

Putting fist-over-fist, Reed made stacking motions with his hands. "You trained us well, Dad. Sometimes I still do it in my sleep."

Drew was uncharacteristically silent. There was a low-key, running rivalry between my two sons. Two years separated them in age, but light years stood between them in their attitude toward the grocery business. From the time he was a little boy, Reed had been fascinated with building things. First it was tumbling towers of blocks, then he graduated to complicated Lego buildings, and more than once he'd demonstrated his interest in architecture by constructing elaborate floor displays at the store using cases of pop or laundry detergent boxes as his building tools. There was no surprise when he announced architecture as his future career.

Drew, on the other hand, seemed to have a love-hate relationship with Westin Foods. His interest in all things financial stemmed back to sixth grade, when I allowed him to help tally up the inventory totals, and demonstrated how those items directly related to how much money the store took in that day. Over the years his math teachers commented on Drew's ability to grasp bottom-line thinking. Financial skills were a must in my business, but the area where Drew really differed from his brother was his social skills . . . and it didn't matter if it was with customers or the store's suppliers, Drew had a natural ability when it came to schmoozing. Not the artificial "howareyouI'mfine" kind of talking, Drew excelled at finding out what made a person get out of bed in the morning.

That kind of gift wasn't given to everyone, and I'd long had the sense my oldest son was the kind of young man who would find meaning being involved in a "people" kind of business. A business much like the one he grew up in. My grocery business. But who was I to try and convince him of that?

"What do you say, Drew?" Reed said. "Wanna see who can empty a case of soup the fastest?"

Not rising to the bait, Drew poured a few swallows of orange juice into his glass. "Let's see how Mom's book signing goes."

"You're afraid I can beat you." Reed knew exactly how to push his brother's buttons.

Drew threw back the last swallow of juice as if it was something much stronger. "You're on, little brother."

Drew and Reed stood in the soup aisle of Westin Foods, red and white Santa caps poised on their heads, box cutters held like cowboys ready for a showdown.

"One . . . two . . . three . . . go!" Trisha cut her hand through the air like a knife.

With a box cutter in their right hands, Reed and Drew each slit open a case of soup cans, tossed the cutters to the side, pulled open the flaps, and started transferring the cans onto the shelf space they'd cleared.

As the owner of the store I should have probably put a stop to their friendly competition, but as the dad of these young men, I was tickled to see them acting like two kids again.

I couldn't resist adding my two cents to the competition. If they were going to do this, I wanted them to do it right. "Labels out."

"What's going on?" A shopper stopped her cart to watch. "Is soup on sale?"

"No," I said, nodding my head in the direction of my two boys, "but my kids might be as soon as they're done."

Drew and Reed were starting to breathe deep, their faces flushed. A can fell out of Reed's hand and fell to the floor. His Santa hat fell off as he grabbed up the can and clanked it onto the shelf. Drew fumbled a can but caught it before it dropped.

Reed taunted his brother. "Reed has speed."

Drew didn't miss a beat. Reed dropped another can. This time he let it roll while he positioned the cans in his hands on the shelf. A shopper toed the can back his way and Reed snatched it up. I looked around. The commotion was starting to draw a crowd.

"Look at them go."

"Wow, they're fast."

Who knew? Maybe this little contest might prove good for business.

The only sound around was metal against metal and the huff of breath as the boys worked. Drew spoke for the first time since the game had started. "Three. Two. One. Done!" Drew stood straight, two fists in the air. A ripple of applause erupted from the shoppers. "Big brother *and* champion," he crowed, bowing to the crowd.

Reed put his last two cans on the shelf, grinned, and then held out his hand. Drew clasped it as they bumped shoulders in a man hug. There were chuckles all around as the shoppers dispersed. I couldn't help noticing many of them reached for a can or two of the soup on display. More proof that my boys, at least *one* of my boys, belonged in the grocery business.

With a hand to each of their shoulders, I clapped both of my sons on the back. "Great job, guys. Be sure those box cutters get put in the back room, and grab those empty boxes out of the way, too.

I'm going to spend a few minutes in my office, so I'll meet you back at—"

"Jim!" My banker and business friend, Bob Marsden, stepped out of the group of shoppers and held out his hand as if to shake hands. He chuckled as he realized he held a can of mushroom soup in his right hand. Transferring it to his left, he shook my hand. "Merry Christmas."

"Merry Christmas," I repeated. "What are you doing in here on a Saturday?"

"Oh, my wife wanted to stop in at the Book Nook for a book signing this morning and didn't want to drive over by herself in case the wind picks up. Snow's in the forecast, you know."

I often forgot that Bob and his wife lived in the nearby town of Brewster. I didn't envy Bob his forty-mile commute, but I imagined living that distance from work made it easier to separate business from home life.

"Book signing?" A slow smile crept onto my face. "Uh, I think that just might be my wife's book she'll be getting signed."

"Are you kidding? Small world. My wife is a writer, too."

I knew that Bob's wife had experienced a measure of success with her books. You couldn't live in a state this small and not hear news like that. "Then they should have lots to talk about."

Bob went on. "Libby wanted to browse downtown a bit. Last minute Christmas shopping. I stopped by the bank to get some work done, and she asked me to stop by the store and pick up a few things we can't get at the Brewster grocery store. The kids will be coming over to the house tonight." He lifted his can of soup. "I'm sure the Brewster store carries soup, but after that impressive shelf-stocking exhibition, I couldn't resist. Quite the floor show there." He nodded in the direction of my boys and the shelves of soup.

I laughed and lifted my eyebrows. "Kids. What we don't let them get by with."

"These are your boys?" Bob asked.

Our paths crossed often enough in our business dealings that it hadn't occurred to me that Bob hadn't met my children. Of course, both Drew and Reed had been gone from Carlton almost a decade. Even if Bob had met them years ago, they'd turned into grown men since then.

Bob held out his hand, first to Reed, then to Drew. "Glad to meet you. Bob Marsden. I'm on the bank board with your dad."

Reed shook Bob's hand and greeted him. Drew snatched the Santa hat off his head, then shook Bob's hand. "Drew Westin. Nice to meet you."

Drew dropped his Santa cap into one of the empty soup cases as Reed turned to pick the empty cardboard boxes off the floor. Typical of him, Drew started making small talk with Bob. "How's Dad doing on the board? Did he approve my million dollar loan, yet?" he joked.

Bob laughed. "That loan was *yours?* Your dad said it was for an island in Tahiti."

"Oh, no," Drew joked back, throwing a crinkle-eyed grin my way, "he's planning to spend that on restoring an old junker car he bought."

While I stood on the sidelines, they bantered back and forth, fun-loving conversation I didn't pay much attention to until I heard Bob ask, "And what is it that you do, Drew?"

"I'm in finance," he replied. "Banking, as a matter of fact. I'm in New York."

Bob's eyes cut to mine then back to my son. "Is that so? Did your dad happen to mention that we're looking for two loan officers to add to our lending team?"

Now it was Drew's turn to shoot me a quick look. "No," he said, stuffing both his hands in the back pockets of his jeans. "He didn't."

I hoped Drew was chalking up a point for his old man. I deserved some credit for not tossing that juicy bone at his feet the moment he walked in the door for the holidays.

Bob ventured where I didn't dare tread. "Any chance you might consider taking a look at our operation?"

I sent a quick prayer heavenward, thanking God it was Bob doing the asking and not me. Drew would have no reason to tell me to get off his case. This was all Bob's doing. In a matter of a millisecond I added to my plea. If Drew had no trouble telling me he didn't want to live in Carlton, he had absolutely no allegiance to Bob whatsoever. *Please let Drew at least be polite when he says, "No way."*

Drew cleared his throat. Ran a hand through his hair. "Um . . ." he hesitated. Once again his eyes flicked to mine, then back to Bob. "Uh, I just might."

Over the loudspeaker system came the page, "Mr. Westin, line one." Only the fact that I was wanted elsewhere kept me from having to scoop my jaw up off the floor. I hurried to my office, leaving Bob talking shop with Drew.

My son would consider moving back home? A Christmas miracle if there ever was one. And I didn't have to say a word.

Drew

"Great to meet you, Drew. I'll be in touch." Bob Marsden tossed the can of soup from his left hand into his right, then lifted it in a semisalute as he walked toward the front of the store.

A light sheen of sweat dotted my upper lip and I wiped at it with the back of my hand. I expected I'd perspire during my can competition with Reed and I had, but what had me in the wringer now was my response to my dad's friend's on-the-spot job interview. In the middle of the soup section, no less. Well, maybe it wasn't an official inquisi-

146

tion, but I'd definitely let him know I was interested in the job at the bank.

I looked around the now-empty aisle, scratched at my head, and automatically reached out to straighten a few cans whose labels weren't perfectly centered on the shelf. What had come over me? After years and years of telling my dad there was no way I would consider coming back to Carlton, I'd more or less told Bob Marsden that if the hiring committee and I could hammer out an employment agreement, I would be on my way back to North Dakota.

I put my hands on my hips and did a slow, three-sixty turn in the aisle as if I were surveying the remains of a landmine incident. Funny, nothing looked different, and yet in some odd way it all did. Soft, elevator-type Christmas carols hummed through the store. Every now and then a page for a carry-out or a price check filtered through the music. At the end of the aisle, two women stopped their carts to chat. The tangy smell of Westin Food's famous smoked sausage tinged the air. I breathed deeply. The sounds and smells of this store were old acquaintances. I'd practically grown up here, which was the very reason I didn't want to work in the grocery business. I'd seen how owning his own business had consumed my dad. Our whole family. Everything we did revolved around the store. If there was a nation-wide trucking strike, Dad would fret about keeping the shelves stocked, or about produce spoiling somewhere along the highway. If the price of gas went up, our dinner table conversation was peppered with shipping costs that were sure to get passed along with the groceries. The idea of getting a part-time job at another Carlton business wasn't an option . . . it was all-hands-on-deck when it came to the kids in our family. Reed, Kaylee, and I were expected to pitch in whenever school activities weren't keeping us busy. By the time I finished high school, I was already burned out on the grocery business. I had bigger things in mind. I always knew I'd manage to put food on my table, but it wouldn't be in the form of groceries from my dad's store.

Out of habit I bent to pick up a couple small pieces of cardboard lying on the floor, debris from our box-unpacking race. Dad was a stickler about keeping the store spotless. As I walked toward the front of the store I chided myself. So much for refusing to help out.

Now that I had some job experience on my resumé, I realized my refusal to consider coming back to the store had been my way of rebelling. Some kids drank too much. Others got into drugs. Or driving too fast. Me? I simply put my foot down over joining my dad in business. I wanted to prove to myself and, yeah, to my *dad,* that I could be successful on my own.

As I tossed the remnants of cardboard into a

garbage bin near the entrance of the store, an image of my office in New York formed in my mind. Dad had been to visit me there. He knew where I sat every day. Even he had to admit I'd done okay without the family business.

Don't you think the work ethic your dad taught you served you well in your profession?

I turned and faced the row of check-out stations. All but one had customers checking out or waiting in line. The constant beep of the scanners under-lined the busyness of the afternoon. There had been many a Saturday when I'd stood at the end of those counters, bagging groceries, chatting with the regulars, carrying bags out to their cars, all under my dad's watchful eye. He wasn't always right there, but I'd wanted to please him all the same. So, yeah, now that I'd hit my thirties, I could admit Dad had taught me well.

The space under the Christmas tree that had been filled with gifts was empty, but the living room looked as if a bomb had detonated. The soft lights on the tree and the fire crackling in the fireplace did nothing to mask the wrapping paper and boxes littering the room. You'd think eight grownups, counting my grandpa, could be a little neater on Christmas Eve. I wondered what the room would look like a year from now when we added a baby to the mix.

Bending to pick up some paper, I sucked in at

the sides of my cheeks, doing my best to hide a smile. I could already imagine what my mom would say when we told the family we were expecting a baby. I tried to catch Trisha's eye. I was ready to spill the beans as soon as she gave me the nod. Not yet. She was busy sorting through our gifts.

I handed her a pair of gloves I'd unwrapped earlier, hoping she'd look my way. Nope. *Sheesh.* As if I didn't have enough on my mind, knowing we'd be making our announcement sometime tonight. I ran a hand along the back of my neck. Ever since my talk with Bob Marsden in the grocery store yesterday, I'd had a hard time focusing on much else than his hint that I could have a job at the bank if I wanted it. The big question was: Did I? Working at a bank in Carlton had seemed like a good idea yesterday, maybe not quite as good today.

I cast my eyes toward the ceiling. I wasn't the greatest when it came to talking to God, but this was one time when I found myself asking for direction. Trouble was, I wasn't the greatest when it came to hearing God answer back, either. I was going to need some divine guidance. *Hurry, Lord.* Bob was sure to share his tentative offer to me with the board sometime soon. And my dad was on that board.

It's Christmas, I reminded myself. Christmas Eve. I had at least a couple days before I'd be forced to decide if I wanted to pursue this job. If I didn't decide, and my family found out, they might decide for me.

Mom and Kaylee were busy gathering the torn wrapping paper and stuffing it into a large garbage bag. Trisha was trying to stack the gifts she and I had received into as compact a bundle as possible. We'd brought along a nearly empty suitcase on the flight from New York to Carlton, but the gifts we'd opened weren't suitcase-shaped. It looked like we might need to ship back a box full of gifts.

Then again, if I was going to be taking the job at Bob Marsden's bank . . . maybe we could leave them here. A nervous tick pulled at the corner of my lip. Why did I feel such hesitation about telling my family, my *dad,* that there was a possibility we might be moving home?

Home, is it?

Yeah, I had to admit, Carlton was still *home* in my mind. You'd think after living in New York all this time, I might have switched my allegiance. But, I hadn't.

I sat back against the couch, watching my family enjoy Christmas Eve night. Trisha laughed at something Kaylee said. Brad went to get another glass of punch. Dad and Reed were busy examining a wild game cookbook Dad had gotten as a gift from Mom. I found myself humming along with the Christmas carol playing on the

151

stereo. "Joy to the World." What would it be like if Trisha and I lived in Carlton? If family time wasn't confined to major holidays?

My thoughts were bouncing around like a ping-pong ball. One minute I was sure I'd take the job if offered. The next I'd think, *there is no way I am leaving New York.* I hadn't even told Trisha that I'd practically had a job offered to me in the soup aisle. Trisha would do backflips if I told her moving back to the Midwest was a possibility. But I didn't want to get her hopes up until I decided this was a step I was ready to take. Would moving back to Carlton be a step down on my career ladder? Or would moving closer to family be a step up on another sort of measuring scale?

Maybe it would be best to keep the news to myself until I had more time to think it over. Time that wasn't filled with the emotional baggage a family Christmas produced.

I rubbed my fingers across the soft silk of a blue tie Kaylee and Brad had given me. My career dilemma could wait. Tonight Trisha and I had another kind of news to share. I cleared my throat and cast my eyes around the room. No one seemed to notice I had something to say. I cleared my throat again.

"I hope you're not getting a cold," Trisha said.

"No, I—"

She caught the look in my eye. "Oh," she said softly, raising one eyebrow. "You want to . . . ?" A slight tilt of her head let me know she was ready for us to tell my family the news.

"Here you go," I said a little too loudly, trying to get everyone's attention without flat-out saying *listen up.* I balled up a wad of paper and arched it toward the bag Kaylee held. "Nothing but net," I said as the paper swished into the sack.

"Show off." Kaylee smiled.

"Hey, look at this." Reed grabbed a ball of paper and under-armed it into the bag.

Under any other circumstances, I might have turned Reed's comeback shot into a friendly game of one-on-one . . . with wrapping paper, no less. Tonight I simply grabbed Trisha's hand and said, "We have something to tell you."

Kaylee squealed. "You're going to have a baby!" She dropped the garbage bag and held her fists up in a *touchdown* position. "Pressure's off." She flopped onto the arm of an overstuffed chair beside Brad and gave a huge sigh.

Mom rolled her eyes and gave Kaylee a long, silent glance before saying. "I have *never* said one word about you having a grandchild for us."

Kaylee rolled her eyes right back. "You didn't have to."

"Hey!" I pointed a finger at my chest. "It was *me* who had something to say."

A slow, expectant grin covered my mom's face. "So . . ." she asked, her eyes dancing between me and Trisha. "Is Kaylee right?"

"So much for our big announcement," I said, grinning back. "Yes, we're going to have a baby."

As if everyone in the room had practiced together, all six of them said, "Congratulations!" at the same time. Laughter all around. Then Mom asked, "When are you due?"

That was Trisha's cue to explain. "I'm due in May. We—"

"May?" Mom interrupted. "That's practically right around the corner. You're not even showing. Are you?"

All eyes seemed to land on Trisha's stomach. "Not too much," she said, holding her stomach as if she was trying to gauge the pressure in a basketball. "Winter sweaters are good camouflage. We wanted to tell you sooner, but . . . well . . ." Trisha glanced down at her lap. "I've known too many friends who've had early-term miscarriages, and being I'm thirty-three . . . Well, we wanted to wait to make sure everything was going to be—"

Mom didn't wait for the rest of the explanation. She grabbed Trisha off the couch and gave her a big squeeze. "Everything is going to be just fine," she said. "I'll be praying every day from here on out. I am *so* happy." She held Trisha by the shoulders and smiled at her, then pulled her back into another hug. "I can't believe it. I'm going to be a grandma. *Finally.*"

"See?" Kaylee chimed in, going over to hug Trisha. "No pressure, right?"

Trisha hugged Kaylee, then my dad, Reed, and my grandpa. Even Brad stood in line.

Trisha looked back at Mom. "I'm glad we waited to tell you in person. This is so much better."

"It is," Mom agreed.

"What about me?" I said, suddenly feeling left out of the congratulations parade.

My mom giggled in a way I hadn't heard in years. "My son is going to be a daddy. Oh, Drew . . ." She held out her arms to me.

When Mom released me from her big hug, my dad clapped me on the shoulder and then pulled me into his chest for a quick clasp. "Congratulations, son."

Kaylee's questions filled the air. "Do you want a boy or a girl? Have you thought of any names? I'm going to be an *aunt*." She gave her husband a little nudge with her shoulder. "Uncle Brad."

Mom stood in the middle of the room with her fingertips pressed to her cheeks. "Is it okay if I tell Julie?"

"Tell anyone you want," I said, a magnanimous feeling of joy filling my lungs.

Mom headed for the kitchen. "I'm going to call her right now."

"Mom," Kaylee called, "it's Christmas Eve. You can wait until—"

Mom didn't break her stride. "No, I can't."

The rest of us got busy cleaning up the

remaining bits of paper and boxes. From the kitchen I could hear Mom laughing with her best friend as she shared our news. It didn't take long before Mom was back in the living room, an odd sort of quiet taking the place of her earlier excitement.

Trisha gave me a *what's wrong with your mom* look.

I don't know, I shrugged back.

"Claire?" Trisha put down a sweater she was folding. "Is everything okay?"

Mom didn't cry, but her eyes looked as though they were holding back a dam of tears. "I'm just happy," she said. And then she added, "I just wish you weren't so far away."

Heavy silence hung in the air until Mom waved a hand, as if pushing her words away. "I'm so excited about you two having a baby. Don't worry, we'll find plenty of time to see him . . . *her.*" She smiled and switched the subject. "Time for homemade ice cream. Who wants to start cranking?"

"I will," I said, raising my hand to volunteer. Anything to get away from all that wasn't being said.

Mom got the creamy mixture out of the fridge, while Dad went downstairs to get extra ice from the chest freezer. I stepped out into the cold garage and pulled the old-fashioned ice cream machine from a battered cardboard box on a shelf. In place of the Christmas carols that had been background music all evening, in my mind I heard the insistent beat of an old Queen song. *Under pressure.* Thump. Thump. Thump.

Kaylee might have felt Mom's unspoken wish for a grandchild, and now Trisha and I were making that wish come true. Who knew there would be another kind of pressure along with that announcement?

"I just wish you weren't so far away."

Mom's words echoed in my brain. All I had to say was, *"we're moving home,"* and I could make everything about this night perfect, for everyone.

Everyone?

That was the rub. I knew once those words were out of my mouth, the die would be cast. Mom, Dad, Trisha, Kaylee, even Mom's friend Julie, would have us up and packed in a blink. We'd be on the road back home before I knew for sure if this is what I really wanted. I'd been resisting living in Carlton for the past umpteen years. It had something to do with proving myself . . . but to whom? Who was left to impress? As Trisha had said about herself, I'd sort of done the whole New York thing. Was it plain old habit that was keeping me from saying the words? That kept me from telling Trisha—my family—about the job offer?

Whatever my hesitation, I'd have to tell Trisha and my dad soon. Bob said he'd like my resumé and a phone interview with the hiring committee as soon as I returned to New York after the holidays. I knew he'd share his impression with the bank board. And then my dad would know I'd been working behind his back.

Oh, if I *took* the job, it would be a great surprise. But if I turned it down? I had a hunch my dad might feel slighted that I hadn't asked for his input.

And then there was Trisha. If I said "no thanks" without even running this by her, I'd—Well, I didn't even want to imagine that.

I needed to wrestle my feelings about this *before* everyone else decided things for me. And before anyone got hurt.

JANUARY: A NEW YEAR AND NEW CHALLENGES . . .

Claire

An icy gust of January wind blew under my wool coat as I opened the car door and leaned across the driver's seat. Putting my briefcase full of class notes for the new semester onto the passenger's seat of my car, I quickly climbed in and pulled the door closed beside me. I tucked my arms close to my sides and shivered. Brrr . . . it was seriously cold outside. Well below zero, if I had to muster a guess. The perfect kind of night to hunker down at home and get some reading done. I was using a new textbook this semester, which was going to require extra preparation on my part.

I fumbled with the jumble of keys in my cold hand, finally unearthing the ignition key and starting the car. As soon as I got home I was going to change into a pair of baggy pants and a sweatshirt. For supper I'd make one of those fancy soup mixes I'd purchased at a Tastefully Simple party last fall . . . if I didn't freeze to death on the drive home before then. Man, it was cold. I snapped the heater fan on *high,* although I knew it wouldn't do a bit of good until the car engine had time to warm up. The best antidote to the cold was not thinking about it. So . . . okay . . . I wouldn't mention to Jim that the fancy soup mix didn't come from Westin Foods. It was from one of those in-home sales parties one of my faculty friends seemed to be addicted to throwing . . . and inviting me to.

I pulled my right hand from the steering wheel and held it close to my mouth. Maybe if I blew some warm, moist air onto my fingers I could actually *move* them. So much for not thinking about the cold. Or for forgetting my gloves in my office. It didn't do much good having an auto-start remote for my car when the signal didn't reach from the front of my classroom to the faculty parking lot.

Shifting into reverse, then drive, I made my way out of the lot. One of these days Jim and I would be spending our winters somewhere warm. Say, Arizona, or Florida, or anywhere but the frozen tundra of Carlton, North Dakota. Why in the world our ancestors thought this would be a good place to stop a covered wagon was beyond my capabilities as a sociologist. Right now my brain cells couldn't move enough to think. All I wanted was to be warm and at—

Oh! Oh! Oh! With the cold heel of my hand I hit myself in the forehead, as if I could knock some sense into myself. I didn't have the luxury of hunkering down at home. Tonight—I glanced at the clock on the dashboard—in two and a half hours, I would be speaking at the Carlton Community Club meeting. For good measure I clunked myself on the forehead again.

This whole day had been discombobulated. An early morning faculty meeting started the day with an announcement from the department dean, who said that due to legislative budget cuts there might be some changes in staffing. Everyone, including me, had been thrown by the news. I'd be turning fifty-three in early April, young enough to know that finding a new career at my age might be difficult, old enough to know that I didn't want to reinvent myself. Still reeling with *what might happen,* I went off to teach two sections of Sociology 101, and a 300-level class on Social Issues and Poverty. A steady stream of student appointments and classroom preparation had filled the hours in between. And now I was faced with making a presentation to the Community Club I hadn't prepared for nearly enough . . . and with my mind cluttered with all sorts of campus goings-on that had nothing to do with the women who would be at my talk this evening.

As I maneuvered my car through the streets leading from campus to my house, my mind raced with the possibilities of what I planned to say to a group of young professional women who would be looking to me for a message that was wise, witty, and wonderful.

I kept my hands firmly gripped on the steering wheel. I'd done enough bonking myself on the head already. But I was questioning why in the world I'd said yes to this speaking engagement and why I'd thought I had anything to share. Just because I'd written a book on the dynamics of friendship didn't mean I had anything profound to say.

Usually I made a point of not driving and talking on my cell phone at the same time, but I couldn't help myself, I needed to hash this over with my best friend. With my thumb I hit Julie's speed dial number. *One.*

"Help!" I cried the moment I heard her familiar voice.

"Sure," she replied without a moment's hesitation. "What do you need?"

"Argh," I sighed. "Do you remember last month when someone called me from the Community Club and asked me to speak to their group in January?"

"Yeeessss?" Julie drew out the word as if she knew there was something coming.

"It's tonight."

"What! You've got to be kidding. Don't tell me you forgot."

"I didn't forget," I admitted as I turned the car into our driveway. "I made some notes shortly after I spoke to the woman who called me, but now everything I wrote down seems . . . I don't know, *lame,* or something." I paused in the driveway, watching as the garage door slowly opened. "Remind me. Why am I doing this?"

"Because you're a world famous author-in-training and your public is demanding to hear from you."

"Very funny." I pulled the car into the garage, turned off the engine, and waited while the garage door lowered. My mind was racing. "They're going to think I'm some kind of imposter. What was I thinking?"

"Listen, Claire." I could almost feel Julie patting my hand, calming my thoughts. "You have taught sociology for . . . what? Twenty years?"

I did the math in my head. "More."

"You've written a book on friendship. Taught about it for decades."

"You make me sound like Methuselah."

Julie laughed. "Well then, you have a wealth of wisdom. Share it."

As I held my cell phone to my ear, I pulled my

briefcase across the seat and into my lap, then slid out of my car and let myself into the house. "You make it sound so simple."

"Believe me," Julie said, "friendship is anything but simple."

There was a long silence between us as her words settled. She spoke a truth I already knew. I remembered the days after my mother died when my sister, Kathy, arrived and took over, driving me crazy in the process. Julie was the one person I could vent to. The one person I knew who could listen to me gripe about my sister and still understand that I loved Kathy in spite of her quirks . . . without me having to say so. Julie was the person who shared my joy when Drew and Trisha announced their pregnancy. Then she listened to me in the days that followed as I unloaded my sorrow that they didn't live close by and my grandchild might be a stranger to me. *You're not going to let that happen,* she assured. Julie listened to more than my words, she listened to my heart.

"What would I do without you?" I asked.

"I'll tell you what you're going to do," Julie answered. "You are going to change into whatever clothes you want to wear tonight. You are going to freshen your makeup. In the meantime I'm going to swing by Quizno's and grab us a sub to share. I'll be over at your house in . . ." There was a pause, and I imagined Julie was doing some quick calculating ". . . in twenty minutes. Then, we are going to go over the outline of what you'll speak about tonight."

"You sound like a military general."

"Desperate times call for desperate measures."

Now it was my turn to laugh. "Am I really that desperate?"

"Okay, so maybe *desperate* is a little dramatic. Think of this as a reality show and you just got a new challenge dropped in your lap. Let's say we're going to do an extreme makeover on information you already know."

"An extreme makeover?" The wheels were beginning to spin in my head. "Oh-oh. Wait. I think I've got something." I paused as a new direction swirled my thoughts around. "How about if I take extreme makeover and change it to . . ." I felt my heart skip in anticipation of my next idea. "What if I call my talk: Extreme Friendship?"

There was silence. Maybe it was a dumb idea. If anyone would tell me, it was my best friend. "Julie? What are you thinking?"

"Wow," Julie said. "Will you take me along when you get on Oprah?"

A wash of relief flooded warmth through my chest and down into my arms. Even my fingers tingled. Now that I had a focus for my talk, ideas started to explode like popcorn on a hot stove. "I need to grab a pen," I told Julie.

"You write. I'll be over ASAP."

We didn't need to say goodbye.

Extreme friendship.

"Thank you so much for being such an attentive group." Looking out at the group of about thirty women, I slid the last page of my notes to the center of the podium. Julie sat in the back of the room beaming as if she were my mother. I smiled at the women in front of me. This half-hour presentation had felt like a conversation between friends. So different from the lecturing I did in front of a classroom each day. Maybe there was a side benefit to this author business I hadn't anticipated. I glanced down at my notes. "In conclusion, I'd like to remind you that the best way to *have* a friend is to *be* one."

There was an uncertain pause. So, okay, maybe I needed to learn a better way to conclude my talks. I nodded. *Done.* "Thank you."

A ripple of applause filled the room. I hesitated, my eyes seeking Julie. My students *never* clapped at the end of a lecture. From the back of the room Julie gave me a thumb high up. An unexpected thrill pushed at the inside of my chest. What a difference it had been talking to a group who had invited me to speak to them. Bending my head I focused on the podium, gathering my notes and tucking them into the blue file folder I'd brought. I wasn't quite sure what the protocol was after a presentation like this . . . did I simply grab Julie and head for the car? The appealing aroma of coffee just done percolating hung in the air. Was I expected to stay and mingle? I wasn't part of the group, and what if my presentation hadn't been what they were expecting? Maybe I should—

"Mrs. Westin?" One of the young women who had been sitting in the front row stood to my right. "I wanted to thank you for what you said. I—I—"

Oh goodness, were those tears in her eyes? Not knowing what to say, I put a hand on her arm.

She gave me a sheepish smile. "I recently moved to Carlton for a new job, and I'm so missing the friends I left behind in Wisconsin. What you said . . ." She curled her fingers and laid her fist against her heart. ". . . well, you challenged me to seek out some new friends. Thank you."

"You're—You're welcome," I stammered, noticing there was a short line of women behind her. Why did they want to talk to me? It was one thing when students stopped by at the end of class; I knew what they wanted . . . a better grade. But I had nothing to offer these women. Did I?

The next person in line stepped forward and held out her hand. "Hi, I'm Amy. I wanted to thank you for your presentation tonight. I really liked what you had to say. And I was wondering . . . ?" She paused and quickly glanced back over her shoulder. She leaned close and lowered her voice.

"I had a falling out with my best friend a couple weeks ago. I was wondering if you had any suggestions about how I could make things better between us."

"Better?" I repeated as if I'd never heard the word. This Amy-girl was asking me for advice? "Well . . . I—" Actually I had no idea what to say. I scrambled for an answer. *Help me, Lord.* "Have you tried talking to her about what happened?"

Amy stared down at the floor for a bit. "No. I was kind of hoping that maybe we'd both just forget about what happened."

"It doesn't sound like you have. Forgotten, that is."

She shook her head. "I've been waiting for her to call me."

"And she's probably waiting for you to call her."

Amy nodded slowly. "Probably."

I repeated the closing words of my talk. "To have a friend you have to *be* a friend."

"And I haven't been acting like a very good friend." Amy pressed her lips into a tight smile. "Thank you," she said, pulling me into a tight hug. "I needed to hear that. I'm going to call her when I get home."

"You do that," I said. I was tempted to ask Amy to call me and let me know how her friend responded, but before I could say more another young woman stepped into her spot.

"Thank you for what you had to say tonight."

The tall redhead stuck out her hand. "I'm Beth. I wanted to tell you that I've read your book." She held a copy of *The Friendship Factor* in her hand. "I was wondering if you could sign it for me?"

"Uh, sure. Let me get—" I looked to the podium for a pen. Empty. My purse was in the back with Julie. Obviously, it had never occurred to me that I would be asked to do more than give my speech. I held out my empty hands. "I don't have anything to sign it with."

"Here." The gal standing behind the young lady handed me a pen. "I came prepared," she said, holding up her own copy of my book.

I could feel a flush rising from my neck into my cheeks as I opened the book to the title page. I put the pen to the page and realized my mind had drawn a complete blank. It was my turn for sheepish looks. "Could you remind me your name?" At this point in the evening I was surprised I remembered *my* name.

"Beth," she said.

Beth, I wrote, trying to remember what I'd written inside the books at my book signing at the Book Nook a month ago. *Friendship is a gift. Cherish it.*

I handed the book to Beth. She turned to the title page and read what I'd written. "I will," she said as she turned to go.

The lady-with-the-pen stepped up next. "Thanks for your talk," she said. "I'm Kim, but you can sign that book to Patti. I'm going to give it for a gift."

Kim. Patti. Kim. Patti. Amy. Beth. Kim. A flurry of names tripped through my mind as if a stock market ticker tape had taken up residence in my brain. For the life of me I couldn't remember what this woman in front of me had said her name was. A slow trickle of sweat ran down my spine. This was going to be embarrassing but I had to ask, "I'm sorry. What did you say your name was?"

"Kim," she said more graciously than I deserved.

I put the pen to the page and made the first stroke of her name.

"But I wanted it signed to my friend, Patti."

"Oh, that's right." I did my best to turn what started out as a *K* into a *P*. "P-a-t-t-y," I said as I wrote.

"Oh, no!" Kim said. "It's Patti with an *i*."

I stopped my pen as fast as I could. "An *i*?"

Kim nodded as I did my best to make an over-long downstroke into a small letter *i*. "Is that okay?" I asked, showing her my botched rendition of her friend's name. I was totally and completely blowing this. Who did I think I was to be standing here signing books? Pretending I was some sort of expert on friendship?

"It'll be fine," she said. "It's just a privilege to have you sign it."

I resisted the urge to roll my eyes. Except for

possibly twenty years, I was no different than the young woman at my elbow. I felt like an imposter. Someone posing as an author. Someone who had friendship all figured out? Julie knew better. I scrawled my signature, handed the book to Kim, and did a quick search of the room for Julie. She was standing in the back of the room talking to a cluster of people, a cup of coffee in her hand. Her eyes caught mine and she made a series of undecipherable gestures with her hands. How she managed not to spill a drop of coffee was a feat in itself. I shook my head. *Something big? Wide? Something to do with writing? What?*

I exchanged a confused glance with the next person in my line and shrugged my shoulders at Julie. *I don't know what you mean.*

Julie excused herself from the group and hurried to the front of the room. "Excuse me a sec," she said to the woman waiting to talk to me. Julie gestured with her head to the women she'd been talking to in the back. "They're wondering if you brought along some extra books. They'd like to buy some and have them autographed."

Did I bring along extra books? I almost laughed. I was lucky I even remembered to come to the event myself.

"Do you have some in your trunk?" Julie sounded as if she thought I had all my bases covered. "I can run and get them. Where are your keys?"

This was proof. Proof that I had no business standing here pretending I was some sort of professional writer or speaker. "No, Julie. I don't have extra books with me." I left out the part that I didn't even have extra books at home. Wasn't it my small publisher who was supposed to be responsible for seeing that my books got sold . . . in *bookstores?* There was a whole other side to this business that I didn't know about. But it looked as though I was going to have to learn in a hurry.

Ginny Black, the president of the Community Club, stepped next to Julie. She eyed the three women still waiting to speak to me. "Don't leave before I talk to you," she told me. "I have something for you." She and Julie walked away chatting.

Ginny had something for me? Possibly advice that I shouldn't attempt anything like this again. I avoided the urge to puff out my cheeks with a burst of frustrated air. If Ginny told me to stick with my day job, I'd agree with her in an instant.

I visited briefly with each of the women in line. One thanked me for my message. Another wanted a copy of my book. Which, *duh,* I didn't have. And the last woman wanted advice on how she could get a book published. When I told her I had no magic formula for publication, she seemed more than a little disappointed. As if I was withholding a secret I refused to share with her. If only she understood how fluke-like this whole process had been, she wouldn't press me for information I didn't have.

"Good luck," I said as Miss *I-want-to-write-a-book* turned away.

All these women had wanted something from me. A signature. Advice on friendship. And publishing. Something about what I'd had to say, what I'd written, had struck a chord in ways that seemed a mystery to me. As hard as I'd tried to communicate my research and thoughts on friendship, I now stood alone, thinking that whatever I'd said hadn't been enough. I wished I had something more concrete to offer.

As I picked up my notes, I glanced about the room at the small clusters of women chatting with one another. Some were animated and engaged. A few stood on the fringes of a group, not quite included, and yet still here. I was exhausted and ready to be home and in bed. What kept these women hanging around on this cold winter night?

They want what you talked about. They're looking for friendship.

An odd mix of emotion—satisfaction laced with a tiny bit of fear—pushed its way into my tired thoughts. If everyone was looking for friendship . . . what if they looked to *me* for the way to find those friends? Could I possibly live up to the expectations I'd written about in my book? The things I'd talked about tonight?

172

I had so much on my plate already. Teaching full time at the university. Wife, mom, friend. And all the responsibilities that went along with those roles. But what if God was calling me to this, too?

"Claire?"

I jumped at the sound of my name. I'd asked God a question, but hadn't expected an answer. At least not right now . . . and not coming from Ginny Black. "You startled me," I said, half-laughing at my jumpy response.

"I wanted to give you this." Ginny handed me a pale green envelope with my name written on the front.

I took the envelope from her. A thank you note I assumed. "Thank *you*," I responded. "I hope I—"

"We can't afford much," she said. "It's only a small honorarium—"

"A—" I looked down at the envelope in my hand. They were *paying* me for that off-the-cuff verbal tango I'd done? No matter how much money was in this envelope, I felt as though I should give it back. I knew better than anyone that I needed *practice* doing this way more than I needed money.

"Come join us." Ginny put a hand on my shoulder and steered me toward the clusters of women standing near the coffee pot and cookies. "It's an honor to have you with us tonight. Thank you so much for your message."

The inside of my head felt like a tennis match was being played with my thoughts. *You-blew-it* got served into the far corner, only to be slammed back by *I-think-you-did-okay.* I had absolutely no perspective on what had just transpired.

Someone put a cup of coffee into my hand. "Your talk was wonderful."

Someone else held the tray of cookies out for me to take one. "That was just what I needed to hear."

"Thank you," I murmured. "Thank you so much." I blew across the top of the coffee. Took a small sip, followed by a bite of molasses cookie. It would be easy to get a big head collecting all the compliments being passed my way. But, really, what else *would* they say about my talk with me standing right there?

The one person I knew I could count on was Julie. As soon as we got out to the car, she'd tell me how I'd really done.

"You were *fab*ulous!" Julie waited until we were inside my car before she high-fived me. "Except for the fact that the *author* forgot to bring actual *books* along to her book talk."

I tossed my purse in the backseat. "I guess I thought my trustworthy assistant was in charge of incidentals."

Julie laughed as she buckled her seat belt. "You call *books* at a book talk incidentals? Ha! I guess you haven't quite mastered the learning curve on this speaking-thing. You'd better let me continue to tag along."

"Okay," I said, starting the car and holding my breath. Did I really want to hear the answer to the question I was going to ask? "Really, how do you think it went?"

"Honestly?" The laughter left Julie's voice. "Wellll. . . ."

I could feel dampness beginning to slather my palms against the steering wheel. Honesty was Julie's theme in life. Whether I wanted to hear it, or not, it was coming my way.

"Here's the deal," she said, turning a bit in her seat so she was angled toward me. "You're going to have to work on your opening. The sociology of friendship is interesting, but you've gotta start with something practical. A story. Something people can relate to. Like the time you bought that fuchsia pair of flowered capris. 'They were on sale,' you said." Julie's voice rose as she imitated me. " 'They're so *springy,* ' " she went on, making me laugh as I remembered that fiasco. "And I flat out told you, *'No.'* " Julie made quote marks in the air. *"No."* She paused, tilted her chin down, and gave me her wide-eyed *I did you a big favor* look. *"That's* what friends are for."

"You're right," I admitted, wiping the palm of my hand against my wool coat. "Starting out with a funny story would be better."

"And . . . ?" Julie prompted.

I shot her a quick, puzzled look. "And, what?"

"Admit it," Julie said. "Those capris were a huge mistake."

"Yeah, I owe you," I said as we laughed together.

A comfortable silence wrapped us in the darkness of the car. An occasional streetlight guided our way back to my house where Julie's car was parked. As I drove I replayed the parts of my talk I could remember. Julie was right. When I told stories to illustrate a point, my audience seemed the most engaged.

I pulled the car into the garage and turned it off. Even though it was freezing out, I'd wait to put down the garage door until I walked Julie to her car.

"Thanks," I said, pulling Julie into a quick hug as we stood on the curb in the cold night. "Talk to you tomorrow."

She climbed into her car as I walked back up the driveway. The long school day, and the unusual way I'd spent my evening, had caught up with me. I was completely exhausted. I couldn't wait to climb into bed and turn out the light. Lucky for me this whole speaking-thing had been a one-time fluke. By tomorrow I'd be back to my old teaching routine and life would be same-old, same-old, again.

"Claire! Wait."

Almost slipping on an icy spot on the driveway, I turned at the sound of Julie's voice. She had rolled down the passenger window of her car and was leaning over the seat, waving something at me.

"I almost forgot to give this to you," she called.

I shuffled my way across the snowy walk to her car. "What?" I asked, leaning my head toward the open window and the piece of paper Julie held out to me.

"After your talk," she said, "there were two people who wanted your business card, and I figured if you didn't have books along, you didn't have cards, either. Was I right?"

"Yeah, but what—"

"Don't worry," Julie said, as if she had my life under control for me. "I took down their names and phone numbers. Here." She thrust the paper into my hand.

I squinted at the paper in the dark. "What am I supposed to do with this?"

"Call them, of course."

Of course. I had no idea what Julie was getting at. "Why?"

Julie sighed deeply. My ignorance was nothing but a thorn in her ever-lovin' side. "They want you to speak again. At a different event. Meeting. Whatever."

"Me?"

"Yes, *you.* I told you, your talk was fabulous. Tweak it a little bit and you're going to be a busy woman."

As Julie drove off I stared at the piece of paper

in my hand. As if I wasn't busy enough already. And yet, tonight had been oddly exciting. A kind of challenge I no longer found in my classroom.

What if Julie was right? What if my talk was fabu—Well, *good,* anyway? What if other people did want to hear it? What if . . . instead of looking at the next years as winding down my career I started a whole new one altogether?

Jim was pouring a glass of milk as I walked into the kitchen from the garage. Apparently, he'd rummaged around in the freezer and found my stash of Christmas cookies. I was tempted to reprimand him, but I was in too good of a mood to get upset over three measly sugar cookies.

"So? How'd it go?" he asked as he pushed half of a frosted snowman into his mouth.

I plopped my purse on the kitchen table and, suddenly exhausted, sat myself down, too. "According to Julie I was . . . get this—" I made quote marks in the air. "Fabulous." I found myself grinning. "I don't think I was quite *that* good, but it seemed to go well. At least as good as could be expected for as nervous as I was."

"Why were you nervous? You talk in front of people every day."

Easy for Jim to say. I lifted a shoulder. "I don't know. This was . . . different. More . . . personal somehow."

"So," Jim said, devouring a snowflake in one big chomp, "did you like doing it?"

I traced a finger along the edge of the table, thinking. "Actually," I said, looking up at Jim, "I did. I really, really did."

And something about that scared me.

Jim

Hands on my hips, I stood staring at the two end cap displays on aisles five and six. The Big Five we called them. Five items in the store, in *any* grocery store, that were the bait we used to lure customers inside. Tide. Miracle Whip. Toilet paper. Cheerios and Frosted Flakes. These were staples in any kitchen. Price-sensitive items that customers watched like hawks. And the products we priced at or below cost, to make sure customers kept returning. The hope was that when they came in to stock up on laundry detergent or cereal, they also filled their carts with items the store actually made a profit on.

Walking over a couple aisles, I surveyed the seasonal loss leaders: tomato and cream soups. How many pallets of those had we gone through this winter? If I was in my office I could look it up. But I didn't need to do the math to know we'd sold a lot. But was it enough? That was always the question.

I scratched at my head and did some mental rearranging. We were heading into spring. Ready to switch out the soups on the end cap and replace the items with pork and beans and Heinz ketchup. Funny how I marked the changing seasons not by leaves on the trees, but by the items we featured in the store.

April meant Claire's birthday and the first of the tender stalks of spring asparagus. She loved them steamed. Add a little butter and a grating of parmesan and my wife couldn't ask for a better birthday meal. "Cheap date," she often quipped as she dug in.

I reached out to realign some of the cans at the front of the display. *Cheap* was a word a few of my customers would beg to differ with. According to some of them there was *nothing* cheap about the price of anything in my store.

Ah, well, I long ago learned I would never please everyone. But pricing was one area where I had to be on my toes. The scuttlebutt around town was that the groundbreaking for the SuperTarget would be any day now. I doubted I'd be able to match their prices across the board, but I was going to do my best to give my customers the best values I could, price-wise and with customer service.

A shopper paused her cart near where I was standing. "Do you work here?"

I glanced down at the long-sleeved denim shirt I was wearing with the Westin Foods logo on the front placket. *Work here? Actually, I live here.* "What can I help you find?"

She looked down at her list, then up at me. "Wheat germ?"

I pointed. "Aisle eight. Left hand side. Bottom shelf. Near the oatmeal."

As she did a one-eighty with her cart, I laid my hands against the small of my back and leaned into the pressure . . . or was it pain? Some days it felt like I was getting too old to—

You're not old.

Here I went again, debating with myself. If age really was just a state of mind then why did my knees ache when I got out of bed this morning? Why was my back hurting now? Who knew what constituted *old* anymore? If fifty was the new thirty, then sixty must be the new forty . . . or something like that. I was creeping up on fifty-six, a number that I knew wasn't *young,* but didn't classify as decrepit, either. Then again, I was a card-carrying member of AARP. Not that I'd demand a senior discount at the pancake house, but if it got me a discount on a hotel room, that was another thing.

Maybe that was the trick. Age slowly crept up on you so a person had a chance to get used to it. First it was a few gray hairs. Then you needed to hold the phone book four feet away so you could read it. After you admitted you needed bifocals, then your joints started aching. About that time, an AARP magazine came in the mail, and that threw you for a loop until you started paging through the articles and realized you were part of a vast majority of people experiencing the same things. And then there was a slow realization that the work you were doing would be there long after you weren't. And that made you start wondering . . . maybe you should start enjoying what's left of your life a little more. But the catch was—

"Excuse me." A shopper stopped her cart and reached around me for four cans of tomato soup.

I stepped aside. "No, excuse me." Here I was, blocking the busiest aisle in the store. Possibly proof that my brain cells were dying off as I stood there. I tugged at the cuffs of my shirt and headed for the produce department. I certainly didn't have time to figure out the aging process now. It was the end of another long day. I'd been at the store since six-thirty this morning. Not quite a twelve-hour day. No wonder my mind was wandering and I was ready to go home. Maybe it had nothing to do with *age* and everything to do with being plain old tired. Even toddlers got tuckered out at the end of a busy day.

I paused to straighten some product in a discount bin in the aisle. Someone had put a cake mix into a wire basket of Raman noodles. Tucking the cake mix into the crook of my arm, I rounded the aisle and put the box where it belonged, then redirected to the produce department.

It would be good to get home, have dinner with Claire, and catch up on our respective days. As soon as I picked up a bunch of Claire's favorite spring asparagus I'd—I stopped short in front of the banana bin. Claire wasn't going to be home tonight. Not until much later. She had a speaking engagement in Brewster.

There went my idea of a good dinner with Claire. Brewster was far enough away from Carlton that she had to leave straight from her last afternoon class to get set up in time for her talk. I turned and looked at the large clock hanging above the entrance of the store. According to my quick calculation, Claire would be getting to Brewster right about now. She'd loaded several cases of books into her trunk last night. Had her notes and a change pouch ready to go. Between driving the forty miles to Brewster and then getting her book table organized, I doubted she'd even have time to grab a bite to eat. Here I was lamenting my long day, and Claire was just getting started on the second half of her day. Without supper.

Which left me with a problem. What was I going to eat? Something from the deli department that I could grab to go? I headed that direction. There was a store full of food at my fingertips but nothing appealed to me, knowing I'd be eating alone.

Alone. A word I tried not to think about. I was a big boy. Fully capable of entertaining myself. It wasn't that I begrudged Claire her speaking engagements. Ever since her talk to the Carlton

Community Club, she had been receiving more offers to speak to a variety of groups in the area. I was glad for her. Really I was.

But . . . ?

Staring at the food behind the deli counter, I scraped a hand against my cheek. Her speaking engagements took place in the evenings or on weekends—the exact times we had to spend with each other. Twice her speaking events were far enough away that she'd had to spend the night away from home, arriving back when the weekend was mostly over, and our hectic work week was about to begin.

There was something that didn't quite seem right about it all. We were at the ages when we should be enjoying life more. Instead, I'd added the Emerson store to my mini-chain, and Claire had started a second career in addition to her teaching. Make that a second *and* third career. At the request of her publisher, she was writing a companion book to her first one, and her speaking schedule was filling up. Both of us were running like hamsters in a cage . . . but were we getting anywhere?

"Hey, Jim! How's it going?" Larry Ritter clapped me on the back.

"No complaints," I answered, even though I'd been running through a litany of them. Including what to have for supper. With Claire gone there was no need for me to race home for dinner. I stuck my hands in my pockets and turned Larry's way. I had time to chat. "What's up?"

"Oh," he said, eyeing the deli counter, "my wife went over to Brewster with a friend for some kind of women's thing tonight, so I'm batching it for supper."

"No kidding?" Brewster wasn't that big. I had a hunch his wife and mine were at the same event. "I'm on my own, too."

A half-grin spread over Larry's face. "Would you be at all offended if I didn't buy something from the deli and you and I went out for burgers instead?"

"Offended? I was about to suggest it myself." I pointed in the direction of my office. "Let me grab my jacket. Meet you at Bruno's in ten?"

"I'm on my way."

Larry and I went way back. We'd joined the Carlton Jaycees around the same time several . . . well . . . decades ago. When we aged out of that organization, we rolled ourselves right into the local Lions Club. We'd flipped pancakes together at the annual fund-raising breakfast more times than I could count. Spending an evening catching up with Larry would be a good diversion from a long night at home alone.

"Over here." Larry waved me over to a booth.

Before I could even get an arm out of my jacket, a waitress was at our table. "What can I get you?"

It didn't take us long to order. Larry asked for a burger with mushrooms and swiss. I put in my order for a German burger complete with sauerkraut and cheese.

Larry pushed a set of napkin-wrapped silverware to my side of the table. "I suppose we should be watching our cholesterol, or something."

I was glad the server had taken our order before we'd had time to feel guilty. "Too late," I replied. "And thank goodness." We laughed together. "Seems like a guy would die of starvation if you followed all the health guidelines out there."

"Speaking of health . . ." Larry unwrapped his silverware and spun the spoon between his thumb and index finger. "Did you hear Dan Jackson has colon cancer?"

My eyebrows rose as I leaned forward. "He does?" Dan was a Lions member and the football coach at North Carlton High.

"Got diagnosed last week. He's having surgery on Monday. It doesn't sound good."

We stopped talking and sat back as our waitress put two small napkins on the table and topped them with our two glasses of beer. I stared at mine, suddenly not very thirsty. I'd meant to have a colonoscopy when I'd turned fifty. Then at fifty-one. Two. I was fifty-five now. Five years past the expiration date, so to speak. But, man, who wanted to plan for one of those? I picked up my beer and took a long swallow. At least I didn't have any symptoms.

"Didn't have any symptoms," Larry said, lifting his glass to his mouth.

I put mine down. "How old is Dan?"

"Fifty-five."

Sheesh. I supposed if I believed in signs, this could be considered one. I'd talk to Claire about it.

Claire?

Okay, my doctor. Really I would. Maybe not tomorrow, but soon.

Larry wiped at some condensation on the side of his glass. "And I suppose you heard about Bill?"

A bus boy clattered dishes as he cleared the booth behind me. I turned one ear toward Larry. "Bill . . . Nyguard?"

Larry nodded grimly.

"What about him?"

"Had a heart attack two weeks ago. He's doing okay. But still . . ."

No kidding. Talk about expiration dates. Were all of us reaching ours? I took another swallow of beer. Maybe a night at home alone would have been better than trying to choke down a drink along with the bad health news of my cohorts in Lions.

"News like Dan's makes me want to retire right now. I mean, really." Larry sat across the table and shook his head. "What's the point of working like a maniac and then, *boom,* you're just about at the age to start enjoying it all and something like colon cancer happens? Or a heart attack?"

What could I say? Larry wasn't saying anything I hadn't thought myself. But what was a guy supposed to do when he was neck deep in a business that never stopped demanding more? And, besides, if I ever did sell my stores . . . what would I do? Sit home and knit? Ha. Maybe the best option was keeling over on the job. "Can we change the subject?"

"Perfect timing," Larry said, as a new server put two plates on the table.

My burger was big enough to feed a third-world family, and I didn't even want to think about the grease-factor in the fries. I'd make up for tonight's meal tomorrow. Nothing but high fiber. Fruit and veggies.

Since when did you start eating like a Beverly Hills starlet?

Since practically everyone I knew was becoming sidelined by health issues. I pushed aside the thought, dumped some ketchup on my burger, and took a big bite. If this was what life was coming to, I'd do my best to enjoy what was left of mine.

"Hey," Larry said around a mouthful of burger. "How are you coming with that old car of yours? Didn't you buy an old . . . Mustang to restore?"

I swallowed then replied, "It's a Dodge. Charger."

"Right. Sweet. How's it coming?"

I wasn't sure I liked this topic any better than our previous conversation. "It's not."

Larry wiped his mouth with his napkin and reached for the ketchup. "Having a hard time finding parts?"

I pushed a French fry into my mouth. "Finding time."

He nodded as he sipped. "Yeah, what's with that *time* thing anyway? My wife swears I've got control of the remote and I've got my thumb on the fast forward button."

I pointed across the table at Larry. "So, let up then."

"I wish I could."

A familiar face appeared at the edge of the booth. "You two in charge of cooking tonight?" Myron Addison stuck out his hand.

I swiped my hand on my napkin and shook Myron's hand. "Long time, no see."

"Yeah, that's what happens when you've gotta work for a living." He shook Larry's hand as he spoke. Then he motioned for Larry to move over a bit and sat on the edge of the cushioned seat. "I'm counting down the days until I'm done teaching. Thirty-five days and I'm outta there."

I didn't mean to talk with my mouth full, but I couldn't help it. "What?"

"Yup." Myron tapped the rim of the table with his fingers. "I'm hanging it up at the end of the school year. I'm going to *reeee*-tire."

"How's that work?" I asked through a French fry. "You can't be—" I was trying to do the math.

The way I had it figured Myron was younger than me by a few years. I flat out asked. "How old are you?"

"Fifty-three."

"And you can afford to retire?"

"Teacher's retirement plan," he said. "My age, plus 30 years teaching and a couple of good investments add up to early retirement. And I'm taking advantage of it. Enough putting up with hormone-fueled teenagers. I'm going to fish and hunt and . . . well, I'm not sure what all I'll be doing. But that's the point. I'll have time to do whatever I want." Myron pushed himself out of the booth and stood. "Gotta run," he said. "School day tomorrow. But not for much longer." He lifted his eyebrows and flashed us a goofy grin.

I pushed a French fry through some ketchup. What would I do if I wasn't compelled out of bed each morning by a demanding business?

I didn't have time to answer my question, Larry interrupted my thoughts. "Man, that kind of announcement gets the wheels turning. Makes me wonder where I went wrong. I'm going to have to work until I'm sixty-five before I can even *think* of hanging it up."

Larry had a crooked line for a career path. He'd started out in construction, went back to school for plumbing, then worked for a couple different outfits before going out on his own. I knew plumbers made pretty decent money, but I also knew Larry liked new pickups and trips to Vegas. In addition to having a second wife and three kids, one still at home.

I tossed my napkin onto my plate, covering up the remains of the hamburger I couldn't finish and a few soggy fries. "Seems like working, or *not* working, is all anyone talks about these days."

"Yeah, well, at our ages, what's left? We're not exactly going to set the world on fire." Larry looked down at his work rough hands. "I'm not sure I'd even want to anymore. What about you?"

With the back of my fingers, I nudged my plate a few inches away and pulled what was left of my beer into my hands. Larry was in the same boat I was. We both had businesses we'd built up and no one who seemed to want to continue our legacy. The question really was, what to do with what we'd worked so hard to build. Did a guy just turn and walk away from all those years? Just like that?

Larry wasn't exactly my idea of a therapist. I didn't want to get into a philosophical discussion and I knew if I opened *that* particular Pandora's box we could sit here all night. More and more often, I wrestled my thoughts about work. I'd held out the hope that maybe one of my boys, or even Kaylee, would show some interest in the store. I'd convinced myself that somehow it would be easier to walk away from all I'd worked for if I knew the store was going to stay in the family. But would it be that simple?

That was a question I'd never have answered. None of my kids were going to step into their old dad's shoes.

As Larry chomped on the last bites of his burger, I stared into my glass. Over Christmas I'd held out a faint hope that Drew might take Bob Marsden up on his offer of a job as a loan officer at the bank in Carlton. I pretended I didn't know the two of them had talked, but a phone call from Bob had led me to believe Drew was considering the offer. Until Drew called home the middle of January with the news he'd been promoted at his New York firm.

Reaching for the check, I picked up my glass and tossed back the last swallow of beer. Kudos to my son. I was ready to call it a night.

MAY SHOWERS BRING MUCH MORE THAN FLOWERS . . .

Drew

"Drew, your ten-thirty appointment is here."

I glanced up from the papers on my desk. Mary, my assistant, stood in the doorway of my office. Well, technically she wasn't *my* assistant. Mary was the admin for three of us who'd been promoted to the position of Senior Lender. A title I'd been flattered to add to my business card, only to discover hardly anyone but me ever saw my business cards. The title, and a raise that barely covered the increased insurance premiums that had been added in the new year, were my reward for doing the same-old, same-old. I wasn't sure what I'd been expecting with my new position, but it hadn't been sitting in my same lumpy chair.

"Okay," I said to Mary, tapping together the loan papers I'd been reviewing. "Let me make a quick phone call and then send him in."

"Will do." Mary partially closed my door on her way out.

I set the closed file on a neat stack beside my computer and tapped at the speed dial on my desk phone. *Home . . . Trisha.* The phone rang once. Twice. Where was she? A twinge of worry pinged in my stomach. Trisha could have our baby any day. The phone rang again. Ring number three. Trisha was supposed to be in bed. Certainly she'd have her cell phone right by her. She'd worked at her marketing position at the bank until last week, when early contractions led to her doctor ordering bed rest. She wasn't due for another three weeks. If she'd moved to the living room couch she would have moved her phone along with her. Where in the wor—

"Hello!" Finally. Trisha's familiar voice.

"Hi," I said, instant relief flooding me, but only for a second.

"You have reached the voice mailbox of Trisha Westin."

I let out a low groan. I didn't want to leave my wife a message. I wanted to know where she was, and if she—and the baby—were okay. "Trisha," I said into the phone. "It's me. Where are—"

Mary poked her head around the door. She put her closed fist near her ear and mouthed, *"Trisha, line two."* Mary knew we were counting down the days to delivery as seriously as a NASA launch.

I quickly cut myself off of line one and punched into my second line. "Are you okay?"

Trisha laughed. "I'm fine. I was in the bathroom, and by the time I got to the phone, my voice mail picked up. I figured it was you."

"It is." I smiled into the receiver, inordinately glad to hear her calm voice. "How's the morning going?"

"Long. Boring." Trisha wasn't the best candidate for bed rest. "If you need an update on the *Today* show or *Regis and Kelly*, I'm your ticket."

"I'll keep that in mind. Are you in the bedroom, or on the couch?"

"The couch," she said. "It's sunnier in here."

In my mind I could see Trisha relaxing in our small living room. Another apartment complex blocked most of the light coming into our bedroom. It was great for sleeping, but not so great for someone having to spend an entire day on her back. "Well, you take it easy. And next time you head to the bathroom, take your cell phone with you. It's probably not the best idea to make a mad dash to the phone."

"Yes, Doctor Westin." I could hear the tease in Trisha's tone. "Wow." Her voice was more serious now. "I think this little guy is going to be a professional football player. He just kicked a field goal through my belly button."

It didn't take much imagining for me to know Trisha was running her hand over her abdomen. Ever since we'd found out we were having a boy, we'd been giving him potential employment opportunities. Acrobat was near the top of the list.

"So, you're feeling okay?" I asked.

"Like a slug with a bowling ball stuck inside."

"That's good," I said, my thoughts moving ahead to the client waiting to see me.

There was silence from Trisha.

"Or maybe not," I corrected. It was hard to put myself in Trisha's bedroom slippers. Or to completely decipher her changing emotions. One minute she'd be on top of the world, laughing at her ungainly stomach and dragging home baby supplies from Target. The next she'd be in tears, lamenting her elephant-like profile and the fact that once this baby was born there would be no family close by to help raise him.

"It's raining in Carlton this morning," Trisha commented as if we'd been talking about the weather in North Dakota all along.

"How do you know that? Did my mom call?"

"No," Trisha said. "I checked on the computer."

"Oh." This didn't seem like a good time to remind her that our computer wasn't anywhere close to the couch.

Ever since I'd turned down the loan officer job in Carlton there had been an uncomfortable silence whenever we talked about what the future held for our child. Trisha made no effort to hide the fact that she wanted to move back to the Midwest. Either closer to her parents, or mine. In spite of the little time they'd spent together, my mom, Kaylee, and Trisha talked like long-lost girlfriends whenever they were together or on the phone. If I wanted to climb the corporate ladder in New York and keep my wife happy, I'd have to import our family . . . and, obviously, that wasn't going to happen.

Once again, our conversation was at a stalemate without even saying much of anything.

"I have someone waiting to see me," I said, guilty that my day would fly by and Trisha would have long hours on the couch ahead of her. "I'll check in later."

"Sure . . . bye," Trisha said.

I placed the phone back in the holder and breathed a deep sigh. I only hoped once our little guy showed up, Trisha would be so involved in motherhood that she'd forget about moving completely.

I held down the intercom button on my phone. "Mary, go ahead and send in my appointment. Thanks."

In seconds my office door swung open, and I walked around the desk to meet my loan client. "Justin," I said, shaking his cold hand. "Good to see you again."

"You, too." He handed me a manila folder, wiped his palm against his slacks, and took a seat in the chair in front of my desk.

As I walked around the desk to my chair, Justin shifted uncomfortably. I didn't blame him. It wasn't every day a person applied for a half-million dollar loan. Justin owned a small restaurant and was looking to upscale, both in size and atmosphere. The future of his business depended on the strength of the financial statement I held in my hands.

I settled into my chair and folded my hands on top of Justin's file. Some polite chitchat was in order before we got to the bottom line. I liked my clients to know I really was on their side, even if I sometimes had to turn down a request for a loan. A banker did a customer no favors loaning them money they couldn't pay back.

According to my memory, it had been about three weeks since Justin had come in to ask for a loan. That's when I'd given him the financial statement to fill out. "So, how's business?" I asked.

He hesitated as if I'd asked him a trick question. Sitting in a lender's office might be a bit like waiting to talk to a doctor. What were you supposed to say when the doctor asked, "How are you?" "Fine" didn't quite fit. Obviously, something was wrong or you wouldn't be there. The same way Justin wouldn't be in my office if he didn't need my help.

I opened my mouth to rephrase my question, but before I could, Justin said, "Good." Then he added, "It could be better. If I had a bigger place, that is."

This guy was serious about expanding his business, and I liked his attitude. I opened the file in front of me. "Let's crunch some numbers and see what we can do."

Scanning the rows of figures in front of me, I couldn't help but think of the number crunching Trisha and I had done when we found out she was pregnant. Having a child was the least of the cost; it was *raising* a child that took some creative accounting. Once this baby was past the crib stage, we were going to need a bigger place, and one with grass outside—instead of concrete— would be nice. Of course, a bigger place meant more money. If Trisha had her druthers she'd stay home with our little guy for at least six months. But she was already hedging her bets and wondering whether she might like to stay home full time. When we tallied up the cost of day care, staying home didn't seem like a bad option, but then our income would be cut almost in half. Could we live on what I made alone? This was when Trisha made sure to point out that the cost of living in North Dakota was a fraction of the cost of living in New York City. Our discussions on the subject were a merry-go-round that wasn't so merry.

A cough from Justin snapped my thoughts back to *his* money issues. "Umm," I said, "let's see here." I ran a mechanical pencil down the forms in front of me as if I'd gotten lost in Justin's financial future instead of mine. "It looks like your food costs are within industry averages and you seem to have good control of your labor costs." I punched some numbers into the calculator near my elbow. "Your profit margins are tight, but I think with some—"

There was a quick rap on the door and then Mary stepped into my office. "Drew, could you pick up line one?"

I could feel my eyebrows puzzle together. Mary knew when I had a client in my office she was supposed to take a message. If I let every phone call interrupt my appointments I'd never get anything done. The look I tossed her wasn't my best. "Tell whoever it is that I'll get back to them. *Please.*" I didn't mean to be short with her, but she knew better.

"It's Trisha," she said.

"I just talked to her fifteen minutes ago," I replied, casting an apologetic look at Justin. This wasn't the way I liked to conduct a business meet—"Oh!" Trisha wouldn't be calling back unless—I lunged for the phone. "What?" I shouted into the receiver.

"Drew?" Trisha's heavy breathing filled the connection between us. "I think—" She pulled in another long breath. "I think it's happening. My . . . my water broke. And it—Hurts. Come get me."

I was already standing. "Fifteen minutes," I said, silently praying for a taxi to appear outside my office building, for light traffic, and stoplights that were green. I hung up the phone and then stood still by my desk, paralyzed by all I should be doing.

"Drew?" Mary asked. I hadn't noticed she was still standing by my office door. "Is everything okay?"

"I'm having a baby." I ran a hand through my hair, not sure if I was ecstatic or terrified. "I'm mean *we're* having a baby."

Mary stepped to my side and put a hand on my shoulder. "Then you'd better go."

I stared down at my loan client. "But Justin—" My head was spinning. I was every rattled-new-dad-to-be-from-the-movies come to life.

Justin jumped to his feet. "Don't worry about me. I'll come back." He clapped a hand on my back, giving me a small push. "You go have your baby. I mean your wife should have it. I—" He snorted a small laugh. "Go."

"Yes," Mary chimed in. "Go. Now."

"You're doing great, Trisha. Great job." I ran the back of my hand over my damp forehead. I had no idea whether my wife was doing fine or not. I was only repeating the words the nurse kept saying. If Trisha's grunts and moans were signs of a "great job," I didn't even *want* to know what a "crummy job" would sound like.

"Ohhh . . . hhhh!" Trisha curled onto her side. She closed her eyes and grimaced through a contraction, then looked up at me. "Next time it's your turn."

Next time? *Me?* There was no way I'd ever put myself through—

Trisha winked at me.

I felt a hot flush rise into my neck. She was joking. Of course she was. At a time like this. And for a split second I'd believed her. As if *I* could have a baby. Sheesh. This kid didn't know what kind of family he was getting born into.

I rubbed a cool cloth over Trisha's face, wishing someone would rub one over mine. At this point I felt as though I'd been through the wringer myself. I wasn't sure I was even thinking coherently, or whether the voice in my head was mine, Trisha's, or if it came from somewhere . . . or Someone else.

Please, Lord, let this baby be okay. Help Trisha not be in so much pain.

There wasn't much more I could do. In all the reading Trisha had done about pregnancy and labor, why hadn't I ever thought to ask her if they said anything about expectant dads? The only thing I knew at this point was that I wanted this part to be over.

Trisha puffed through a contraction, then laid back and relaxed . . . if you could call anything about this process *relaxing*. One side of her mouth turned up. "I want my mom."

"I want my mom, too." I was only half-joking.

"Your mom. My mom. I'll take either one right now." Trisha gasped, squeezed her eyes tight, and started panting.

Even in the midst of hard labor, we'd somehow entered the familiar territory of having our parents close by. I wasn't about to start an argument with my wife in the labor room. I only hoped that once our little guy was in her arms, Trisha wouldn't care where she lived as long as the three of us were a family.

The nurse coached Trisha through the contraction. "There you go. The contraction's over. Lie back. Whoa!" She looked at her own hand that rested on Trisha's abdomen. "Here comes another one." She did some quick checking of her watch, took a peek under the sheet that covered Trisha's lower half, then said, "I'm calling the doctor. This baby is coming now."

• • •

From her hospital bed Trisha gazed over at the blue bundle in my arms. "I think he looks like you."

It was on the tip of my tongue to deny it, but she was right, our little guy did. A football-sized piece of pride pushed at the inside of my chest. Did every new dad feel like this? Proud. Happy. Lump in the throat. It was hard to imagine I hadn't heard a word about this part of being a dad.

With the tip of my little finger, I nuzzled the corner of William Westin's miniature mouth. His eyes were closed, but he turned his head toward my hand, his mouth moving in a suckling motion. How in the world could such a tiny person already know where to look for food? *Amazing* was the only word I could come up with to describe how it felt to hold my son in my arms. Well, make that in my hand and forearm. Will was unbelievably small. And yet perfect.

I found myself blinking against the sting in my eyes. *Thank You, Lord.* In all the commotion of the labor and delivery, and then getting Trisha and the baby cleaned up and tucked into bed, I'd forgotten to say thanks. It seemed impossible to me that anyone could look at a newborn and claim not to believe in God. There was no way a random burst of particles could spontaneously create my son. "Thank You, Lord," I whispered as I lifted my son and held him close to my heart.

"Drew? Could you come here?" Trisha's uncertain voice called from our bedroom.

Laying down the morning paper and taking a quick sip of coffee, I pushed myself away from the kitchen table and headed to the bedroom. Trisha was standing by the changing table, in the middle of putting an impossibly small disposable diaper on Will.

I paused in the doorway and took in the scene. "Picture perfect" came to mind. My wife and son. It was our second day at home with our baby, and the fascination of having a baby in our midst had not worn off. I'd taken a week of paternity leave so we could both get used to this mom and dad business.

"What's up?" I asked, walking in and standing next to Trisha.

"Look at him," she said, nodding her head in Will's direction.

He looked pretty darn near perfect to me. "What?"

"Doesn't he look . . . I don't know . . ." She put her index finger under our son's fingers and lifted them a bit for me to see. "Don't they look kind of . . . blue . . . or something? And look at his legs." She eased her fingers from his palm and moved her hand to his thigh. "His legs seem, I don't know, like . . . *puffy*. Don't you think?"

I scratched my forehead as I gave my son the

once-over. His fingertips did have a bluish cast. "He's probably cold lying there stark naked," I said.

"But his fingers were like that before I started to change his diaper. And then I noticed his legs and—"

"He's growing," I added. "All that good mother's milk and all."

Trisha kept one hand on Will as she turned to look at me. "Drew, it's only been two days since we brought him home. I doubt my—" She made two quick quote-marks in the air "—'good mother's milk' went straight to his thighs. Do you think I should call the doctor?"

"I don't know. He looks okay to me."

"Well, he doesn't to me."

"Trish." I leveled a look at her. If she was going to turn into one of those overprotective mothers who ran to the doctor for every little thing, this boy of ours was going to grow up to be a wimp. "I really don't think there's anything wrong. Why don't you finish changing his diaper and wrap him in his blanket. I'll hold him for awhile. You go shower. You'll feel better."

Trisha gave me a hard nudge with her shoulder. "Stop patronizing me."

"Patronize—" I lifted my hands in the air, then let them drop. Okay, so maybe I was. The fact was, I didn't know much more about this parenting business than Trisha. If Trisha was worried, maybe I should be, too. Or maybe not. I knew enough to know that my wife's hormones had run amuck. She was crying as often as the baby. Speaking of which . . . she was at it again.

This situation didn't call for a lecture, it called for a hug. "Come here." I held out my arms. As Trisha leaned into me, we both looked down at Will, making sure our hips formed a barrier to keep him safe on the changing table.

Trisha cried softly against my shoulder. "I'm scared I'm—I'm—not doing everything right."

I rubbed comforting circles into my wife's back. "You're a great mom."

"I don't feel like one. What if something's wrong?"

"There's nothing wrong." I put my hands on her shoulders and eased her away from me enough so that I could look into her eyes. "Are you going to get mad if I tell you to go take a bubble bath?"

A small smile curved along Trisha's lips. She glanced down at our baby and then up at me. "Promise me he's okay?"

I kissed the top of Trisha's head. "He's okay."

And then, as if to prove I was right, a pale yellow stream of pee arched from our son into the air and right back down onto the changing table.

Trisha nudged her head against my shoulder. "I think I'll go take that bath and let you handle this."

"Gee, thanks," I said, but I couldn't help but laugh.

The noise from the running bathwater formed a soft soundtrack as I grabbed a damp baby wipe and sopped up the piddly mess. In the two days we'd had Will home, I'd become expert at whipping a diaper onto my son. In no time I had him in one of his sleeper-things.

"How's that, Buddy? Your old dad did okay." I lifted Will off the table and into my arms. He was almost too small to hold comfortably, so I laid him on our bed and grabbed a blue blanket from the shelf beneath the changing table. "I'll get you wrapped up and then we'll go finish reading the paper. Sound like a plan?"

I pitched my voice high. "Sounds good, Dad." I sounded more like Alvin the Chipmunk than a little kid. Okay, so maybe I had a few new-dad hormones floating around making me slightly crazy.

I carried Will to the kitchen table with me, settling him in the crook of my arm while I attempted to read the paper one-handed. However, instead of reading, I found myself doing nothing but gazing down at my son. With the side of my index finger, I chucked him under his tiny chin. "Hey there, Fella. You ready for a whole day in your new home?"

In response, he lazily yawned and stretched his skinny arms above his head. On the way down, I caught his tiny hand and let his fingers curl around my little finger. Playing a gentle version of tug-of-war, I teased and tested my son's grip. "Gotta learn how to hold onto a football," I said. "No letting go until you're in the end zone."

Smiling at my years-ahead-of-itself imagination, I bent to kiss Will's impossibly small fingers. They were cool against my lips. Too cool for a baby wrapped tight. I pulled my head back and studied his hand. Then examined the other one. Trisha hadn't been imagining things. Will's fingertips were definitely blue tinged. Now that I was looking closer, even his face seemed drained of natural color. A pang of fear seared beneath my ribs, burning and settling like a hot coal in my stomach.

"Trisha!" I pushed myself away from the table and hurried the short distance to the bathroom. Without knocking on the door, I burst in. "I think we should take Will to the clinic."

"What?" Trisha had been leaning back in a cloud of steamy bubbles. She sat up. "What's wrong?"

I held Will to my chest, trying to stay calm. "I think you were right. His fingers are blue. They're cold. And look at his face." I turned our baby so she could see his face. "It looks gray, or blue, or . . . not right."

Instant tears flooded Trisha's eyes as she pushed her way out of the tub and grabbed a towel. "Oh, God." She looked upward. "Should we call first?"

"I'll call while you get dressed." I looked down at myself. I was wearing nothing more than gym trunks and an old T-shirt. "Let's both get dressed and just go."

"This is your son's heart." Dr. Thomas held his clenched fist out for us to see. He didn't seem to notice that the size of his fist was almost bigger than Will's whole chest. Dr. Thomas slowly pulsed his hand. "The heart beats to pump oxygen through the blood. Occasionally, during pregnancy as the heart forms in utero . . . ," Dr. Thomas extended the fingers of his hand, "the heart starts out as a simple tube. As it develops it turns back onto itself, forming a loop." He gradually bent his fingers back into his fist. "This action creates chambers on each side and forms blood vessels to carry blood in and out of the heart." He paused as he looked to Trisha and me, gauging to see if we understood what he was saying.

We'd spent most of the day at the hospital, standing by as our small son was checked and rechecked. He'd been poked for blood samples, hooked up to monitors, scanned, and had a cold stethoscope put to his chest at least a dozen times. I glanced over at Will in Trisha's arms. He looked no worse for the experience, but Trisha and I looked as if we'd been run over by a truck. A *big* truck.

Dr. Thomas cleared his throat. "Are you following so far?"

Even though my thoughts were screaming, *No! No!* I nodded.

He went on. "Sometimes during this complicated process of forming the heart and its chambers, not all of the structures join together completely. In your son's case, he has what we call atrial septic defect. More commonly referred to as a *hole* in his heart."

At his words, a block of cement dropped into my stomach. It felt as if I had a hole as wide and deep as the Grand Canyon inside me. I wanted to turn back the clock to yesterday, or the day before, anytime but right now. There was something wrong with my boy and I couldn't fix it.

Trisha looked at me, eyes wide. Her mouth opened, then closed. She looked down at Will as she blinked back tears.

I ran a hand along the back of my neck and blew out a lungful of air. Nothing had prepared me for this. None of my college classes, or the specialized banking school I'd attended. I'd solved all kinds of lending dilemmas in my office, but I sat here, helpless to help my son.

Help us, Lord. Help him.

I held my empty, open palms out to the doctor. "What can we do?"

"You're in luck," he said, going on to describe a catheterization technique that didn't sound lucky at all. "We will thread a thin tube through a vein in your son's leg up to the heart. We'll monitor the progress through X-ray images. Then, when the tube is in the proper place in the heart, I'll insert an expandable disk into the opening." He paused and plucked a piece of fuzz from the knee of his black slacks as if what he'd described was nothing but routine to him. "Not all that many years ago, the *fix* for this procedure meant open heart surgery."

"Open heart surgery?" I felt the blood drain from my face. If the doctor wasn't careful, he was going to have a second patient on his hands.

Dr. Thomas held up one finger. "That was in the past. Nowadays, the procedure is much less invasive. Like I said, you're lucky."

If this was his idea of luck, I wouldn't advise a trip to Vegas anytime soon.

"What now?" Trisha asked, her voice tight.

The doctor ran his hand along his jaw line. "I'd like to schedule the procedure as soon as possible. This condition can lead to congestive heart failure, and we're already finding some signs of some respiratory distress. I don't want your son to have any undue stress put on his heart. We'll have him fixed up and back home in no time."

I thought of my pat assurances to Trisha that there was nothing wrong with Will. How could I have been so blind? My son was possibly dying, and I'd brushed off Trisha's concern. Guilt weighed on my shoulders. I wasn't going to let anything like that happen ever again. I had to ask. "Should we get a second opinion?"

Dr. Thomas gave me a quick nod. "You're entitled to that, but the tests we ran are pretty standard and the results clear. Your son needs this procedure, and the sooner we get it done the better off he'll be."

I nodded back. That's all I wanted . . . for Will to be better.

I paced across the waiting area. Twelve steps in one direction, about-face, twelve in the other. *Please, God. Help him.* About-face. Start walking again. Twelve steps. *Please, God . . .*

"Drew," Trisha said, patting the padded chair beside her, "sit down, you're making me more nervous." She lowered her voice. "You're making everyone nervous."

I glanced at the other people in the waiting room. One woman was knitting. Another man was paging through an old *People* magazine. A couple obviously younger than Trisha and me sat with their hands clasped together. It seemed like hours since we'd exchanged tense greetings as the early morning surgeries started.

I dropped into a chair and tried to unwind. I hadn't done this much praying ever. It was amazing how that little boy of mine had worked his way into my heart in such a short time. *Make him better. Heal him. Please.* I jiggled my knee up and down. Jell-O-on-speed.

Trisha reached over and put her hand on my leg, stilling my knee with her fingers. "Drew."

As if my nervous energy had to go somewhere, the tip of my shoe started tapping out a rhythm that would rival a tap-dancing pro.

Trisha rolled her eyes, half-smiled, and shook her head, the first bit of lightness I'd experienced in two days. The doctor had kept Will in the hospital overnight, scheduled surgery for first thing this morning. We'd spent the night in the pediatric floor waiting room, taking turns dozing and going to check on Will in the nursery. It had been a long night and a longer morning.

In between pacing and praying, we'd kept our families updated with an ongoing flurry of phone calls. Everyone was praying. Even people we didn't know.

The door leading from the operating area opened, and I jumped from my chair as a doctor stepped into the waiting area. A buzz of silent tension hovered in the air as he looked around the room. The young couple stood up as the doctor approached them. If I'd taken a second to look past the scrubs he wore, I would have known this wasn't Dr. Thomas. Breathing a heavy sigh, I sat back down. *Please . . .*

I closed my eyes and pressed my fingers hard against my brows. What would we do if this procedure didn't fix Will? What if this hole in his heart caused him permanent damage? Trisha and I would somehow learn to cope . . . wouldn't we? But what if Will needed more surgeries? I had to work, we needed my income and insurance benefits, and even if Trisha did stay home full time, she couldn't do everything by herself. What would we do? *Oh, Lord . . .*

Family.

The one word answer to my prayer slammed into my turbulent thoughts. Family. The thing Trisha had wanted, begged for, all along. *I want to be close to family.*

It had taken this—a possible life-or-death situation with our son—to get it through my thick head that *family* was where we would find help, comfort, and support.

"Are you the Westins?"

I'd been so engrossed in my thoughts I hadn't seen the surgical waiting room attendant coming our way. I jumped to my feet. "Yes. I am." I held a hand toward Trisha. "We are."

The older woman smiled. "The doctor will be out to see you in a minute. He said to tell you the procedure was—and I'm quoting here—'a piece of cake.'"

A surge of welcome, hot relief flooded through my chest, running down my arms, making them feel as limp as overcooked spaghetti. I closed my eyes. *Thank You, Lord. Thank You.*

Without thinking, I reached out and pulled the woman into a too-tight hug. "Thank you," I said.

It was only when I felt her shaking with laughter that I realized what I'd done. I laughed along, as I released her. "Sorry," I said, dipping my head and smiling. "I—"

She held up a hand. "Yours isn't the first hug I've had here. And I hope it's not the last. Good news is sweet."

"It sure is." I sat down beside Trisha and gave her a big kiss on the cheek, then noticed the tears slipping from her eyes. "What . . . ?"

"I was scared," she said, her voice scratchy. "We're so far away from everyone, and if something happened, I didn't know—"

"Shh . . ." I wiped a tear away with my thumb. "Everything is okay. I promise, everything will be okay."

I put an arm around Trisha's shoulder and held her close. Everything would be okay. I had a plan. I knew exactly what I would do as soon as we brought Will home from the hospital. I only hoped Bob Marsden still had a job open.

Claire

I sat at my office computer and clicked through the latest batch of digital photos Trisha had e-mailed. In spite of little Will's precarious start on life, the tiny trooper was thriving. *Click.* I enlarged the photo that showed a close-up of Will wrapped in a blue blanket with an impossibly small, blue knit stocking cap on his perfect little head. Home from the hospital after his heart procedure. The urge to hold him was so strong I almost had to fight with myself to keep from reaching out to my computer screen. If only I could hop on a plane and be in New York tonight.

I turned my head and studied the calendar on my desk top. Of course, I knew that babies didn't follow anyone's schedule, but having little Will arrive three weeks early threw a curveball into my carefully made plans. His original due date would have meshed perfectly into the end of the college spring semester. While I hadn't booked a ticket, I'd reserved a spot on the calendar I kept in my head that would have put me at my new grandson's apartment within a week of his arrival home.

Instead, I was stuck in my office, or a classroom, trying to concentrate on sociology when my whole being cried out to meet my oldest son's son. *Grandma* was a word I was getting used to the more I thought about it.

I took one last look at my favorite of the new photos on my computer and then clicked over to my Word document. I didn't like to mix my duties as a college professor with my obligations to my publisher, but there were only so many hours in the day and I had a night class to teach tonight. If

I was going to get the draft of my second book off to Wesley by the end of the week, I had to work on it during my office hours.

Concentrate. The images I'd viewed of my grandson seemed superimposed on the computer screen in front of me. As hard as I tried to focus on the pages of manuscript in front of me, all I could think of was Will.

I reached for the phone. "Julie," I called into the receiver when she answered. "Help! I need new-Grandma therapy."

Her laughter bubbled through the phone line. "Think of sticky fingers on your face and changing dirty diapers. That should cure you for a little while."

In my mind's eye, I did exactly what Julie advised. Her remedy didn't work. "Oh, but imagine how cute that little handprint would look. And remember that phrase? 'As smooth as a baby's bottom.' Even that seems cute to me right now."

"Man," she said, "you do have it bad."

"I know." I sighed into the phone.

"Why don't you see if you and Jim can get a flight out this weekend? Don't analyze it. Just go. Check online and see if you can find a deal."

Even though Julie couldn't see me, I rolled my eyes. "Two problems with that. For one, there are no deals flying out of North Dakota. And two, I have speaking engagements on Friday night and Saturday."

Shortly after my talk to the Carlton Community Club, I'd started getting phone calls to speak to other groups. It hadn't taken long for my spring weekends to become completely booked. Julie should remember, she'd been the one to encourage me to do this. I reminded her. "It's not really the money, it's the time."

"Speaking of which . . . I was going to call and see if you'd have time on Saturday to run to the mall with me. I need a dress for my niece's wedding in June."

"This Saturday?" I asked.

"Well, yeah. I know you said you have a speaking engagement, but I'm flexible. If it's in the morning we'll go in the afternoon, and if it's in the afternoon we'll go in the morning. How's that for planning?"

"It'd be great if my speaking engagements were in Carlton. They're not. I have a hundred miles to drive before I speak Friday night, and another seventy-five to get to Saturday's event. That means I have almost two hundred miles to drive to get home. I'll be staying over Friday night in a hotel. Coming home Saturday, probably late."

"Two hundred miles? Where are you going?"

I recited the name of two small towns in the middle of the state. "Ever heard of them?"

"I've heard of them," Julie replied. "But I wouldn't know how to get there."

"Want to come along and find out?"

"Uh, sorry. I really can't be gone all weekend. I've got too much to do around the house. And Saturday night Greg and I are going out for dinner with his sister and her husband. It's her birthday. But have fun. I'll miss you when I go shopping."

"I'll miss you, too." I hung up the phone and pressed my fingers hard against the bridge of my nose. Now that I thought about the weekend ahead of me and weighed it against the outing I'd be missing with Julie, staying home felt like the option I preferred. But I'd already made these two weekend commitments. There were a business fund-raiser and a church women's group planning their weekend events around having me as their speaker. I couldn't back out. They were paying me decent money to be there.

It's not about money . . . My earlier lament to Julie still held true. It wasn't about money, although I'd raised my speaking fee considerably since my first talk at the Community Club. My years of college teaching gave me a comfort in front of a group that made the time I spent away from home worth something. But what motivated me more than what I got paid was that I felt I had a message to share. One about the importance of friendship. And that God was nudging me to share it. While my book and talk weren't overtly religious, they did have a faith-based outlook that seemed to strike a chord with my audiences. I was getting asked more and more to speak at church women's events. Like the one on Saturday. But, first I needed to finish this new manuscript.

I jiggled my computer mouse to get the screen-saver off and my manuscript back in front of me. Where was I? My eyes skimmed the paragraphs I'd written as I scrolled through the pages of this follow-up book. *The Friendship Factor for Twenty-somethings.* It was a perfect piggyback book to follow my first one, and perfect for me to write considering I'd spent most of my career teaching college-age students. Plus the fact that Wesley was anxious to capitalize on the success of my first book.

"I've never seen anything like it," Wesley had told me more than once. In all his years as a small-press publisher, he'd never gone back to press three times in five months. The initial print run of two thousand had been doubled and then tripled. And still, booksellers were having a hard time keeping up with the demand. At least that's what Wesley told me. It seemed strange to be slaving away at my computer in relatively small Carlton, North Dakota at the same time my first book was selling out in places I'd never even heard of . . . like a bookstore in Howick, New Zealand. The only reason I knew that was from the reader mail I'd been receiving. My e-mail address had been included in the back of *The Friendship Factor*, and each day I turned on my computer to be greeted by letters from readers, thanking me for writing about friendship in such a personal way.

For not the first time today, I felt the tug to check my e-mail. *No.* I would force myself to get to the end of editing this new chapter before I changed screens. I read through a page and a half before I gave in. I knew I should be spending my computer time more productively, but I couldn't help it. I clicked over to my Yahoo! e-mail account. Sure enough, I had eight new e-mails since I'd checked an hour ago. Two I deleted without reading . . . spam. Two had similar headings: *Speaking inquiry.* The other four had variations on the title of my book . . . reader mail.

I opened one of the speaking inquiries first. My spring schedule was full, so it would be easy to quickly write back and tell them I wasn't available.

Good morning, Claire. (I hope it's okay for me to call you that . . . after reading your book, *The Friendship Factor*, I feel like I know you.) I am the director of the women's ministry at our church. I'm writing to ask about your availability to speak at our annual Mother-Daughter Tea held each spring.

Ah-ha. Just what I thought. I was already booked. This would be easy enough. I moved my cursor to reply. Before hitting the "reply" icon, I scanned the rest of the e-mail.

I am currently looking to book you as a speaker at our annual event in May, "spring" of next year. Please let me know of your availability and your speaking fees at your earliest convenience. Many of the women in our church have read your book and would so love to hear you speak.

It was barely May *this* year. I didn't even have a calendar for next year, yet. How in the world would I know my availability a year from now? I'd have to wait to answer this e-mail. I clicked on the second speaking inquiry.

Ms. Westin. I'm writing about the possibility of having you speak at the banquet for our Hospice Fundraiser in October. Your name was mentioned by several of the people on our committee as a possible keynote speaker. We have some flexibility as to scheduling. If you could get back to me with openings you might have in October, we can start from there. Hope to hear from you soon.

What openings did I have in October? How about any day? Who thought about what they'd be doing in October when it was barely May? I pulled my yearly planner near and flipped through the summer months to fall. Other than the fact that I knew I'd be teaching classes come September, my days and nights were wide open. I picked up a pen and clicked it open and shut, open and shut. A thrum of nervous anticipation hummed in my stomach. What if I scheduled a speaking event on a particular evening in October and something else came along that I should be doing instead?

Like what?

What if Jim and I decided to go visit Drew, Trisha, and Will in New York?

You wouldn't schedule your trip when you already had a booking.

Well . . . what if someone in our family got sick and needed me to be there?

You can never plan around everything. If an emergency comes up, people understand.

What if it's not an emergency? What if it's something I want to do more than head to an unfamiliar town and speak?

That's the deal breaker. These people will be counting on you to head-up their event. If you commit, nothing but a true emergency can change your plans.

A deep breath of air filled my lungs, and I slowly released it as my mind tumbled around the pros and cons of making a commitment so far in advance. I had my teaching schedule to consider. And then there was Will. I had no idea what being a Grandma entailed. At least I knew enough not to book anything on his birthday . . . who knew . . . we might decide to make a trip to New York for birthday number one.

I reread the e-mail. Both of these requests had just come in. I didn't have to answer them in a nanosecond. I would talk things over with Jim. See if he had some wisdom—or objections—to my making plans so far in advance.

Jim pulled back the covers on his side of the bed and crawled in. He punched at the pillow and then lay on his back, hands behind his head. "Where did you say you're going, again?"

The small suitcase I was packing anchored down the blankets on my side of the bed. I paused in the middle of folding a light sweater I planned to wear on the long drive home from my speaking engagements. "I'll be in Wallace tomorrow night and Clayton on Saturday. It's a luncheon, and then I speak after we eat." Mentally I tallied up the time it would take for me to chat with people afterward, get my books packed up and hauled out to my car, stop at a local gas station for a Diet Coke for the road, and then head home. An almost four-hour drive. "I'm guessing I'll be home around seven, seven-thirty."

"Oh." The single word dangled with something unsaid.

I rested my hand on the edge of the suitcase. "Did you have something planned?"

"No, not really. I thought maybe we could go out for dinner when you got back. But it might be kind of late."

"We can still go. We'll be fashionably late." I forced a smile. It hardly seemed fair to leave Jim sitting home alone most of the weekend. I'd been gone last Saturday, too. "It'll be nice to have that to look forward to on my drive home."

Jim reached out and turned off his bedside lamp. "When are you leaving?"

"I'm going to have to head out straight from campus tomorrow." That's why I was packing tonight. "I have a class at eleven, then I'll grab some lunch and head out. I want to be in Wallace by around three. Their event starts at five and I need to have my book table set up earlier. Then I'm going to want to check in at the hotel and change clothes before the thing starts."

Jim nodded as if everything I'd mentioned was already done. "Night," he said, turning onto his side and pulling the covers to his chin.

"I'll be done in a minute." Staring into my suitcase I reviewed my schedule, trying to put myself into all the clothes and shoes I'd packed, making sure I'd included everything I'd need. The suit I'd wear to speak in was hanging in dry cleaner's plastic on the closet door. I reminded myself to not forget it. All that was left was my makeup case. I'd throw that in, in the morning. I lifted my suitcase and put it on the floor, out of the way in case I needed to use the bathroom during the night.

Ah . . . it felt heavenly to finally slip into bed, feel the cool covers against my legs. I turned out the light and lay on my side and tried to relax. My thoughts shuffled through the intro to my speech. I'd given it enough this spring that I didn't feel the need to rehearse the whole thing, but I liked to remind myself how it started. One of my nightmares was standing up to speak and going completely blank. Which is why I had my talk printed out word for word. I didn't use my notes all that much, but they were there if I needed them.

I turned onto my stomach, my now-it's-time-to-get-to-sleep position. But, instead of dreamland, I found myself mentally tracing the highway system I was going to have to navigate over the next two days. The little towns where I'd been invited to speak weren't on any of the major roadways running through North Dakota. I was going to have to rely on my map to get me there.

I flipped over on my side and reached for a sip of the water I kept on my nightstand. Maybe now I could settle down. It wasn't that I was nervous about the drive . . . or maybe I was, a little. I certainly didn't have to worry about heavy traffic, not on the county highways I'd be driving, but if I had car trouble, there would be no Jim to rely on to bail me out of a flat tire. I'd be lucky if I could get reception on my cell phone to call for help.

If I was going to worry, I might as well be comfortable. I turned onto my back and stared at the dark ceiling. I'd give myself ten minutes. Why was I doing this? It wasn't as if I didn't have enough to do teaching full time. We didn't need the little bit of extra money my book sales and speaking brought in. I'd turned fifty-three in early April, an age when I thought my career would be winding down, not gearing up. So why . . . ?

Because I've called you to this.

I felt the tense muscles in my shoulders relax. There it was. The only reason that made sense. God had somehow nudged me into this. Who was I to question His plan?

Lifting the covers, I turned onto my side, and then fully onto my stomach, pulling the blankets over my shoulders and tucking myself in. I was ready to sleep.

I let my mind drift. A mental slideshow of pictures of Will was better than counting sheep. Ah, Will. My grandchild. Soon . . . soon . . . I'd . . . hold . . . him. I could feel myself drifting off—Oh my goodness!

My eyes popped open, and in the same motion I hurtled out of bed. I'd forgotten to pack my hairdryer! The little-town hotels I'd been staying in rarely provided anything but hot and cold running water . . . a hairdryer was a bring-your-own necessity. I stumbled into the bathroom and then remembered, I'd need my hairdryer in the morning to get ready.

Rather than write myself a note, I grabbed a washcloth from the bathroom drawer and tossed it on top of my suitcase. The unusual spot for the light blue cloth would serve to jog my memory in the morning. A reminder to include my hairdryer before I zipped up.

Crawling back into bed, I glanced at the clock. The ten minutes I'd given myself to worry had long passed and now I was wide awake again.

Go to sleep, I ordered myself. *Go to sleep. You've got a long day ahead of you. A longer weekend.*

I tossed and turned and tried to find dreamland. Jim's gentle snoring was not helping. I gave him a nudge with my foot. He turned over and went right back at it.

The people who were paying me to come speak at their events deserved a rested speaker. But here I was, on my way to being exhausted before I even left the house.

I knew Jim was being nice by suggesting dinner out when I returned on Saturday, but after two back-to-back speaking events, plus all the driving, not to mention sleeping in an unfamiliar bed, I knew I'd be exhausted by the time I got home. And then there would be books to unload from the car and a bank deposit to prepare. All things that could wait until Sunday.

So much for a day—or night—of rest.

Bzzz! Bzzz! Bzzz!

"Umm . . . What . . . ?" Fighting my way out of a deep sleep, I flailed at the air, trying to turn off my alarm clock. Why did I have to wake up now? After what seemed like a whole night of restless tossing, I was finally getting the rest I'd craved all the long night.

Bzzz! Bzzz! Bzzz!

"Hey, Sleepyhead." Jim was cutting me no slack. He stood near the bottom of the bed and gently shook my foot through the covers. "Rise and shine."

"Ugh," I mumbled, finally finding the alarm shutoff switch. "I might rise, but I don't think I can shine." I swung my legs over the side of the bed and raised my arms into a lazy stretch. "I slept terrible."

"You could have fooled me." Jim buttoned the cuffs of his white cotton shirt with the Westin Foods logo on the front placket. "You were snoring like a bear."

I stood up and reached down to touch my toes, getting out the kinks in my legs and lower back. "How would you know what a snoring bear sounds like?"

"Like you." Jim chuckled at his lame joke. "Well," he said, looking into the dresser mirror and tugging at his collar. "I'm heading to the store. I'll grab something to eat there. I already fed Pesto and let him out. See you tonigh—" His eyes flicked to my open suitcase on the floor and he corrected himself. "Saturday." He stepped close and puckered his lips. "Drive safe," he said, after he'd given me a peck on the lips. "Do a good job."

I groaned. In my fog of sleep, I'd momentarily forgotten about the two long days I had in front of me. Teaching this morning, followed by a hundred-mile drive and a speech. A night in a small hotel, another drive, another speech. All on a lousy night's sleep.

But still, in spite of my tiredness, a thrum of excitement pulsed in my chest. In all my career planning, I'd never once imagined a step up the ladder that included writing a book and traveling around the state speaking. Many of my colleagues were talking about retirement, and here I was being handed a completely new opportunity. Suddenly I felt alert and more than ready for the two coming days.

Standing at the kitchen counter, I tossed back the last sip of my favorite blend of coffee. I did my best to savor it. I'd be lucky if I had anything better than gas station coffee from now until Sunday. I turned my mug upside down and put it in the dishwasher. "No, Pesto," I said, shooing him away from licking the dishwasher door. The pesky little terrier had his name for a reason. "I'm going to work. You go lie down." I pointed to the family room and his favorite chair. At age ten, our dog was content to stay alone and sleep the day away. Something I would have relished when I woke up this morning. I unplugged my coffeemaker and surveyed the kitchen, making sure everything was in its place until I returned. The morning paper was folded and sitting in a corner of the table, waiting for Jim in case he hadn't had time to scan it before he left for work. *Ready.* I slipped into my coat, pulled my purse onto my shoulder, picked up my briefcase in one hand, my suitcase in the other. Yes, I'd remembered my hairdryer.

Fumbling with the doorknob, I managed to make my way out to the garage. There. Suitcase in the backseat . . . the trunk was crowded with four cases of books. Briefcase on the passenger seat beside me. I punched at the garage door opener as I did a mental checklist. Books. A copy of my speech. Underwear. Makeup. Toothbrush. Shoes. Jeans for the drive home. It felt like I was leaving for a month instead of only overnight. Sticking the keys in the ignition I was about to start the car when I remembered—my speaking outfit was still hanging on the edge of the closet frame!

A hot flush rose in my neck as I barreled out of the car and back into the house. "Sorry, Pesto," I called, as our dog jumped from his chair. "False alarm. No treat."

I dashed through the kitchen and into my bedroom, snagging the hanger off the closet. What else was I forgetting? Oh sure, the outfit I was wearing to teach this morning would do in a pinch, but I didn't want to imagine how wrinkled and bedraggled I'd look by Saturday night. Most of the little-town motels I'd stayed in didn't offer amenities like an iron or an ironing board.

When I got back to the kitchen, I stopped. It was now-or-never if I was forgetting anything else. Nope, I convinced myself, I had everything. If I didn't get a move on I was going to be late for work. Once more I reached for the doorknob—

Brrr-ring. Now it was the phone. I did a small stutter-step, as if dancing between the idea of answering it or leaving. Curiosity won out.

"Hello."

"Claire? Wesley here."

What was my publisher doing calling so early in the day? "Yes?" I pressed the receiver to my ear, holding my plastic-draped suit in the crook of my finger. Our communication was mostly by e-mail and, try as I might, I couldn't imagine what would be so important to warrant a phone call at not-quite-eight in the morning. Just as quickly, it dawned on me it was nearly nine out east where Wesley lived, but still early.

Wesley answered my question with one of his own. "Are you sitting down?"

"Goodness, no, you just caught me. I'm heading to work. What's up?"

Wesley laughed. "This is going to . . . Make. Your. Day." His odd phrasing coupled with his excited tone sent an anticipatory thrill running down my spine. Was it possible my book was going into *another* print run? So soon? I didn't have any experience to gauge the success of this book against, but Wesley assured me what was happening with my book was unusual. "The *Today* show called," he said. "They want you."

Somehow what he said didn't make sense. "Want me for what?"

"As a guest on the show."

"On the show," I repeated, carefully laying my speaking suit on the top of the kitchen table, as if it was suddenly much too heavy to hold along with this news.

"Yes, on the show. They're doing a series on friendship in the technological era and they want you as a guest."

"Me?" I pulled a chair out from the kitchen table and sat down.

"A talent booker for the program just called. They like what you said in your book, and they love the fact that you're a sociologist, too."

"How in the world did they get a copy of my book?"

"I have no idea, but they did. Claire, this is *fantastic* news. Your sales are already through the roof, but this is the kind of exposure a company can't buy. I'm going to go back to press over the weekend. Hopefully, by the end of next week, we'll be ready for whatever happens after your appearance."

"Next week?" I was having a hard time absorbing all he said.

"They want you on the show a week from today."

"It's Friday." I suddenly seemed incapable of putting together more than a two word sentence.

"Yes, it is, and a week from today you'll be on national television."

"National television," I echoed.

"They're going to fly you in. Me, too. Put us up in a hotel. Send a car." Wesley paused. "I've never had anything like this happen with any of my authors."

"I have classes to teach," I said. None of this was sinking in.

"You'll have to get someone to cover for you." He paused, quickly added, "You can get someone to fill in, can't you? I mean, this kind of opportunity doesn't come around—"

"Yes, yes." I waved my fingers through the air as if swatting away the idea that I couldn't make it. Of course I'd make it. Nervous excitement bubbled in my stomach. Who ever thought I'd be invited to be a guest on the *Today* show? Oh, my.

Oh, Lord, I found myself praying as I tried to take in what Wesley was saying. *This is so much more than I ever dreamt . . . or prayed for. Did You plan this? I'm scared. And excited. Go with me. Please.*

As Wesley went through the details of the trip,

my eyes traveled to the calendar I had hanging on the wall near the phone. A week from today I'd be on national TV. A week from today was the day my little grandson was *supposed* to have been born. *Will!* If I was going to be in New York I could see my grandson.

Did You arrange this, too? Thank You!

"Wesley," I interrupted. "Do you think it would be possible for me to stay over in New York for the weekend? My son lives there. My grandson was just—"

"Claire," Wesley said, "you can do whatever you want. I'll see to it."

So this is what it felt like to hit the jackpot.

I drove to campus on a cloud of exhilaration, calling Jim from my cell phone to share the news.

"Wow, Claire. That's great," he said, his enthusiasm sounding forced. "I guess that means you'll be gone next weekend, too."

How could my husband think of something so . . . so . . . *practical* when it was obvious I was in demand somewhere not nearly as small-town as North Dakota?

Irritation scratched my breastbone. "Yes, but think of what the exposure could do for my book."

"Sure. Sure. It'll be great."

How could Jim sound so distracted when this was the biggest thing to happen since Wesley agreed to actually publish my book? It was time to change the subject before his lack of excitement ruined Wesley's news for me.

"And guess what?" I asked. Not waiting for a reply I went on. "I'm going to stay through the weekend and see the baby."

"Have you talked to Drew?"

What was with Jim? He should be exclaiming over the fact that I'd get to hold our grandson, not wondering if I'd talked with our son. "No, not yet. I just got off the phone with Wesley."

As I spoke, I could hear a *beep* on the line. Another call coming in. I pulled the phone away from my ear and glanced at the display: Drew.

My arms felt unusually weak. Was something wrong with Will? Did Jim know something I didn't? I hadn't even met my grandson, yet, but I was unaccountably attached.

"Drew's calling," I said into the phone.

"Then I'll let him tell you the news."

If there was something more wrong with Will I wanted to know *now*. "What news?"

"Drew's taken a job at the bank. Here in Carlton. He'll be flying home to look for housing."

"Drew? Coming home? When?"

"Next Friday."

Jim

I placed the phone in its cradle and sat back. I needed a few minutes to gather my thoughts. In the background, soft music played over the store's speaker system, interrupted by a page for a price check on aisle two. This morning had barely begun and already my mind was spinning with all that had happened.

I tilted my head from side to side, trying to release the tension. Two hands of guilt pressed on my shoulders. I should have been more enthusiastic about Claire's big news. It was a huge deal that she'd been invited to be on a national TV program, but I'd just gotten off the phone with Bob Marsden, who'd told me of his decision to hire Drew. One of the open lending positions had been filled long ago, but the right candidate hadn't shown up for the second spot after Drew turned it down the first time around. Drew had been talking to Bob all week by phone while they hammered out the fine points of his employment.

I massaged the tight muscle at the base of my neck. Why hadn't Drew called to tell me he was reconsidering the position?

Because you might have tried to talk him into working at the store instead.

Would I have? Drew was thirty-two, old enough to make a decision without running it by me. And yet, I would have relished a debate over the pros and cons of moving back home. Although in my mind there wouldn't have been much to argue. I'd always dreamed of having my family nearby. Not to mention my new grandson.

I put my hands behind my head and gazed at the ceiling. Drew was going to be moving back to Carlton. I smiled to myself even as I felt a bit left out of the loop. Next thing I knew, I felt my eyebrows puzzle together. A cauldron of mixed emotions burbled inside me. Of course I wanted Drew in Carlton. He'd have a good career and a good future at the bank. And, maybe now I could get some help at restoring that old Dodge rusting away in my garage. But, if Drew was going to live in Carlton, I couldn't imagine anything better than if he'd join me in the grocery business. What was I working for if not for my children's future?

A soft chuckle escaped my lips. Drew had done the right thing making this decision on his own. No doubt I would have thrown in a suggestion— or three—about joining me in the store. And Drew knew that.

"Jim, call on line one. Jim, line one." The page from the loudspeaker system caught my attention and I quickly sat forward and picked up the phone.

"Dad." It was Drew.

I knew why he was calling. Once more I sat back in my chair. I'd let him take his time telling me the news, and I'd listen with more than just my ears. Unlike the half-baked enthusiasm I'd mustered when Claire called, I would let my son know how proud I was, and how happy I was that he, Trisha, and Will would be moving home.

"When's she coming on?" For the umpteenth time I looked at my watch, at the TV, and then at Drew leaning forward on the couch, his elbows resting on his knees.

"Dad. Relax. I think you're more nervous than Mom."

Maybe I was. Claire's segment on the *Today* show was supposed to air between eight and eight-thirty. They'd been promoting the friendship series all week and this was the wrap-up. They'd saved the best for last . . . at least that's what I was telling myself. Which only set me more on edge.

Reaching down, I scratched Pesto behind the ears. If he wasn't careful, and if Claire didn't come on soon, our poor dog would have bald spots on both sides of his head. I'd postponed going in to work this morning so I could watch the interview live. But now I was wishing it was already over. I wiped my palms against my slacks. If I was feeling this anxious, I could only imagine how Claire was feeling.

She'd called last night, bubbling over with excitement at holding our grandson for the first time. Trisha and the baby had stayed in New York while Drew flew to Carlton. The doctor hadn't given the okay for Will to make the trip so soon after his heart procedure, which gave Claire a double reason for being in the Big Apple. I hoped she—

"Dad. Here." Drew pointed to the television.

My heart did a flip as I concentrated on the TV host.

"After this commercial break, to conclude our series on friendship in the computer age, we'll be talking to sociologist and author, Claire Westin."

They flashed a picture of Claire's book cover, and then a fade-out, with a shot of Claire sitting on the studio couch looking calm. A commercial for some sort of bathroom tile cleaner filled the screen.

Oh great. More waiting.

Finally, the television host was back. "Welcome to the *Today* show, Claire."

There was my wife. Sitting and chatting on national television as if she did it every day. I leaned forward, scrutinizing my wife's image on the television screen. We'd been married for thirty-plus years. If she was nervous, I couldn't detect even a tremble in her hands, or her voice. And I was a basket case.

"Friendship is one of those topics that's hard to define," the interviewer said. "I found a quote that stated . . ." She read from her notes ". . . everyone wishes they had more and better friends." She pointed to herself. "I have lots of wonderful friends and I'm . . ."

Blah. Blah. Blah. In my opinion the show host was talking way too much. It was obvious Claire knew her stuff, why didn't they give her more time to talk? Okay, now Claire got a chance to say something. And here was the host, jumping in again.

It seemed Claire had been on the program mere seconds and the interviewer was winding up. She looked down at her notes, then at Claire. "I understand you have a new book on friendship set to release, well," she corrected herself, "a whole series of books in the works and an upcoming book tour."

"Yes, I do," Claire responded as a website address for *ClaireWestin.com* was displayed at the bottom of the screen. She reached out and shook the interviewer's hand as a commercial filled the screen.

In an instant the phone rang. Logic told me it couldn't possibly be Claire. She could have never gotten to her cell phone that quickly, but still I hoped. I had some questions for my author wife.

I reached for the phone. "Hello."

"Dad!" It was Kaylee. "Did you see Mom? Well, I know you did. Didn't she do great? I didn't know she had a series of books. Or a book tour. Did you?" She didn't give me time to answer before babbling on. "And when did she get a website?"

241

Kaylee had taken the words, and questions, straight from my mouth. I was wondering the same things. Just *who* was the woman I'd watched on TV? Right now she didn't seem at all like someone I knew.

SEVEN MONTHS LATER: HEAD OVER HEELS IN "LIFE" . . .

Drew

"Have a good day." I leaned over and gave Trisha a peck on the lips, then I tousled the fuzz on Will's head that Trisha insisted was hair. "You, too, Mister."

Trisha held the spoon holding Will's creamy breakfast cereal in midair. "Say 'bye-bye' to Daddy."

Nine-month-old Will gave me a sloppy smile as I left through the kitchen door. I sidled around Trisha's vehicle in the garage and tossed my brief-case onto the seat of my pickup. Living in North Dakota, a four-wheel drive pickup wasn't an indulgence, it was a necessity. Especially in January. At least that's what I told Trisha. The fact was, after riding New York's subway and taxi system to work for the past several years, I enjoyed the freedom of climbing into my new-to-me pickup and driving myself to work.

I waited while the garage door completely

raised, then I backed out of the driveway and pointed my truck toward the bank. Shifting into "drive" and pressing on the accelerator, I enjoyed the comforting sensation of being in control of my own way to work. Most days I headed straight to the one-way running north and south through Carlton, the most direct route to my job. At least two inches of snow had fallen during the night, coating the trees in a thick blanket of white. It would be a shame not to appreciate God's handiwork. I had time to take the side streets to work this morning.

Even though I'd been driving these familiar streets of Carlton for the past seven months, I still marveled at the laid-back pace of life I had forgotten existed here. Even if I meandered, like a little kid jumping into every snow bank he saw, I still could make it to work in less time than my daily New York commute.

I took a left turn, and as I rounded the corner, the back of the pickup spun into a quick semicircle across the snow-covered ice on the road. "Whoa!" I quickly corrected to accommodate for the conditions. In New York that spin might have resulted in a five-car pileup. In Carlton it only made me grin.

I eased up on the brake and then gently accelerated. It was hard to believe how much life had changed in the past seven months since we'd moved back to Carlton. Having Will had been the tip of the iceberg. His medical challenges had thrown us for a loop, making Trisha and me realize that the important things in life weren't *things*. It was the *people* in our lives who mattered. Once we'd figured that out, the rest went fast. While much of the country was suffering from a housing recession, the housing market in Carlton was holding its own. It seemed Trisha and I weren't the only folks looking for a more relaxed way of living. We weren't the only couple bidding on the house we'd flown back to look at . . . but we were the winning bidders. By the end of June the belongings of our cramped New York apartment were headed west, and Trisha, Will, and I weren't far behind. Will's doctor had given him the all-clear to travel, in addition to making some phone calls and finding a specialist for him in Carlton.

It hadn't taken us long to set up house. What had seemed like too much stuff in New York barely filled the nooks and crannies of our new home. What we liked best was that we had room for our extended family to come and visit. Trisha's parents were only a four hour drive away. A trip they'd made twice in the seven months we'd been living in Carlton. Kaylee was a regular drop-in. Trisha and my sister were on their way to becoming close friends. A friendship that would have been unlikely if we'd stayed a thousand miles away.

Sheesh, it was getting warm in my pickup. I turned the heat control down a notch and took off my gloves. Was it really the heater that made me boil, or the thought of my mom and dad?

I negotiated around another corner, letting up on the accelerator as I felt a slick of ice beneath my wheels. Sure, settling in had gone fine . . . but then there was this thing with my parents. Of course I didn't expect my dad to quit work and hang around with his grandson, but I had expected that we'd spend more time together. Dad kept mentioning that we should get busy and restore that old Dodge he'd bought. I was ready, but he always put it off. It was always, "*Someday* we're going to have to get at that old car." At this rate Will would be old enough to drive the thing by the time Dad got serious.

And then there was Mom. Oh, she'd said all the right things when I'd told her we were moving home. *Oh, I can't wait to see Will as much as I want. It'll be so much fun to have you guys living so close. I can't wait.* She'd been so enthusiastic I'd worried that maybe she'd be *over*-involved in our lives. *Ha.* The intervening months had proven her words false.

The eager grandmother, who had made promises to dote on us after our arrival, was now very, very busy. Too busy to spend much time with Will, or the three of us.

Everyone is busy, I reminded myself. I shouldn't

begrudge my mom her new career as a writer and speaker, in addition to her teaching. But the fact remained that we'd moved back to Carlton to be closer to family, and *Grandma* wasn't around much.

Oh, she tried to make an effort. We'd rung in the New Year at my parents' place last week, the invitation coming from Mom two days before the end of the year. Kaylee and Brad joined us at Mom and Dad's house for a later-than-usual dinner, then they were off to a party at a friend's. Trisha and I weren't sure how Will would react to all the people, and all the attention, so much past his bedtime. But he was a trooper. We laughed when Will's head started bobbing, and then simply dropped, as if he'd been knocked out by the clock. It wasn't quite so funny when Mom fell asleep with her head on her hand while I was telling a story about one of my coworkers at the bank. Oh, we chuckled, but the fact of the matter was that Mom had spent a good part of the night talking about her new book, the e-mail she was getting from her readers, and about the Friendship Factor seminars she was in the process of developing. It seemed the least she could do was to listen when I had something to say.

Carlton isn't Mayberry and grandmas don't sit around knitting and baking cookies anymore.

I knew that. It wasn't that I expected her to be a full-time babysitter; all I wanted was for her to get to know her grandson. Part of me knew I should be thanking my lucky stars that my mom wasn't the kind of woman who acted like being a grandma was a full-time, 24/7 career. I should probably be grateful my mother had a life of her own. But still—

You're a grown man.

Of course, I was.

You don't need your mom's attention to be happy.

No, I didn't. But, somehow, I'd hoped for more from my mom. For Will. For Trisha. And for me.

Good grief. Once again I reached to turn down the heat. This kind of thinking was getting me nowhere. I knew my mom, or my dad, didn't mean to blow us off . . . but that's what it felt like.

Maybe this idea of taking the side streets to work was giving me too much time to think. I glanced in the rearview mirror—no one was behind me—and made a quick turn to the right. I'd be on the one-way in a couple blocks, straight to work and on with my day.

I stopped behind a few others cars at the traffic light and tapped my fingers against the steering wheel. Only when I started humming along to the beat did I realize I was singing one of the silly songs from a CD Trisha played for Will. Good thing I was safely enclosed in steel and glass where no one could hear me.

The light turned green, and I slowly followed a

line of cars left onto the main thoroughfare. As I moved forward, I could hear the crunch of frozen snow beneath my tires. The quietness of my morning commute continued to amaze me. Barely any traffic or the continual honk of car horns. No people to shoulder through or panhandlers begging for spare change. There was something to be said for—

"Stop-stop-stop!" I yelled, even though I knew no one would hear. As if in slow motion, I watched on my left as a car slid through the red light and smacked into the side of my pickup. *Crash!*

The force of the impact tossed me to the right as far as my seatbelt allowed, then I bounced back to the left, smacking my head against the side window. *Ouch.*

In just a few seconds the collision was over, and I was left gripping the steering wheel of my smashed pickup.

Wonderful. The understatement of the New Year.

With some prodding from my shoulder I was able to muscle open my truck door. The accompanying screech let me know I probably wasn't going to be able to get it closed.

The other driver, who looked to be another guy like me—on his way to work—was walking toward me. "I hit a patch of ice," he explained. "Are you okay?"

I touched the side of my throbbing head. No blood. "Yeah, I'm fine. You?"

He looked himself up and down. "Not a scratch . . . unless you count . . . ," he pointed to our two dented vehicles, ". . . those. Hey, I'm sorry."

In a matter of minutes we'd exchanged phone numbers, and two police cars pulled up. One officer got out and started directing traffic around the crumpled vehicles and the other one took down information about the accident. A tow truck showed up, and before I knew it I was standing in the chilly office of a repair shop with no way to get to work.

I pulled out my cell phone and stared at the screen. No way would I call Trisha to come get me. I didn't want her and Will out on these icy streets. My mom was more than likely heading into a classroom right about now. That left a taxi or my dad.

Calling a cab might be the quickest way out of here, but now that I'd had a little time to get used to the idea that my pickup was smashed, I wanted Dad's input on what to do about the repairs. A quick call to work let them know I'd be unavoidably late.

With my index finger, I punched in the number of Westin Foods. I listened while the clerk who answered the phone paged, "Jim line two. Jim. Line two."

"Dad?"

"Reed? Drew?"

"It's Drew," I explained, not sure if I should be

irritated or laugh. My parents almost always got my brother's and my voices mixed up on the phone. They had a fifty-fifty chance of getting the first guess right, yet they were usually wrong. I rolled my eyes. Maybe this is what came along with parents getting older.

"What's up?" My dad sounded distracted, but so would I if I got a call at my office about the same time I'd walked in the door.

A puff of frustration filled my cheeks. I blew it out. Now that the adrenaline had worn off, I was starting to realize all the hassle my next words would put into action. "My pickup got smashed up."

Dad didn't hesitate. "What about you?"

"I'm fine. I didn't realize how icy the roads were, and, apparently, neither did the guy who smacked into me. I need a ride to work." I told him where I was . . . not too far from the store's south-side location. I'd worry about a ride home later.

"I'm on my way."

In spite of my grumbling about my parents not giving my little family the attention I expected now that we'd moved home, deep down I knew I could count on my dad . . . and my mom.

The store wasn't more than a mile from the auto body place. It wouldn't take Dad long to get here. Stuffing my hands in my coat pockets, I walked back outside to survey the damage.

My pickup was wrecked all right. The way it was sitting, it looked as if the frame might be bent. But then, what did I know? I was a banker, not a mechanic.

Tom Morgan, of Morgan's Auto Body, came out from the garage. "Looks like the frame might be bent."

Then again, maybe there was a future for me in auto body.

We both stood there and stared, our breath making small white clouds in the frosty air. I had a hunch Tom was sizing up the work it would take to fix the thing. Me? I was sizing up my insurance premiums and wondering how Trisha and I were going to manage with only one vehicle between the two of us.

I stomped my feet against the snowpack paving the parking area. My dress shoes slipped crazily against the icy surface. Automatically, I grabbed at the sleeve of Tom's jacket to keep from falling.

He chuckled as he helped steady me. Glancing down at the ground he said, "Still got those New York shoes, I see." One of the disadvantages of moving home was the fact that I couldn't escape with anonymity in Carlton. With three kids in our family, this wasn't the first fender bender Tom Morgan had repaired for the Westin clan.

I shuffled my feet, trying to find a secure place to stand. It wouldn't do much good to explain to Tom that it also snowed in New York. The thing was, there were so many people that the snow never lasted long on the sidewalks of the big city. All I could do was agree with him. "Yeah. These darn New York shoes."

The faint sound of a phone ringing came from the repair shop office. "Better get that," Tom said. He clapped me on the back before moving away and sent me into another scuffle to keep my feet beneath me. "Glad to have you back home."

An icy gust of wind scattered snow pebbles against my back. Okay. It was getting seriously cold standing out here, and the thin soles of my New York shoes weren't providing any insulation against the hard-packed snow. And come to think of it, the tops of my ears were turning into Popsicles. I cupped my hands over my ears for a second. As I turned to head back to Tom's office, I saw my dad's vehicle turn into the lot.

He pulled his car near the wreck and I jumped into his car. We could look at the damage out of the wind.

"Better get out and take a look," Dad said, opening his door, but leaving the car running.

What kind of wimp would I be to sit in the car while my dad surveyed the damage? Reluctantly, I slid out of the warm car.

I shuffled over to stand shoulder-to-shoulder with my dad. He pointed to the crumpled metal on the driver's side door. "You're lucky your leg didn't get broken."

Come to think of it, I *was* lucky. I'd been so caught up in the condition of my pickup, I'd forgotten to be thankful for what *didn't* happen. Other than the bump on my head, I was fine. *Thank You, Lord.*

"What about the other side?" Dad asked as he headed around the front of the pickup. "Did it get bent up?"

I did my best to keep close behind him. "Not really. Kind of."

As Dad rounded the passenger side headlight, Tom stepped out of the office and came our way. "Morning," he called to my dad. "Don't dare say 'good morning' on account of . . ." He nodded his head at the bent metal.

Dad lifted a hand in greeting. "I'd say it's a good morning. No one got hurt."

"True." Tom stepped into our little gathering paying respects to the damage.

After a few seconds, Dad clapped his gloved hands together. "Guess we'd all better get back to work."

"Call me with the estimate," I told Tom as we began to move away from our spots.

"Whoop! Whoa!" My New York shoes flew out from under me. My reflexes sent my arms flying, grabbing at whatever was near to steady me. Dad's jacket was closest. I managed to grab tight. My right leg swung around and clipped Tom at the knees. In an instant three grown men were lying on the ground. Somehow, my dad had ended up on the bottom. We were a lopsided sandwich with me in the middle.

"Yup, it's broken." Dr. Godfrey pointed to a spot on the X-ray where even two laymen like me and my dad could see the jagged line. "You did a pretty good job of it, Jim. We're going to have to put a pin in there to stabilize things."

A hot flush rose into my neck, and I felt my Adam's apple bob as I swallowed. "How long will it take to heal?"

"These kinds of fractures? Oh . . ." Dr. Godfrey tapped his finger against his chin. "I'd say we're looking at ten to twelve weeks."

"Twelve *weeks?*" My dad's jaw practically hit the floor.

"That's not a number written in stone," Dr. Godfrey said. "But when a person gets to be a certain age these sorts of things take a little longer. Now if it was your *son's* leg we were looking at . . ."

I didn't hear the rest. I stared at my dad's elevated leg. His low groans as the EMTs had lifted him into the ambulance still rang in my ears. I'd followed the ambulance to the emergency room in my dad's car. Somehow I'd managed to wreck my truck and mangle my dad's leg in the course of an hour.

Earlier I'd been so sure God had orchestrated

my move back to Carlton. Now I was wondering if I should have stayed in New York.

"Drew?" Dad's voice penetrated my far-off thoughts.

"Sure," I said. I had no idea what my dad wanted, but whatever it was, I'd take care of it for him.

"I'm going to need you to run over to the store and take care of a few things on my desk. There are a couple invoices that I was going to pay today and I need to get payroll ready for the end of the week."

"Whatever you need, Dad. Anything at all."

Somehow it seemed everything always came back to me, my dad, and the store.

Claire

"Are you ready?" Instead of tapping his foot, Jim tapped his crutch impatiently against the kitchen floor. "I need to get to the store, you know."

"And I need to find the car keys," I replied as evenly as I could between my clenched teeth. I rummaged in the bottom of my purse, then my coat pocket. "Here they are."

"Let's go then." Jim pegged his way out the door and down the one step into the garage.

Although it was easy to pretend everything was fine and dandy with Jim stretched out in the back seat and me behind the wheel in the front, an uneasy silence settled between us in the car as I drove to Westin Foods.

I could hardly blame Jim for being crabby. No one in his right mind would want to spend the winter months in North Dakota on crutches. He'd been hobbling around for thirty long, long days. With many more long days ahead.

His temporary handicap might not have been so bad if he'd broken his arm instead of his leg. A full leg cast made driving impossible, and left him at the mercy of me . . . or Drew . . . or Kaylee . . . or whoever he could round up.

I glanced in the rear view mirror and caught Grumpy's eye. "What time do you think you'll want a ride home?"

Jim shook his head. "I don't know. I'll give you a call." He wasn't going to make this easy. If he had to suffer it seemed we all did.

Oh, come on. All in all he's been a pretty patient patient. I bit at the inside of my lip and chided myself. Under the circumstances, Jim had been surprisingly uncomplaining. If I were the one hobbling around in a cast and on crutches . . . well, I didn't even want to contemplate what Jim might be thinking about me if he were the one doing the chauffeur detail.

He's the lucky one. Having a broken leg would be a relief. I brushed an imaginary hair off my face as if I could push away the guilty thought.

What was I thinking? I didn't want a broken leg.

256

Maybe not that, *but admit it, part of you would welcome an excuse to slow down. To have a reason to cut back on all you've been doing.*

Gripping tight to the wheel, I tried to do nothing but concentrate on the road in front of me. This feeling of being overwhelmed was coming more and more frequently. Ever since my appearance on the *Today* show, life had gone into fast-forward. I felt like a juggler who'd started out with an easy three balls. And then some invisible helper tossed in a fourth ball, and then a fifth, and suddenly I was scrambling to keep up. There were too many balls to count and no time to count them. And if I wasn't careful, the whole, crazy mess would drop down all around me.

Help me, Lord. I'd been praying those three words more and more these days. If God had given me all these opportunities, He was going to have to help me juggle them all.

Do the first thing first.

That would be to get Jim to the store. He could bide his time there while I stopped to check in on my dad. There would be time for a quick cup of coffee with Julie at the Book Nook . . . I couldn't remember the last time she and I had sat down together to chat. Then I wanted to swing by and say hi to Will . . . Trisha, too. It had been at least two weeks since I'd seen either of them. And then I was going to need to spend the rest of the day working on the format for the second Friendship

Factor seminar next month. This one would be in Minneapolis, a big step up from the first one I'd held in Carlton in January. Oh, and I needed to map out the rest of the books in the friendship series Wesley was proposing I write. I glanced at my watch as if the day was already getting away from me. This Saturday had barely begun and I felt tired. I'd been so looking forward to having a whole weekend free. No speaking engagements. No book signings. No papers to correct since the new semester was just underway. Now it seemed I was going to spend the day simply catching up on everything I didn't have time for on the other days.

I drove the car to the back entrance of the store and hit the unlock button on the armrest. The sooner Jim got on his way, the quicker I'd be on mine. "Can you give me a ballpark idea when you might be done? I've got a bunch of errands and—"

"I said I'd call. You're not the only person with a schedule." Jim yanked on the door handle, drawing a cold blast of air into the warm interior. The air wasn't the only thing icy between us. A wall of stubborn self-righteousness formed firm inside my chest. Jim might be busy, but I was busier. If this was how he wanted to start off the day . . . fine. A good dose of anger would help fuel me through all the hoops I had to jump through today.

Jim pulled his crutches across the seat as he maneuvered his way out of the car. Hopping on his good leg, he moved away from the open door. I waited for the door to slam so I could shift into drive and be on my way. When the sound I waited for didn't come, I ventured a look behind me.

Jim was tucking a crutch under each arm. The frigid February air whipped at the open ends of his unzipped jacket. It was on the tip of my tongue to say, "get inside where it's not so cold," but I was too angry to give him any sort of warm advice.

Hands on the wheel, I clenched my teeth together and stared straight ahead.

"Claire?" Jim's voice startled me. I'd expected the steely slam of metal, not this soft question. I turned to look at him over the seat. "I'm sorry," he said. "Thank you for driving me." He hopped back a step and closed the door, not a slam, just a firm push.

Instead of pulling away, I sat and watched as he slowly made his way across the parking area and up the several steps leading to the door. Twice his crutches seemed to slip on the ice, and I found myself gasping, praying he wouldn't fall again.

I'm sorry. His words echoed in my ears. I was sorry, too. Even though I hadn't said anything to give away how irritated I was with him, I was sick at heart over my begrudging attitude. If I was too busy to help my husband when he was recuperating from a broken leg, well, then, I was too busy.

Tears stung my eyes and I did my best to blink them away. Instead of viewing the rest of my day as a series of hoops I needed to jump through, I was going to do my best to enjoy the minutes I had to spend with my dad, with Julie, and with Will and Trisha. What was life all about, anyway? What mattered most? A seminar that I'd be giving to a bunch of strangers, or making a difference in the lives of the people most important to me?

"Dad. It's me . . . Claire." Since I'd dropped Jim at the store a light snow had started falling. I stepped into Dad's house, stomping my feet on the scatter rug in the entry. I'd told Dad a dozen times that ratty old rug was a fall waiting to happen. But I saw his point, where would a person wipe their shoes if it weren't there? I dried my shoes and noticed how dirty the rug was. If I threw it in the washer now, would Dad remember to take it out and put it in the dryer? Would he even think to put it back in front of the door? In the three years since Mom had died, my dad hadn't managed to pick up much in the housekeeping department. It seemed I was always reminding him what needed to be done . . . or doing it for him.

I bent to pick up the rug. *How much can one person do?*

"Hi, Honey." Dad came around the corner from the kitchen. His eyes dropped to the rug in my hand. "What did I forget now?"

As I lifted the rug I could hear small grains of sand and pebbles drop onto the small, tiled entry. "I think the entry needs to be swept, Dad. Get me the broom and then I'll throw this in the washer." I stepped outside onto the step and gave the rug a good shake. I wondered if any of the neighbors were watching. Would they see right through my dutiful-daughter exterior to the resentful thoughts peppering my actions? Seven months ago I'd been a guest on the *Today* show, now I'd been reduced to nothing but a scrub-woman for my dad.

Reduced? What has more lasting value? A TV program or your relationship with your father?

In spite of the cold, a flame of heat seared my cheeks. I knew the answer, but being on TV felt so much headier than this kind of daily drudgery.

Daily drudgery? When was the last time you stopped by your dad's house?

I didn't want to know the answer to that question. With a final shake of the rug, I turned and went back into the house. Dad was busy sweeping the dirty entry.

"Your mom always kept things so nice and clean," he said. "Of course I might do a better job if I could see better." He paused and leaned against the broom. "Did I mention the eye doctor said I need cataract surgery?"

"Yes, Dad, you did." Another wash of guilt assailed me. What my dad didn't mention was that I'd been with him at that appointment. When was it . . . a month ago? Two? He was waiting on me to make the follow-up appointment. I'd said I needed to check my calendar before we scheduled anything . . . and then I'd forgotten about it completely. *Throw another ball into the juggler's act.*

"Here, Dad, let me do that." I reached for the broom.

"No, no, I've got it." He held onto the broom with one hand and slowly knelt on one knee, holding the dust pan with his other hand.

I held my breath. Part of me recognized how simple it would be for me to take over. I'd have those dirt particles swept up and tossed outside in ten seconds. Another part of me knew it was important to let my dad take care of this simple task. He'd recently turned eighty, a milestone that left him shaking his head. *"Where did it go?"* he'd asked when we'd presented him with a cake with eighty candles to blow out. My sister, Kathy, and my brother, Gary, who had come back to Carlton for the small celebration, exchanged a puzzled look at the comment.

"It's right here," Kathy said, pointing to the cake as if my dad couldn't notice eighty burning candles in front of his face.

Let Kathy think what she wanted, I knew what my dad meant. He was wondering where all that time had gone. Eighty years passed by in a breath.

I watched my dad now, down on one knee, taking pride in the simple act of cleaning his entry.

Oh, to have life be so uncomplicated. I swallowed against the lump in my throat. I couldn't even imagine what it would be like to have cleaning my entry as my challenge for the day. My mind raced ahead at all I had left to do before I could call it a day.

"Uh-umpf." My dad grunted as he pushed himself back into an upright position and handed me the dust pan. I opened the front door and threw the dirt back out where it belonged. "We make a good team," he said, smiling.

Oh, if only I could learn to take such joy in a task so small. But there would be time for the small joys later. Right now I had a teaching/writing/speaking bandwagon to jump on. The busier the better. Right? Wasn't the goal to climb as high on the ladder of success as I could?

But what are you missing while you're busy climbing?

Maybe it was a good thing I didn't have time to consider the answer. "Let me throw this rug in the washer," I told my dad as I headed for the laundry off the kitchen. Right now I wasn't worried about what I might be missing while I was busy climbing, I was worried about what I'd miss if *I didn't* head up the ladder of opportunity. I well remembered Mom's basket of unfinished projects. That basket had kept me going on my book during all those times I wanted to procrastinate. Even now, with the book completed and selling well, I didn't want to get to be eighty someday, cleaning my entry, and wishing I had done more with the opportunities I'd had when I was younger.

No, I'd make sure that didn't happen. I threw the rug in the washer, then realized the thing might be off balance during the spin cycle. I hurried to Dad's bathroom and picked that rug off the floor. Back to the laundry room. A little detergent, a spin of the dial. There, ready to head out. I'd call Dad later and remind him to put the load in the dryer. In the meantime I wouldn't have to worry about him slipping and falling on the rugs. Okay, there was a small joy I could appreciate. One less thing to worry about.

"Do you have time for a cup of coffee?" Dad asked as I rounded the corner into the kitchen. He held up an almost-full pot he must have brewed right before I arrived.

I made a show of looking at my watch, but I knew the answer. "Actually, Dad, I told Julie I'd meet her at nine-thirty for coffee at the Book Nook. She's probably already there waiting for me."

I pretended not to notice the way his smile faded. "Maybe I can stop by later." An empty promise and I knew it. I wasn't sure which was wound more tightly around my neck, my winter scarf or the guilt I felt for not giving my dad more of my time.

You spend a lot more time with him than either

Kathy or Gary. Usually that mantra made me feel better. Today it didn't.

"Oh, I almost forgot," I said, pulling on my gloves, "can you come over for dinner after church tomorrow?" I hadn't planned on having company for dinner. Truth be told, Jim was lucky if I cooked a meal at all these days. He'd be thrilled.

My dad didn't need to check his schedule. "Sure," he said, his smile back in place.

I pecked him on the cheek. "How about if we pick you up for church, too?" At eighty, Dad still had his driver's license, even if I wasn't completely sure he was safe on the road, cataracts or not. I could only imagine how complicated my life would get if Dad had to rely on me for all his transportation needs. "See you tomorrow then."

I closed the door behind me and speed-walked to my car, making a mental grocery list in my head. When I went back to pick up Jim from the store, I'd have to pick up some groceries along with my husband. Spaghetti, salad, and garlic toast. Ice cream for dessert. Now all I had to do was to keep juggling the items in my head until after I met Julie for coffee.

"Sorry I'm late," I said, as I pulled off my gloves and unwrapped my scarf from around my neck.

"That's okay," Julie replied. "I haven't been here that long." She had her hands wrapped around a white, ceramic coffee mug. It was only half full, meaning she'd been here longer than she'd made it sound.

"Let me get you a refill while I grab a cup for myself." I slipped my coat over the back of a chair, picked up her mug, and hurried to the coffee counter.

A couple minutes later I was back. "Here you go." I handed her the mug and slid into the chair across from her. "Whew," I said, "it's only nine-thirty and I already feel like I put in a full day."

"It's almost ten," Julie said.

A quick glance at my watch told me she was right. "I'm sorry," I said again. "I had to drop Jim off at the store, then I ran by my dad's." I stopped to take a sip of the strong coffee the Book Nook was famous for. A shot of caffeine was what I needed. I took another sip, waiting for Julie to start filling me in on all that had happened since the last time we'd chatted.

Silence. Julie matched me sip for sip.

"So . . ." I said, tilting my head side to side, trying to stretch out the tension in my neck. "What have you been doing lately? Did you—" I was at a loss for words. For the life of me, I couldn't think of a thing to ask Julie about.

"You've been really busy," Julie finally filled in.

"Busy is an understatement. Ever since the *Today* show things have been nuts. My agent has been taking calls—"

266

Julie leaned forward. "You have an agent?"

I nodded. "I told you about that."

"No," Julie said, sitting back, "you didn't."

"I must have. I signed with him shortly after I was on the *Today* show."

Okay, I'd said "the *Today* show" twice in the span of ten seconds. If I wasn't careful, Julie would think I was trying to brag myself up. I picked up my mug and held it, letting the warmth from the cup help me unwind. If Julie didn't know I had an agent, she probably also had no idea of all the opportunities that had come my way in the past several months. Where should I start?

Without taking a sip, I set down my mug and leaned forward. "Did I tell you about the radio interview I did on the Sirius radio network? You know, that satellite radio that gets broadcast around the nation?"

"I know what Sirius radio is."

"It was a call-in show and they asked me back for another interview when my next book releases."

"That's good." Her brows puzzled together. "You have another book releasing? I thought there were two already."

"Well, yes. The two I have out now and then— uh—" My eyes darted away from Julie's puzzled look. Had I really not told her about all this? "I thought I told you. Wesley wants a whole series of Friendship books. The *Friendship for Twenty-*

somethings was the start of an age-related series. I'm working on *Friendship for Thirty-somethings* and then we'll do *Forty-somethings* and . . ." I let my words trail off. Maybe I hadn't told Julie about this because I imagined she'd react the exact way she was . . . her glance bouncing over my shoulder as if she really wasn't interested.

I tugged at my earring. Usually it was Julie who said-things-like-they-were. Well, I'd give it right back. "I'm sorry. I'm boring you."

"No, no." Her eyes darted back to me. "There was someone over there I thought I knew. No, really." She leaned toward me. "I want to hear what's been going on."

Okay, then. "Did I tell you about the Friendship Factor seminar I'm holding in Minneapolis next month?"

"I don't think you did, but I get your e-mail newsletter so I read about it there." Julie gazed at me over the top of her mug as she took a long sip of coffee.

"There are already over a hundred women registered and it's still a month away. We're hoping for five hun—"

"Excuse me." A woman stood near my elbow. "Are you Claire Westin?"

"Yes?" I gave Julie an embarrassed glance.

"I thought I recognized you from the photo on your website. I knew you live in Carlton so I've kind of been keeping an eye out for you." The unfamiliar woman stuck out her hand. "It's a pleasure to meet you. I've read your book. And loved it." She laughed as she shook my hand. Turning to Julie she said, "You are so lucky to have someone like her for a friend." She angled her body back my direction and lowered her voice. "I have a friendship story I thought you might be interested in hearing about. You might want to use it in one of your books."

"Uh . . . I . . . I really don't have—"

The woman didn't seem to hear my protests. She pulled a chair over from another table and sat down, leaning my way. "I was best friends with Theresa from first grade through high school, and then we both went off to different colleges . . ."

The woman proceeded to tell me a story filled with details only a close friend would care about. The fact that they'd purchased the exact same sweater, or had their hair cut in the same style, even though they lived in different towns, was riveting only to her.

I shot Julie an "I'm sorry" look. What could I do without being rude? Julie lifted an eyebrow and then stared off into the recesses of the bookstore.

"Thank you for sharing that," I said when the woman came up for air. I touched her on the arm. "If you'll excuse me, I think I'll get a warm-up of my coffee." I looked down at my mug. It was full minus a swallow or two. Busted.

Luckily, the woman didn't pay any attention to

what I'd said. "If you want to know more, I have all kinds of other things I can tell you."

"Another time, maybe." I gestured to Julie. "I'm here with my best friend. We're trying to catch up. I hope you understa—"

"Oh," the woman said. "Don't let me keep you." She pointed a finger at me. "You keep writing those books."

"I will. I will," I said, wondering if she could hear the fake enthusiasm in my words.

An amused twinkle danced in Julie's eyes. "So you're famous now. You're going to have to start wearing sunglasses and a hat in public."

I rolled my eyes and took a sip of coffee. "This is stone cold."

"See what fame will get you?" Julie replied.

Julie had a wry sense of humor, but instead of making me laugh, her words hung in the air like an omen. A prediction of sorts that made me squirm.

I grabbed the handle of my mug and stood. "Let me see if they can warm this up for me."

A minute later I slid back into my chair. "Where were we?" I asked.

"I think we were talking about your seminar in Minneapolis. The big time, huh?"

I smiled and lifted a shoulder. "Kind of. For me, anyway."

Julie wrapped her hands around her cup and slid it forward, resting her forearms on the table, ready to listen. "Tell me."

"We're not talking *Women of Faith* size. Not yet, anyway." A bubble of excitement expanded in my chest as I told Julie about my plans. My spring series of seminars would be the tiny rock on the surface of a lake. Wesley, my agent, and the PR person I'd hired were hoping the ripple-effect from my five-city tour would propel my books, and me, to the next tier of publicity. A book on the bestseller list would give me name recognition and authority. Not to mention the ability to ask for higher speaking fees, which would lead to bigger venues. What we were planning went far beyond the perimeter of North Dakota.

I drained the last of my coffee and sat back in my chair. "Maybe you could come along with me on one of my trips sometime." It would be fun to have more time to spend with my friend.

"That would be interesting," Julie replied.

I noticed her coffee cup was empty, too. "Would you like more?" I asked, reaching for her cup.

Before she could answer, another woman interrupted. "Claire? I thought that was you." I recognized the store manager, but her name escaped me. The name tag she wore on a lanyard around her neck was flipped backward. No help at all. She put a hand on my shoulder. "I don't mean to interrupt, but I was wondering . . . as long as you're in the store, can I ask you to sign some copies of your books? Ever since your second book released I've been meaning to call and ask you to have a book signing. But, frankly, they've been selling so well—and I know how busy you must be—I've let it slide. Do you have a little time?" She nodded to our empty coffee cups. "I'd be glad to get you refills."

Signing books was part of the territory. And it was something I could do while I sat and visited with Julie. We could make it fun. I'd sign, she could put the "Autographed Copy" stickers on them.

"I guess I have a few minutes," I said.

The legs of Julie's chair squeaked against the hardwood floor as she pushed back her chair. "I really need to run," she said, standing. "It's my mother-in-law's birthday and I've got a cake to bake."

Julie scooted behind the store manager and gave me a quick hug. "This was fun." Three words that didn't sound fun at all. "Call me," she said over her shoulder as she walked away.

"I hope I didn't—" The store manager looked at Julie's departing back and then back to me.

"Oh, no." I waved my hand through the air. "We were getting ready to leave soon, anyway."

"Well then, let me get you some books and a pen and you can get started."

As I waited for the store manager to return, I lifted my cup to my lips. Empty. Like the conversation I'd just had with Julie. Why had our conversation felt so strained? As if we didn't know how to be friends anymore?

It's hard to have a relationship with someone if you don't spend time with them.

I fingered the pendant on the necklace I wore. A gift from Julie. It wasn't that I didn't want to spend time with her. I was giving her the spare minutes I had.

Maybe that's the problem. You're giving her leftovers.

That wasn't true. If anyone was getting leftover time, it was me. I had no time for myself anymore. If it wasn't Jim tugging at my time, it was my dad. Or Wesley. Or one of my kids. And I didn't even want to think about my grandson. He changed by the day, and I was missing it. And then there was my website to keep up, and answering mail from my readers. Not to mention plotting out the next book in the series, and the workshop tour. And—

What about Me?

I closed my eyes and breathed deep. That's all I needed. A guilt trip from God. Oh, I prayed all right. Prayed for time enough to do it all.

What about your relationship with Me?

What relationship?

Exactly.

I was only one person. I couldn't do it all, all by myself. Someday. Someday when I had more time, I would get back to my devotion time. My Bible reading. Right now God had given me deadlines and expectations to fulfill. Who had time to sit around and meditate? I trusted Him to help me . . . if He could keep up with me.

"Here you go." The store manager appeared at my elbow behind a metal cart loaded with my books. "Sign as many as you have time for."

"Wow," I said, eyeing the stack, "you're sure you'll sell all these?"

"Oh, we will." She nodded to my empty cup. "Let me fill that for you."

I exchanged my cup for the pen she held out to me. In seconds she was back, my cup full. "I really appreciate this."

"No problem." I took a sip and then pulled a stack of books onto my table. I'd said "no problem," but it kind of was. It was going to take more than a few minutes to sign all these. Time I'd planned to spend with Will. The store manager said to sign what I had time for, but it seemed silly to only sign a handful. It would seem ungrateful to drink her free coffee and then slip out the door without accommodating her request.

I opened the first book to the title page. *Become the friend you long to have,* I wrote. *Blessings, Claire Westin.*

Two books. Three. Four. Too many to count. The fleshy part of my hand grew tender from sliding along the surface of the paper. I paused to take a swallow of lukewarm coffee, wishing Julie were still here to keep me company, or that I was spending this empty hour with Will. Other people in the bookstore eyed me curiously as they passed by my table. Did they recognize me? Or were they wondering why I was sitting at a table piled with books all by myself?

As I began signing another stack of books, Julie's words echoed in my ears. *So you're famous now.*

If I was so famous, everybody . . . somebody . . . should want to be with me. If I was so famous, then why did I feel so completely alone?

Jim

What I was doing was more than likely illegal, but I planned to plead ignorance if I got stopped by a cop. For the hundredth time I checked my rear view mirror . . . no sign of the law in sight. So far, so good. I waited while the stoplight turned green and then slowly pressed the accelerator with my left foot. My right leg was at a cockeyed angle, stretched out stiff as a board across part of the front seat of my car and the floor. *Ouch.* Good thing I didn't have much farther to go until I reached the back entrance of the store.

My flexibility wasn't what it used to be, but it was getting better the more I drove. Claire about had a fit when she saw my attempt to drive myself for the first time a few weeks ago. "You're going to get arrested," she warned. "Or kill someone."

I was being as careful as I could under the circumstances, and sick and tired of depending on others to lug me around.

Moving my left foot over to the brake, I tapped at it. *Whoa.* So, okay, I had a way to go in the soft-touch department, but at least I was here and could put the car in park. I puffed up my cheeks and blew out a huge sigh of relief. I'd done it. Gotten myself from home, to my doctor's appointment, and over to the store . . . all in one piece. As proud as I was of myself for being so resourceful—and so bendable—I knew I didn't dare drive much further than the few, slow, backstreet miles I'd attempted. I was proud, but not stupid.

I hobbled my way up the back stairs to the back entrance of the store and made my way to my office, greeting employees as I passed by. It was a good thing I owned the place. I wasn't so sure another boss would give me as much leeway as I'd needed with my injury. I settled myself behind my desk. The morning was almost gone, and I had a stack of mail and phone messages to return to prove it.

Two hours later, I came up for air. I'd missed lunch but made a dent in all I had to do. Other than one more small pile of mail to sort through, I'd gotten a lot accomplished. I'd gone to the website and downloaded the manufacturer's price changes, I'd selected the ad items I wanted featured in our flyer next week, and I'd met with one of the DSD guys. The technical term was Direct

Store Delivery, but I called them the "chip guys." It seemed they always wanted more shelf space. It was getting ridiculous. After all, how many ways were there to manufacture a chip? More than I thought necessary, that was for sure.

I shifted uncomfortably in my chair. Sitting still had never been high on my priority list, and sitting this long in a leg cast only made matters worse. I'd be lucky if my left hip didn't need replacing after bearing the extra burden of weight these past weeks.

A broken leg. Hip replacement. You sound like you're getting old.

As much as I hated to admit it, some days it *felt* as if I was getting old. I grabbed a pen and tapped it against the calendar lying on my desk. The doctor had predicted I'd be in this stupid leg cast for twelve weeks. I'd been hoping to be an exception to the rule, but after my follow-up appointment today—ten weeks and counting—it looked as though I'd be in for the duration. Which meant I needed to find someone to drive me to the store in Emerson tomorrow. It had been three weeks since my last trip there, and if I didn't show my face soon, they might think I'd abandoned them. Compounding the problem was that I couldn't drive myself that distance, and with Claire in Minneapolis at her seminar, I needed to find someone to watch Pesto. The mutt was sleeping like Rip van Winkle these days, but who knew how long I'd be out of town. At his age all he seemed to do was eat, sleep, and, of course, pee.

Kind of what it all boils down to, doesn't it?

I smiled to myself. My leg injury had made me realize just how much effort went into the everyday things of living. It wasn't hard to understand why so many older people simply wanted to stay home. Going outside in the winter meant taking the risk of a fall like mine. And I knew all too well how the results of that had impacted my life. If I'd been much older, or in not quite as good shape, a fall like mine could sideline a person for the duration. This cumbersome cast had taught me a lesson . . . I would no longer take my mobility for granted. When this thing came off, I was going to get back in shape. And I'd never ask anyone to drive me anywhere again.

Sheesh. I hit the tip of my pen hard against the paper. As much as I hated to impose on Drew again, I was going to have to ask him to run me up to Emerson tomorrow. There were a host of little blazes up there that needed me to put them out. One of my part-time checkers had sold cigarettes to a minor. I had a policy that, if the store got the five-hundred dollar fine for selling illegally, the checker who did the deed would have to pay up. We'd been hit with a fine and I needed to have a sit-down with the kid who did it. " 'Splain" things, as Ricky Ricardo would have said. Of course, this kid would have no idea who Ricky was. You had to be my age to understand the reference. Back in my day, we could refer to someone like that, and everyone knew who we were talking about. Kids these days had so many cable channels to watch, there were no commonalities anymore. Sometimes I felt kind of sorry for kids nowadays.

I gave my head a shake. How on earth did I get off on that rabbit trail of thought? The store in Emerson needed my attention, not the kids-culture of today.

Back to business. I pulled a notepad toward me and started making a list.

One: Talk to Samantha about paying fine.

Two: Grocery scanner on aisle two on the fritz. Check it out. Set up service call.

And, three, my biggest headache of all.

Chester. Retirement. *NO!!*

I underlined the word . . . as if I'd forget. Ever since the woman I'd tried to make my Emerson store manager resigned shortly after I'd purchased the store, I hadn't been able to find a capable replacement. Poor Chester somehow inherited the title. Butcher and Boss. Well, the "boss" part when I wasn't around, anyway. Which, unfortunately, was most of the time. I was hoping to have a talk with him . . . stall him with a pay increase until I could find and train someone to take his place. Chester was no dummy. He'd know I was talking about having him hang around for another year . . . or more.

I reached for the phone. I hated to call Drew at work. I also hated to take him away from Trisha and Will on a Saturday. I paused with my hand in midair. Maybe Kaylee could drive me. Nah. I pushed that idea aside. We'd had an unpredictable month of March. Snow and wind every other day, it seemed. Sexist or not, I didn't want my daughter out on the road in a blizzard. I'd ask her to watch Pesto, and Drew to drive me.

It was either that, or face the possibility of having the Emerson store close its doors. I hated to admit it, but some days having the store doors close, *all* my stores' doors close, sounded awfully appealing.

Are you losing your drive?

I sighed. Some days it felt like I was. But . . . in the meantime I still had three stores to manage. Once again, I reached for the phone. Ever since I'd joined the bank board I'd had the bank number programmed into my speed dial. Never did I think I'd be using it to call my son to haul me around the state.

"I'm sorry," the receptionist said when I asked to speak to Drew. "He's with a customer right now. May I take a message?"

Of course he was busy. He had work to do just like I did. The spot where I'd had a pin put in my leg throbbed. "Have him call his—" It was embarrassing to be so dependent. I cleared my throat. "Have him call Jim Westin. He has the number." The receptionist might not know the difference, but I did.

I sorted through the stack of mail on my desk and stopped with a brochure in my hand. *Palm Desert, California.* Here was the convention Bob Marsden had been talking about. The annual banker's convention he'd suggested I attend this year. They were offering several workshops of special interest to board members. *"I think you'd find it interesting,"* Bob had said. *"Libby and I are going, and it would be fun to have you and Claire along."*

And it would be fun to be out of this cast, and get away from the store and the never-ending cycle of work it entailed. When was the conference? I scanned the information. September. Six months from now. Perfect.

I picked up my pen and filled in the blanks. There were some spouse functions Claire could attend. If I told her about it now, she could block off some vacation days from the college. It was about time we did something fun together. This was the time in our lives when we were supposed to be kicking back and starting to appreciate some of the fruit of our work. Starting when this cast got off my leg, I planned to do just that.

"I appreciate this, Drew." It wouldn't hurt to say it twice. "I really appre—"

"Dad, really, it's okay." Drew caught my eye in the rearview mirror and then focused on the snowy road to Emerson.

I'd tried sitting in the front passenger seat, but even putting the seat back as far as it would go, my board-like right leg stuck out at an odd angle, with no room to maneuver. Too uncomfortable to ride seventy miles. I sighed quietly and leaned my head back against the seat. I wasn't used to taking a backseat to my son.

I watched Drew in the seat in front of me. Snow was falling at a pretty good clip, but the weather didn't seem to faze him.

"Do you have your lights on?" I asked. Even though it was broad daylight, the blowing snow made it difficult to see in places or, more importantly, *be seen.*

"Yes, Dad." His tone told me I could save myself some breath if I quit backseat driving.

"Good." I felt bad enough taking him away from home for the day. He worked hard and deserved a Saturday day off. And then the weather had to go stormy on us. I turned my head and stared out the side window through the falling snow.

I wasn't *that* old—I remembered what life with a ten-month-old was like. Trisha was a stay-at-home mom and probably looked forward to

Saturdays when Drew could share some of the parenting duties. And I knew Drew needed time with his family. I'd thought of asking them along, but what fun would an hour car ride and sitting around in a grocery store be for Trisha, or Will. Not to mention Drew.

I opened my mouth to say "thanks" again, but then thought better of it. In the past two and a half months it was obvious that Drew felt completely responsible for my broken leg. He had practically done backflips to make things easier for me. Driving me to Emerson was only the tip of the iceberg. Since my accident, he stopped by the store almost every day, sometimes on his way to work, other times during his lunch hour, or, often as not, on his way home from work. "Anything I can do, Dad?" he'd ask. Or, "How're things going?" Sometimes I'd look out the window in my elevated office that overlooked the store, and I'd see him stop to straighten a display or help one of the stock boys refill an empty place on a shelf. Yesterday I saw him lead Mrs. Jenner down an aisle and around a corner to the powdered sugar, pointing out the brand that was on sale.

Claire and I had done a pretty good job of raising a responsible kid. Well, I could hardly call him a "kid" anymore. Drew was thirty-three, the same age I was when my dad had his first heart attack. The age when I realized running the store would be my lifelong career. Unlike Drew, another line of work had never been an option.

Did you miss something?

Who knew? I'd worked in the store with my dad from the time I was old enough—make that *tall* enough—to stock shelves. I went off to college, majored in business, and then came right back to Carlton to show my dad ways we could expand and improve the store. Funny, we'd never talked about me taking over, it was simply assumed. And I'd never questioned it. Maybe that's why it hounded me so much that Drew had taken a different path. I'd never had that chance.

But I was ready to let Drew go his own way.

Are you?

I thought about it for a minute. Did I really *want* Drew working in the store with me?

Yes, I did. But more importantly, I wanted *him* to do the work he was called to do. And if that work was banking, then so be it.

I cleared my throat. "Do you like your job?"

"What?" Drew gave his head a small shake as if he'd been lost in thoughts of his own.

"I asked if you like working at the bank."

Drew's eyes darted to mine in the mirror. He was probably checking to see if this was going to turn into another *"why don't you come work with me"* conversation. I met his gaze full-on. No hidden agenda. Not anymore. Drew was entitled to live his own life the way he wanted.

"Do you?" I repeated.

Drew's eyes crinkled a bit at the corners. "Yeah, I do."

A gust of wind pushed at the side of the car but I wasn't worried; we were in capable hands. "What do you like about it?"

He took his time answering. "Well . . . I like working with numbers. But . . ." His voice trailed off. It was a comfortable silence. I could wait. ". . . I think the thing I like best is that I'm helping people. You know . . ." He paused. ". . . with their dreams and stuff."

Once again it was quiet. The wind and snow wrapped us in a cocoon that made a conversation like this easier than if we'd been sitting eye-to-eye at home.

After a while I said, "Dreams, huh?"

Once again Drew caught my eye, one eyebrow raised as if laughing at himself. He lifted one shoulder. "You know, helping someone get a loan for their first home. Investing in a business. That kind of stuff. I like driving around Carlton and knowing that I'm making a difference."

There was a full feeling in my chest. I knew what he meant. I sometimes felt like that at the store. Oh sure, there were days, lots of them, when all the store seemed like was work, but the sense that I was contributing to the community came often enough to make the work worth it. "That's important work you're doing," I said.

Drew avoided my eyes in the mirror, but I could see his shoulders straighten a bit. "Thanks."

Drew ran ahead and held the door of the Emerson store open for me to peg my way through. While my Carlton stores had automatic door openers, the Emerson store was too small to justify the cost of installing them . . . at least for now. I was still waiting to see what kind of fallout we were going to get in Carlton now that the SuperTarget had opened its doors. The threat of that megastore had hung over my head for more than a year. There had been countless construction delays, which only served to prolong the agony of the unknown.

I wasn't running scared from the megastore. There had always been competition in my business, and now we'd added another player to the mix. The advantage of being in the grocery business was that people had to eat.

But they didn't have to shop in my store.

"Drew could you—" I stopped mid-sentence. Drew had already grabbed the snow shovel tucked near the door and was heading outside to clear the sidewalk in front of the store. The kid had read my mind.

I stopped in the entry area and looked over the notices taped haphazardly to the floor-to-ceiling windows separating the store from the elements outside. There were a couple auction sale posters of farm land and equipment for sale. A puppies-to-give-away sign. A notice for the annual Lions Club breakfast in two weeks. And several outdated posters for a host of community events. I tugged down a church bake sale sign . . . those goodies were goners by now. Another for the school spring concert that had been held the previous week. I read over a sign advertising a house for hunters to rent. Hunting season was months away, but even so, there might be someone passing through who would take the number and make a call. I left it up.

Tucking the outdated posters in my hand, I hobbled into the store. *Whoops!* The rubber tip of my crutch dipped into a puddle caused by tracked-in snow and sent me hopping on my good leg to keep my balance.

"I got you, Dad." Drew was right behind me, steadying me with a hand to my back. "I'll get a mop," he said, one step ahead of my thoughts.

Carefully, I made my way over to the checkout aisle. There was a garbage can under the counter, and I handed the posters to the checkout clerk. "Toss these for me?"

"Sure," she said, sounding bored.

I read her name tag: Samantha. Uh . . . might as well get the dirty work out of the way first. "Samantha," I said, standing as straight as I could, considering I was on crutches. "I'm not sure if you remember me. We met several months ago. I'm Jim Westin."

She barely lifted her hand in greeting. "Oh, hi."

I had no clue if she knew I was her boss. "I'd like to talk to you for a minute."

"Well, uh . . ." Her eyes darted to the empty aisle. "I'm sorta supposed to be working."

What did she think I was? Some kind of dirty old man who got his jollies out of harassing high school checkout clerks?

Thinning, graying hair. A broken leg. Hunched over on crutches. To her, you probably do look like an old man. You are *an old man compared to her.*

I'd made a seventy-mile trip to set Samantha straight, and I was the one being put in my place. If the facts weren't so true, I would have been tempted to laugh.

"Samantha," I repeated. "I'm here to talk to you about selling cigarettes to a minor."

She rolled her eyes, as if what I'd said was the lamest thing she'd ever heard. One tough cookie. She set her jaw and stared me down.

What she didn't know was that I could be one tough cookie, too. I had years and years of experience on this kid. Over the years I'd had to let go more employees than the years she'd lived.

"Let's go back to the office." I motioned toward the back of the store with my head.

Her eyes widened for a second, then filled with tears. "I'm sorry. I didn't mean to do anything wrong." Her voice notched up an octave. "Are you going to arrest me?"

I couldn't help it; I chuckled. Maybe I was getting jaded after all my years in business, but it struck me as funny that one of my employees thought I was a plainclothes policeman . . . not her boss.

Not so funny. It means you haven't been around enough for her to recognize you.

The truth sobered me. I'd always prided myself on the family-like atmosphere among the staff members of my stores. Buying the Emerson store had been a step outside of the comfortable cocoon I had with the staff at my two stores in Carlton. Obviously, if an employee didn't recognize me, I wasn't doing all I should here.

I made my way back to the office, Samantha dragging her feet behind me. Maybe I'd overstepped my limits by thinking I could efficiently operate a store this distance from home. I wanted to be an asset to the community, but it was difficult to stay plugged in from seventy miles away.

If it's too hard, maybe you should think about selling this store.

Selling? I'd barely owned it two years. Of course there were still kinks to work out. That was to be expected.

But you're only one person. You can't possibly be in three stores at the same time.

No, but there was a time when I thought nothing of driving between my north and south stores a couple times a day. It didn't seem like it should be that difficult to get to Emerson at least once a week.

You had more energy earlier in your career. More drive.

I stood aside and let Samantha walk into my office ahead of me. Just thinking about the logistics of my life was making me tired. It would be good to get the situation with Samantha out of the way. Then I could concentrate on the *real* problem, talking Chester into staying on as store manager. And *then* I could try and figure out why these problems drained me of energy, instead of charging me up like they used to. There was a time when I viewed the problems at work as challenges, mountains to be conquered.

Pushing aside the thought, I motioned for Samantha to take a seat, and I settled myself into the chair behind the desk, propping my crutches against a nearby file cabinet. Buying myself a little time to gather my thoughts, I rearranged the pens that were standing in a ceramic mug on the desktop. I lifted my eyes, ready to tackle the problem at hand. Samantha sniffled and swiped at her nose with the back of her hand.

"Samantha," I said, then stopped. *She's a little girl.*

The girl sitting across from me had dumped her tough-girl persona and looked to be no older than twelve, thirteen at the outside. Logically, I knew she was older, but not by much. Why did I think someone her age was qualified to check out groceries, much less enforce the laws concerning the selling of tobacco products? If some tough-looking dude walked into the store and asked her for cigarettes, I couldn't blame her for being intimidated.

You're getting soft in your old age.

I cleared my throat and started again. "Samantha—" *Go easy. She's old enough to be your grandkid.*

That fact was . . . she was. I couldn't help it that my kids had wisely waited until they were a bit older to start their families. If Drew had followed my footsteps, I could easily have a grandchild about old enough to be a checkout clerk in my store.

Someone had fortuitously put a box of tissues on the desktop, and I nudged it toward Samantha. She reached for one and blew her nose.

"When you're my age," I explained, as if I had the corner on wisdom, "you'll understand that these laws are put in place to *protect* people."

"How old are you?" Samantha asked, missing my point completely.

"Fifty-seven," I answered, without thinking. Or was I fifty-eight? And did the fact that I didn't know off the top of my head prove the point I'd been trying to deny during this whole conversation?

"You're almost as old as my grand . . . pa." She

hiccupped as I cringed inside. "But not quite," she added. "He's fifty-nine."

I was getting old. Too old to relish reprimanding a teenager who'd made a mistake.

A teenager who could qualify as your grandchild.

"I'm sorry I did something wrong." Samantha looked at me, her eyes wide and teary. "I'm kinda new, and I can't tell how old people are. Everyone seems older than me, you know?" She looked down at her lap. "I'm still in high school."

She looked like she was in junior high.

"I'm really sor—ry." She burst into tears. "I can't afford five—" She gasped for air. "Five hun—dred dollars."

Sheesh. Of course she couldn't. Wasn't that the whole point of having my policy in place? If a clerk knew they were going to have to pay the fine out of their own pocket, it would serve as a deterrent to selling to minors in the first place.

Samantha reached for another tissue and dabbed at the mascara running down her cheeks. Her voice squeaked between her tears. "Do you want me to quit?"

If help were easier to find, the easy answer would be "yes." But in a town the size of Emerson, we were constantly advertising for help. And I could hardly fire her when she was so distraught . . . and sorry. She sat across from me, her head hanging low.

A heavy, weary sigh pushed its way out of my chest. "Tell you what, Samantha." She risked a glance from beneath her lowered eyes. "You're young." *No kidding.* "And I know you didn't mean to break the law."

She shook her head. "I didn't."

I must be nuts for what I was about to do.

I leaned forward, my forearms on the desk, my hands out in a sort of offering. "How about if we split the cost of the fine? I'll pay two-fifty, and we'll take your half out of your paycheck over the next few months."

"Okay." Now she sounded about five.

At least I did the payroll for all the stores at the Carlton office. No one would have to know about this but Samantha and me. If the other employees got wind of this, I might have a free-for-all on my hands.

I had to show I had a little backbone left. "But if it ever happens again—"

Her eyes locked onto mine. "It won't. Promise."

I nodded as if I was still in charge. "Well then. Uh . . ." I scratched my finger against my cheek. "Uh, you've got a little mascara . . . here." She wiped at her skin. "There. You got it."

She put her hands on the arms of her chair. "Should I go back to work now?"

"I think that would be a good idea." And her leaving would give me time to think about what just happened. If I wasn't careful, by the end of the day I might be offering to fill in behind the butcher counter for Chester.

"What about that son of yours?" Chester was now sitting where Samantha had been in the hot seat.

"What about him?" I asked.

Chester cast a glance down at his stained butcher's apron. "Don't you think he'd make a better manager than me?"

I wasn't going to go there with Chester . . . or myself. "Drew doesn't work for me. He—"

"Could of fooled me."

"What?"

"Sure seems like he knows what he's doing." Chester tilted his head in the direction of the store's main floor. "He's out there rearranging the end caps. And before that, he was mopping up the snow that got tracked in this morning."

"He was helping me out."

"That's the kind of stuff a manager notices when the rest of the staff don't."

Poor grammar aside, Chester was right. But I was going to let my son follow his own path. In the meantime, I had three stores to run. By myself. My broken-legged, overworked, mushy-hearted self.

A wry laugh pushed at the back of my throat. With that kind of resumé, I'd better keep my nose to the grindstone. No one else would have me.

Drew

"Are you new here?"

I looked up. The warbling voice was directed at me. I was at the Emerson store, squatting down and restocking cans of diced tomatoes onto a lower shelf, trying to make good use of my time while I waited for my dad to finish his business. Pushing myself to my feet, I found I was staring down at what could only be described as the shortest older lady I'd ever seen. She was four-foot-something, for sure. "Excuse me?"

"I asked if you were new here?" She didn't wait for my answer. "Used to be I knew everyone in town. And nowadays they come and go so fast it would make your head spin. You don't look like the kind of young man whose head would spin very easy. You seem like a nice, solid kind of person. I can usually tell that right off." She squinted up at me through thick glasses. "Who are you?"

"I'm Drew," I said, holding out my hand. Turnabout seemed fair play. "Who are you?"

She grabbed my right hand with her left. "Bum hand," she said.

For a fleeting second, I thought she meant her first name was Bum. I was doing the best I could not to laugh when I noticed her raising her right arm a bit.

"Stroke," she said. "Back about ten years. Can't do much about it, so I do what I can. Who did you say you were?"

"I'm Drew," I said again. She had a death lock on my hand. For a little thing, she had quite a grip. "And you are . . . ?"

"Liddie. Short for Lydia. Well, it's really not much shorter, but that's what folks call me." She let go of my hand, but kept herself planted right in front of me. She nodded her head toward the space where I'd been squatting. "You work here, I take it."

"Well, not really. I—"

"Then what are you doing monkeying around with the tomato cans?"

Before I had time to explain myself, she fired another question at me.

"Do you know where the cornmeal is? Ever since that new guy took over, he changed every-thing around and it's a scavenger hunt coming to this place." She waved her good hand through the air. "It's not like it was when Ted and Millie ran it."

"Is that so?" At this point I wasn't so sure I wanted to tell Liddie my dad was the new guy. A diversion might be best. "I think the cornmeal might be over by the flour. Aisle . . ." Quickly I scanned the overhead aisle markers ". . . three." I started walking down the aisle. As long as Liddie was talking, I figured she'd follow.

As we walked slowly through the aisle, Liddie kept up a running conversation. "Ted used to deliver on Wednesdays. But, you know, since that new guy took over, they can hardly keep the place manned as it is. They cut out the delivery, which is why I had to come out in this blizzard. An old person like me should stay home on days like this. I could fall and break something."

"Uh-huh," I said, chuckling to myself. I was getting an ear full.

"When Ted had the store, I never had to worry about firing up the Buick just so I could eat. He'd bring me whatever I wanted. I'd call it in, and he would drop it off. His wife, Millie, she was good about making sure the fruit was good. I told 'em I wouldn't pay for any of those tasteless cardboard bananas. Now the tomatoes!" Liddie was so wound up, she managed to lift her bum right hand in the air. "They couldn't help it with the tomatoes. I understood about that. Not their fault. That's all a person can get this time of year. Unless you buy them canned. I suppose that's why you were thumbing through those cans yourself. Trying to—"

If I was going to get a word in, I was going to have to interrupt. "Here's the cornmeal." I leaned over and picked a round container off the shelf for her.

For a second she was actually speechless. "Did I say *corn*meal? I meant *oat*meal. Don't tell my kids; they think I'm losing it the way it is. Next thing I know they'll be trying to take my driver's license away. Then what would I do? Did I tell you that the new guy doesn't deliver anymore?"

"Uh . . . yes, you did."

She laid her left hand on my arm and lifted her chin seemingly as high as it would go. Finally she managed to look into my eyes. "If you work here, you should tell them they should start delivering again."

I wasn't about to disagree. "I'll do that."

"Good. Now where did you say the oatmeal is?"

"The oatmeal is in the cereal aisle." At least it always had been in the Carlton stores. "Do you want me to show you?" I had nothing else to do.

"That would be very kind of you." Liddie shuffled along as I led the way.

I wasn't sure if Liddie needed the direction or if she just wanted someone to talk to. Either way, she kept up a running monologue. "Back when Ted owned the store, I used to see him every time I came in here. Millie, too. Now this new guy, I've never once set eyes on him. What kind of deal is that, I ask you?"

Yeah? I found myself wondering . . . what kind of deal *was* that? The owner of the store should be around to hear what the customers wanted.

Your dad can't be in three places at the same time. He's already spread as thin as rice noodles.

"There are a lot of widows in town," she went

on. "We all need to eat, but we can't get around like we used to. If they'd start up that delivery service again, they could keep one person busy full time by taking our orders over the phone and then delivering them. At least on Wednesdays. I know, because we talk about it all the time. Like it *used* to be, anyway."

Liddie's babbling had given me an idea. But there was no time to mull it over now because we'd finally made it to the oatmeal.

"Here we are." I waved my hand in front of the Quaker Oats containers lining the shelf. "What kind are you looking for? Quick cooking? Old fashioned?"

"Pfhhff! I knew you'd try and sell me the expensive stuff. Store brand is all I need. It's only going in oatmeal cookies. Who'd know the difference?"

How Liddie managed to make oatmeal cookies one-handed I wasn't about to ask . . . mostly because I knew she'd tell me, and that could take the rest of the day.

"Is there anything else you need?" I wanted to be polite—she was a customer, after all.

"Canned tomatoes," she said.

"Why didn't you—" We'd been right there, back when she'd latched onto me. I had a feeling it wouldn't pay to remind her. Biting my lips together, I said, "This way."

"Seems like we just came this way," she said.

I wasn't about to correct her. "Did you need a

cart or anything?" Maybe I could make a getaway.

"A cart? Well . . ." She paused. "I had a cart. I think it must be back by the tomatoes. My purse is probably there, too. At least I hope it's there. With this bum hand of mine, grocery shopping is next to impossible. That's what made it so nice back when Ted had the store. Did I tell you . . . ? He delivered. On Wednesdays."

If I didn't know better, I'd swear I was getting punked.

"Are you coming?" Liddie waved me along with her good hand.

Then again, following Liddie around the store was only a small price to pay for the guilt I felt over putting my dad on crutches for two-and-a-half months.

I'd never thought of my dad as *old*. It always seemed he had energy to burn. I respected the years he'd put into building his business. Work seemed to fuel him, not wear him down like it did a lot of people. Until lately. Until I'd gone and knocked his feet right out from under him. Now, it was easy to see what an effort it was for him to manage three stores. There was enough work for three people, three *healthy* people . . . and Dad was doing it all alone. Since I'd gone and broken his leg, I was doing all I could to help until he got his cast off. It was the least I could do.

"There she be." Sounding like a pirate sighting

land, Liddie laid claim to her cart. I placed the cardboard container of oatmeal into the cart while Liddie pulled a list from her purse. "Now, maybe you can help me find bran flakes."

I suppressed the urge to roll my eyes and pointed Liddie back the direction we'd just come. The cereal aisle. She trotted on ahead and I followed behind.

These past couple months had given me a glimpse into my dad's world. His work challenged and excited him as much as it demanded of him. He felt a responsibility for his customers . . . and his staff. And after talking to Liddie, I could see what a service a grocery store was to a community. People had to eat, and my dad made it possible for them to do that.

Forty minutes later, I had Liddie's groceries bagged and carried out to her Buick. With my back to the blustery wind, I opened the driver's door and helped Liddie inside. No wonder her kids worried about her driving. The weather and her age had nothing to do with it. She was so short she could barely see over the steering wheel. I had an urge to run back inside the store and grab a phone book for her to sit on. Or drive her home myself.

Liddie reached out her left hand and grabbed mine. "Thank you, now. You tell that new guy I like his new service. Having someone to help me shop was very nice. But I'd still like it if he delivered." She let go of my hand and gestured to the air. "For days like this."

"Don't worry," I said. "I'll tell him."

"Here, let me get that." I held the outer door of the store open so Dad could work his way out, then hurried ahead of him and got to the car. A small, pillow-drift had formed on the driver's side, and I did my best to kick it away with my foot.

Dad handed me his crutches, and I held them as he maneuvered himself into the backseat.

"Be careful," I cautioned. "Don't slip—it's icy here." I felt an odd protectiveness, much like I did when I was with Will. The irony that it was *me* acting like a hovering parent over my dad didn't escape me. "Here. Let me . . ." I angled the set of crutches along the backseat floorboard as my dad attempted to buckle his seat belt.

"They don't make this easy," he said.

Somehow, he managed to buckle himself in. I doubted the car manufacturer had engineered the seat belt to guard someone sitting nearly sideways in the seat, but with snow continuing to fall and blow, I was thankful Dad had managed to buckle up.

I slid into the driver's seat, started the engine, and headed out of the parking lot onto the highway. "Home," I announced.

"Actually," Dad said, "I'm going to have to spend the rest of the afternoon at the store. Swing by my house when we get back to Carlton. I'll get my car and I can drive myself from there."

I'd left Trisha with my pickup truck for the day, knowing my dad would have a hard time situating himself with his cast in the narrow cab.

"I don't mind dropping you off at the store and picking you up. But, don't you think you should get some rest?" Here I was, acting like a parent again.

Dad was quiet.

"You okay?"

"Just tired."

In the rearview mirror, I could see him close his eyes and lay his head back against the seat. My urge was to talk, to fill the silence with words to mask my concern. Instead, I decided the best path was to let Dad rest. But that didn't do a thing to silence the incriminating voices inside my head. A father-lode of guilt hung heavy on my shoulders.

Your dad wouldn't be so tired if it weren't for you.

Your dad has worked his whole life to make life better for you.

On and on my thoughts raced, as I drove down the snowy highway. After awhile, I hardly noticed the self-criticism because what caught my attention was the absence of one thought I'd had for years.

Your dad hasn't mentioned you joining him in the business since you've moved back to Carlton.

He hadn't. I'd spent so much time automatically rebuffing his offers over the years, that when they stopped coming I hadn't noticed. Until now.

Maybe he doesn't want you working with him any more.

The thought left me feeling strangely empty.

I reached to turn the radio on, then thought better of it. It wasn't often Dad admitted to being tired. I would let him rest. Which left me with only my thick thoughts to keep me company.

Dad's voice from the backseat startled me. "How much farther?"

The normal landmarks along the road had nearly vanished in the blizzardlike wind. "Twenty minutes?"

There was rustling from the backseat as Dad adjusted his position. "Do you have the heat on?" he asked.

Of course I did. We were driving into an icy wind. "Yeah," I answered. "Are you cold? I can turn it up."

"Thanks."

I glanced at Dad in the mirror. "Did you get things worked out with your store-manager-slash-butcher?" I tried to make light of the unusual job description. It was kind of funny when you thought about it.

A heavy sigh came from the backseat. "Yeah, he agreed to stay on for now. I think he feels sorry for me in this . . ." There was a knocking sound. Two sharp thumps on Dad's cast ". . . thing," he finished.

My laugh hid my real emotions. "You'd better milk it for all it's worth. You won't have it on much longer."

"Thank the Lord for that."

I knew Dad meant it.

A gust of wind hit the car broadside as I plowed through some finger-drifts on the highway. "I'll be glad when we get to Carlton. It's kind of getting ugly out here."

"I hope it doesn't get much worse. Your mom's coming in on the last flight tonight."

Mom had been gone since Thursday at her Friendship Factor seminar in the Twin Cities. The sessions started Friday night and ended sometime this afternoon. "Do you need me to pick her up?"

"No. I offered," Dad said. "But she insisted on driving herself to the airport. She said she wasn't going to take a chance on my one-legged driving. Something about not being an accomplice to a crime. Ha."

For a while we were both quiet. The sound of the howling wind was our background music. We'd be back in Carlton soon—if I was going to bring up the idea that had been simmering in the back of my brain ever since I'd had my conversation with Liddie, now would be a good time to do it.

"Dad?" I caught his gaze in the mirror to make sure he'd heard me, then I focused on the snowy road ahead. "Have you ever thought about adding a delivery service to the Emerson store?"

I could hear Dad shifting around, trying to make himself more comfortable in the backseat. "Oh . . . the thought's crossed my mind, but this is such a labor-intense business the way it is. And it's hard enough to keep the stores staffed. Why?"

"When I was in the store today, I talked to this lady. Liddie." I smiled, thinking about my extremely short new friend. "She's old and has one arm crippled from a stroke and she was telling me about when Ted owned the store . . ."

I spent the next minutes telling my dad about my convoluted conversation with Liddie. "And she kept saying how much better she liked the store when she knew she could get her groceries delivered."

"The idea is great in theory, Drew, but I don't have the manpower to make it happen."

"It's not just that, Dad." I paused for a second while I tapped on the brakes. There was a highway snow plow ahead of us, kicking up drifts with its huge blade. I dropped back to avoid the snow fog. We weren't in that much of a hurry to chance passing blind. And besides, we were almost home, and I had another idea to run by my dad before we got there.

I kept both hands on the wheel as I explained what I'd been brainstorming. "I was wondering what it would be like to offer a delivery service in Carlton."

"In Carlton? I don't thi—"

"Hear me out, Dad. It's not only the widowed ladies who want their groceries delivered. I'm thinking of people like Trisha. It's hard work to shop with an eleven-month-old. If she could call in an order and have it brought right to the house, I think she'd jump right on the idea. And think about all the families with two working parents. If we could offer to do the shopping for them—"

For a second my words stopped. *We?* Had Dad noticed?

Quickly I reframed the sentence. "*You* could offer to do the shopping and the delivery. You could have a call-in service and set up an online ordering system through the Internet." More ideas were coming as I talked. "You'd have to set up a website, but think of it, Dad, you were worried about competing with the SuperTarget and this is one way you could. They're too big to offer such a personalized service. Our stores—"

I was at it again. "*Your* stores are the perfect size to put a system like that into action. Talk about specializing in customer service."

We were at the city limits now, and I felt stored-up tension release from my shoulders. I didn't know if I was tense from driving in a near blizzard, or from being so keyed-up about my ideas for the stores.

I drove through the outskirts of town, past a couple car dealerships and the very SuperTarget I'd been talking about. The more I thought about my ideas, the better they seemed. I was anxious to get my dad's opinion. "What do you think?"

As I waited for his answer, I turned off the main road running the length of Carlton and headed into the residential section where Dad and Mom lived. Dad was the kind of guy who thought things out before he spoke. It might take him a day or two to think them through. I understood a system like the one I'd been describing didn't happen overnight. But if my ideas could help Dad's stores compete with the big guns, I'd be a happy camper.

And so would he.

I was about to pull in the driveway to drop Dad off when I noticed the large snowdrift across the cement. Driving through it would only make the driveway that much harder to shovel. A task Mom had been attempting to keep up with since Dad's fall. It didn't help that Dad's car was parked outside on one side of the driveway. It served as nothing but a snow catcher. The old Dodge Dad bought to restore—was it two years ago?—took up one half of the double garage. It had been sitting in there so long, untouched, it had become a permanent fixture. One of those topics our family didn't even talk about any more. Although I had a hunch Mom would have a few choice words to say about it if she arrived home and couldn't get in the garage.

I pulled in at the base of the driveway and put the car in park. "Let me grab a shovel," I said to Dad. "I'll dig a path for you into the house." I knew I'd end up clearing the whole half of the driveway before I was done. Dad couldn't do it, and Mom would have a conniption if it got left for her to deal with at midnight.

"Here's the garage key." Dad handed me a ring of keys over the backseat.

Jumping out of the car I high-stepped through the snow bank, let myself into the garage, and found the shovel. Dad watched from the car as I tackled the snow. When I had made some headway on getting the far end of the driveway cleared, Dad got out of the car, and observed on one foot and two crutches. It was cold and windy, but I understood his need to stand outside with me. If Dad could be doing the shoveling, he would. Freezing in the wind was his sacrifice for just watching.

"Done!" I tossed the last shovelful of snow onto the snowbank I'd created at the edge of the driveway. I had worked up a sweat, but I knew my dad had to be chilled to the bone. "Let's get inside."

Dad pegged his way into the garage. I followed,

and returned the snow shovel to its corner. Hands on my hips, I stood and huffed and puffed, trying to catch my breath.

"Thanks, Drew."

"No problem."

Dad tilted his head toward the driveway. "Not just for shoveling, but for taking me up to Emerson today. I really needed to spend some time there."

I shrugged off his thanks. "So, you still plan on going to the store? I should check and make sure your car starts. It's been sitting outside since last night." Earlier in the winter Dad made sure to plug his car in overnight, but this time of year the temps didn't make the boost seem so urgent. But this cold snap hadn't been expected. I dug in my pocket for the keys he'd handed me earlier.

My dad held out his hand for them.

"That's okay," I said. "I'll do it."

"No," he said, taking the keys and searching for the house key. "I think I'm going to stay home. My leg is—" He stopped. "You'd better get on home. I'll bet Trisha could use a break about now. Give Will a high five from his grandpa. And tell Trisha 'thanks' for letting you go for the day. I appreciate it."

"Well, okay." I waited while my dad made his way up the three stairs to the landing and put his key in the lock. "Glad I could help."

"Drew," he said, turning, balancing on the

crutches. "About those ideas of yours . . . for the store. They were good. Really good."

He paused so long I thought he'd said all he was going to. I was turning to go when he added, "I never thought I'd say this, but the thing is, I just don't have the drive to implement them."

Another long pause. He looked down at his crutches. His broken leg. I willed him not to say what I knew was coming. *Don't say it. If you don't say it, it won't be true.*

Dad sighed, then looked up at me. "I'm sorry, Drew. I must be getting old."

Claire

"Where are they?" I dipped my hand into the bottom of my purse and rummaged around for my car keys. Standing outside in the cold, in the wind, in the parking lot of the dark Carlton airport was a quick ticket off the adrenaline high I'd been on since winding up the Friendship Factor seminar in Minneapolis. *Here!* I wrapped my fingers around the key fob. In two quick punches I'd unlocked the car doors and the trunk. I tossed my purse on the car seat and then turned to my heavy suitcase. I'd had no other option than to drag my suitcase through the several inches of snow that had fallen while I'd been gone. Balancing the suitcase half in and half out of the trunk, I did my best to brush off the snow that had accumulated on the bottom while I'd pulled it from the terminal. No wonder it looked so battle scarred. I was thankful there wasn't a full-length mirror close by because I sure didn't need a glimpse at what I looked like after three days of full-tilt conferencing. I only hoped I didn't look as tired as I felt.

I slammed the trunk and then reached into the backseat for the combination long-handled brush and snow scraper. Maybe I should have taken Jim up on his offer to come pick me up from the airport. The car was covered with a layer of snow that would have to be brushed off if I hoped to be able to see to drive home. I started with the driver's side windows, then the rear window. I made my way around the back of the car. *Whoosh!* Great. A gust of wind blew the snow right into my face. With the sleeve of my wool coat, I wiped the cold, wet mist from my face. So much for the glamorous life I imagined a seminar speaker lived. This was the behind-the-scenes glimpse that the people in the seats never got to see.

Finally, I climbed behind the wheel and started the car. I should have thought to start it before I began scraping, then it would at least have been lukewarm. But, all things considered, I was thankful it started after sitting in the cold for three days. Scrunching my neck down into my scarf for warmth, I backed out of my parking space. As soon as I paid for parking, I'd be on my way home and that much closer to sleeping in my own bed.

Minutes later, I mouthed "Thank you, Lord" into the air as I spied my shoveled driveway. I didn't know how Jim had managed to clear the snow, but I was grateful he had. I'd done enough traipsing through snow for one night.

Lugging my heavy suitcase into the kitchen, I let it drop to the floor with a thump. I glanced at the clock hanging on the wall. My plane had arrived at eleven-fifteen, but by the time I'd picked up my luggage, scraped off the car, and then driven home it was already the start of the next day. Now that I was this close to my bed, a yawn pushed its way from my throat. Man, I was tired.

"Hey there, Pesto." Our aging terrier waddled into the kitchen from the family room to investigate. Putting one knee to the floor and pulling off my gloves, I ruffled my hands into his wiry fur. I'd been gone so much the past couple months I was relieved to know the dog recognized me. Hopefully, my husband would, too.

A small finger of guilt rubbed at my breastbone. Lately, between Jim and me, it seemed one of us was always on our way somewhere. Always in the opposite direction. For years our schedule had been predictable. Each morning Jim would head to the store, and I'd hit the road to the college campus. We'd meet at home for dinner, unless I had a night class to teach. We'd lived that same routine for years. It was comfortable, maybe too comfortable, and—if I was honest with myself—I

was more than a little ready to shake things up. We might be sailing into the nether regions of middle-age, but I wasn't quite ready to tie up at the dock and grow barnacles.

The fact that my first book had seemingly hit it big had been a welcome surprise . . . the extra income was nice—not that we *needed* it—but who wouldn't welcome a little extra cushion heading into the retirement years? My second book was doing well, too. What had really rocked the boat in all this were the invitations I was getting to speak all over the country. Since my appearance on the *Today* show not quite a year ago, I could be on the road every week if I wanted to. I was already doing some creative time management, scheduling my speaking engagements around my teaching schedule when possible, or using accumulated vacation time and professional days in order to be gone. In spite of Jim's wrinkled nose at the idea, I'd requested a leave of absence from the sociology department, starting at the end of spring semester in May. Who knew what lay ahead?

A sense of anticipation bubbled inside me, although I couldn't put a finger on the reason, other than I was beginning a new phase of my life with my writing and speaking. I put my face close to Pesto and nuzzled him. "Who knows what's next? Hmm? Who knows?"

Pesto looked up at me and wagged his tail.

I gave his head a pat. "At least someone in this house is excited for me."

Pesto went to his water dish and lapped at it a few times, then trotted back into the family room where a cozy chair waited.

Unbuttoning my coat, I hung it in the closet near the door. One look at my suitcase and I knew I wasn't going to attempt to drag it upstairs to the bedroom tonight. It was too heavy. I was too tired. And Jim would be sound asleep. Tomorrow—make that *later today*—would be soon enough to unpack.

I switched off the light Jim had left on over the kitchen sink, then headed into the family room to turn off the small, decorative table lamp burning there.

As I made a beeline into the family room, I sensed a dark presence on the corner of the couch. Before I could make sense of what I'd seen, I jumped and let out an "Oh!"

"Huh? What?" Jim jerked awake, his head snapping up.

"You scared me," I said.

Jim stretched his arms and yawned. "Didn't mean to. I guess I fell asleep."

"What are you doing down here so late?" Jim was an early to bed, early to rise kind of guy. And not the kind of husband who felt the need to wait up if I'd be coming home late. I noticed his leg propped on the coffee table. With the heel of his hand, Jim rubbed the spot where his cast and skin met up under the cloth of his baggy slacks. "Is your leg bothering you?"

He shrugged. "A little." Nothing more.

There was something he wasn't saying, and if it had to do with me being in Minneapolis the past three days, I didn't want to get into that tonight. But it would be rude to say a quick "good night" and head upstairs. After all, we hadn't seen each other for three days.

I perched myself on the opposite end of the couch, sitting on the oversized arm. I didn't plan to spend any more time than I had to outside of my bed. "Anything special go on while I was gone?" There, that was a general enough question to be polite. If anything extraordinary had happened, Jim would have called my cell, or Kaylee would have filled me in when I called her as I was waiting for my flight.

"Not really," Jim answered. "Drew ran me up to Emerson this morning."

Other than the Grand Opening I'd helped Jim host when the store changed ownership two years ago, I hadn't had reason to drive seventy miles to get groceries I could get in Carlton. "Everything okay up there?"

Jim waved his hand in the air. "I could use someone to manage the store. Chester's getting bullheaded about pulling double duty."

"Got any prospects?"

"Unfortunately, no."

Staffing problems at the stores were a constant source of frustration. A problem we were not going to solve at one o'clock in the morning. Once again a yawn pushed its way from my throat as an uneasy silence fell between us. I'd only been gone three days, but suddenly it felt like we'd been apart for weeks.

Ask me how my time in Minneapolis went. I wanted to share with Jim how it felt to stand in front of five hundred women and share my friend-ship theories and stories, but I didn't want to have to *beg* him to listen about my past three days. *He should know I have things to talk about, too.* Why didn't he ask? Didn't he care? Didn't he wonder what my first big conference was like? How nervous I'd been before my introduction? I wanted to tell him how the women laughed and cried as I'd shared my stories. The mistake I'd made in underestimating how many books to have shipped in. I'd sold out far too quickly. For three days I'd given everything I had in me to make that conference a success. I wanted to share the details with Jim, but all he cared about was staffing his store in Emerson.

"Well then," I said, pushing myself from the arm of the couch, standing behind the wall I'd just built between us, "I'm going to get to bed."

I'd only taken two steps—

"Claire?"

I stopped. *Now what?* If Jim was going to start talking about his personnel problems at the stores, now wasn't the time. Even though my name was on the deed to the stores, I'd never taken much of a role in running them. The stores were Jim's "baby," and teaching and homemaking were mine. Now, with my writing and speaking thrown in, I had more than my hands full. This was one problem Jim was going to have to solve on his own. But first, I'd bite my tongue and see what he wanted. Maybe it had actually occurred to him that I might have something to say, too. I turned his way and raised my eyebrows. *What?*

"How would you feel if I sold the stores?"

I took two steps back his way and sat down on the couch. "Sell the stores?" I was practically whispering. "What happened?"

For a second Jim closed his eyes and touched his head back against the couch. "I don't have it in me anymore."

"You don't have it in you?" I was nothing but an empty echo.

Jim blinked slowly and shook his head. "I was talking with Drew on the way back from Emerson today and—"

"He didn't tell you to sell, did he?" I couldn't imagine Drew doing such a thing. He knew how important the stores were to his dad. But where else had this half-baked notion come from?

Again Jim shook his head. "No, Drew didn't tell

me to sell. In fact, he told me just the opposite."

I sat back, then forward. "He wants you to buy *more* stores?"

"Not exactly." Jim pulled at the left side of his neck as if the muscles there were screaming along with my racing thoughts.

"Well then . . . what?"

"Drew had some ideas to improve the stores. Make them more . . . I suppose you'd say 'customer friendly.'" Jim made quote marks in the air.

"And that made you want to sell out?" What would my husband *do* if he didn't have his stores to run? Here I'd been brainstorming about my career taking off and he was thinking about cashing it in altogether. Suddenly I was no longer sleepy. Something *had* happened while I'd been gone. I needed to figure out what it was. "What does making the stores customer friendly have to do with selling them?"

Jim was pushing at his broken leg with the heel of his hand again. Massaging the ache along with his thoughts. "When Drew told me his ideas, I knew he had something. I've been wondering how to stay competitive now that the SuperTarget has opened. Drew wants me to add online grocery ordering. On the computer," he added, in case I didn't understand. "And a delivery service."

I thought of all the working women I knew. Getting to the grocery store was a ball they were constantly juggling. "That's a great idea."

Jim gave me a half-smile along with a raised eyebrow. "I know." His expression told me he was proud of our son.

I turned my hand and wiggled my fingers, urging Jim to keep talking. "And . . . ? If it's such a great idea, what's the problem?"

Jim stared off somewhere over my shoulder, his eyes not meeting mine. "If I'm going to stay competitive in this business I'm going to have to get bigger, which *would* mean buying more stores, or . . ." He let that key word linger in the air ". . . or I'm going to have to get really creative on customer service. Kill 'em with kindness, or something like that." He paused as his glance met my eyes. "Isn't there something about that in the Bible?"

"There is, actually. It talks about pouring heaping coals of kindness on our enemy's heads. I use the reference in one of my seminar sessions on friendship." I lifted an eyebrow. "Not sure how it applies to grocery shoppers."

Jim's jaw tensed and flexed, a sure sign he was worrying about something. "I'm not so sure. Staying in business feels like a battle these days. One I'm not sure I want to keep fighting." He looked down at his broken leg.

Now I got it. Where all this was coming from. I reached out my hand and wrapped mine around his. "Jim, you've had a rough winter. You're tired."

"You can say that again."

"Once you get your cast off and get that leg back in shape, things will look different." At least I hoped they would.

"I don't know, Claire." Jim squeezed my hand and let go. "When Drew ran his ideas past me, all I could think was how much more *work* it would make for me. Instead of feeling excited about doing something new, all I felt was exhausted. I've never run away from a challenge." His eyes locked onto mine. "And that scares me." Quickly, he glanced away, as if he was afraid of what he might see in my eyes.

There was something in Jim's voice, in his eyes, I hadn't heard or seen before. Over the years I'd seen him worried about the business, heard him complain about the long hours. He often got fed up with employees who didn't show up on time . . . or didn't show up at all. He'd grumble and then tackle whatever it was that made up the problem. Never once had I heard him say he simply wanted to quit. I didn't know why, but his revelation made me feel scared, too.

Moving over on the couch, I turned and leaned into Jim. His arms came around me, and I laid my head against his chest. How long had it been since we'd been together like this? We'd been so busy chasing our separate careers, somewhere along the line we'd missed connecting with each other.

I murmured into the cozy night. "We should do this more."

"Um-hmm." Jim's chest vibrated with his assent. "We can do this all the time if I sell the stores."

The contented smile on my face froze. *All the time? Sell the stores?* What about *me?* What about all the plans *I* had?

"Want a refill?" I did my best to keep my tone neutral as I held the half-full coffee pot near Jim's cup.

He covered the top with his hand. "No thanks, I've got to get to the store."

I frowned. "It's Sunday. Aren't you going to church with me?"

He tossed back the last swallow in his cup, pushed his chair away from the table, and reached for his crutches. "I'll try to meet you there. But being I was out all day yesterday . . ." He let his words trail off. We'd been through this before. I knew the lay of the land. Owning a business that was open 24/7 meant you needed to tend to it, Sunday, or not.

In spite of our late night we were both up early, doing a delicate dance around each other. Our conversation last night brought no resolution. Only questions neither of us had the answer to. Was Jim really ready to retire? What would he do? What about me? My career? Even *if* Jim would sell out—and that was a big *if*—would we have enough money to take us through into our old age? And then it came right back around to . . . what would we *do?*

Eventually we'd both fallen asleep on the couch. At some point during the night, we roused and made our way upstairs, only to tumble back to sleep.

For no reason I could put my finger on, I felt crabby this morning. Tired and out of sorts. The questions of last night cartwheeled around in my head. I was unreasonably irritated with Jim. Why did he have to go and throw the *R* word around just when the doors of my career were opening wide? On the other hand, Jim had worked hard at that store his whole life. I could see why the idea of being *done* with the stores was appealing.

I ran water over my cereal bowl and then crammed it into the dishwasher, adding the coffee mug Jim handed me as he walked by. This circle of endless thoughts and questions was getting me nowhere. If nothing else, attending church this morning would be a diversion.

A diversion? You could pray about all this.

A warm flush filled my cheeks. *Pray.* A concept I had too little time for these days. How in the world was I supposed to find time to pray when I didn't even have time to see my grandson? Or spend time with Julie? Or any of my kids?

Or your husband?

Yeah, him, too.

Then you're too busy.

Dishwasher soap granules spilled out of the box and overflowed the compartment I was trying to fill. *Slow down,* I cautioned myself. Everything in my life seemed like it was on fast-forward these days. Maybe I *was* too busy. But I enjoyed what I was doing. It was exciting to be invited to speak all over the country. The events were fun and organized by interesting people. It was enticing to stand in front of a group of people and share my thoughts. To have their full attention directed at me.

Enticing. Interesting word.

Well, I admitted to my internal antagonist, it *was* enticing.

Like the Siren's song?

Oh, good grief. I wasn't going to get sucked into some mythical vortex and lose sight of everything that was important.

Are you so sure?

I slammed the dishwasher door closed with my hip. If I was going to shower and get to church on time I needed to get a move on.

"Praise God from whom all blessings flow . . ." The memorized words fell from my lips. I'd stopped watching for Jim after the opening prayer. In my frame of mind, it might be best to worship alone. The acerbic thoughts going through my head hadn't settled down a bit.

After the doxology concluded I settled into the

pew, ready to continue my internal argument right through the sermon. As the pastor paged through the Bible in his hand, I crossed my arms over my chest. What right did Jim have to *declare* he was done with it all . . . without even consulting me?

"Good morning," Pastor Rudy said, looking out at the congregation.

"Good morning," I mumbled with the rest of the folks in the pew, wondering what was good about it.

Hey there, I reminded myself, *you're in church.* Okay, I would make an honest effort to listen. After spending the past three days being the one in front of a group and in charge of informing my listeners, it might be a nice change to sit back and let someone else do the teaching. I uncrossed my arms and clasped my hands in my lap. That small attitude adjustment and already I felt calmer.

"I'm reading today from Second Corinthians, chapter four, verses sixteen, seventeen, and eighteen." Pastor Rudy held a finger in the air. *Listen up.* "This is why we never give up."

My ears perked up at the words he read. Jim should be here to hear this.

"Though our bodies are dying, our spirits are being renewed every day. For our present troubles are small and won't last very long. Yet they produce for us a glory that vastly outweighs them and will last forever!"

Pastor Rudy went on to explain the verses.

About the meaning of work and the troubles that came along with our daily lives.

"About that first verse I read," he went on. "It talks about *renewing* our spirits. This is something God does for us, and that we need to be mindful to do for ourselves. Remember, even Jesus took time away from his ministry to refresh and renew. When the everydayness of life gets to be too much, instead of letting it get you down, don't forget it's okay—even necessary—to take some time to recharge."

Time. *Time,* I repeated to myself. That's what Jim needed. Time away. He didn't need to sell out completely. What he needed was time to recharge. And I'd be sure to tell him my solution as soon as I could. We'd plan a trip. A getaway. We'd both get a new outlook on our lives. I knew Jim might protest at first. A trip was a luxury we'd seldom taken. A couple times we'd taken the kids along to the National Grocer's Convention, tacked on a couple extra days for swimming and sightseeing and called it a vacation. But this time we'd plan a real excursion. Just the two of us. How could he argue with the pastor . . . or the Bible?

But *when* could we go? I thought about my planner. How scribbled up it appeared every time I opened it. I was teaching and speaking through the month of May. There were a couple women's conferences I'd be speaking at over the summer, but my schedule wasn't packed.

Sometime this summer, then, I'd tell Jim. *We'll go on a trip this summer.* It would be something for both of us to look forward to.

"Claire," Jim said in a placating tone, the kind one would use with a child who should know better than make the suggestion they just did. "I can't take a trip in the summer. That's when everybody in the stores takes *their* vacations. We're always short-staffed. And the stores are busier."

He was standing by the kitchen counter. I'd barely given him a chance to get inside the house when I'd sprung my brainstorm on him. Just as quickly he'd poked a hole in my good-idea balloon.

I leaned against the counter and crossed my arms over my chest, playing the stubborn child. He wasn't going to get off the hook that easy. If I had any say in the matter, Jim was not going to sell the stores. All I needed was to have Jim sitting at home all day, watching me come and go from my speaking engagements, or *worse,* having him *watch* me trying to write my next book. Jim was fifty-seven. He had at *least* a good five years to keep working. And I'd be fifty-four next month, much too young to sit around and twiddle my thumbs into eternity.

I'd try a different tactic. I uncrossed my arms and walked close to Jim. Reaching out, I put a hand on his arm. "I think you could use a break.

And so could I. It would be good for the two of us to get away. Together."

A small smile crinkled the corners of Jim's eyes. Ah . . . it was working. With his upper arm he held one of his crutches steady, reached inside his jacket, and pulled out what looked to be a folded-lengthwise brochure. "Here's where we can go," he said, unfolding the glossy booklet. "Palm Desert, California. Bob Marsden and his wife are going. It's a banker's event and he invited us to go along."

I leafed through the shiny pages. In addition to the seminar schedule, there were images of a bright green golf course . . . something we didn't see much of in March in North Dakota. A woman getting a facial at the spa. *Gala banquet* caught my eye. Even if it was a meeting, a fancy hotel in Palm Desert was somewhere Jim and I could go together and, hopefully, mix in some fun. "I'm already packing," I said. "When is it?"

Jim held up a hand. "Don't worry," he said. "I've got it covered. I've already signed us up."

"When is it? I'll need to—" I stopped. The dates of the conference were printed in bold letters on the front of the brochure. Four days in September. Dates I knew were already booked for a fall speaking engagement. "Jim." I looked up at him. "I can't go then. There's a women's conference in Ohio. I've signed a contract. I . . ." What more was there to say?

Jim took the brochure from my hand. In the silence I could hear him swallow. "I came home because I wasn't feeling that great. I'm going to take a couple aspirin and lay down." He halfheartedly lifted the pamphlet. "We can talk about this later," he said, his voice hard and flat.

I nodded. I already knew there was nothing to talk about, but what would be the point of pointing out the obvious. Jim would be going one way, and I would be going another. The story of our lives these days. The sting of tears stabbed at my eyes. I wanted my new career and I wanted to be with my husband. I wanted to speak in Ohio and I wanted to be in Palm Desert. An impossible wish. Life was getting too complicated.

Now you know how Jim feels.

Maybe I did.

A DIFFERENT SORT OF FALL ...

Jim

After a month of not-so-subtle jabs back and forth—

Claire: "You should have *asked* me before you signed up for this . . . this . . . *thing.*"

Me: "Who in the world has her life booked half a year in advance?"

Claire: "Just for your information, my life is booked a *year* ahead of time, which you'd know if you'd stop thinking about the store and actually *listen* when I talk to you."

—we reached a cease-fire of sorts.

It was easier to talk about other things, namely our grandson. But, unfortunately, most of the *other things* were what had caused the argument in the first place. Claire was either busy working on the manuscript for her next book or driving off to a speaking engagement. After I got my cast off my leg, I hobbled around on a gimpy-muscled leg and did my best to resume my former two-legged pace, running between my three stores.

Somehow, Claire and I raced on parallel tracks through the summer months, pointedly ignoring the fact that both of us would be going our separate ways come September.

Claire walked through the kitchen rolling her suitcase behind her, the wheels humming over the flooring. She paused by the door, adjusting her purse on her shoulder.

"Let me carry that out for you." Extending an olive branch was the least I could do before we spent most of the next week apart. I felt guilty jetting away to Palm Desert to a fancy resort when Claire was heading to Ohio to work hard for the next four days. But it was a self-righteous guilt. Claire could be coming with me if she weren't so wrapped up in her own world.

"Thank you." Claire glanced at me quickly, and then led the way through the garage.

Kaylee had called and was on her way to drive Claire to the airport so we wouldn't have two cars sitting in the parking lot all week. I would be leaving in another hour to take Pesto to the kennel and had packing of my own to do. As we stepped outside into the crisp fall air, Kaylee pulled into the driveway, giving us both a little wave.

I waited while Kaylee tapped the automatic lock release. I put Claire's suitcase into the backseat and closed the door. Claire walked around to the passenger side of the car and looked at me over the roof.

"Thank you," she said, too politely for what I'd done.

"Did you have your books shipped ahead to the hotel?" A smart man would have asked that question days ago, but this impasse had turned me into a stubborn husband. I still hated the fact that Claire wasn't going with me.

"Yes," she said, standing inside the open car door. "Well . . ." She shrugged her purse off her shoulder and put it on the passenger seat of the car. "I'd better get going."

Now, of all times, I wanted to take her in my arms and apologize for the grudge I'd carried the past months. I didn't want this polite cavern hanging between us. But it was too late. Claire had a plane to catch and so did I.

• • •

The hum of a hundred conversations filled the convention hall as I stepped into the large Palm Desert hotel ballroom. How in the world was I going to find Bob and Libby in this crowd? Vendor booths created a small marketplace in the cavernous room. There were aisles and aisles of dealers, all ready to discuss any banking-related business I might have. As an outside director on the bank board, I really didn't have the need to pick up the informational brochures on display, but I would browse the room to get a feel for what the concerns of the banking industry were.

"Want to try your luck?" A vendor held a putter out to me and pointed to the artificial turf creating a putting green in his booth. "You get three tries. Hole-in-one and you can throw your business card in the fishbowl for a chance to win the putter."

What the heck, someday I planned to start golfing more. Grabbing the putter I lined myself up with the cup. My right leg held an awkward stiffness that even my physical therapy sessions hadn't been able to get rid of. But I wasn't complaining. My cast had been off since the end of March and even though it was now September, six months later I was still enjoying the freedom of walking around without crutches. More than once I'd found myself singing my version of a phrase from some old country song . . . "you don't know how good something is until it's gone." I felt that way about those two aluminum sticks I'd balanced on most of the winter. Glad they were gone. I focused on the golf ball in front of me and gave it a solid tap.

"We've got a Tiger here, folks," the vendor called as the ball rimmed the cup and fell in.

A hand clapped my back. "Hey, great shot."

I turned around to find Bob and Libby standing behind me. "Beginner's luck," I said.

The vendor held out a glass fishbowl. "Throw your business card in here for the drawing."

I patted at my sport coat pockets. "I guess I don't have any on me," I said, holding up my empty hands. "Bob, give me one of yours." I turned to the vendor. "He's the bank president. Is that legal?"

The vendor pretended to cover his eyes with his hand. "If I don't see it, it is."

Bob reached in his sport coat pocket, pulled out a card, and dropped it into the bowl. He tipped his head to the vendor and then looked my way. "Now if this guy calls and tries to sell me an expensive check-processing system, I'm going to make you come in and listen to the sales pitch."

"So that's the trick."

"Um-hmm," Bob confirmed. "As they say, there's no such thing as a free lunch. But—" He motioned for us to start walking down the aisle. "There is such a thing as free drinks at these things."

Bob, Libby, and I maneuvered through the crowded aisles toward a just-as-crowded line at the bar. Along the way, Bob shook hands with a couple men and introduced me as a board member of the bank he represented. While Bob and I shuffled into place in the end of the drink line, Libby stepped aside and visited with a woman she knew from previous conventions.

As we waited, I turned around and surveyed the people waiting in line and those meandering the conference aisles. The conference brochure had said the dress code for most events was business casual. While my grocer's meetings were on the informal side, I'd decided to step it up a notch for the meetings here. It had been a bit embarrassing to double-check my wardrobe choices with Bob while I'd been packing, but I would have been more mortified to stick out like a hick-from-the-sticks-of-Carlton in Palm Desert, California.

Looking around, it seemed as though Bob and I stuck out together. We were both wearing sport coats with open collared shirts, while most of the men around us seemed to be sporting Tommy Bahama-type shirts and Dockers. No one would ever accuse me of being a fashion guru, but even I could tell my outfit was a bit old school for this sports-themed opening event.

I nodded my head in the general direction of the milling people. "Seems like a young crowd."

Bob raised an eyebrow. "You noticed, too, huh?"

He pushed aside the hem of his sport coat and stuck his hands in his pant's pockets. "Didn't used to be." He chuckled. "Twenty-five years ago, when I started coming to these things, it seemed like it was nothing but a bunch of old codgers. They wore three-piece suits and ties to all the meetings. Even the workshops during the day. Heck, even the *women* wore three-piece suits. I remember back then thinking I didn't fit in. That I didn't *want* to fit in if it meant becoming one of those stuffy bankers unbuttoning his suit coat before he sat down. And look at me—" Bob tilted his chin and grazed his eyes down his sport coat and slacks. "I'm guessing over half these guys are looking at me and thinking I'm the stuffy one tonight."

As he spoke, the drink line moved forward, and we moved along with it. When we stopped he shook his head. "Things have sure changed. Up until about five years ago, Libby and I used to come to these events and know a good share of the people here. Now it's as if there's been a changing of the guard or something. The old guys like me are all retiring, and the younger men are stepping in to fill in the gaps. Everything's a young man's game these days." Bob took a hand from his pocket and lightly punched me on my upper arm. "We're getting *old,* Buddy."

As if I needed a reminder. Mirroring Bob, I pushed aside my sport coat and shoved my hands in my pockets. "Given any thought to it?"

"By 'it' I'm assuming you mean retirement?"

Funny how he knew exactly what I meant. We baby boomers seemed to have a collective mind-set, and we were all realizing that time wasn't on our side any longer.

"Got any plans?" I asked.

"Well, I didn't until I started noticing how many of my old banking cronies weren't showing up at these things anymore. I feel like my expiration date is running out."

Bob laughed and I joined in, even though the underlying idea of what he'd said hit all too close to home. Spending all winter and spring in a full-leg cast had done a number on my psyche. I was forced to face the fact that my body wasn't invincible, and even though the rest of me was healthy, my broken leg put a big dent in my ego. Relying on Claire and the kids had taught me the lesson that, as much as I hated to admit it, being dependent was what I had to look forward to.

Thank goodness Bob couldn't read my morbid thoughts. He went on as if I hadn't already practically put myself in a nursing home. "Libby and I have talked about taking a couple weeks in February and heading someplace warmer. I guess it wouldn't hurt to scout out what the future might hold." Once again, we shuffled toward the bar. "It's just that it's so hard to get away from work . . . and so hard to get caught up once I'm back. I guess I don't have quite the drive I used to." He snorted a wry laugh. "Which I suppose is a good indication that it's time to think about finding another pasture for the old gray . . . uh, stallion."

Before Bob had a chance to turn the question back to me, it was our turn at the bar. Bob ordered a white wine for Libby and a beer for each of us. When we had our drinks in hand, I tipped the lip of my bottle toward Bob, happy to change the subject.

"Thanks for inviting me to come along." I left out the part that I was sorry Claire couldn't come. That was still a sore subject and one I didn't care to revisit now.

Before my thoughts could get away from me, Bob and I were approached by a nearby vendor, who challenged us to play a mini-basketball free throw game. Tonight was a night to relax and have fun. I handed Bob my beer and took up the challenge. I used to have a pretty mean free throw shot . . . back in the day.

"Go!" the vendor said as he started the one-minute countdown clock.

I started out at a frantic pace that led to nothing but air shots. Soon enough I found my touch and my rhythm and was netting shot after shot. The buzzer sounded and some people nearby clapped. Apparently I'd done okay.

The vendor handed me the stub-ends of five red tickets. "Check back tomorrow to see if you've won a prize." He dropped the other end of the tickets into a bucket. The young man handed me a letter opener marked with his company's logo. "You're about as good at that game as my dad," he said. "He used to play college ball."

His dad? For a split second, irritation scrubbed at my ego, but his comment about playing college ball pushed it away. I felt my chest fill with pride.

"But the game was a lot different back then," he added.

For his sake, it was a good thing I had no purchasing power on behalf of the bank. This young man's company just got crossed off of any list I might have been making.

Bob was chuckling as he passed me back my beer. "If it's any consolation, if you wait thirty years that kid will be standing in our shoes and some snot-nosed kid will put *him* in his place."

I took a long swallow of my cold beer. The bad news was, I more than likely wouldn't be around in thirty years to see my revenge. I hated to admit it, but my little bout of blitz-basketball had left me winded. I took another swallow, hoping it would help me cool down. A light sweat had broken out on my upper lip.

"What time is dinner?" I asked Bob, looking at my watch, trying to turn his attention away from me and the lousy shape I was in.

"Seven o'clock," he replied.

I made a circular motion with my beer bottle.

"Think I'll go wander around and look things over." I didn't want Bob to see me trying to regain my composure.

"We'll meet you at the main door to the banquet room."

"Great," I replied, my back already facing Bob's way. For some reason, I couldn't seem to draw in a full breath. I lifted my chin and pulled in a long, slow breath through my mouth. Concentrating on the floor, I picked my way along the aisle, waving off vendors who tried to entice me into playing their games. I ditched my half-full bottle of beer into a trash can. Maybe I was experiencing some weird reaction to the few swallows of alcohol I'd had.

The vendor booths on both sides of me faded into the background as I concentrated on filling my lungs. Certainly that grade-school version of a free throw contest couldn't have caused this kind of overreaction. A smothering feeling of claustrophobia sent me elbowing my way out of the overheated hall. A bathroom. That's what I needed. Somewhere I could get out of this crowd and splash cold water on my face.

I stumbled down the corridor, frantically searching for a doorway that would lead me out of my misery.

There! I shouldered my way into the cool, tiled space and made my way to the row of sinks hanging from the wall. The mirror told me what I already knew. A light sheen of sweat covered my face. What was happening to me?

A heart attack?

Oh, Lord. No. My heart was pounding. As long as it was beating, that was a good sign. Right? *Breathe.* As long as I could breathe I'd be okay. I couldn't be having a heart attack . . . could I?

Of course not. I wasn't *that* old. Or that out of shape. What I was experiencing now, had to do with the six months I'd spent on crutches not doing any kind of exercising except for hobbling around. This was ridiculous. How out of shape was I to get in an out-of-breath sweat over one minute of free throw shooting? Maybe the plane trip to Palm Desert had done me in. Getting anywhere from North Dakota was not a simple matter. We'd left well before dawn. I'd been up since three-thirty. Even someone twenty years younger than me would be dragging fifteen hours later. As soon as I got back to Carlton I was going to join a gym. I'd hire a personal trainer.

The door to the bathroom swung open and a young guy walked in. Crisp white shirt, sleeves rolled back to expose his muscular forearms. A guy like him wouldn't be worrying about a heart attack. As he headed to the urinals his eyes passed over me as if I wasn't even there. He had all of life in front of him while I was invisible to an up-and-comer like him. Who wouldn't have a panic attack at a thought like that?

I bent to the sink and splashed cold water on my face. That was better. All I needed to do was calm down. Being overtired and a little exertion had sent my heart racing and I'd panicked. That was all. With my hands I wiped the cool water from my face and looked back into the mirror. I wasn't as flushed as I had been.

"Hey there." The young guy was washing his hands at a sink two down from mine. "How's it going?"

"Fine," I said, yanking a paper towel from the dispenser and wiping off my face. I shrugged out of my sport coat. "It's hot out there." As if I owed the kid an explanation.

"Yeah."

He was being polite. Even in my sweltering state, I was aware that the air-conditioning in the convention hall was set on frigid. Half the women had been walking around with their arms wrapped around themselves and their teeth chattering. If I were a woman, I could claim hormones as the cause of my discomfort. As it was, I had no expla-nation for what had happened to me. But I was feeling better now.

Maybe I was hungry. In the process of arriving at the terminal, getting our luggage, the cab ride to the hotel, and checking in, we'd missed lunch. There had been a welcome-to-the-convention packet waiting for me in my room, along with some odd combination of trail mix that I'd wolfed down. What happened could have been my blood sugar dropping . . . or something. I'd talk to my personal trainer about that. The personal trainer I didn't have but would get as soon as I got home.

In the meantime, I had a *gala banquet* to attend.

"No, thanks." I turned my wine glass upside down as the waiter began serving our table our salads, and another began pouring from the bottles of red and white wine in his hands. I leaned to the banker next to me. "I've been up since three-thirty this morning. If I have a glass of wine I'm afraid my face will be in my mashed potatoes." I wasn't about to admit I'd thought I was having a heart attack fifteen minutes ago.

He laughed and stuck out his hand. "Milt Lindstrom. Iowa," he said.

"Jim Westin," I replied shaking his hand. "North Dakota."

"Any relation to the Westin hotel family?" he asked.

At home no one ever made that assumption. But since I'd been at the convention, three people had asked the same question. No question I was in an arena where the stakes were higher and big business connections were part of the playing field.

"None," I said, nodding to the waiter so he'd pour some thin-looking vinaigrette dressing on my salad of what I knew were expensive greens, not to mention the cost of the edible flower petals as garnish. Whoever supplied the hotel with food for banquets of this size had a good deal going. I was guessing there were almost a thousand people at this impressive event.

The Iowa banker tossed his salad a bit with his fork and then dug in. "What's the size of your bank?" he asked around the lettuce in his mouth.

In North Dakota, we talked about the weather as a conversation opener. Here, I'd quickly learned, people sized you up by the assets of your bank. I had a new respect for Bob Marsden and Carlton bank shareholders. They were relatively small in the scheme of things, and yet they made every effort to operate as if they were one of the big boys.

On the flight out here, Bob had explained the lengthy process it had been for the Carlton bank to offer online banking to its customers. Firewalls. Security passwords. Regulations to meet regulatory requirements. Just hearing about the process made my head spin. I couldn't help but compare it to the hoops I might have to jump through if Drew's idea of online grocery shopping were to become a reality. For not the first time, I felt that the effort of taking my business into the future was more work than I had in me to tackle. And if I couldn't stay competitive . . . well, I knew then it was time to get out completely. Even worse than refusing to keep up with technology would be to see the store my grandfather started get run into the ground. Before that happened, I'd sell.

There were big decisions facing me, but the time to make them wasn't now. I turned my attention back to my dinner companion and explained my position as an outside director on the bank board. "I'm in the grocery business."

With his fork, Milt pushed aside an edible flower petal and speared another mouthful of lettuce. "The grocery business, hmm. Well, that's gotta be a little gold mine. I mean people have to *eat*."

"Yeah, they do," I agreed. "But they don't have to shop at my store."

Milt stabbed at the air with his butter knife. "You got a point there." He broke off a piece of dinner roll and slathered it with butter. "So tell me, Jim, what are some of the challenges facing grocers these days?"

Challenges? How long did this guy think this dinner was going to last? I could talk to him all night about the challenges of the grocery business. I took a sip of water while my mind scrambled to come up with a response that wouldn't qualify as a session on a therapist's couch.

"The thing about the grocery business," I started, "is that in spite of technology, it's a very hands-on business. The product has to get loaded onto a truck and brought to my stores. The trucks need unloading and we need personnel to process the shipment. Boxes need to be carried to the shelves and opened. Then every single cereal box, pickle jar, and can of tomatoes gets put on a shelf by hand."

"Huh," Milt said, "never thought of it that way."

But I wasn't done. "Periodically the shelves need to be stripped and cleaned. And every week the price markers on the shelves need to be updated to reflect the current price of my inventory."

I paused as a waiter came and removed our salad plates and replaced them with plates filled with sizzling steak and shrimp, an overstuffed potato, and a mix of grilled vegetables. Once again, I found myself envying the guy who had this food contract.

"Go on," Milt said as he sliced into his steak. "This is interesting."

Using my fork I picked up a slice of buttery yellow squash and held it above my plate. "What do you think the shelf life is for fresh vegetables?" I supplied the answer. "Shorter than you'd think. Produce is all about *image.* Once the product starts to get even the slightest bit bruised or past its peak, you can forget about it selling. The customer wants *fresh.*" I popped the squash into my mouth. "About twenty-three percent goes to waste."

Milt's eyebrows rose. "That's almost a fourth of the inventory." Leave it to a banker to get right to the bottom line.

"You got it right."

"I suppose meat is the same?"

"Actually," I said, slicing into my steak, "anything that's not selling gets ground up into hamburger or made into sausage. We have more control over our waste costs in the meat department."

"Fascinating," Milt said.

I laughed. "It's day-to-day business for me." I glanced around our table of eight. "I don't want to monopolize your time. I'd talk about my business all night if you'd listen."

He looked at our dinner companions. Bob and Libby were conversing with the couple to their left. There were two other men at our table deep into a conversation of their own.

Milt picked up a shrimp by the tail and bit off the meat. "Have trouble with the light-fingered discount?"

"You mean shoplifting?"

"Yeah. I would imagine kids try to steal candy. Chips. You know . . ."

Before answering I scooped up a bite of the cheese-topped stuffed potato. "Our biggest problem is adults. They take aspirin bottles out of the boxes and stick 'em in their pockets or purses. Health and beauty products are what get stolen the most."

"Interesting." Milt seemed to mull this over as we both concentrated on our meal.

For a time, we visited with the other people at

the table, and then everyone started up smaller conversations with their dinner partners. It was time for me to ask Milt a few questions of my own. A perfect time for me to change the subject. But Milt's questions had sent my mind racing. My thoughts were nothing I didn't already know, but saying them out loud laid my business on the table in a way I hadn't looked at in a long time. The grocery business was labor intensive. Profit margins were narrow. Waste was an issue, as was personnel turnover. At least his questions had pushed aside my concern about the health episode I'd had in the convention hall. I didn't know which was worse, worrying about my health or my business.

Before I could decide on the winner, Milt interrupted my thoughts. "I suppose you have one of those superstores in your town. Have you noticed any changes in your business?"

There we had it . . . for right now, my business worries took first place. They said confession was good for the soul . . . well, if so, by spilling my inside view of the grocery business to Milt, I might be taking care of my health issues at the same time. I rested my knife and fork across my plate, I was finished eating . . . but not done unloading on this poor, unsuspecting makeshift psychiatrist. "Funny you should ask." With my thumbs I nudged my plate away from the edge of the table. "We had a SuperTarget open down the road from us about six months ago."

Milt turned his coffee cup right side up and nodded as a waiter appeared at his elbow with a thermal carafe. "And?"

I waved off the waiter. I'd gotten a second wind and was wound up enough without a caffeine injection. I tilted my hand in the air. "People are going to check things out. Heck, I'll even drop by and take a look one of these days. I'm guessing we'll see a small dip in our business until the dust settles, but I'm counting on people being creatures of habit. We've got a good customer base and I'm hoping they like Westin Foods enough to keep shopping there. Here's the thing . . ."

I leaned back as the waiter put a piece of cheesecake with strawberry topping in front of me. "Sure, the SuperTarget is another player on the field, so to speak. But in the grocery business our competition isn't only other grocery sellers. It's also the restaurant business. People think nothing of eating out nowadays. Anyone who sells food is my competition. I've learned not to lose sleep over it."

Okay, I hoped I could be forgiven a little white lie. Occasionally I did toss and turn over my competition, but, really, what could I do about it?

You could get out of business.

There it was again. The carrot at the end of the stick. Was getting out really what I'd been running toward all these years? The idea that someday my work would be over? Done? Kaput? Finished?

Was that the goal? To someday have absolutely nothing to do?

You'd go nuts.

Yeah, I would. Maybe a heart attack wasn't so terrible after all. At least then the decision would be made for me and I could quit all this waffling.

Now you're losing it.

Maybe I was. Thinking that keeling over was a solution to my troubles. *Sheesh!* Certainly, retirement was a simpler option.

Using the back of my fork, I scooped at the graham cracker crumbs and strawberry sauce dotting the dessert plate. As I put the last sweet bite into my mouth, I realized I'd been so caught up in explaining my business to Milt, I'd barely tasted the meal.

I turned to my dinner companion. "I hope I didn't bore you with details. It's not often I get someone who knows the right questions to get me foaming at the mouth." I was hoping Milt had a sense of humor.

Milt laughed as he pushed himself away from the table and stood. I did likewise. He stuck out his hand and shook mine. "Good to meet you, Jim. I learned a lot tonight. I think we can safely say that you've talked me into staying in the banking business."

And I'd pretty much talked myself out of my business.

· · ·

Holding my cell phone to my ear, I listened as the phone rang once, twice, three times. It looked as though I wasn't going to be able to connect with Claire tonight. Considering the three-hour time difference between her conference in Ohio and mine in Palm Desert, it was late to be calling her, but I'd hoped I might catch Claire at the very end of her evening and before I hit the sack.

Now that I was back in my hotel room and finally had a chance to sleep, I wasn't tired. My monologue to Milt kept running through my head, an endless litany of all that was wrong with being in the grocery business. If I felt that way about things, there was no good reason for me to keep my doors open. And I planned to tell Claire just that—

Claire's voice mail picked up. *Leave a message.*

—But not over the phone.

Even so, I felt the need to talk to my wife. We'd left on our separate business trips on an off-key note. Me upset because Claire couldn't come along. Claire irked because I hadn't checked with her before signing up for the trip. There was no question Claire's new midlife career was taking off. No one I knew had a schedule that was booked a year in advance . . . a fact I didn't realize until Claire pulled out her planner and flipped through the pages for me. If I planned to retire, I was going to have to make an appointment to see my wife.

"Hi, Honey," I said, suddenly missing her. "Thought I might be able to catch you. Hope your conference is going well. I'm sorry I left things—"

There was a catch in my throat. I tried to cough it away, but I had that same sense of not being able to catch my breath that I had in the conference hall earlier in the evening. I shook my head, trying to shake away the light-headedness I was feeling.

I coughed again. "Sorry," I said into the phone. I felt slightly nauseated. "I've gotta go."

I snapped my phone shut and laid back against the pillows, thinking of nothing, trying only to breathe. What was happening to me?

The voice of the pilot came over the intercom. "We're scheduled to land in Carlton in fifteen minutes. Please make sure your seatbelts are fastened and your tray tables are in the upright position. The flight attendant will make a final pass through the cabin to collect anything you might want to discard before we touch down. Flight attendants, we've been cleared for landing."

Bob turned in his seat, kitty-corner across the aisle from mine. "Ready to get back to reality?"

I raised my eyebrows in a you-had-to-remind-me gesture and checked to see that my seatbelt was secured. Bob, Libby, and my days in Palm Desert had been a nice break, but I would have enjoyed the time more if Claire had been along. The fact was, I'd never been so glad to get back home as I was to be returning from this four-day trip. Claire and I had played phone tag the entire time. Leaving each other messages, never connecting.

Checking in with the stores a couple times each day only kept me abreast of which checkout clerks didn't show, and that two of my carry-out kids were quitting. There'd been an unexpected run on Pepsi that left the large space on the shelf empty. Inventory turnover was the name of the game, but you couldn't sell a product that wasn't there. Nothing I could do about any of it even if I'd been right there, but somehow the news left me feeling helpless and out of touch with my business.

My odd symptoms had disappeared, but had concerned me enough that I'd made up my mind I'd go see my doctor as soon as I got unpacked. And checked things out at the store. I might have to run up to Emerson, too. But, I promised myself, I'd go to the doctor . . . soon.

I looked out the window of the airplane, watching the familiar landscape grow closer as we descended. Harvest was in full swing, the golden fields perfect rectangles from my vantage point this late September afternoon.

Getting away from the stores had been a good thing. Much like being this high in the sky, I'd gained a perspective that was hard to see when I was in the thick of things. Talking to Milt that first evening had helped me see that, while I knew the grocery business inside and out, all I was focusing on were the aspects of the business that were negative. If there were things I loved about the business, I'd forgotten them. Hanging on to the stores in the hopes one of my kids would take over was pointless. It was time to make a change. Past time.

As soon as possible I was going to take Claire out to dinner and have a long, uninterrupted conversation. I wanted to lay my retirement proposal on the table and see what she wanted to do next. Take a trip to Europe? Buy an RV and travel around the country? I'd had that old Dodge taking up half the garage for almost exactly two years now, and I'd done nothing but walk past the rusty old thing. All I needed now was time . . . and I planned to have that in short order.

Claire would be arriving back in Carlton tomorrow afternoon. Kaylee had driven Claire to the airport so we wouldn't have both our vehicles sitting in the parking lot. I'd planned to pick Claire up and drive her home. But possibly a detour was in order. I could meet her plane. Whisk her off to dinner. My plan could be underway by as early as tomorrow evening.

As the plane touched down and the pilot applied the brakes, I was pushed back into my seat. A mild tightness pressed against my chest. The plane slowed and turned off the runway. I waited for the pressure to lift from my chest. It didn't. Taking long breaths, I tried to calm myself. *Breathe. Just breathe.* Whatever this was, it wasn't going to happen to me again.

The plane taxied to the terminal and the *fasten seatbelt* sign blinked off. I forced myself out of my seat. Maybe I wouldn't wait to call my doctor until after I checked things out at the stores. If I called as soon as I got home, maybe my doctor could squeeze me in yet today. I pulled my briefcase from the overheard compartment and joined the line leading from the plane into the terminal.

Libby had ducked into the bathroom, and Bob waited for her outside the doorway.

"Nice flight," he commented.

"Yeah," was all I could manage. Now familiar sweat popped out on my upper lip. I debated between ducking into the bathroom to ride this wave out or heading straight to the baggage claim. The sooner I could collect my suitcase, the quicker I could get home. If I could lie down and rest . . . certainly this would pass. I motioned that I'd meet Bob at the luggage claim.

Normally I'd take the flight of steps down rather than the escalator, but the pressure in my chest hadn't let up, and the idea of even that small bit of effort seemed too much.

As I approached the baggage area, a loud buzzer sounded and suitcases starting appearing on the moving track. One advantage of flying in and out of North Dakota was that the small size of our airport made luggage retrieval a quick job. The airport personnel had done themselves proud this trip.

"Mmm . . ." I hummed against the fullness in my chest. *Man, that hurts.* Rubbing my knuckles against the thickness pushing at my breastbone I watched for my black bag. In my peripheral vision I saw Bob and Libby join me, but it was too much effort for me to acknowledge them.

"There's mine." Libby pointed to an oversized brown suede bag.

Bob stepped forward and easily pulled it from the moving rack. The way I was feeling, I couldn't imagine lifting anything right now. I moved my fingers from my chest to massage my jaw. A sudden pain in the joint of my mouth left me feeling as if I'd chomped down hard on a walnut still in the shell. The ache seemed to radiate down into my neck.

Bob pulled his own bag from the line of luggage and set it beside me. "You going to head into the store this afternoon?"

"No." One word was all I could manage. My head was spinning. I should thank Bob for the trip. I should tell him how much I enjoyed my time with them. But my bag was heading my way. How was I going to lift it? What was happening to me?

It took an effort, but I managed to step forward and grab the handle of my suitcase. I yanked it from the conveyor belt. Whew, I'd done it. For a brief moment the pressure in my chest let up. I held out my hand to Bob. "Thank—"

In the next instant, a crushing, squeezing pain in the center of my chest knocked me to my knees. I gasped for air. My eyes met Bob's, registered his expression of puzzlement and then alarm. His arm reached toward me as I fell forward.

A buzz of frightened voices surrounded me, but I couldn't make out what anyone was saying through the whooshing in my ears.

Oh, Lord. Help!

I had a sensation of falling onto my side, then flopping over onto my back.

Help me. Had I said the words out loud . . . or to myself? Was I talking to Bob . . . or God?

Anyone. Help me.

This couldn't be happening. *God, please.* Irrational thoughts pummeled along with the crushing pain. I was supposed to pick up Pesto from the kennel. Who would meet Claire tomorrow? I had to check on the stores.

I'd wanted out of my responsibilities, but not this way. I didn't want to die. I had too much to do. Too much life to live. I had an old car to restore. And a grandson to watch grow up. I was going to improve my golf game. And what about growing old with Claire? And traveling? I wanted all that . . . and more.

The viselike pain wouldn't quit.

My voice was a moan. A sound I couldn't imagine coming from me.

Oh, Lord, let me live. I have work to do.

My hands raked at the shirt covering my chest, as if tearing it away would get rid of the pain.

From close by, I heard Bob yell. "Someone call an ambulance!"

For the past year I'd been looking to leave my work behind, but now I wanted nothing more than to get up every day and do it.

Drew

"Thanks for coming in." I followed my loan customer out of my office and into the bank lobby. Our meeting had taken longer than I'd expected, and I knew my next client, Todd Wilson, would be waiting. Sure enough, there he was. Knowing Todd, he'd been on time, and then was forced to cool his heels for a good twenty minutes.

"Hi, Todd." I stuck out my hand as I tilted my head in the direction of my office. "Come on. Sorry to keep you waiting."

"No problem." Todd tucked a folder under his arm, grabbed a baseball cap off his head, and shook my hand. He didn't even wait until we were halfway down the hall. "I got those figures put together that you wanted." He was a go-getter and anxious to get the paperwork done, so he could transfer ownership of the business he was buying into his own name.

"Great," I said, motioning Todd to have a chair

in front of my desk. I walked around to the opposite side and sat down.

Todd wasted no time. He slid a manila folder across the desk top, did a quick one-eighty with it, and then flipped it open in front of me. Using my pen, I tracked my way through the pages, taking a few minutes to go over the numbers he'd penciled in on his financial statement, and the projections he'd made.

When I got to the end, I tapped at the last figure. "Looks good."

Todd gave a quick nod. "I thought so, too."

"Have you negotiated the final purchase price?"

"Yup." Todd named a figure.

I raised an eyebrow and cocked my head. "Sounds like you're getting a good deal."

A slow grin spread across Todd's face. "I know." He leaned forward, forearms on the edge of my desk. Excitement pulsed in his expression. "Bruce wants out and he's glad to see me take over."

Todd had been working at an auto body repair shop since he'd been in high school. Time marched on, and Todd acquired a wife, three kids, and a promotion to foreman. Now in his late thirties, Todd had a chance to buy the place from his boss. The way Todd told it, they'd been dickering out a deal for years.

Todd sat back in his chair. "I feel kind of bad that the only way I can buy this is because my grandpa died."

"I have a feeling your grandpa would think it's a great way to spend your inheritance."

Todd nodded slowly. He had been one of my first clients when I started work at the Carlton bank. He'd first come to talk to me about buying the repair shop nine months ago. At that time, he had only a pittance for a down payment, not enough to make the business cash flow. I urged him to wait. The reason most businesses failed is that they were under capitalized, and I wanted to see Todd succeed. It was no secret that Bruce did too. He was willing to bide his time while Todd tried to save more money.

Todd's dad had died when he was in junior high, and his grandparents did everything they could to help Todd's mom raise her kids right. When his grandpa died three months ago, Todd found out he'd been left a modest inheritance. The sum might have been fairly small to many people, but to Todd it was a fortune, because it meant he had enough to finalize a deal with Bruce.

"I've thanked Bruce a million times for being willing to wait. For giving me a chance." Todd shook his head as if he couldn't believe his luck.

"He's been good to you."

Todd pressed his lips together, as if trying to hold back his emotions. "He has." Todd covered his mouth and gave a short cough. "Did I tell you that Bruce was the one who encouraged me to go to mechanics school?"

Todd had told me the story . . . twice, but I'd learned some things needed repeating. I often told Trisha that I should have a counseling degree to go along with my finance background. I spent more time listening than talking to loan customers. I sat back and let Todd talk.

"Bruce even helped me fill out the application to go to school. And then he promised me a job when I came home on weekends, and after I was through." Todd scrubbed at the side of his cheek. "All I ever wanted to do was work on cars. And Bruce let me." His Adam's apple bobbed as he swallowed. "He's been like a dad to me."

Todd blinked, cleared his throat, and glanced down at his hands folded on my desktop. Todd looked up at me quickly and then away. Two grown men getting emotional over a loan deal. Sheesh. I reached for a paper clip and got busy fastening together his financial statement.

He sat back. "Anyway, I'm glad this worked out. I'm glad I can do this for Bruce. He didn't want to sell the shop to just . . . anybody. He knows I'll treat it like he did. Heck—" Todd gave a short laugh. "The place has felt like mine for years already."

Kind of like the store does to you . . . right? Where had that thought come from?

I tried to brush away the idea that had been running through my thoughts more often than I was willing to admit. Ever since my dad had broken his leg—or since *I'd* been the one to break his leg—I'd made a point of stopping by the store to see if there was any way I could help my dad out. By the time his cast had come off, my daily stop by the store had become a habit. I enjoyed kibitzing with the checkout clerks. I liked stepping behind the butcher counter and grabbing a taste of the home-smoked sausage the store was known for. And I found myself looking forward to my daily visit with my dad. Not once in all those months did he even hint that he wanted me to take over the business. And now that the pressure was off, I found myself toying with the concept at night when I tried to fall asleep.

But now wasn't the time to wrestle with that idea. Todd was sitting across from me, waiting for a check so he could buy his own business.

Todd scratched the back of his head, pulled his baseball cap on, and tugged at the brim. He grinned. "It's going to be great to have something to leave my kids, you know?"

I nodded in agreement, but his statement sent my thoughts scrambling. What was I going to have to leave Will? All my hard work at the bank was in exchange for a salary and a decent benefit package, but when it came right down to it, I wasn't building up any kind of equity. I didn't own the business . . . I just worked here.

But if you went into business with your dad . . .

There it was again. And once again, I pushed the thought aside.

I closed the folder Todd had given me. "I'll get the paperwork drawn up and have Melissa cut you a check. We should have everything ready by Friday. Can you stop by after lunch?"

Todd pushed himself to his feet, the wide smile still on his face. "I'll stop by whenever you want me to."

We shook hands. It felt good to help a client fulfill his dreams, but I had a hunch Todd was feeling even better than I was.

I walked Todd down the hallway and into the bank lobby. We chatted for a bit and then shook hands again.

A husky-looking, middle-aged man came up and clasped Todd on the shoulder. "Did you get it done?"

Todd turned. "What are you doing here?"

The man lifted a hand toward the teller stations. "I . . . Uh . . . I had to make a deposit."

"You could have sent it with me," Todd said.

"Well, I, uh . . . didn't think of it until you already left."

It took me a second to recognize Todd's employer, Bruce. I'd only met him once, back when they were still in the talking stages of transferring the business ownership. I wondered if Todd could see right through Bruce's flimsy excuse. The way Bruce was fidgeting, it was obvious he was in the act of checking up on his favorite employee. If he wasn't careful, Bruce would burst right out of his coveralls.

"So," Bruce said, turning his attention to me, "did you help this kid out?"

Before I could even nod, Todd spoke up. "Got 'er done."

Bruce clasped Todd's hand and pulled him into a quick guy-hug. He released Todd and looked to me. "Can't wait to see how my kid is going to do."

My kid, he'd said, as if Todd really was his son. *Imagine how your dad would feel if you took over his business.*

No, I didn't want to imagine that. Not right now. I wanted time to think things over, time to decide if that really was an offer I wanted to make . . . because *if* I took over the business—and that was a big *if*—I'd be committing myself for life.

Todd tugged at the brim on his hat, still grinning at Bruce. "Come Monday you'll be a free man."

Bruce's smile matched Todd's. "You're not going to get rid of me that easy. You're still gonna need me to crack the whip. Show you how things are done."

Todd leaned his head back and looked to the ceiling as if pleading for help, but it was easy to see this was a game the two of them played. I had a hunch Bruce would be around to give Todd a helping hand, and Todd would be glad to have him pitch in.

The way it should be with family.

Todd and Bruce weren't related by blood, but they were *kin* all the same. Their bond was obvious in the way they interacted with each other.

Like you do with your dad?

Yeah, kind of like that.

Only without the business changing hands between you.

I closed my eyes and allowed myself an eye-roll behind my lids. It always came back to that. Which reminded me . . . I glanced at my watch. My dad should be getting back to Carlton about now. Knowing him, he'd head straight to the store to check on things.

I waited for a break in Todd and Bruce's bantering. "I'm going to get back to my office," I said, throwing a thumb in that direction. I nodded to Todd. "See you Friday."

"Won't miss it," he said.

I turned and walked through the bank lobby. Other than a couple loan customers dropping in, this afternoon had been slow. If I cleared up Todd's paperwork, I could call it an early day. On my way home I would swing by the store and catch up with my dad. I'd missed him while he'd been gone. Missed our daily chats. Oh sure, I'd stopped by the store while he'd been gone—

Keeping an eye on things?

Sheesh. My conscience wouldn't let me get by

with a thing. Yeah, okay. So I felt a little responsibility to the business while my dad was away. No one would sue me for that. But, even so, things weren't the same without my dad front and center. Maybe I was fooling myself that I had a place there. Dad had carved out a nice niche for himself. He was doing what he was supposed to be doing.

And you?

I blew a puff of air from my mouth. *I wish I knew.* I was more confused than ever. Banking was fine. I enjoyed the work, but there was always this tug pulling me toward . . . the store.

Lord, help me to know. Really know *what it is You want me to do.*

"Drew!" The bank receptionist, June, called to me from across the bank lobby. "There you are." She hurried toward me. "You weren't in your office and you weren't in the break room. I had someone check the men's room, but you weren't there, either." She stopped in front of me. "Bob called for you."

"Bob?" The only Bob I could think of was Bob Marsden, the bank president, but he was at the same meeting my dad had attended. Today was a travel day for both of them. There would be no reason for him to call me. And even if he would have called, I could think of no business so pressing that it would send June on a wild goose chase around the bank to find me. Taking a message would have done the trick. "Bob who?"

"Bob Marsden," June confirmed. Her face was pale.

A finger of unexplained worry suddenly prodded inside my stomach. *Something's wrong.*

Before I could voice my questions, words tumbled from June's mouth. "He said you should get to the hospital immediately. Your dad's been taken there by ambulance."

"Ambulance?" I sounded slow. Dumb.

"Yes, by ambulance."

"But—" Questions swarmed through my head. I turned my head to the left, right, looking to make some sense of this. "Where is he? Are they home? Did they leave Palm Desert?"

June's eyes grew wide. "I don't—Oh! Bob said you should get to the hospital. They must be back in Carlton. Otherwise you couldn't—" June pushed at my arm. "Go." She pushed again, harder this time. "Go now!"

Claire

"Ugh." I moaned and rolled over in bed, groping in the dark for the bedside phone in my Ohio hotel room.

"This is your six-fifteen a.m. wake-up call." The automated voice blabbered on about today's weather while I lay on my back, trying to convince myself it really was time to get up. The last day of the conference was ahead of me and I was already exhausted. The weather report didn't matter. My day was so packed, I'd be lucky if I had one second to stick my head out the door to see if the sun was shining.

I fumbled to hang up the phone, then laid back and threw my arm over my eyes. A couple more minutes, then I'd get up. Foggy memories of last night floated through my mind like a dream. My hotel room was near the elevator, a mistake I hoped never to make again. The keynote session last night had ended at nine. By the time I'd finished up at my book table, it had been after ten. Out of the corner of my eye, I noticed a woman hovering off to the side, glancing my way. I recognized the posture . . . she was waiting to talk to me. Inwardly, I sighed. I knew whatever she had to share would be emotion-packed. My Friendship Factor seminars always seemed to touch something in women, something that oftentimes brought up hurt feelings and troublesome relationships. And for some reason, these women thought I was the Friendship Doctor. It wasn't unusual for me to spend the time between sessions handing out tissues and listening to stories of friendships gone bad.

I'd been right. By the time I'd been able to extract myself from the late-night conversation and make my way down the wide hotel corridor, two other women cornered me along the way. It was nearly eleven-thirty by the time I'd made it back to my room. And I still had my notes to review for the seminars that would go on most of the day tomorrow.

Make that *today.*

I threw back the covers and forced my legs over the edge of the bed. Now the hotel hallway outside my room was quiet, a quality that had been lacking last night. It seemed that every time I'd start to doze off, the elevator doors would open and deposit another group of boisterous women into the hall near my door. I hardly dared complain, because most of the rooms on this floor of the hotel were occupied by women attending the conference. My talks centered on friendship, and part of me was glad the women were using their spare time to share and bond . . . but did they have to do it at midnight? Or after? Right outside my door?

Sometime after two a.m. I'd shuffled into the bathroom, rummaged in the bottom of my cosmetic bag, and unearthed a bottle of prescription sleeping pills. As often as possible, I tried not to take them, but there were times when I realized sleep would not be coming anytime soon. These women were paying to have a quality program, and they deserved a rested speaker. And I deserved some sleep.

But now I needed to wake up. It was so tempting to lay back down on my pillow, but I pushed myself into a standing position and stretched. Once I got going I'd be fine. Coffee would help.

Squinting against what I knew was coming, I turned on the bedside light. Slowly I opened my eyes, blinking against the brightness. I hated to wish the day away, but I was already looking forward to tonight. To climbing right back into this bed and getting a good night's sleep. The conference ended with my final session right after supper. Since most of the registered women lived in and around Akron, the majority of them would be leaving after the keynote speech. Lucky Jim, he would be heading back to Carlton from his banking meeting later today. I would spend tonight and tomorrow morning packing up any books that didn't sell and going over notes from the conference with the committee who helped sponsor my event here. They were already talking about doing another seminar next fall. We were going to have to get dates on the calendar very soon because my schedule for next year was filling fast.

I slipped into my slippers and scuffed my way to the small coffeemaker sitting in a corner of the bathroom counter. Opening both the regular and decaf packets, I put both of them into the basket— my trick for making hotel room coffee palatable. In short order, I had the coffee brewing and got in the shower. Every morning, I cautioned myself about drinking too much coffee. Once I set foot out of my hotel room I'd be lucky to get a bathroom break.

As I soaped up, rinsed off, and shampooed my hair I thought about the day ahead. What I would wear. What I would talk about. The times in between sessions when I knew I'd be waylaid by women wanting more of my time. Alone in my hotel room was the only time I'd have by myself all day. The minute I set foot outside this room I considered myself "on stage." My focus was friendship, and I knew I was expected to practice what I preached. I was well aware of the fact that eyes were on me, whether I was behind the podium, at my book table, or simply walking down the hall. Attention came with the territory, and I didn't fault people for their scrutiny. I'd be the same way if the high heels were on the other feet. I wanted to live up to what these women had made me out to be, but by the last day of a conference I was more than ready to head home, slip into a pair of jeans, a comfy T-shirt, and a *flat* pair of shoes.

Rinsing the conditioner from my hair, I reminded myself that I was about thirty hours ahead of myself. Before I could slip into those comfortable clothes, I needed to finish up this full day of seminars and workshops, give the final keynote talk after dinner, and pack up my things. Tomorrow morning I'd lug the books I needed to ship back home to the hotel business center. After a breakfast meeting with the committee members, one of them would drive me to the airport, and by noon I'd be on the flight back to Carlton. With a stop to change planes in Minneapolis, as always. Getting anywhere from North Dakota—and back again—was not an easy endeavor.

I stepped from the shower, toweled myself off, and slipped into the terry robe provided by the hotel. Now I could have my first sip of coffee. And another. Ahhh . . . I was starting to feel halfway awake and ready to tackle the day. As much as I enjoyed these seminars, I recognized that I couldn't keep up this pace forever.

I set down my cup and began putting on my makeup. Foundation. Blush. I leaned into the mirror to apply eyeliner. Even before my first conference nine months ago, I'd been on the run, saying yes to any speaking engagement that came my way. Wesley had advised me that the best advertisement for my books was word of mouth, and making personal connections was the way to get people talking. And then we'd come up with the idea of turning my *Friendship Factor* books into an event that people could attend.

Life had been on fast-forward ever since. And when I wasn't actually *at* a conference, I was busy making arrangements for the next one. There was so much work involved. More than I'd ever imagined. We'd hired a publicist to guide us through the process, but even so, the bulk of each event fell on me.

The first thing always involved finding a local

team to lay the groundwork. Since my books held a faith-based look at friendship, it was natural to team up with an active church women's group. They were able to supply local helpers to conduct some of the break-out sessions, and a core group of women to help arrange a block of hotel rooms, process registrations, and line up meals for the attendees. But it all fell back on my plate to make sure it all got done.

I wasn't complaining. I'd met some of the coolest women ever in these past months. But the fact was, I was never in a town for more than three or four days. My relationships with the women I met were as heartfelt as one could get in conversational moments snatched to and from the airport and between workshops at the seminars. The irony was, my *real* friendships were something I hardly had time for when I was home. Which reminded me—

I poured another cup of coffee and carried it to the desk near the bed. My cell phone was plugged into the charger. I'd been too tired last night to check for messages, but this would be my only chance to dial in before my day took off. I punched in my PIN and waited while my messages were retrieved.

"You have four unheard messages." As I listened, I sat in the desk chair and sipped my coffee.

A pang of guilt shot through me as my dad's familiar voice came through the phone. "Hi,

Honey. I . . . uh . . . well I know you're busy. I was calling to tell you I got the results of my blood tests and the doctor thinks I'm borderline diabetic. What next, huh? Your dad is falling apart." He gave the kind of laugh that meant what he'd said wasn't the ha-ha kind of funny. "I forgot when you're coming back. In fact, I forgot where you're at. See what I mean? Well, call me when you get this."

I tilted my head back and stared at the ceiling. It would have been too late to call him last night, and I didn't have time to spare this morning. And even if I did, the hour time difference would make it five-thirty a.m. back in Carlton. My early-bird dad wouldn't be awake quite this early.

The second message was from Kaylee. Asking when was I coming home. Asking when her dad would be home. Chiding both of us for being too busy. I couldn't tell if she was being funny, or dead serious. Add another layer to the guilt-coat I already had on.

Ah, here was a message from Julie. If there was one person I could count on to understand how busy I was, it was my best friend. Julie was a saint to put up with my crazy life these days. Funny how I talked about her all the time in my seminars, using examples from our real-life relationship, but the times we'd actually hung out over the past year were minimal.

"Hi! I figured I wouldn't catch you. I can't

remember when you said you'd be back in town, but thought I'd check. Mary's having a CAbi party at her house tomorrow night, and I thought we could go to it together if you're around. Call me when you have time." There was something about Julie's voice that sounded resigned, or disappointed, as if she didn't expect much from me anymore.

Julie's invitation for *tomorrow night* would now be tonight. Wednesday. No, I wouldn't be back in town. I'd call Julie later.

You won't have time.

Well, I couldn't call her now. It was too early back home, and I knew Julie rarely turned her cell phone off. As much as I missed talking to her I knew a predawn call wasn't what Julie had in mind. With my thumb, I pressed the number seven to delete the call. I wouldn't forget to call my friend later.

One more message to listen to. I smiled as I heard Jim's familiar voice. We'd played phone tag the entire time we'd been apart. The three hour time difference made catching up with each other nearly impossible. I pressed the phone closer to my cheek as if I could hold him close. "Hi, Honey. Thought I might be able to catch you. Hope your conference is going well. I'm sorry I left things—" There was a cough on the other end of the line. "Sorry," he said into the phone. Another catch in his throat. Then, "I've gotta go." The call was disconnected. Pulling the phone from my ear, I glared at the screen, wishing I could see right through it to my husband. No good-bye. No "love you."

A disquieting feeling settled into my stomach. I hoped Jim wasn't catching a cold. No, my instincts told me, not a cold. It was hard to pinpoint the source of my anxiety. Jim felt a thousand miles away. He *was* a thousand miles away. Too far. We'd spent almost four days on opposite ends of the U.S. in addition to the distant way we'd left things between us before we went our separate ways. *I'm sorry I left things*—I knew what he meant, but why did he feel the need to bring it up now? We'd been married long enough to know that disgruntled feelings passed. Suddenly I couldn't wait to get this conference over and be home.

I looked around my hotel room. This was one of the nicer places I'd stayed over the past many months, but it didn't make up for being away from everyone I loved. I'd done my share of tossing and turning in small-town hotels, too . . . wishing I was in my own bed next to my husband. When I got home it might be time to sit down with Jim and draft a plan that would guide us into the future. He'd flat-out said he wanted to sell the stores, and while I wasn't quite ready to chuck it all and sail off into the sunset, I was ready to agree that the way we were living—each of us going our separate ways—was not how I envisioned our life together. I loved what I was doing, but the newness was wearing off. Instead of veiled complaints about each of us being too busy, it was time for us to sit down like mature adults and be intentional about our careers . . . and our life together.

Together. That was the key. What was the point of all my busyness if I ended up in a hotel room by myself? Life *alone* wasn't what I was after. If I didn't have time to spend with Jim, my kids, my grandson, or my best friend, well then, what was the point of all my speech-making on friendship?

I gave my head a shake. I certainly didn't have time to solve my dilemma in the next few minutes, or even today. What I needed was to get dressed and get downstairs for the Continental breakfast. Muffins and more coffee. And then I'd step up on stage and tell these women how to be better friends to each other.

And you won't tell them how you no longer have time for your own friendships.

No, I would leave out that part. I pushed myself out of the chair. Wallowing in hypocrisy wouldn't get me through this day. In a rush I got dressed and then stood in front of the full-length mirror giving myself a once-over. Everything was buttoned and tucked. My hair was sprayed into place. It would have to stay that way because I'd be lucky to set foot back in this room for another fourteen hours.

I tucked my talk notes into a folder and stuck the folder into the small, wheeled briefcase that held everything I needed for the day. The last thing I did was to slip my feet into what I called my "big girl" shoes. Three-inch heels that filled me with a sense of authority and competence, but left my toes numb by the end of the day. If only I could cop a lesson from *Barbie*. Plastic feet would come in handy on a day like today.

Ready. I grabbed my cell phone, turned it off, and slid it into a pocket in my purse.

Aren't you forgetting something?

What? I scanned the room one more time. Nope. I had everything.

What about Me? Remember?

I closed my eyes and forced myself to take a calming breath. It was only by the grace of God my books had hit the bestseller lists, that I had the privilege of sharing my message in front of so many people. The irony of it all was that I was so busy I rarely had time to say thanks. My prayer time was at a premium, and I didn't have more than a couple seconds this morning to whisper, "Be with me. Be with the women here today."

I lifted my head and caught a glimpse of my face in the mirror by the hotel room door. I had that deer-in-the-headlights look . . . as if I needed to hurry up and run. Which is exactly what I'd have to do if we were going to keep this seminar on track today.

. . .

"Mrs. Westin? Claire? I hope it's okay if I call you that?" A wide-eyed young woman fell into step beside me as I entered the banquet hall where a breakfast buffet was set up. "After listening to you for the past two days, well, you seem like my friend." She giggled nervously. "I mean, I know you don't really know me, but I feel like we're friends. You know?"

She was right about the part that I didn't know her, but what could I say? I smiled politely. "I know," I answered noncommittally.

"I have a story about a friend of mine that I wanted to tell you. Do you mind if I sit with you for breakfast?"

I picked up a small plate from the buffet line. "That would be nice," I said to my newest friend. "Tell me, what's your name?"

"Beth."

And so my day began. Every second spent focused on everyone around me. On their need to share personal stories with me. Wanting at the least, a sympathetic ear. At most, advice on what to do about a broken relationship.

As I broke apart my blueberry muffin—I'd have to be sure and slip into the ladies room and make sure I didn't have blueberry bits in my teeth before I got on stage—Beth's eyes filled with tears. I put down my muffin and laid a hand on her arm. "Oh, no, what's wrong?"

Beth waved a hand in front of her face and half laughed, half cried. "I didn't think I'd—"

"It's okay," I said, leaning close. "I'm used to tears."

So much for eating my muffin. Beth cried as she told me about her rocky relationship with her mother. In the middle of her story, a women tapped me lightly on the shoulder. Couldn't she see I was in the middle of an intense conversation? I held up a finger, letting Beth know I needed to turn away for a second.

"Yes?"

The woman beside me was holding what looked to be a heavy, brown grocery bag. "I was wondering if I could talk to you sometime this morning? I need to leave the conference early and I have something I know you'll be interested in hearing."

Okay . . . "Um . . ." I looked toward Beth. She wasn't eating, she was looking down at her folded hands, blinking at her tears. It didn't look like she would be wrapping up her story anytime soon. I turned back to the woman. "There's a break after the first session. Why don't you catch me then."

"I'm Marion," she said, shifting the grocery bag from one arm to the other. "Do you want me to meet you by the stage?"

She was going to make sure she didn't miss me.

"Sure." There went my chance at a bathroom break.

• • •

"Here I am." Ms. Grocery Bag lady was standing at the bottom of the steps leading from the stage, waving one hand. I would have had to trip over her to get past her, but she seemed to think I might not see her.

I wracked my brain, trying to remember her name. I'd probably talked briefly with at least twenty women already this morning. Names were running through my mind like a stock market ticker tape and I was coming up blank.

Grimacing as if in apology, I touched Ms. Grocery Bag's hand. "Remind me of your name again."

I didn't miss her quick look of annoyance. "Marion."

"Oh, that's *right.*" I rolled my eyes to illustrate to her that I was a hopeless case. "Marion. Now what was it you wanted to talk to me about?" I tried my hardest to concentrate on the woman in front of me, but out of the corner of my eye I could see a couple other women standing nearby. They were chatting with each other as if they'd just met, and both of them kept casting glances my way . . . a sure sign they would jump in as soon as Marion was through. In the back of the room, there were several women browsing at my book table. Thankfully, a couple of the conference-sponsor women were there to make change, but they couldn't autograph the books for me.

". . . and that's why I thought of you." Marion passed the heavy grocery bag into my arms.

I looked down into the bag. It was filled with scraps of paper and small old-looking books. And that was only what I could see at the top. The bag was packed solid. "What's in here?"

Marion smiled and sighed as she pressed her open palms together and brought her fingertips to rest under her chin. "These are diaries and letters that my great-grandmother left behind. She has an amazing story, and I *know* you're going to want to write it."

I couldn't help myself. "Me?"

"Oh, yes." Marion's tone held no doubt. "I wouldn't trust anyone but you."

"But I—"

"My great-grandmother was a fascinating woman. This book will be a bestseller. Of course I'd share the royalties—"

"I'm sorry." I thrust the bag back into her arms. "I'm honored you thought of me, but, really, I can't do this. This isn't the kind of story for me to—"

Marion's expression shifted from hopeful to hesitant. She held the bag toward me again. "If you'll look through her papers, I know you'll want to . . ." Her words trailed off.

I shook my head. Time for damage control. "I'm sorry, Marion. I have contracts to fulfill with my publisher. This isn't my story to tell. Why don't *you* work on writing the story of your great-grand-mother's life?"

"I'm not a writer." Marion was turning snippy.

"I'm sorry," I said, again. "This isn't the kind of project I do."

She shifted the grocery bag onto her hip and pressed her lips into a thin line. "No," she said, "I'm the one that's sorry." She turned on her heel and stalked off, leaving me feeling like one big failure.

It wasn't enough that I'd shared from my heart for two-and-a-half days. That I'd stayed up talking with a number of women until almost midnight every night, listening to them pour their problems out to me. That every meal set in front of me was left mostly uneaten because I'd been expected to listen to another stranger's life story. No matter what I did, it wasn't enough.

With my fingertips, I pressed hard against the bridge of my nose. I couldn't cry now. Marion hadn't meant to hurt me. I was tired and oversensitive. By this time tomorrow, I'd be on my way to the airport. Almost home. Then would be the time to take a hard look at how much more, how much longer, I wanted to keep this up.

"Claire?" One of the women who'd been standing off to my side approached. "I hope I'm not—Is everything okay?"

"Fine," I said, plastering a quick smile on my face. "Just a little tired." At least that part wasn't a lie. "What did you want to talk to me about?"

"I have a funny friendship story to tell you. I thought you might like to use it in one of your talks."

This time tomorrow, I repeated like a mantra. *This time tomorrow.*

I flushed the toilet, made sure everything was pulled down where it should be, and that my skirt wasn't tucked into the backside of my panty hose. I then hurried out of the bathroom stall. As I washed my hands I grinned into the mirror, doing a quick check to make sure there was nothing stuck in my teeth. Ahead of me were the last two hours of the conference. The final session. The time I'd been waiting for all day.

Briefly I closed my eyes, trying to focus on the talk I'd be giving to close out the conference.

Call home.

My eyes flew open. I didn't have time to call home. I needed to remember the opening lines of my speech. My mind might be jumbled with the many events of the past few days, but I knew for a fact the opening lines of my final session did not include the words "call home."

Call home.

Wherever that random thought was coming from, I didn't have time for that luxury right now. Reaching into my jacket pocket, I pulled out my lipstick and ran the color across my lips, smacking them together to seal in the color. What was the first sentence of my talk? I couldn't go blank now. This was the—

Call home.

A nervous sensation crawled across my stomach. I always had a few butterflies before I went on stage, but this was different. I pulled in a deep breath, trying to calm my anxiety. If anything was wrong certainly—

Someone would call you.

Of course they would. But there was nothing wrong. I was overtired. Four days away from home had taken their toll. Even if "fifty was the new thirty," I had to remember I was fifty-four, on the upper end of middle age. I might have been able to burn the candle at both ends twenty years ago, but these days I was lucky to have the stub end of a candle left by the end of one of these conferences. What I needed was a good night's sleep and a week at home to refuel.

I applied another layer of color to my lips. In spite of my little pep talk, the urge to check in at home still nagged. There was a singing and door-prize time starting in a few minutes. If I timed things right, I could dial in and check my phone messages, and see if there were any fires to put out once I returned home tomorrow. I did some quick time figuring. With the time change between here and Carlton, Jim's plane should have landed about the time I had wrapped up the afternoon session and gone in to dinner. Knowing Jim, the first place he headed was to the store. I smiled to myself, imagining him rifling through the mail that had piled on his desk while he was gone. It was somehow comforting to think about both of us getting back into our old routine. Right about now I could use a little same-old, same-old. By this time tomorrow, I'd be at home with Jim. He'd be in his recliner. I'd be curled up on a corner of the couch. The tension that had hung between us when we both went our separate ways four days ago would disappear just by the fact that we were back home together. Why didn't we make more time for little things like that? When I got home, I was going to take a good long look at my schedule. What was the point in all of this if I didn't have time to spend with the people who mattered most in my life?

Pocketing my lipstick, I glanced at my watch. Maybe I had time to make a quick call home. It would be good to hear Jim's voice. Set my anxieties to rest. The only glitch was that I'd left my phone in my purse, which was tucked into a back corner of the stage where I'd be giving my final presentation. No one would notice if I wasn't there for the singing. I usually only mouthed the words anyway, saving my voice for the talking I needed to do in the hour ahead. Maybe I could sneak in a side entrance near the stage and snatch my purse from the corner.

"Claire?" A woman at the sink next to me caught my eye in the mirror. She squirted soap onto her hands and began washing them. "I want to tell you how much I'm enjoying the conference. When you talked about your mother's death and all those unfinished projects she had, and how that had led you to write your friendship book . . ." She paused as she pulled her hands from the stream of water and grabbed a paper towel. "That story was so inspiring. Oh—" She blushed and hurried on with her words. "I didn't mean about your mom dying. Oh, goodness, I stuck my foot in my mouth again."

"Don't worry." I touched her arm. "I think I know what you mean."

"Thank you," she said. "For understanding. And for sharing so honestly with us."

Now it was my turn to feel warmth creeping into my neck, onto my cheeks. If I was going to be perfectly honest with these women, I would get up on stage and tell them about the way reaching for my dream had distanced me from the really important people in my life. But, I didn't think that was a story they would pay money to hear. I pushed a smile onto my face. "I'm glad you're enjoying the conference."

"Oh, I am. I'm just sorry it'll be over tonight."

I was glad she felt that way, but I didn't quite share her sorrow . . . of course, I wouldn't tell her that. "It's been fun." That much I could say.

I walked with her out of the bathroom, listening to her compliments about the conference, all the while plotting for a way to get to my cell phone. That nagging sensation to call home hadn't left.

"I'm going to head this way," I said, pointing to the right, as the woman waited for me to turn left, toward the hotel ballroom entrance. After four days in the hotel, I'd learned the shortcuts to where I needed to be. And right now I was needed by my purse.

"Claire! There you are." Elaine, one of the women who helped organize the conference, grabbed me by the arm and turned me around to walk with her the opposite direction I'd been headed. "They're looking for you by the book table. There's a line of women waiting for you to sign books. And the next session is almost ready to start."

Which is exactly why I wanted to get to my phone now. Instead, I hurried along beside Elaine. A line at the book table took precedence over a vague sense that I should call home.

"Here she is." Elaine pulled me to the book table as if I was a prize-sized trout she'd caught. The women waiting in line looked anxious, as if they were afraid they were going to miss out on the session by standing in line.

I could put them at ease with a practiced line. "The good thing about being the speaker," I said, as I picked up a pen, "is that the event can't start until I get there."

They laughed as I began signing books. Even though the music and singing had started, that didn't stop other women from jumping into the book-signing line. I would have loved a moment to myself. To gather my thoughts. Say a quick prayer. Not to mention give my tired legs a break. My feet, tucked into my three-inch heels, were killing me, and, while the ladies standing in my line would get to sit down for the next hour, I'd be standing on stage delivering my talk, my toes going numb.

The persistent sensation that I should call home snapped at the edges of my concentration. I needed to focus on the task in front of me. No matter what was going on at home, I couldn't do anything about it from here anyway.

You could pray.

No, I couldn't do even that. Not with a line of women in front of me. What I needed to do now was sign books. Make chitchat.

Call home.

I could feel tension tugging at my neck, clamping around my temples. The sure signs of a headache coming on. "Elaine?" I turned to seek her out behind my book table.

"Yes." Instantly she was at my side, as if I was some kind of celebrity.

"I wonder if I could ask you to do a favor?" As an explanation for my request, I glanced at the women still waiting to have their books signed. It was obvious I was stranded here for a while.

"What can I get you?" Elaine asked.

"My purse. It's up there, next to the stage. On the floor."

"Got it," Elaine said, already on her way.

Okay, so there were some perks to this gig of mine. Having a person like Elaine ready to do my bidding could get addictive.

In short order Elaine was back with my slouchy bag. I whispered to her, "I really need to check my phone messages. I haven't had a moment all day, and . . ."

And what? How to explain an obscure urge to call home?

Elaine didn't need an explanation. She held her arm behind the second person in the book signing line. "We're going to have to cut things off right here. Claire will be back to sign your books after the closing session."

I could use a little of Elaine's moxie.

Thank you, I mouthed to her. Grateful beyond words for the couple minutes she bought me. I scrawled my name into two copies of my books and then grabbed my phone out of my purse and stepped into the hotel hallway, away from the singing inside.

I flipped open my phone. *Ten missed calls,* the screen read.

Ten calls? There must be some mistake. The only person I could think who might call was Jim, to let me know he'd gotten back to Carlton. But he would know I'd be at my sessions. He'd leave a message and wait for me to get back to him.

My heart took up an ominous thump. The music inside and the voices of others in the hall drifted into near silence as a cold, distant ringing filled my ears. Something was wrong.

I bypassed the time it would take to check my messages and called Jim's number at the store.

"Westin Foods, how can I help you?"

There was no time for niceties. "Is Jim there? Jim Westin?"

"No," said whoever it was who answered, "he hasn't come back from his trip, yet."

But he should have been back a couple hours ago. The Jim I knew would head straight to the store. In the midst of our quick conversation, I heard the insistent beep that told me I had a message waiting. I said a curt "good-bye" and cut off the call. A thousand possibilities swirled through my brain. It always seemed as if it took forever to jump through the cell phone maze to retrieve messages, and I was expected on stage in a couple minutes. Calling Jim would be faster. I punched in our home number. Once again, as I listened to the unanswered ringing, the message signal beeped. When our answering machine picked up I disconnected the call. Now what? Jim rarely had his cell phone on when he was in Carlton.

The loudspeaker system in the ballroom carried the sounds of the conference out into the hall. The singing had been replaced by a woman giving some end-of-the-session announcements. Putting in a plug for the possibility of having another Friendship Factor seminar next year. There would be one more song and then I'd be called to the stage.

I pressed the speed dial number that would connect me to my message in-box, then punched in my PIN number. If I had ten messages, there would be no time for me to listen to them.

The recorded voice announced, "You have ten unheard messages. Message number one."

"Mom." Drew's familiar voice came on the line, except there was an edge to it I hardly recognized. There was a long pause, then a rapid flow of words. "Call me when you get this."

"Message number two."

"Mom." Drew again. "I'm at the hospital. Call me-e." His voice cracked.

The hospital? A heavy lump pulsed in the place where my heart was supposed to beat. Had something happened to Will? He'd been born with a hole in his heart, but after his operation as a newborn he'd been given a good-to-go designation from his doctor. Had something gone terribly wrong?

"Message number three."

I wiped a sweaty palm against the side of my skirt, not so sure I wanted to hear any more.

"Mom!" It was Kaylee now. "You have to get

here. Where are you? Why aren't you answering your phone? We need you!"

"Message number four." How could even an automated operator sound so calm in the midst of what was unfolding on my cell phone?

Oh, Lord. Please.

The first word I heard was a mild curse. Drew, again. Whatever was happening, it had to be bad. I had no illusions that my son was a saint, but he never swore in front of me. Not until now. "The doctor is going to do surgery. You need to get here." He snapped off the call.

From the conference hall, I heard the music stop and an expectant quiet settle over the crowd inside. Someone in front of the microphone cleared her throat and began my introduction. There was no time to listen to the rest of the messages. No time to pray. Right now all I could do was stride to the front of the room and give my speech. There would be time for phone calls, and praying, when I was done.

If it wasn't too late for prayers by then.

I powered down my phone, entered the ballroom, and slipped my phone into my purse. All I could do now was pace at the back of the large room. It was time for the program to begin, and all I could think about was how far away I would be from my cell phone. About how far away I was from whatever was happening at home. Where I *should* be.

392

"I'm so honored to once again be introducing our keynote speaker for tonight." The woman who had picked me up from the airport looked up from the microphone and smiled at me in the back of the room.

I gave her a little wave to let her know I'd heard. What was her name? Linda? Cindy? *Come onnnn.* I squeezed my eyes shut and tried to remember. Her name would come to me. Maybe. This wouldn't be the first time I'd blanked out on a name. I knew how to handle it. *"Oh, good grief, I know I know your name but it flew right out of my head,"* I'd say. *"Half-heimers,"* I'd add, pointing to the side of my lame-brain. Everyone would laugh at that. After all, who in their right mind had never forgotten a name?

But forgetting the name of the person who had picked me up at the airport? Sheesh . . . that was different. There were too many distractions pounding inside my head right now. *Concentrate.* Miss No-name had met me at baggage claim, with bottled water and a flower-stenciled "Welcome Claire" sign. She'd insisted on lifting my overpacked suitcase into her car trunk, even after I told her I wouldn't pay for hernia surgery. *Ha, ha.* I'd spent almost an hour in the car with her, listening to her talk about what a difference my books had made in her life. I'd listened to her from-the-airport-to-the-hotel length story about the discussion she and her best friend had after they'd read my latest book. There were some names a person *should* remember, and I couldn't. Not tonight.

Nervously, I rubbed my fingers across my heavy necklace, fingered my earrings, touched the thick, gold bracelet on my wrist. Everything was in place . . . except my train of thought.

My eyes flicked to my purse tucked under a corner of my book table. My cell phone was in there, a potential time bomb waiting in my message in-box.

I shouldn't be here. I should be—

". . . I can't begin to tell you what this woman has meant to my life." There was a catch in Miss-Suitcase-Lifter's throat.

Oh, please, don't cry. If you only knew. I'm not half the person you think I am.

The lady at the podium lifted her hand my way, as if her audience had the same view of me she did. I turned up the corners of my lips . . . I knew what was expected of me.

An hour. In one hour I'd be done. Then I could check the rest of my messages. It seemed that was all I'd been doing lately.

She turned back to the group, hardly looking at her notes. "As you may know, Ms. Westin's first book, *The Friendship Factor*, went on to top the charts of bestseller lists across the country. She has appeared on the *Today* show and *Good Morning America*, and has been invited to share her message to women's groups around the country. Her Friendship Factor workshops are sold out almost before the tickets go on sale."

There was a knowing bubble of laughter from the women in the audience. They could laugh, they'd been lucky enough to get those tickets.

"When she's not writing and speaking, Ms. Westin teaches sociology at a university near her home. In her spare time, she enjoys having coffee with friends and playing the piano. She also loves to spend time with her husband, three grown children, assorted in-laws, her grandson, friends, and a pesky dog named Pesto."

Another ripple of laughter. They were listening to every word. Thank goodness they didn't know how *little* time I had to spend doing any of those *things I enjoy* listed on my bio.

Miss Speaker looked down at her notes and gave a chuckle into the microphone. "Let's put it this way," she went on, "if I stood here and told you all of our presenter's accomplishments, we'd be here all night. You know her name as well as I do. So please join me in giving a warm welcome tooooo . . ."

There was an orchestrated pause as I began striding toward the front of the ballroom.

"Here she is, ladies, everyone's best friend, the Friendship Doctor . . . Claire Westin!"

Waving my right arm, the arm *upstage* from the audience so they could see my face, I grinned toward the vast, dark, applauding mass and strode across the stage.

Energy, I reminded myself. *Project energy.* I couldn't see a thing with the stage lights blinding me. But my audience didn't know that. I paused beside the podium and lifted my hands toward the conference room filled with applauding women. I turned to the woman who had introduced me. *Linda!* That was her name. "Linda. Thank you," I whispered into her ear, and gave her a hug before she left the stage.

"Goodness," I said, stepping behind the podium and arranging the notes I'd already placed there. "Linda made it sound like I know what I'm doing."

Right on cue they laughed.

I could do this. I *had* to do this. I would put myself on autopilot and somehow get through this hour. *Game time.* I pressed a smile onto my lips and slowly turned my head from one side of the auditorium to the other, pretending I could actually *see* the people in front of me. Logic told me there were more than likely a few men in the vast arena, but at a Friendship Factor Women's Conference, chances were the estrogen in the room far outweighed the testosterone.

What am I doing here? Once again, the dogging thought scratched through my concentration. I should be at the hospital. Back in Carlton. With . . . who? My son? My grandson? My dad? Was

Jim there, too? Of course I was supposed to be here, too. Two places at the same time. Impossible. I looked down at the notes in front of me. I knew what they said. I'd repeated the words hundreds of times, and yet right now, I couldn't remember even the first one.

Stalling, I reached below the podium and pulled out the glass of water someone had placed there for me. I smiled as I sipped, patting at the air with my free hand to let the women know they could stop clapping and sit down. They were paying me very good money to be here. I'd worked hard to have an opportunity like this. But right now, I was wishing I was anywhere but here.

I drew in a deep breath. *Focus.* I closed my eyes for one, brief second. *Oh, Lord. Help me.*

I looked out at the sea of expectant faces all centered on me. I knew the words that came next, and the ones after that. I could recite this speech in my sleep if I had to. And so, I would begin.

My amplified voice carried through the large room. "Ladies, are you living the life you want?"

The laughter quieted as my audience took in the question. The words I knew would make them think. Start examining their lives. Their relationships. Were they living the life they imagined? Only they could know.

As for my answer to that question . . . ?

The only answer I could come up with was . . . *no.*

• • •

"Loved. Loved the conference. Every minute of it."

"I can't tell you what listening to you has meant to me."

"I want to be a better friend. The way you talked about your friend Julie, made me want a friend like that."

"Thank you. Thank you." I shook hands. Smiled in a way I hoped was gracious, deflecting their praise. No matter how many times I did this, I never felt I'd done as well as my listeners seemed to think. And that story about Julie and me was ancient history. If these women knew I hadn't checked in with my best friend in weeks, well . . . I didn't want to hear what they'd have to say then. I pushed my hair back from my face. Every time I finished one of my talks, I felt warm. Make that *hot*. The combination of adrenaline and nerves served as instant menopause. Tonight I could add "imposter" to my resumé. A woman who preached friendship, but didn't have anything to show for it. I hadn't talked to my husband in four days. My dad had to leave his medical test results in my voice mail in-box. My daughter couldn't even remember where I was . . . or when I was returning. I hadn't seen my daughter-in-law or my grandchild in much too long. And all of that paled in comparison to the urgent phone messages I'd ignored right before stepping on stage. If only these women knew the truth. Then I might get all that free time I'd been wishing for.

On autopilot, I stood at the end of my book table, chatting, signing books, accepting thanks for a great conference. My cell phone was on vibrate inside my purse. If I had the slightest break in the line, I planned to grab it and call Drew. Maybe by now, the emergency—whatever it was—had passed. In the back of my mind I sent up a silent prayer that my wishful hoping was true.

Tomorrow would be a travel day for me, but I was going to clear my calendar for the rest of the week, and weekend, and do nothing but devote my time to the important people in my life. Jim and I could go out for a long dinner and catch up. I'd invite Dad over for a meal. I'd offer to take Kaylee shopping on Saturday. Julie and I could meet for coffee on Sunday afternoon. And the first thing I'd do after I unpacked would be to make a date to play with my grandson.

Before I could do any of that, I needed to bring this night to a close. There were small groups of women standing near me, visiting with one another. No doubt a few of them were waiting to purchase books before they left. But there was no one standing in front of me right now. I bent to pull my purse out from beneath the table and caught Elaine's eye.

"I need to make a phone call," I said. "I'm going to step into the hall. If anyone wants a book signed, I'll be right back."

"Go on. Do you want me to start packing things up?"

"You can wait a few minutes." I knew once the books started to be put away, another small wave of people wanting to pick up books would flow toward the table. It would be best to wait until I was back in place.

The screen of my phone showed that I'd missed another two calls while I'd given my talk. Using my thumb, I flipped the phone open and speed-dialed Drew's number. It rang several times and then went to his voice mail in-box. Now it was my turn to snap the phone shut. Why had he been so intent on reaching me, and then wasn't around to pick up when I called?

If he was at the hospital, maybe he was in an area that didn't allow cell phones. Didn't hospitals limit the use of cell phones in the heart-care areas? *Will. Something's gone wrong with Will.* Frustration wrestled with worry and anxiety inside my chest. What more could I do but keep trying to reach someone?

I opened my phone and tried our home number. This time as it rang, an incoming-call signal beeped in my ear. I pressed the button to transfer lines. "Hello?" I could hear the anxious sound of my voice.

"Mom, where in the heck have you been?" Drew's tone was filled with aggravation, but I had to give him kudos for not swearing. He didn't wait for me to answer. "You have to get home. Dad's in surgery. We're waiting for the doc—"

"Dad's in surgery?" The words weren't making sense. In the quick imagining I'd done, I thought something might be happening to my grandson or my father . . . not my husband. My hand turned icy as I clung to my only connection to home. "What? Why? Surgery?"

"Dad had a heart attack, Mom. At the airport, when he came back from his trip." The rest of the conversation filtered through in frantic bits and pieces.

"Ambulance," Drew said.

"Triple bypass," I heard next.

"It's bad. You need to come home."

It's bad. It's bad. Drew's words rang in my ears as I assured him I'd get home as soon as possible. In a flurry of hurried sentences, I explained to Elaine what had happened at home in the past few hours. She offered to pray and pack up my things while I went back to my hotel room to call the airlines and book the next flight home.

"Argh!" I stabbed at the "end call" button on my cell phone, stopping the automated recording mid-sentence. What was so wrong about having an actual *human* answer an airline phone number?

I rummaged through my flight information, looking for an alternative phone number. I'd booked my flight online directly through the airline, but the number on my travel voucher matched the one I'd found in the phone book.

Lord, Lord, please, Lord. The prayer ran parallel with my thoughts, as I powered up my laptop to try and find another option. I wasn't sure which I was praying for more, for Jim in surgery, or for me to find a way to be by his side.

Ten minutes of digging through the airline website led me to a new phone number. I punched in the numbers as fast as I could. This time, I was determined to stay on the line until I talked to a person who could help me get home. Punching my way through an automated routing system, I was finally connected to a real, live, living, breathing airline worker. *Thank you, Lord.*

"Please," I started, "I need help."

Within five minutes, I'd been told there were no more flights to my destination tonight. There was an early morning flight that would get me as far as Minneapolis, but it was fully booked. I could show up at the airport and hope someone didn't show, or I could take my scheduled early-afternoon flight home.

"I'm sorry," the airline call-center employee said as if he heard these kinds of stories all the time.

I closed my eyes and closed my phone. The thought of getting a rental car and driving back to North Dakota flitted across my mind, but I rejected it as impossible. Not only was I too tired to drive through the night, the distance made flying from Ohio—even by waiting overnight— the only reasonable option.

I set my phone on the table by my laptop and pressed my palms together, touching my fingertips to my lips. I'd spent all day on my feet. Now it was time to get on my knees. The only option now was to pray. Something I'd done way too little of lately.

I planned to make up for that tonight.

Jim

"Jim!" Someone shook my shoulder, rousing me out of a deep, deep sleep.

"Uhh-hh." I moaned, fighting to open my eyes. *Ohhhh.* Pain. Bright lights. Too bright. I didn't want to wake up.

"Jim! Try to wake up now."

There was that loud voice again. An antiseptic smell. Soft beeps I couldn't make sense of. It took a Herculean effort, but I managed to open my eyes and peer through the slit of my lids. A blurry, unfamiliar face looked back at me. My eyes drifted shut.

"You're doing fine."

Why didn't she leave me alone?

"Wake up."

Once again, I tried to open my eyes. I could feel

my eyelids flutter as my eyeballs rolled back into my head. Why did I need to wake up?

"We're taking you to ICU now."

Fine. I didn't care. Whatever. I had no strength to do anything for myself.

I had a vague sense of being wheeled down a hallway. Was I in an elevator? Going up? Down?

"I'll be your nurse tonight." A woman was speaking loudly in my ear. "My name is Doris." Soft hands adjusted my covers and positioned my arms just so on top of them. All I wanted was to be left alone. To sleep away the heavy, burning pain in my chest.

"I'm going to let your son and daughter in to see you." Doris was standing at the foot of my bed. "They can only stay five minutes. Don't try to talk. Take it easy."

What did she think? That I was going to get up and dance the rumba?

Through the covers I felt a hand on my foot.

Claire. Had I said that out loud? Maybe not. There was something helping me breathe. "Claire?" Oh, how I wanted it to be her.

"Dad, it's me, Kaylee."

"Ah." Or did I only manage to groan?

"I'm here, too, Dad." Drew's hand touched my leg.

Neither one asked how I was. Somehow I managed to raise my eyelids half-mast. No wonder they hadn't asked how I was feeling—their pale, drawn faces told it all.

"Your . . . Mom?" Two words were the best I could do.

"She's going to get here. As soon as she can. She said to tell you she's praying. She's got the women from her conference praying, too."

I let my eyes fall shut. If Claire had strangers several states away praying for me, I must be really bad off.

When had the kids left?

My room felt brighter. Daytime? Or maybe my awareness was the anesthesia wearing off. Yes, that must be it. I had a vague recollection of nurses coming through the night. Checking my blood pressure. Taking note of the monitors hooked to my body. I remembered Drew and Kaylee standing at the end of my bed . . . didn't I? Had my son, Reed, been here, too? Had Claire sat at my side, or did I only dream her?

No, Claire hadn't been here. I would have remembered that. Panic rose behind my aching breastbone. Where was she? An elephant was sitting on my chest. What if I died before I got to see Claire again? My eyes darted from side to side, searching the sterile room. Wasn't there anyone watching over me? Where were they? Didn't they know I needed help? The steady beat of the monitor seemed to grow faster. My breath came short, shallow. Even with oxygen assisting my breathing, I couldn't fill my lungs. Was I dying?

405

Help! Why couldn't someone see I needed help?

"Good morning, Jim." A new nurse walked into the room. "How was your night?"

Was she kidding?

She checked the monitors. Changed the IV bag. Chatting all the while, as if this was an ordinary day. Maybe it was . . . for her.

"We're going to be moving you out of ICU into the cardiac care unit. You're doing great."

If this was what great felt like, I wasn't sure I wanted to get any better.

"It's time for your pain medication."

The magic words I'd been waiting to hear.

"I'm going to let your son in. Only five minutes. Don't overdo it."

Right.

"Hey, Dad." Drew lifted his hand half-mast. It didn't look as if he'd had a much better night than I had. He must have spent the night at the hospital. Either that, or he'd decided to go for the scruffy look.

"Mom?" I asked, the single word an effort.

"She's coming. She couldn't get a flight home until this afternoon. She'll be here."

"Good." Knowing she was on her way was enough. I closed my eyes and let the morphine do its trick.

I was at the store. Or maybe I was in the bank board room. If it was the bank, there were groceries on the board room table. I needed to get to them and put them on the shelves. How could people buy groceries if they weren't on display? But there were bars across the door, keeping me away. Grasping the cold bars in my hands, I rattled them as if in a cage. They wouldn't budge. "Let me in," I hollered into the empty room. "I need to get in." A person I didn't recognize appeared inside the room. "Go away," he said. "You're not needed here."

My eyes shot open. I wasn't at the store. I was in the hospital. The morphine had done more than numb my pain. The drug had reminded me my days of working nonstop at the store were over. This suffocating pain was proof of that. Who would I be now . . . what would I do without my work at the store?

The answer came in an instant. An invalid. I'd sit around the house and do nothing but nurse my injured arteries. My heart attack had appeared without warning. Who knew what else lurked in my body, ready to strike when I was least expecting it. I was going to have to slow down. Sell the stores. A concept that had been fine when I'd been in charge of the plan, but something altogether different when it felt as if my work was being ripped from me.

A watery, cold fear washed from my chest down into both arms, up into my neck, rushing into my ears. My fingers were icy. Why couldn't I get warm?

"Jim." Another new nurse appeared in the doorway. What did they do? Change shifts every fifteen minutes? Or maybe I was sleeping through their shifts. I had no idea what time meant anymore. "We're going to get you up walking now."

Now? No way. I could barely breathe. How could I possibly get up and walk? It would take a miracle to get me out of this bed.

The nurse approached the bed and carefully pulled back my covers. She stayed busy arranging and rearranging the various tubes connecting me to my lifelines . . . or whatever they were.

"Let's get your legs over the edge of the bed now," she said.

Where was Drew when I needed him? I didn't have the strength to argue, much less get up and walk.

The nurse was gentle . . . but firm. There was no stopping her. Somehow I was standing.

She pulled a rolling stand, with an oxygen canister attached, near me. "Your son said to tell you he was going home to shower. He was here all night and most of today."

Fine for him to ditch out right when I needed him at my bedside.

"We'll take it slow."

I had a choice of giving the nurse a look-to-kill or breathing. Lucky for her I chose to breathe.

It seemed to take forever for me to shuffle as far as the door. The nurse was patient as I stopped

between each step to power up ...
cule shuffle. We turned into th...
escaped my lips as I took in t...
front of me.

"Don't worry," she said. "I'm no...
you walk the whole way. We'll on...
the elevators."

She might as well have told me I w...
walk to California.

My room was one of the closest to th...
bank, a small fact that had me sending up...
of thankfulness.

"See," the nurse said, when we'd reache...
goal. "That wasn't so bad."

I was ready to give her a smart remark when...
elevator doors opened. I was busy focusing on t...
carpet, willing myself to take one more ste...
before I could turn around. A man stepped out—I
could tell by his shoes. Then, a quick gasp and a
cry of surprise caused me to look up.

"Claire."

My wife was standing in the elevator. Her eyes
were wide, and her hands pressed to her mouth as
she got a good look at me. I could only imagine
what she saw. Tubes running from my body to the
pole accompanying my shuffle. My wrinkled,
light blue hospital garb. An oxygen hose hanging
from my nose. I hadn't showered or shaved in
almost two days. I had to look like a caricature of
the man she married.

n the other hand, looked like a small piece
en.

e elevator doors began to close she held out
and stopped them from closing. Stepping
f the elevator, she stood in front of me.
ly, carefully, first one side, then the other, she
er soft hands on either side of my face. She
them there, cupping my face, letting her skin
m mine.

Oh, Jim." Her eyes filled with tears. Mine did,
She leaned forward, tilting my head with her
nds, and gently kissed me on the forehead.

For the first time since I'd been stricken at the
airport, since I'd woken up from surgery
wracked with pain, since I'd taken my shuffling,
agonizing steps . . . for the first time, I thought I
might live.

TWO MONTHS LATER:
THE WINTER OF DISCONTENT

Drew

"Thanks, everyone." Bob Marsden closed the file
folder on his desk as the other members of the
loan committee picked up their printouts and files
and left the bank president's office.

I lingered behind, taking my time stacking my
papers into a much-too-neat order. There was
something I wanted to ask my boss, but crossing

the line between business and personal issues didn't come easy.

He beat me to the punch. "I've missed your dad at the last two board meetings. How's he doing these days?"

I filled my lungs before answering. "I was going to ask you the same question. Well," I corrected, "I wasn't going to ask about *your* dad . . . I wondered what you thought about mine. How he's doing? You know . . ."

The trouble was, I didn't know. Didn't know what to make of the way my dad was acting . . . or more accurately *wasn't* acting. It had been two months since my dad's heart attack and surgery back in September, and it was all my mom or I could do to coax him out of the house. At least lately he'd been going into the store for a couple hours each day, but his afternoons and evenings were spent in his recliner, or bed, "resting," he called it. "I don't want to overdo."

There was no chance of *overdoing,* the way he sat around. My dad was fifty-eight, old enough to recognize how lucky he was to be given a second chance. But, apparently not smart enough to take it.

Bob Marsden tapped at his desk with a pen, thinking before speaking. "Your dad has had a major life change. A wake-up call, so to speak. It's going to take some time for him—"

"The doctor said six to eight weeks."

"Well, it's been . . . what?"

"Eight weeks exactly."

"You have to remember, Drew, everyone heals differently."

Frustration pushed the words from my mouth. "But my dad's not everyone."

My words were too loud, and they hung in the air. I had no business challenging my boss's diagnosis. I'd asked for his opinion, but as it turned out, I didn't want to hear what he had to say.

Picking up my papers, I pushed myself out of my chair. "Sorry. I didn't mean—"

Bob lifted his fingers from the desktop, stopping my words. "It's okay." He nodded for me to sit down again. "What has you worried?"

Looking at the floor, I shook my head, shrugged a shoulder. "He doesn't want to *do* anything. Mom's been driving him to and from the store. I took him up to Emerson the Saturday before last. And I ran up there myself last week. I stop by the store here every night on my way home to check on things. Heck—" I waved a hand in the air, proving how worked up I was getting, talking about what I'd been holding inside, "—I'm doing everything I can to keep it running." I took a deep breath. "I might as well own the store myself."

A long silence held my words in the air as what I'd blurted sunk in. My eyes widened, locked on my boss. Had he heard what I'd said? Of course he'd *heard,* my volume alone would make not hearing impossible. But had he put any stock in what I'd so cavalierly spouted?

I might as well own the store myself. The idea I'd been running from my whole life.

Bob cleared his throat. "Have you given that idea any thought?"

I ran a hand through my hair, scrubbed at the side of my face. "I've spent my whole life trying *not* to think about it."

"Ahh . . ." Bob lifted his chin as if he understood. "And why is that?"

I stalled a few seconds, wondering if it was appropriate to use my boss as a makeshift therapist. But I'd already laid my cards on the table, so I might as well turn over the rest of my hand. I ran my finger around my collar, loosening my tie a bit. "My dad's wanted me to join him in the store since I was tall enough to stock shelves." Over my boss's shoulder, I looked out the window at the world outside this office. "What kid wants to do exactly what their dad wants them to?" My eyes shifted to Bob, my look the next thing to a challenge. "Especially right out of high school?"

One side of Bob's mouth turned up in understanding. He nodded as I continued. "Dad wanted me to go to college and get a business degree, which I did . . . but not because that's what my dad wanted, it was because that's what *I* wanted. For

413

four years, Dad dropped hints about me coming back to Carlton and joining him in the store. So, of course, I did the *you-can't-tell-me-what-to-do* thing and moved to New York."

"Couldn't get much further away."

"You got it."

"So what brought you back?"

"Besides this job, you mean?" I smiled at what I meant as a little humor in this heavy conversation. I grew serious again. "My son was born with a hole in his heart. All the stuff Trisha and I had to go through with him made us realize we wanted to live closer to family."

"And how's that been for you?"

I caught my lips between my teeth and thought for a minute. "Initially I wanted to say *great,* but honestly? My mom's been so busy with her new career we hardly see her. And my dad has been busy managing the three stores, serving on the bank board, and other stuff. We don't see them nearly as much as I thought we would. But . . ." I paused while I weighed my words. "Knowing they're close by is better. I know if we really needed them, they'd be there."

"Just like you are for your dad now?"

Another long silence let his words sink in. Slowly, I nodded. "Yeah, like that."

"What noise does a cow make?" I trotted a plastic cow up Will's leg. He was eighteen months now, and this was one of the rare minutes when he was sitting still.

"MOO!" he screamed, laughing and grabbing for the toy.

"Are you sure?" I teased. "I think a cow says, 'woof-woof.'"

Will looked at the toy in his hand, and then at his mom, who was sitting on the couch. Trisha looked at him out of the corner of her eye and raised an eyebrow.

"No!" Will shouted. "Moo!"

"You're right, Buddy." I grabbed Will into my arms and gave him a loud raspberry on his stomach. His giggles turned to screams . . . the overly-excited kind.

"You boys." Trisha raised her voice to be heard. "Settle down."

I pulled Will onto my lap and whispered loudly. "We'd better be careful. We're going to make Mom mad."

Will pointed at his mother. "Mom mad."

Trisha laughed. So much for teaching Will what "mad" meant. Will squirmed from my lap and toddled over to a large laundry basket we used to keep his toys corralled. He proceeded to take them out, one by one, examining each as if it was the first time he'd laid eyes on the stuffed animals, blocks, and plastic trucks and cars.

Picking myself off the floor, I slid onto the opposite end of the couch from Trisha. I had things to read that I'd brought home from work, but I didn't have the desire to do anything more than watch my son.

Will grabbed a stuffed lion from the laundry basket and held it my way. "Whi-on," he said, holding it up for me to see.

"Yup, that's a lion," I affirmed, my chest filling with pride. How could such a little thing as hearing my son correctly identify a stuffed animal make me feel like crying out of sheer happiness?

Think about how your dad feels when he sees you as a banker, a husband . . . a father.

A lump pushed its way into the back of my throat, and I blinked at the stinging in my eyes. Oh, man, if I was getting choked up over a stuffed animal, I was going to be a basket case when Will got older.

You're not getting choked up over a stuffed animal. You're emotional thinking about your son becoming an accomplished young man. The way your dad sees you.

Turning my head so Trisha couldn't see, I swiped at my eyes with the back of my hand. Dad's health scare had thrown him for a loop . . . and me along with him. What would I do if I lost my dad?

Funny . . . I hadn't shed a tear when I'd been called to the hospital after my dad had been brought there by ambulance. I'd made the decision to operate when we couldn't reach my mom.

I'd stood by his bedside in the ICU. And then I'd taken on the responsibility of the stores when my dad was out of commission. All that without shedding a tear. Why now?

Because it's too much for one person to handle. And maybe that's how your dad feels, too. Like it's too much.

I pushed myself off the couch and made a beeline for the bathroom, where I could close the door, grab some tissues, and try to make some sense of my overwhelming emotions.

The bathroom was cooler than the rest of the house, a perfect respite for me to think. I blew my nose, and then closed the lid on the toilet and sat down. As I hung my head, more tears came. A sob pushed its way out of my throat.

I didn't want to lose my dad . . . and I hadn't. At least, not yet. But the way he was acting, afraid to do much of anything, made it seem that even without dying, I was losing him a little bit at a time.

You can help him.

But how? I was already doing everything I knew how.

You know how.

Silent sobs doubled me over. I did know. I could quit my job at the bank and join my dad in business. I could do what he couldn't. There was a Bible verse Trisha and I had read at our wedding. I didn't remember it exactly, but it was something about two being better than one, and *three,* meaning God, was even better. It was the same with my dad and me. Both of us together in the store would be better.

God, I cried, *is this really what You want?*

Is it what you want?

I grabbed the hand towel off the edge of the sink and pressed it to my face. Why was He leaving this up to me? All I wanted was an answer. A "yes" or a "no." I wanted someone to tell me what to do.

Tell me, Lord. Tell me.

Your Father has been telling you all along.

Through my tears, I drew in a shaky breath as the words settled in my soul. I wasn't sure if the answer I heard meant my dad or my heavenly Father had been telling me. All I knew was that my answer was clear. Everything I'd ever done . . . going to college for business, moving to New York and then marrying a girl from the Midwest, Will's health issues that had brought me back home, Dad's heart attack . . . everything, absolutely *everything,* had brought me to right now. All my running had brought me full circle. And the strange thing was, knowing the answer, getting back to where I knew I belonged, made me feel incredibly free.

I stood up and stepped to the sink, splashed icy cold water on my face, then dried it with the hand towel I'd used to soak up my tears. I looked into the mirror and watched as a slow grin spread across my face with the realization: *I was going to go into business with my dad.* A business I had a knack for. The job I'd been training for my whole life. Finally, I was going to do what I'd been put on earth to do.

I high-fived myself in the mirror. All that was left was to tell Trisha, and then seal the deal with my dad.

Claire

I held the cell phone to my ear as I watched the back door of the store from inside my car. Jim had called me a half-hour ago to tell me he'd be ready to come home at two-thirty. Well, it was two-thirty-seven, according to the clock on my dash-board, and he hadn't shown, yet. As the phone rang, I tapped my foot against the floorboard of my car. It wasn't as if I had all afternoon to sit in the alley and wait for Jim to show up. I was working on another book in the Friendship Factor series . . . *Friendship for Forty-somethings* . . . and it was hard to get much accomplished when I had to play taxi driver. Not to mention having him around the house practically round-the-clock. It would be different if he really needed me . . . but the doctor said Jim could resume driving weeks ago. But without saying a word, Jim had let me know he didn't feel confident enough to drive. I was doing my best to be supportive. After all, I'd promised "for better for worse." But I'd never said anything about being a chauffeur.

"Jim," I said into the phone when he picked up, "I'm waiting out back." I did my best to keep my irritation from my voice. It had been eight long weeks since Jim's heart attack, two months that changed the go-getter man I married into a shell of his former self. I was at my wit's end what to do with him. This wasn't the man I married.

Before I had a chance to really work myself up, Jim stepped out the back door and carefully made his way down the steps. I held my breath as I watched him grab onto the railing for support. If I didn't know better, I'd swear the man moving slowly toward the car was seventy-eight, not fifty-eight. He walked as if each step might break the eggshells he was treading on.

"It's normal for someone who's had a heart attack to be apprehensive about getting back into normal activities," his cardiac care nurse told me when I'd snuck behind Jim's back during one of his follow-up appointments to ask a few questions of my own.

I understood that, really I did. I'd had my own fears in those early days when Jim was released from the hospital. But after eight weeks of tip-toeing around, I was ready to have my old husband back. In my living room as well as our bedroom.

"Hi." Jim opened the passenger door and stood for a moment, as if trying to figure out how to get in the car.

He leaned inside and laid a bank deposit bag on the seat, then turned his back to me and sat down, finally bringing his legs into the car, one by one. I fought the urge to roll my eyes. What could be so hard about getting into a car?

"Could you swing by the bank?" he asked. "I need to drop off the deposit."

"Sure," I said, biting back irritation. I'd been hoping to get back to my manuscript as soon as possible.

"Do you want to go in?" I asked as we approached the bank, hoping against hope that today would be the day Jim would decide to get out of the car and do his business.

"No, go through the drive-up."

No surprise there. Although the nurse had told me his fears were normal, what she hadn't told me was what to do with my urge to throttle him.

"Hi, Mrs. Westin." The drive-up teller knew my name, which was all the more evidence this little routine had gone on much too long.

Jim handed me the bank deposit bag, and I did my best not to fling it into the deposit box. Jim and I waited in silence until the transaction was complete.

"Ready to go home?" I asked.

Jim sighed as if he had run a marathon. "Yeah."

I maneuvered through the streets, working my way back to our neighborhood. Now was as good a time as any . . .

"You remember I have a speaking engagement this weekend, don't you?"

"This weekend?" I could hear the slight panic in his question. "Where is it? Here?"

Now it was my turn to sigh. "No. I'll need to spend Friday night away. I speak first thing Saturday morning at a women's retreat in South Dakota a hundred and fifty miles from here."

The words were barely out of my mouth when Jim countered, "When will you get back?"

"It'll be late Saturday. After supper time, I'm guessing."

"What am I supposed to do?"

What was he supposed to do? I had all kinds of suggestions for what he could do. How about turning back into the man I used to know?

I played dumb. "What do you mean?"

"Well . . . I . . . uhh . . . I . . . it's just that I don't want to . . ."

I looked at him out of the corner of my eye. He was looking down at his hands clasped on his lap. *Like an old man.* I knew what he was trying to say. He didn't want to stay alone. A pang of guilt stabbed my stomach. It was mean of me to make him put his fears into words.

As luck had it, or God arranged it, I'd had a two-week gap in my speaking schedule when Jim's heart attack happened. It was time I had planned to begin the new book, but the weekends following had become jam-packed with events I'd agreed to speak at. Reed came home from Minneapolis that first weekend I'd needed to be away and spent the time with his dad. From then on, Kaylee, Drew, and I had cobbled together a check-up-on-Dad plan. Jim didn't like the fact that I was so busy, but I had signed contracts to fulfill, and the doctor assured the both of us that Jim's healing was progressing right on schedule. But, no matter what the doctor said, that didn't change the fact that Jim was afraid to be alone.

"Do you want me to call and see if Kaylee can come . . . *visit* . . . while I'm gone?"

"Yeah." He sounded defeated, and that only made me feel worse.

I pulled the car into the garage, parking beside the old junker—Dodge Charger that had been decomposing on the floor, untouched, for two years now. That pile of rusted metal didn't even bother me . . . if only he'd get interested in *something*. "Maybe you should—"

Jim's look cut my words right off. He slid out of the car, and slowly walked around the back of the car and into the house, leaving me alone with fears and frustrations of my own.

"What're you doing?" Jim was standing over my shoulder, looking down at my keyboard.

I bit back the smart remark on the tip of my tongue. "Working on my new book." If they gave out awards for restraint I'd win one for sure.

"Oh."

I reread the paragraph I'd just written and typed an additional line.

"What's for supper?"

Could a person pierce her tongue with her teeth? I might be the first. "Not sure. Do you have any ideas?" If Jim was so changed by this heart attack of his, maybe he'd morphed into a chef, as well.

"No. I was just wondering."

What he was, was *bored*. And who wouldn't be, sitting around the house for two months? An idea played in my mind. As I spoke, I transferred the file I was working on onto my flash drive stick. "How about if we go to the Book Nook? I'll take along my laptop and get some work done in the coffee shop, and you can browse, or sit and read. Then afterward, we can stop somewhere to get a bite to eat." I wasn't about to give him time to think up an excuse. I stood up and headed for the coat closet near the door.

Twenty minutes later I was powering up my laptop in the Book Nook coffee shop, and Jim was somewhere in the stacks of books. I only hoped he stayed there long enough for me to get some work done.

As I sipped a late-afternoon decaf, I transferred my work-in-progress to my laptop. Waiting for the

Word file to open, I glanced around at my fellow coffee drinkers. A young couple near the wall looked like former students of mine, but they were so engrossed in each other I didn't need to worry they might want to chat with me. There was a man reading the newspaper, and two women standing in line to order coffee. They were talking up a storm, laughing together in the way only really good friends could. The woman first in line, standing so I could only see her profile, reminded me of my friend Julie. But it couldn't be her, because at this time of day, Julie would be at home getting supper started for her and Greg. All the same, the resemblance to my friend made me miss her. We hadn't had a heart-to-heart for . . . well, I couldn't remember the last time we'd sat down face to face to chat. Julie had called a couple times since Jim's heart attack, but each time I'd been in the middle of something . . . heading to a doctor appointment, or getting ready to leave for a speaking engagement. *I seem to pick the worst times to call,* Julie said as I begged off from our last conversation. *Why don't you call me when you have time?*

A flush warmed me as I realized I hadn't ever called her back. Oh well, Julie had to know I was swamped right now. A friend like Julie would understand. I'd call her tonight after Jim and I got back from eating out. In the meantime, I had a book to write.

"Claire?"

I looked up from my computer. "Julie? Julie!" Pushing my chair back, I stood and pulled her into a hug. "I thought that looked like you."

Holding her coffee to the side, Julie stepped out of my embrace. "I'm surprised you recognized me." She smiled, but I caught the edge in her words.

It would be best to pretend I hadn't heard. "What are you doing here?" For the first time, I noticed the woman she'd been in line with right at her elbow.

"Oh!" Julie seemed to remember the woman at the same time. "Claire, I'd like you to meet Melissa. We just got done with our watercolor class and stopped to have coffee."

"You're taking a watercolor class?"

"Yeah. Don't you remember, I asked you back at the end of August if you wanted to sign up with me? You already had a full schedule of speaking. And a book to write." Julie put her hand on Melissa's arm. "I met Melissa at the first class and we've sort of made stopping here our thing."

Melissa had a coat draped over her left arm, and a cup of coffee in her right hand. She gestured as if she'd like to shake hands, but both of hers were occupied. She smiled. "So you're Claire Westin, Julie's famous friend?"

My eyes darted to Julie. She wouldn't describe me like that . . . would she? I looked back to her new friend . . . the friend I'd never heard about until now. Warmth flooded my cheeks. "I suppose that would be me."

"Glad to meet you," Melissa said. "I've been teasing Julie that I didn't believe she really knew you. She talks about you so much, but I've never met you." She nudged Julie with her shoulder. "I guess now I'll have to believe you."

After a brief laugh, there was a slightly longer, almost uncomfortable pause. Then . . .

"How've you been?"

"How are you?"

Julie and I spoke in unison, as if we still thought alike. But, obviously way too much time had passed for us to be asking each other something as generic as "how are you."

"Fine," I said. "Jim's here . . . somewhere."

"Then he's feeling better? That's good."

Oh, how I wanted to tell Julie about the fearful way Jim was acting. About how I felt more like his babysitter than his wife. But how could I tell her all that, when I hadn't talked to her in weeks?

Melissa lifted a finger, pausing Julie's and my self-conscious conversation. "I'm going to let you two visit a bit. I want to look for a couple books." She smiled my way. "If I buy one of yours, would you sign it for me?"

"Of course." I could feel my cheeks turning red. Right now I didn't want to be Julie's "famous friend." I wanted to be "Claire" . . . Julie's best friend. But perhaps Melissa had taken over that role.

Melissa walked off. I motioned to the chair opposite mine. "Do you want to sit down?"

Julie glanced at my open laptop. "I don't want to interrupt if you're busy."

"No. Not yet. Jim and I just got here."

"Well, okay then, just for a minute."

We both sat down, sipping from our coffee cups in tandem. My mind scrambled for what to say next. Ask her about her kids? About her husband? Or about the watercolor class she was taking without me? Anything I came up with sounded weird. As if I barely knew what was going on in my best friend's life.

You don't.

"How are your kids?" Julie asked, her mind still working like mine, after all.

"Fine," I said. The truth was I hardly knew how they were doing. I'd spent the past two months treading water trying to keep my head afloat. Between Jim's heart attack, keeping my speaking engagement commitments, and trying to work on the next book for my publisher, I hadn't had much time for anyone. "The kids are fine," I repeated, hoping what I'd said was true.

Julie nodded. "That's good."

She tilted her head down and stared at the table top. What happened to the easy way we used to chat? In the past, we'd hardly had time to breathe in between all we had to say to each other.

"Listen, Claire." Julie pushed her coffee cup aside and put both her hands on the table. "You know I've never been one for small talk. This is just too weird. Both of us sitting here like we hardly know each other."

A wave of relief washed over me. Leave it to my old friend to clear the air. "I know," I said, leaning forward and resting my fingers on the tabletop, too. Maybe if we talked about the obvious, we could get back to the way things used to be.

"Here's the deal," Julie said, staring me straight in the eye. "I used to feel like your best friend. I know you were mine. And I miss you. But the thing is, you're too busy to need a friend. The best way I know to be your friend right now is to leave you alone."

The legs of her chair scraped loudly against the tile as Julie pushed herself away from the table, and left me with her words. *The best way I know to be your friend right now is to leave you alone.*

All the times in the past months I'd begged off her invitations to get together saying, "I'm too busy," rang in my ears. *Too busy. Too busy.*

The irony didn't escape me. I'd been too busy talking and writing about friendship to make time for my best friend. It was almost funny.

Almost.

"How much longer till you're ready to go?" Jim was at my elbow.

I hadn't typed one word in the half hour we'd

been here. I'd planned to work for at least an hour before we went out for supper, but now I reached up and closed my laptop. "We can go now."

Jim started wrapping his wool scarf around his neck. "I'm not too hungry. I think going in to the store and then this was more than I should have done today."

I swallowed against the tears forming in my eyes. "I'm not very hungry, either. Let's go home." What I didn't say was that this little outing to the bookstore was more than I should have done today, too.

Now there were two people in our family with broken hearts.

I didn't write a word the next day, either. Julie's declaration about me being too busy to have a friend festered, an open wound. Every time I tried to pray about our friendship, my words hit a glass ceiling, coming right back to convict me.

The truth hurts. It sure did.

The truth will set you free. No, it didn't.

I kept waiting for the phone to ring. Hoping Julie would somehow know how badly I needed to talk to her. Twice I picked up the phone to call her, but put the receiver back in its cradle. What would I say?

When the phone rang late that afternoon I raced to answer it.

"Hello!?"

"Mom?"

I shouldn't have been disappointed to hear Drew's voice instead of Julie's, but I was. "Oh, hi." I did my best to sound upbeat, even though I was anything but. "What's up?"

"Ummm, I was wondering . . . well, *we* were wondering if you'd mind if Trisha and I stopped by the house after supper tonight?"

There was something in his voice . . . something I couldn't quite put my finger on. "You and Trisha? What about Will?"

"Oh! Yeah, we'll bring him along, too. We . . . ah . . . have something we want to talk to Dad about. And you."

Why did he sound so nervous? "Sure," I said, my mind shifting into overdrive. "Does seven work?"

"See you then."

Ooooh . . . I knew. That wasn't nervousness I'd heard in Drew's voice, it was excitement. They were having another baby! For the first time today my heart lifted. Goodness knew, we could use some good news around here.

Carrying Will in his arms, Drew stomped snow from his shoes as he stepped in from the November cold outside. Trisha stepped in after him, and began unzipping Will from his winter gear.

"Ga-pa!" Little Will crawled out of his puffy

snowsuit and barreled toward his Grandpa Jim. Rather than scoop his grandson into his arms, Jim took Will by the hand and led him to the recliner. He sat, then patted his knees. "Up here, Buddy." Will scrambled onto Jim's lap as a little pin-prick of jealousy poked at my heart. Why hadn't Will run to me?

Too busy.

I wasn't going to think about that tonight, either. As soon as Drew and Trisha made their announcement—Put it this way, by this time next year, we'd have *two* grandkids. One for each of our laps.

"Anyone want coffee?" The heartburn from my late afternoon brew with Julie still bubbled. And it had nothing to do with coffee. Come to think of it, I didn't need coffee to remind me of what I was trying to forget. "Or I've got some Coke in the fridge."

"Coke!" shouted Will. I doubted he even knew what Coke was. But then, how would I know what he knew these days, as little as I'd seen him?

"No Coke for you." Drew leveled a look at his nineteen-month-old son.

Trisha looked my way. "Do you have any juice? He could have that."

"Deuce!" yelled Will, as if he held a winning poker hand.

"Let's go see if Grandma has some juice." I held my arms his way. Thank goodness little boys

432

didn't know how to hold grudges. Will twisted his way off of Jim's lap and ran my direction.

I led Will into the kitchen with a promise of a cracker to go along with his juice. In the background, I could hear Drew making chitchat with his dad. Allowing myself a smug smile, I took my time getting Will his snack. I knew Drew and Trisha would hold their new-baby announcement until I returned to the living room.

As I walked into the room, I had Will on my hip, and balanced a cup of apple juice and a couple crackers in my other hand. I smiled and wrinkled my nose at my grandson, who tried his best to wrinkle his nose back at me. I was distracted, and only now caught a snippet of what Drew was saying.

"Trisha and I have talked this idea over for a couple days. We've been praying about it, too. And the reason I—*we,*" Drew grabbed Trisha's hand, "wanted to talk to you tonight was to tell you that we'd like to buy the stores."

"Westin Foods?" I blurted. "What about the baby?"

"What baby?" Drew asked.

"Isn't that why you came over tonight? To tell us you're going to have a baby?"

Drew lowered his chin and leveled a look at me. "No-ooo."

"Baby," Will parroted, reaching for a cracker.

I set him on the floor by the coffee table and

arranged his snack. My mind scrabbled to make quick sense of the conversation I'd walked in on. "You want to buy Westin Foods?"

Drew let out a chuckle . . . or a sigh. "Yeah. I know it took me a long time to come around. But after working in the bank and helping other people go into business for themselves . . . well, as much as I like my job, I'm not ever going to be able to get any equity in the bank. All I'll ever get is a salary. I won't have a business where Will can come work with me if he wants to someday. And I want that for him." Drew paused, his glance falling on Will, Trisha, Jim, and me. "For *us*."

Trisha smiled, and a big grin lit up Drew's face. Drew continued talking, telling Jim and me more about his decision to buy the business from his dad. I only caught part of the conversation as my mind grabbed onto what Drew was proposing. Before his heart attack, Jim had been talking about getting out of the business. Maybe selling the stores to Drew would kick Jim out of his postheart attack funk. *Thank You, Lord.* Having Drew buy the business was the answer to my prayers. Instead of playing nursemaid to Jim, I'd finally have a chance to get my old life back again.

Are you sure you want your old life back?

Yes. Yes, I did.

What about being "too busy"?

Too busy was better than having Jim following me around like a lost puppy.

And what about Julie?

Why was I thinking about *her* now? I should be rejoicing that Drew wanted to buy the stores. Instead, I had an inordinate urge to go into the other room. To run away from thoughts about the best friend I might have lost with all my busyness.

"I'm going to get a paper towel to clean off Will."

"He's okay," Trisha said.

Pretending I didn't hear, I hurried into the kitchen and stood near the window, pressing my hands against the cold glass, and staring into the darkness. My life had been on fast-forward the past few years. Teaching, writing, speaking, in the midst of trying to be a wife, mother, and friend. I'd given up teaching to fulfill my writing and speaking contracts, and somehow in the process I'd alienated my husband and my best friend. And my relationships with my kids and grandson were cordial, at best. I tried to do it all, but somehow my efforts weren't enough. There simply wasn't time to do it all. I closed my eyes. *Help me, Lord. I can't do this anymore.*

Time is a gift.

What? I shook my head against the unlikely thought. Of course time was a gift. I understood that. And I'd been using my time to the max.

And where did it get you?

Random thoughts swirled through my mind. The awkwardness between Julie and me in the coffee shop. Will running to Jim, not me. My resentment toward Jim for depending on me to drive him around and keep him company after his heart attack.

I use all things for good. This time of Jim's recuperation could have been a gift. Instead, you squandered it.

Sudden warmth flooded my face as I understood the many ways I'd misused the time I'd been given. Not only the time after Jim's heart attack, but the time before that, as well. I'd let my striving after a new career come before my relationships.

Lifting my hands from the cool glass, I pressed them against my cheeks. I didn't want to live like this anymore. Here I was . . . the Friendship Doctor, and all the important relationships in my life needed repair. There was something very wrong about that.

I closed my eyes and whispered a prayer. "No more, Lord. Help me change. Help me to use my time the way *You* would have me spend my minutes."

I knew it would take more than simply praying for me to reorder things, but now I was ready to go back to the living room. Ready to figure out, along with Jim, how we'd use the time ahead of us. I knew making a deal with Drew to purchase the stores might take a little time. But that was okay. Jim wasn't anywhere near recovered, yet. We'd use this time as transition. I still had a calendar of speaking events to fulfill and another book in the Friendship Factor series under contract, but I was ready to reexamine my priorities. It would be exciting to watch Drew and Trisha take over the stores. Watch them work side by side, the way Jim and I had started. For the first time in too long, I was actually looking forward to the days and weeks ahead.

"Got the deal hammered out, yet?" I joked, as I stepped back into the living room with the paper towel I'd used as an excuse to leave.

Drew's and Trisha's heads whipped my way. Their bewildered, wide-eyed stares stopped me in my tracks.

"No!" Jim said, I realized now, for a second time. He pounded his clenched fist against the padded arm of his chair, the first real emotion I'd seen him display since his heart attack. "No!"

"Dad," Drew said, his voice rising, "I thought that's what you wanted. I thought I'd be helping you out."

"No." Jim pushed himself out of his recliner and walked out of the room, leaving only stunned silence in his wake.

"No!" Will mimicked, pounding his cracker against the table. None of us even cracked a smile at his uncanny imitation of his grandpa.

I had no idea what was going through Jim's head right now. I only hoped whatever it was, it didn't go to his heart.

Jim

Fueled by unexpected anger, I marched down the hall and into our bedroom, closing the door firmly behind me. I hoped Drew, Trisha, Claire, and even Will heard the finality in the sound. Who were they to push me out of the business I'd worked my whole life to build?

No! No! The words echoed in my head as I walked a quick circle around the foot of the bed, pounding my clenched fist into my hand. I didn't need my son feeling sorry for his poor old dad. Was everyone ready to assign me to the junk heap?

The sound of my blood pumping thundered in my ears. *Ba-boom. Ba-boom.* I stopped pacing and concentrated on breathing. *Calm down.* If I wasn't careful, I might have another heart attack right now. *Ba-boom. Ba-boom.*

This couldn't be good. I sat on the edge of the bed, braced my hands on my knees, and stared at the floor. I'd spend the past two months tiptoeing through life, doing my best to avoid what was happening right now. *Ba-boom. Ba-boom.*

A heavy hand of panic pressed against my breastbone. Would all the work my doctor had done repairing my heart hold up? *Ba-boom.*

I pulled in another deep breath, and then blew it out. Did it again. My heart rate seemed to be slowing and I was still upright. I was going to live through this, after all.

From outside the door, down the hall, I heard the murmur of voices. No doubt Drew and Claire were tossing a coin to see who dared check on me.

I waited for a knock on the door. What would I say? I didn't feel ready to apologize for anything. Oh, maybe I could have used a little more finesse in telling Drew I wasn't interested in his offer. Shouting, "No!" hadn't been my finest hour. But after years and years of brushing off my suggestion he go into business with me, I'd come to terms with the fact my son had no interest in my life's work. And then to have him sit in my living room and tell me he wanted to buy my business—why now? I didn't need his pity.

He was trying to help. Offering you what he thought you wanted.

His timing stunk. Nothing like kicking a guy when he's down for the count.

I held my hand against my heart. Sure enough, thinking about all this made my heart rate increase.

Through the door, I heard a muffled shout from Will. "No!"

Was he still imitating his grandpa's tantrum? Or throwing one of his own? Nothing like a chip off the old hereditary block.

Come to think of it . . . why hadn't Drew or

Claire come to check on me? For all they knew I could be lying here inert. Dead and gone.

The way you've been acting, you'd given up on life anyway.

For the first time since my little tirade in the living room, I felt the sting of embarrassment. What must I have looked like? Sounded like?

Your nineteen-month-old grandson?

I tugged at the back of my neck. So I'd been the one imitating *him*. Real mature.

Another flurry of muffled voices. The sound of the front door closing. A car starting outside. So, they'd gone home and left Claire to find my body by herself.

I waited for Claire to knock on the bedroom door. Poke her head around the door jamb. I lay down on top of the covers, resting my hands across my abdomen. Let her find me like that. Maybe she'd realize—

What? What life would be like without you?

I laid my arm over my eyes, as if I could shield myself from the many ways I'd shied away from life—from the people in my life—these past months. Claire was upset with me for sitting around the house so much. After tonight, Drew would certainly be angry. I'd missed the bank board meetings two months in a row. Things at the stores were cobbled together just enough to keep them limping along. But how much longer would that last?

440

For a fleeting instance, I wondered if maybe it would have been better if I'd died on the airport floor. Then I wouldn't have so many burned bridges to tread back across.

I opened one eye and peeked around. I was still lying on top of the covers, fully dressed, and from what I could tell in the darkened bedroom, Claire was under the covers on her side of the bed, sleeping. I opened my other eye and looked at the clock. Five-thirty a.m. I'd fallen asleep after the kids had left and slept the whole night through, waking long before sunrise.

My outburst the night before must have worn me out. I ventured a stretch, reaching . . . reaching for something outside my grasp. Whatever it was, it eluded me. Well, then, I was going to have to get out of bed and try to find whatever it was I was trying to seize.

If I was very careful, I might be able to get up, put on some fresh clothes, and get to the store without waking Claire. It would be best if I could avoid talking to her while I was dressed in my tantrum clothes from last night. The sting of embarrassment pricked at my cheeks, but surprisingly, an ember of anger burned inside. So what if I'd languished too long in a post-heart attack pit? Maybe Drew had done me a favor last night. He'd given me a wake-up call I badly needed.

I swung my legs over the side of the bed and sat

up. For the first time in weeks, I was anxious to get up and tackle the day. Come to think of it, Drew really *had* done me a favor last night. Kicking a guy when he's down leaves him only two options . . . stay down . . . or get up and fight back. I'd show him. I'd show them all that Jim Westin still had a little life left in him.

"Good morning, Mr. Westin." I didn't miss the look of surprise on the stock boy's face as he greeted my early-morning entrance from the back of the store.

"Morning." I nodded sharply at my employee and headed through the swinging doors at the rear of the store onto the shopping floor. This early in the morning there was only one checkout aisle open, and from what I could see, only one unshaven dad buying a carton of milk. I was determined to walk every aisle. The exercise would be good for me, but I planned to kill two birds at the same time. I was taking stock of my inventory. Seeing the damage that had been done while I'd spent two months wallowing in my pit of self-pity.

Hmmm. Surprisingly, the cereal aisle had held its own. The high-turnover items frequently ran low, and little hands often grabbed at the sugary-cereals on the lower shelves, begging to take home the brands they recognized from their favorite TV commercials. My hands on my hips, I stopped at the end cap of the aisle. It looked like there was a new brand being featured this week. Who had ordered that in?

I shook my head and continued my walk. There were simply too many items in the store for me to remember each and every one. In my absence, my floor manager possibly pulled a slow-selling brand from the shelves and moved it to the end of the aisle in an effort to get it out of the store. It was amazing how a little product placement could move a product.

The baking supplies were all in order. I quickly took stock. Flour, sugar, powered sugar, brown sugar. Nothing was missing or looked picked over. Rounding the aisles, I found the chips and crackers neatly displayed. I plucked an overripe banana from the fruit bin and looked around to see if there was anything else that needed my attention in the produce department. Nope. I continued my walk. The floors were clean. The checkout stand areas were neat and tidy. I poked my head into the bathrooms. They'd obviously been cleaned during the night, as scheduled.

I headed to my office and flipped on the lights. Even though I'd managed to drag myself into work a couple hours most days over the past weeks to do the bank deposit and pay bills, there was a stack of mail that had piled up in the hours I hadn't been here. Picking up a handful, I flipped through the mail like a deck of cards, discarding the junk, and setting aside envelopes and invoices that needed attention. The pile left for me to look through was surprisingly small.

Either no one had missed me, or someone had been looking out for things when I was out of commission.

Drew.

I hadn't asked a question, yet an answer came anyway. There was only one way the store could have kept running so smoothly while I was out of commission, and that had to have been thanks to my oldest son. The time I'd spent hobbling around on crutches last winter and Drew pitching in to help, had served as a training ground for the bigger crisis that lay ahead.

I hung my head, trying to puzzle together the many events that led to last night.

Two years ago, Drew still lived in New York, and I'd rarely embraced his work there. Instead, I dropped broad hints that he should move home and join me in business. My first grandchild had been born with a hole in his heart, and that defect had been repaired but, ultimately, led their small family back to Carlton and Drew's job at the bank. What could be better training to go into business than being a small city loan officer? Working with small business owners? Learning the pitfalls and the benefits of owning your own business?

Funny, though, once Drew moved back, I'd quit asking him to come work with me. Oh, sure, Drew wasn't exactly chomping at the bit to join me in business back then. Both of us were stubborn mules. Or completely blind as to God's leading.

He'd—God—had to go and break my leg to get Drew into the store to help me. And yet, we were still so dense not to pick up on that wake-up call. I'd gone and had a heart attack so Drew could keep his fingers in the business.

I raised my head to look up. *Is that how it worked, Lord?*

I use all things for good.

Somehow I could imagine God looking down on me with a sly smile on His face. But I wasn't about to smile back. If I was going to ever get out of the grocery business, it would be on *my* terms. Not by my son feeling sorry for me.

There was a soft knock on my open office door. It was my produce manager, Donna.

"Good morning," I said as if I'd been here every morning for the past sixty days instead of wallowing at home in my recliner.

"It's good to see you here," she said.

I waved off her comment. "Any fires to put out today?"

She rolled her eyes. "There're little blazes every day."

"Well then, we'd better get busy and put them out."

Donna raised her hand to her eyebrow, a makeshift salute. I did likewise, as a slow smile crept onto my face and I turned back to my paperwork. Yup, it felt good to be back in the saddle—make that *shopping cart*—again. Mighty good. I'd missed being engaged in life. I hadn't realized it until my son gave me a kick in the backside. I only wished I hadn't verbally kicked him back.

My outburst was uncalled for. But I wasn't ready to apologize. I was still doing a slow simmer over the idea that Drew, Claire . . . *everyone* seemed ready to give up on me. I'd show them I wasn't ready to be put out to pasture and turned into glue.

"Joy to the world, the Lord is come . . ."

Was the Christmas music playing over the store speaker system turned especially loud today?

Or are you noticing the fact that there isn't a whole lot of joy in your world these days?

I bent over, sliced open a case of kidney beans with a box cutter, and began putting cans on the shelf. One of my stock boys had quit a week ago and another one had called in sick. He'd been out three days now. There was nothing left but for the boss—namely *me*—to pitch in. So much for the *joys* of owning my own business.

The strains of the familiar carol accompanied my work, the words burning into my thoughts as I tried to stay busy and not think. It had been a long two weeks. Two miserable weeks since what I'd started thinking of as *that night.* Claire was barely speaking to me, and my son? We hadn't exchanged so much as a single word in all that time. Sixteen days . . . but who was counting?

In order to exchange actual *words,* we would have had to actually *see* each other, and somehow we'd managed to two-step around each other, even at church last Sunday, where I squirmed through a sermon on forgiveness.

Even if I hadn't seen Drew in all that time, he was on my mind most every minute. I slashed through the sealing tape on another box, this time canned corn, and began unloading. Every day I replayed that last conversation I'd had with Drew. Well, I could hardly call it a *conversation* the way I'd lashed out at him. Even now, two weeks later, I felt the slap that my words must have been to my son. No wonder he'd kept his distance. Embarrassment and self-righteousness helped me keep mine.

My words had been harsh, and I tried to rationalize away my hot-headed response. It was easy to blame my over-the-top reaction on my heart attack and the aftermath. My doctor suggested that my condition exacted not only a physical toll, but also an emotional one. But still, knowing all the facts didn't justify tearing into my son.

"You need to apologize to Drew," Claire announced, after she'd very formally asked me to "please pass the salt."

Yeah, an apology would be good, if only I could bring myself to get off my high horse. There was a part of me that wanted to wash this whole episode under the bridge of life. Drew should understand that his dad wasn't perfect. I was back at work, and wasn't that what everyone had been praying for?

The box of corn was empty, and I straightened and stretched, working out the kinks from a task I didn't do that often anymore. I picked up the two cardboard containers and carried them into the back room. There was a mountain of cardboard back here, boxes that needed to be cut down, laid flat, and recycled. I'd leave that task for Max, the minimum-wage high school student who came in every school-day afternoon to help out. My time was better spent getting merchandise out on the shelves so customers could buy it. I grabbed up two cases of M&M's. Everyone in town seemed to want the special Christmas red and green candies this year.

Carrying the boxes in front of me, I made my way to the candy aisle. There was always a lull in business, after lunch time and before school and businesses closed for the day. The store was relatively quiet this December afternoon, which made it a good time to replenish the shelves. I only wished I had more help to keep up with things.

Drew.

One word. One person who kept dogging my thoughts. Even when I tried not to think about him.

What are you so afraid of?

Afraid? I wasn't afraid.

You are.

I set the boxes of candy on the floor and sank down next to them. The truth settled heavy inside me. Conviction in the candy aisle. If I let Drew take over the business, that meant my work would be done. What would be left for me to do? I'd spent two miserable months doing nothing. I wasn't ready to live the rest of my life in a rocking chair. I wouldn't. *No!*

"No," I whispered. "No."

Now I knew. That's where that word had come from the awful night with Drew. From fear. But what could I do about it?

My contradicting emotions made no sense. Before my heart attack, I'd wanted nothing more than to sell my stores and retire. Be done with all my years of work. And then, when Drew offered to take it all off my hands, suddenly I didn't want retirement anymore. Or did I?

I'd always imagined the future would happen according to my terms, my planning . . . until I'd almost had any future at all yanked away from me by a fibrillating heart.

One thing I did know was that I now had an acute awareness of time. The notion I'd had, that death was somewhere off in the *future,* had been turned upside down. Every minute was a gift, I could see that now. Life should have some sort of *purpose,* shouldn't it? Walking away from every-thing I knew didn't seem like an answer until I knew what I was walking toward.

Drew has offered to help you.

Help me? Help me what?

Find purpose.

I pulled the box cutter from my back pocket and slit open the case of candy as my mind played with those two words. For so long I'd pushed aside the idea that Drew might join me in the store. Now I allowed myself to imagine the possi-bility. I wouldn't have to carry all the responsi-bility for the stores by myself. Drew could share the work . . . and the satisfactions of owning a family business. I wouldn't have to leave my work completely to enjoy the time I had left. We could do this together.

Or, could we? Had my harsh words slammed the door shut once and for all? Or was the door still open a crack?

Lord, show me what to do. For now, all I knew to do was to keep busy.

The M&M's were kept on the lower shelves. They were popular enough that shoppers would seek them out, unlike some of the other items we kept waist high where people might be tempted to try something new. The candy pieces inside the packages clinked against each other as I began shelving the deep brown bags. I wished I could as easily tuck away my fear of what the future held.

Oh, if only it was that easy.

"O little town, hmm Bethlehem, hmm hum we see thee lie . . ." Without realizing it, I found myself humming along to the music being played in the store. Good thing there weren't many people here. My voice was lousy, and would chase customers away if they heard. "Above thy deep hum hmm hum sleep . . ."

Another carol, another reminder. Christmas would be here in two weeks. Reed would be home from Minneapolis, Kaylee and Brad would come over to the house and hang out. And Drew, Trisha, and Will? If they didn't show, it would be my fault. And Claire would never forgive me.

I shelved the candy bags two at a time, working in a steady rhythm.

Wait.

"Ohhh."

I stopped and put a fist to my chest.

Pain!

Cold terror raced down my back. *Not again, Lord. Please, not again.* I didn't want to die. Not now, and especially not like this. Not when I hadn't spoken to my son. When things with Claire were so strained. *Spare me. I'll make things right. I promise.*

There was a gurgle in the back of my throat. *Burp!* The pain disappeared. I sobered in relief. Had I made a rash promise over a gas bubble? Or had God answered my prayer?

What do you think?

I didn't know what to think, but I did know I'd made a promise . . . and now I needed to find a way to keep it.

Off to my left, I heard little feet pattering toward the candy aisle. I turned my head and caught sight of a young man and his son silhouetted in the light streaming in from the large windows at the front of the store.

My damaged heart jumped inside my chest. *Drew and Will.*

"Hey there, kiddo. Slow down." The young man lunged for the little guy before he could grab candy off the shelf.

Now that they were closer, I could see it wasn't Drew, or Will. Logic told me Drew would be at the bank this time of day, but obviously my heart didn't know that. A strange letdown filled my chest.

"M&M's!" The little boy smacked his lips and pointed to the bag in my hand.

I looked to his dad for permission. "Do you want this?" He nodded his okay and I handed over the sweet treats.

"Tank you Mister Grandpa."

The dad lifted one eyebrow and rolled his eyes, a sort of apology in case I wasn't a grandpa, I supposed.

"You're welcome." I reached out and tousled the tyke's hair. Judging by his speech, the little boy was probably a little older than Will, but about the same size, and his dad bore an uncanny resemblance shape-wise to Drew. I watched as he and his dad walked off hand in hand.

As they rounded the corner, the little boy chattering away, looking up at his dad as if he hung the moon, I sat back on my heels and imagined another pair, another time.

Dad, look! I did it! Dad, see? I can do it. A voice from the past echoed. How many times had I walked these aisles with Drew? I'd drafted all the kids as helpers, as soon as they were old enough to be of some real assistance, but it had always been Drew who'd stuck with the tasks the longest. *I can do more, Dad.*

For years I thought nothing would make me happier than to pass my business along to one of my kids, and then when Drew offered, I'd yelled, "No." I'd tossed his offer aside like a crumpled candy wrapper.

I stared down at the candy bag in my hand. The words of the Christmas carol I'd been humming played through my mind. *". . . And praises sing to God the King, and peace to men on earth."*

Peace, the vocalist sang. So easy to sing about. So hard to live out.

But I had to try. I shelved the last of the candy, pushed myself to my feet, and then dusted off my hands. I'd promised God I'd make things right. There wasn't much I could do about peace in the world, but there was something I could do about making peace with my son. And wasn't that what Christmas was all about . . . a Father and a Son . . . and peace?

I took my time walking back to my office. Back to where my coat and car keys were stashed. Back to where my promise to make things right would start.

As I walked, I ran my hand along the grocery shelves, as if I was looking for something. But I knew I could hunt all I wanted and I still wouldn't find what I really needed this afternoon. I sold all sorts of merchandise. Food items so varied it took a computer program to keep track of them all. But even without scanning the shelves, I knew we didn't sell the one product I needed to make the recipe I had to cook up.

We didn't sell "crow," and that was what I was going to have to eat to make things right with my oldest son.

TIDINGS OF COMFORT AND JOY . . .

Drew

"Hey, Todd, how's it going?" I walked around my desk and shook hands with Todd Wilson, the guy I'd been working with on a loan to buy his boss's auto mechanic business the day my dad had had his heart attack. I'd seen Todd a few times since, but I'd never forget that particular day.

Todd grabbed his baseball cap off his head and shook my hand. "It's going great. Better than I could've hoped." Todd laid his cap on the edge of my desk and settled into a chair as I sat down across from him.

I folded my hands and laid my arms on the desktop. "How can I help you?"

He scratched at the back of his head. "I think I'm going to need another tow truck."

If anyone could repair an engine, it would be Todd, and a repair job would be cheaper than a new truck. I was only looking after his best interests. "The one you have giving you trouble?"

"The only trouble I'm having is keeping up with business. I'm talking about buying a second truck."

My eyebrows rose. "You need two tow trucks?"

"Yeah," Todd replied. "And I'm thinking I need to add on another repair stall and maybe hire another guy. That advertising I've been doing has paid off. Bruce never went in much for advertising."

I sat back in my chair. This was big money Todd was talking. Especially big, since he'd just bought the business two months ago. It would be easy to get carried away by enthusiasm and big ideas. The trouble was, big debt walked hand-in-hand with lofty plans.

I turned to my computer and brought up Todd's financial information. After a half-hour of some serious calculating, we came up for air. We were in agreement. His money would best be spent hiring another full-time repairman.

"Bruce can keep the tow truck side of things going, and the new guy and I can do a quicker turnaround on the vehicles that need repair," Todd said. Bruce was now working for Todd for free. According to Todd, the way Bruce rationalized it, Todd was making monthly payments on the business and that was Bruce's paycheck.

Once again, Todd scratched his head. "I'm making payments to the *bank,* so I can't quite figure out how Bruce figures all this. But he says he'd have nothing to do but watch game shows if it weren't for me letting him keep his fingers in the business. Know what he told me the other day?"

I couldn't wait to hear. The dynamic between Bruce and Todd never ceased to amaze me. "What?"

Todd laughed. "He told me I was single-handedly saving his marriage. That his wife would have him frosting cookies or something if he stayed home every day. And he said if *that* happened, he'd have to get a divorce—of course he was joking—but he said then she'd get half of what I'd paid him for the business, and he'd be out all that money."

Todd plucked his baseball cap off my desk and fingered the rim. He looked up, his eyes crinkled in amusement. "I don't know . . . it made some kind of stupid sense when he said it."

We both laughed, and I shook my head. "It kind of does . . . although I can't quite figure out why."

"Well," Todd said, pulling his cap onto his head and tugging at the brim, "I think he likes to have a place to hang out. Somewhere to get up and go to in the morning. Something to *do*. Besides frost cookies." Todd grinned as he stood up to leave.

"Yeah," I said, standing myself. "Frosting cookies isn't exactly my idea of exciting retirement."

And it's not your dad's, either.

Normally, I would have walked Todd out to the bank lobby, but his last words, and the thought that followed, kept me in my office. I didn't know what my dad's idea of retirement was . . . I'd never asked him. Once I'd made up my mind that I really did want to get into the family business, I'd been so intent on my dream, my goal, that I'd never put myself in my dad's place. All I'd done was imagine how good it would be to take over the business for *me* and my little family.

And because of my dad's heart attack, I thought I was doing him some kind of favor by offering to buy him out.

I scrubbed a hand across my cheek. How would I feel if Will—given twenty-some years—waltzed into my home and announced he wanted to do me a favor and take over the business I'd spent my life building?

Even at the far-fetched thought, a small fire of resentment burned in my chest. I'd be mad.

And that's how your dad felt that night.

I sat down in my office chair and rested my forehead against my hand. Yeah, I'd admit it, Dad and I weren't much different. I'd been mad at my dad that night when he'd shot down my offer. I'd nursed a grudge for two weeks. I'd been so sure my dad would embrace my plan as brilliant . . . not once did I take the time to think of how *he* might feel about my offer. I squeezed my fingers against the bridge of my nose. I'd messed up royally. No wonder he'd turned me down flat. *Lord, what do I do now?*

In response to my plea, I heard nothing. I stared down at my desktop as if the answer to my question lay there. I couldn't blame my dad for the way he'd reacted. He'd had his feet knocked out from under him this past year . . . not only by me tripping him and breaking his leg, but also with his heart attack. And then I'd come along and tried to yank the store away, too.

My dad's knee-jerk reaction made perfect sense now. I'd spent two weeks alternating between never wanting to speak to him again and wallowing in the chasm of being pushed away from my dad.

The weeks I'd spent helping him while he'd been laid up had created an easy bond between us that I'd missed more than I knew was possible the past weeks when we'd been avoiding each other. Everything seemed so clear to me now. But, how could I make things right again? *Lord?*

At the thought of making peace with my dad came a calm I hadn't felt in the past many days. *Show me what to do.*

A soft presence whispered into my tumbling thoughts. What sounded like advice from God in my dad's words. *You should always treat customers the way you'd like to be treated. You'll never go wrong if you do that.*

For a moment, I puzzled at the unlikely counsel. *Treat customers the way I'd like to be treated?* What did that have to do with—

And then I knew. I needed to treat my dad the way I wanted him to treat me. And the advice had nothing at all to do with business. Everything to do with matters of the heart.

I pushed myself away from my desk, stood, and reached into my pocket for my car keys. If Dad didn't want to sell the store, so be it. But a business deal wasn't worth throwing away the relationship I had with my father. Our bond went way beyond business.

A quick glance at my calendar let me know I'd miss nothing at work this afternoon other than ever-present paperwork. This close to the holidays, most people weren't thinking about a visit to their banker. On my way out of the office, I stopped by my assistant's desk. "I'm going to step out for a few minutes."

"A little Christmas shopping?" she asked.

"If I can find what I need at the grocery store," I answered. She didn't need to know that the best gift I could get this season wouldn't cost a cent. All I wanted was my relationship with my dad restored.

The familiar, comforting aroma of the store's homemade smoked sausage filtered into the icy December air as I opened the door at the back of the store. Even if this business wasn't going to be mine, I'd learned most everything I needed to know about being a successful business person here. Hard work and putting the customer first went a long way in any profession.

I planned to thank my dad for all he'd taught me here . . . after I apologized for the past two weeks.

"Dad?" I knocked on the frame of his office door and peered around the doorway. His office was empty.

I walked out onto the selling floor of the store. Donna, my dad's produce manager, was coming my way, pushing a dolly-cart stacked high with boxes of apples.

"Have you seen my dad?" I asked.

Donna stopped and pressed her lips into a thin

line, thinking. "Nope. But am I glad to see you. The freight truck just unloaded, and there's a ton of stuff that needs to be put on shelves, and we're short of help. If you've got a few minutes . . ."

I did have a few minutes, but I hadn't planned to put them to use as a stock boy. I'd go in the back and take a look at the freight. Maybe my dad was back there and we could have the talk I'd been rehearsing.

Pushing my way through the swinging doors that led to the freight unloading area, I was stopped in my tracks by the sight of all the merchandise waiting to be put out for shoppers. Christmas might be a slow time in the banking business, but it was one of the busiest times of the year in the grocery business.

I really should head back to the bank. To my *real* job. But the sight of all those groceries that couldn't get sold unless customers could get at them prodded me into action. Taking a Westin Foods apron off a hook near the doors, I slipped out of my winter coat and hung it on the hook. I took off my sport jacket and hung that on top of my coat. The apron would protect my white shirt and blue tie from dust and dirt. I might be a bit overdressed for a stock boy, but no one would accuse Westin Foods of having sloppy employees.

Not that I was an employee.

Loading a push cart with a variety of cases of canned goods, I made my way through the aisles

461

to—I glanced at the box on the top of the stack—*canned peaches* was as good as any place to start. There was a box cutter in the pocket of the apron and I got to work. Quickly I fell into a familiar rhythm, a dance I'd done with thousands of pieces of my dad's merchandise. By the time I'd worked my way down to the third case, to the canned peas, I'd worked up a bit of a sweat. At the end of that case, I stopped and wiped the back of my hand across my brow. After sitting at a desk doing paperwork most of my work days, the physical labor felt good. I unbuttoned the cuffs of my shirt, rolled back my sleeves, and then loosened my tie. If I was going to do this, I might as well get into it.

"Excuse me?" A young mother stopped with a cart filled with groceries and a child as a passenger. "Could you tell me where you keep the candied cherries? I'm baking tomorrow and this recipe calls for—"

"Aisle five," I said, pointing that direction.

"And what about . . ." She consulted a piece of paper in her hand. ". . . draaa . . . gees? Or however you pronounce it."

I didn't know how to pronounce the word either, but I knew exactly what she wanted. Those little silver balls of sugar used to decorate cookies. I'd stocked my share of those over the years. "By the baking goods," I instructed. "Aisle seven. Top shelf."

"Great. Thanks."

I high-fived her little boy as the woman pushed her cart around the boxes I had left to unload. Smiling to myself, I slit open a case of mandarin oranges and began emptying the box, humming along to the Christmas music playing over the speaker system.

As I reached to place the small cans on a high shelf, I sensed, more than saw, someone next to me. Before I could turn to see if another shopper needed assistance, I realized the *someone* was my dad, bent down beside me, handing me two cans so I didn't have to reach down so far to get them.

A warm flush worked its way from my chest into my neck. I'd come to the store wanting to talk to my dad, but now that he was here, I was at a loss for words. This wasn't quite where I'd planned to give my little speech. And if I'd ever really had a speech to give, any of the words I'd rehearsed left me now.

In short order the case was empty. "Thanks," I said.

Dad held out the flat of his hand. Intuitively, I put the box cutter into it and watched while he bent and sliced open the last case on the cart. Canned cranberries. We shifted down the aisle to the cranberry section and silently began working in tandem. What was unsaid hung heavy between us as we passed cans between us in a familiar rhythm. A weight pressed against my chest, words fighting to find their way into the space between us.

"Dad."

"Drew."

We spoke in unison. I cast a glance his way, and our eyes locked as we stopped our work and simply stared at each other. I hadn't looked my dad in the eye for two weeks, and never quite like this. There was a strength in my dad's gaze that I knew wasn't in mine. A resolve that had been missing in his gaze over the past many months. I swallowed and looked away.

Dad handed me a can as he spoke. "I went looking for you. You weren't in your office."

I put the can on the shelf. Straightened it so the label faced out just the way my dad had taught me so long ago. "You weren't in yours, either."

Dad passed me two cans. "But I never thought of pitching in and doing your work for you at the bank. Not like you're doing for me."

"Yeah . . . well . . ." I shrugged one shoulder. What happened to all those words I'd planned to say? Where were they now?

"Drew?"

I stopped stocking the shelves and looked down at my dad squatted on the floor by the case of cranberries. He was looking up at me. "I've been giving what you said the other night some thought." He pressed his hands against his knees and slowly stood, facing me eye to eye. "Well, more than some thought—a *lot* of thought." He drew in a deep breath and I could see his jaw tense and flex.

I might as well get it over with. I swallowed hard. "And . . . ?"

"And," Dad said, reaching out and putting a hand on my shoulder, "I owe you an apology."

The warmth from his hand on my shoulder seemed to sear into me, spreading from my upper arm, across my chest, and right into the center of my heart. "But I—"

Dad squeezed my shoulder, stopping my words. "But nothing. I was wrong to lash out at you like that, and I'm sorry."

I nodded once, my Adam's apple bobbing. "I shouldn't have—"

Once again, he squeezed my shoulder. "You did exactly what I've been wanting you to do for the past thirty-some years. Well . . ." There was a small spark of apology in the way my dad's eye winked ". . . minus a couple weeks when I needed my butt kicked precisely the way you did."

"Dad . . . I didn't mean to—"

"Drew," Dad removed his hand from my shoulder in a way that made me feel as though a heavy weight was being lifted from my back. "I hope you meant every word of what you said that night."

"You . . . what?"

"You heard me." A slow smile crept onto my

dad's face. "Son, nothing would mean more to me than having you in this business."

"But what about—?" The many random thoughts I'd had about my dad's outburst flashed through my mind, but none of what I'd imagined seemed to matter right now. Everything I'd planned to say to my dad had left me. It appeared I was left with nothing but half sentences, sentences my dad seemed to have no trouble completing. "Are you saying . . . ?"

Dad nodded. "I was thinking—"

"Excuse me." A middle-aged woman leaned into our conversation. "Do you work here?"

"Yes." My dad and I answered in unison.

"Could you tell me where I could find button mushrooms?"

"Aisle three." Again we spoke together.

The lady looked back and forth between us. "Wow. You two are good."

"We are," we echoed, exchanging amused glances.

The woman shook her head and walked off down the aisle.

"Here's what I was thinking." As if we'd already wasted too much time, Dad picked up right where he'd left off, handing me cans of cranberries and talking at the same time. "I think I've come to terms with the idea of selling the store. To you, of course. But I was thinking we could kind of make the transition over the next couple years. I'm not ready to sit home and take up knitting quite yet. And there are a few things about the business I think I might be able to show you—"

"You think?" I turned a raised eyebrow his way.

One side of Dad's mouth lifted. "Yeah, I think."

"So I don't know everything, yet?"

Dad laughed and rolled his eyes. "Even I don't know everything about this business, yet." He handed me the last two cans of cranberries. "But what I do know . . ." As he stood, he paused and blinked his eyes rapidly ". . . I'd love to pass on to you."

I nodded sharply. "It's a deal."

I bent and stacked the now empty boxes on the dolly to take back to the freight room. Dad picked up the empty cranberry box and carried it in one hand. The other he threw around my shoulder as we began walking toward the back of the store.

"Got a question for you," he said.

"Yeah?"

"This guy who's gonna buy my store . . . he might need a good loan officer." Dad pulled me close in a sideways hug. "Know any?"

Leaning into his embrace, I replied through my big, silly grin. "I do."

Claire

"Claire? Are you awake?" Jim's whispered voice filtered through the light sleep I was falling into.

"Hmmm?" I rolled over and pulled the covers up to my chin. I really didn't want to wake up. It was late and I wanted to get a good night's sleep. I'd spent most of the day at my computer, putting the finishing touches on the edits for my latest book. Tomorrow I planned to hit Westwood Mall at the crack of dawn . . . well, make that the crack of ten, and make a big dent in the long Christmas gift list I'd made. Jim had put in a full day at the store, and followed that up with a Chamber dinner meeting this evening. The fact that we hadn't talked all day didn't mean we really needed to catch up now . . . did it?

"Claire?" Jim whispered again. I felt the covers on his side of the bed pull back as he crawled in next to me.

This could go either way. I could pretend I didn't hear him and drift off into dreamland, or I could let him know I really was at least partially awake. Right now my brain was voting for the acting job.

Besides, what could Jim have to say that was so important? We'd developed an uneasy truce going into Christmas. I still thought Jim owed Drew an apology for the way he'd shouted at him two weeks ago. But I'd said my piece and the rest was up to Jim. He knew how I felt. But if Drew, Trisha, and Will stayed away from our house over the holidays I'd . . . well, I didn't know quite *what* I'd do, but—No, that couldn't happen. Jim needed to make his peace with Drew before then.

I pushed the covers off my shoulder. "Did you let the dog out?" My sleepy question would let Jim know I was awake enough that if he had something important to say I'd hear it.

"Yeah. Pesto's down for the count on my recliner." Jim lifted the covers and scooted my way. "Can I hug you?"

The fact he had to ask made me feel guilty. My affections of late had been mechanical. Not only had the whole business with Drew affected Jim's and my relationship, his heart attack and bypass surgery had left him keeping a kind of emotional distance of his own. Even though I was still perturbed at him, I'd missed my husband's arms around me more than I cared to admit. And the thought that he could have died while I'd been off speaking and that I might never have felt his caress again . . . ever. *Oh, my.* Maybe it was time to let Jim know that, in spite of everything, I wanted to be close to him. I loved him, stubbornness and all.

"Sure," I said, ready to turn his way. Before I could roll over, Jim snuggled himself up behind me, tucking his knees behind mine and putting a warm arm around my shoulder, cupping my hand in his.

"Feels good," I murmured.

"Mmmm-hmmm." If a husband could purr, Jim was doing just that.

We lay together, comfortable quiet between us. Oh yes, I'd missed this all right. Missed *him.* The Jim I used to know. Ever since he'd gone back to work full time, daily life slipped back into a familiar routine. I had no speaking engagements the month of December, a luxury I didn't understand until I wasn't packing up to head off somewhere every weekend. Once things were smoothed over between Jim and Drew, life might be pretty near perfect again.

What about Julie?

Now why'd I have to go and think about her? My used-to-be best friend.

You're the one who made her used-to-be . . . it's up to you to—

I had enough on my hands with my writing and speaking, not to mention Jim's health issues, and my dad's diabetes diagnosis. Kaylee was talking about starting a family. Reed had a steady girl-friend he was bringing home for Christmas. My life was full. Too full.

Isn't that what Julie told you?

Too busy. My friend's words still stung.

I closed my eyes and curled back against Jim, as if he could shield me from the convicting thoughts. Julie was right. What I needed was a friend I could vent to, share with, hash out the many issues on my plate just now. But how could I turn to Julie when she'd flat out told me I was too busy to have a friend?

Only a true friend dares speak the truth. Even if it hurts. It's you who moved away from Julie. It's up to you to move close again.

But how could I?

Jim nuzzled his mouth against my neck, giving me a kiss, pulling me close, helping to push the thoughts of Julie away. I'd think more about her tomorrow. Tonight I would enjoy falling asleep in my husband's arms.

I snuggled my cheek into Jim's as he planted another kiss on my shoulder.

"This is nice," I said.

Soft moonlight filtered through the bedroom curtains. From deep below the house, the furnace kicked in. Warm air and the mist of sleep sent relaxation through my body. I felt the tug of nearby dreams.

Jim's whisper sifted into my ear. "I talked to Drew today."

My eyes flew open. Had they made amends? Or made things worse? I was walking on eggshells, but I had to ask. "What did you say?"

Jim was quiet for a moment. "That I was sorry."

I stared into the dark. My stubborn husband had really apologized? "Sorry?" I turned a little bit and looked at Jim over my shoulder. "What did Drew say?"

"Well, he didn't say much of anything . . ."

Oh, no. This didn't sound good.

Jim leaned over and kissed my cheek again. "Mostly because I didn't give him a chance. I offered to sell him the stores."

"You *what?*" As if a wave of gladness had come along and flipped me right over, I rolled over and looked into his eyes. In the dimness of the dark night I could feel his smile almost more than see it. "You did?"

"I did," he confirmed.

"What did he say?" I held my breath. If Drew was anything like his dad—and he was—my son might have his own stubborn streak to wrestle with.

"He said he knew a good loan officer who could start writing up the deal."

"Oh, Jim." I reached up and held my palm against his cheek. As happy as I was to know that Jim and Drew had made their peace, I wondered what Jim would do if he didn't have the stores to keep him busy. I wasn't anxious to relive the past months when he'd practically given up on life. "This is what you wanted . . . right?"

The stubble on Jim's cheek rubbed against my hand as he nodded. "It is." He leaned forward and kissed my lips, then rolled onto his back, pulling me into that favorite spot where my head nestled in the curve of his shoulder. I snuggled close as Jim told me his plans. He would work right alongside Drew for a year or two. Then, when he was confident Drew could go it alone, he'd think about cutting back. Maybe he'd take some time to work on his golf game.

I couldn't resist the opportunity. "Or finally restore that old car in the garage?"

Jim's chest lifted as he allowed a small chuckle. "You know what, Claire? I don't think I ever really had a plan for that old thing. I think I was trying to buy back some of my youth. After what I've been through this past year, I'm ready to look ahead . . . not back. Would you care if I sold it?"

In spite of the amusement I could hear in his tone, I swatted at his arm. "Mind? I'll haul it out myself right this minute if you'll let me."

Jim turned, keeping me close but now facing me. "Maybe we can get at that tomorrow. I have another idea what we could do right now."

So . . . my husband—the husband I knew and loved—was back.

Later, when I was drifting off to dreamland for the second time of the night, once again Jim's voice filtered into my sleepy, happy thoughts. "What did you say?" I murmured.

I opened my eyes just a crack. Jim lay beside me, on his back, his hands resting behind his head. "I can't believe how good it felt to say 'I'm sorry.'"

"Hmmm." I smiled as I tucked his comment away. What he'd said was exactly what I needed to hear. I turned onto my side and pulled the covers around my shoulders, snuggling into the warmth of the blankets. More than likely it would take more than a day to get rid of Jim's old car in the garage, but that was okay with me. There was something else far more important on my agenda for tomorrow.

I needed all the sleep I could get to be ready to face the day ahead.

I held the cordless phone in my cupped hands on my lap and stared down at it. Was I really ready to make this call? Closing my eyes, I whispered one more prayer. *Is this what You want, Lord?*

Trust Me.

I thought I had been trusting Him. But my life had gotten so out of whack, my relationships strained—

You weren't focused on My will. You were chasing after yours.

Ouch. The truth had a bite to it.

Okay. I double-checked Wesley's number and then punched it in.

"Claire! How are you? I'm so glad you called." Of course Wesley was happy to hear from me. My books had put his small publishing company on the radar screen of the book world. "Would you believe I was getting ready to call you? I had another idea for the Friendship Factor series last night. Listen to this—"

"Wesley," I interrupted, "uh . . . that's why I'm calling. I—"

"Hear me out, Claire. I think you'll love this."

In my mind's eye, I imagined Wesley pacing with the phone pressed to his cheek. "We've done the Friendship Factor for twenty-somethings, thirty-somethings, and forty-somethings. And, you know we have the rest of the books mapped out for the fifties and beyond. But I was thinking . . ." Now, in my thoughts he stopped and slowly moved his open palm through the air, as if imagining his idea painted in the sky. "How about if we change the concept a bit and do something like *The Friendship Factor for Neighbors?*"

For neighbors? Was he kidding? My silence only spurred him on.

"And then we might look at *The Friendship Factor in Business.* We could start a fresh series of—"

"No."

"Excuse me?"

"No." I hadn't meant to blurt it out quite like that. "I can't, Wesley. I'm sorry. I know you've been pleased with the way this series has taken on a life of its own. But in the process I've been losing mine."

Poor Wesley. He wasn't my therapist. I had no right or reason to dump my troubles on him. But I was grateful for the chance he'd given me, and he deserved to know why I had to back away.

In the briefest way possible, I told him how Jim's heart attack had been a wake-up call and sent me—sent Jim *and* me—on a new journey. A path I hoped would lead back to my family and friends. To the close relationships I longed for. My treasure wasn't in the money I was making, or standing up on a stage with hundreds of people waiting to hear what I had to say. The riches I wanted couldn't be bought. They could only be earned through a different kind of investment.

"It's time . . ." I paused. It was hard to say what came next. Was I really sure this is what God wanted?

"Time?" Wesley asked.

Even though he couldn't see me, I nodded. "It's time for me to step aside and let someone else tell their stories."

"Step aside."

"At least for now."

"You aren't? You can't . . . ?"

"I'll finish up the manuscripts we have under contract." *Please, Lord, let this be what You want. Trust.*

"What about the Friendship Factor seminars we have planned?"

This was getting harder. *Am I supposed to walk away from everything?*

I first called you to teach.

"Wesley, I don't have this all figured out yet." I was praying as I spoke. "But I'm thinking it might be good to keep doing a few seminars a year. Not as many as I've been doing, mind you."

"No. That's okay." There was relief in his voice. "I understand. Maybe I expected too much. I never had anything like this happen before and I got caught up in it all and—"

"So did I." A weight the size of a hundred cases of books seemed to lift from my chest. As I hung up the phone, the smallest of smiles turned up one side of my lips. It hadn't been so hard after all.

I only hoped what I had to do next went half as well.

"Did you find everything you need?"

"I hope so."

The clerk behind the checkout counter at the Book Nook rang up my one item. "Thanks," I said as she handed me my bag.

I walked over to the coffee shop section of the store and sat down at one of the tables. I hoped it was "legal" to sit in the space without actually sipping on anything. "Frosty the Snowman" played in the background. The perfect tempo for the way I was feeling today. Like all things were possible. Even snowmen who came to life . . . and friendships resurrected from ashes.

Reaching into my purse, I pulled out my favorite pen and opened the calendar I'd just purchased. I had an idea . . . what I thought was a good idea. But who knew if Julie would feel the same way?

"I'd like a gift card, please." I named the amount.

The clerk's eyebrows rose. "How much?"

I repeated the figure I'd come up with, and smiled while she rang up my purchase.

Now that I was standing on Julie's doorstep, with a wicked, cold December wind threatening to blow me off her porch, my good idea of the morning was starting to seem not quite so good. In fact, maybe it was stupid. Maybe I should turn around and forget about it.

You'll never know until you ring the doorbell.

I lifted my shoulders and buried my ears into the wool scarf wrapped around my neck. I looked down at my gloves, at the calendar held in my freezing fingers. What if Julie thought—

Ring the bell!

If God was going to yell at me, it was probably best to listen. I pushed the chime before I could talk myself out of it.

Maybe she wasn't home. All this angst for noth—

"Claire! What are you—?" Julie didn't look as surprised as I'd imagined she might. Quickly she stepped back from the doorway. "Come in. It's freezing out there."

"You're not kidding." Whether it was the cold

wind at my back, or my tumbling emotions propelling me, I practically jumped into her house. "Thanks."

Julie closed the door behind me and turned to face me. Now that I was inside in the silence of Julie's entryway, my grand plan didn't seem quite so great. "Are you busy?" I asked, not missing the irony of *me* asking if Julie was the busy one.

"No," Julie said.

Any other time, I would have simply walked right past Julie, into her kitchen, helping myself to coffee, a glass of water, whatever . . . chattering away. Today, all our former familiarity was gone.

I wanted it back.

I lifted the unwrapped calendar in my gloved hands. "I brought you something."

Julie's eyes darted to my gift, then to my eyes. "Oh, Claire. I didn't get you—I didn't know if . . ."

"It's not a Christmas gift. It's a . . ." I didn't know what to call the offering I had in my hand. Julie was the plain-talking, just-say-it person in our friendship. Maybe it was time for me to try her method on for size.

Pressing the calendar between my elbow and my side, I pulled my gloves off my hands. "Here." I thrust the calendar her way. "I know I've been a lousy friend lately . . ."

"Claire, you—"

"Julie. I need to say this."

As if biting back her words, Julie pressed her lips into a thin line. "Okay."

"Do you remember that day at the Book Nook? When I was there with my laptop and you were with—" I remembered, I just didn't want to say the name of Julie's new friend.

Julie nodded.

"You told me I was too busy to be your friend." I couldn't look at Julie when I said this next part. I turned my gaze to the floor. "You were right."

In the silence between us, I heard the sound of a grandfather clock I knew stood around the corner from where we were standing.

Now I lifted my eyes. It was important for me to look her in the eyes when I said what I'd come to say. I drew in a deep breath, steeling myself for what came next. "I'm so sorry."

Julie simply looked at me for what felt like an eternity, then her eyes filled with tears, and the corners of her mouth turned up in a trembling sort of smile. "I've missed you so much."

I was surprised to find tears rolling down my cheeks, too. Jim was right, it did feel good to say "I'm sorry." I held out my arms and Julie stepped into my hug. "I've missed you, too," I said through my tears. "In more ways than you'll ever know."

Both of us sniffling, Julie stepped back a half-step. "What is this?" she asked, holding the calendar between us.

"It's a clean slate," I said. "Well, not exactly 'clean.' Open it."

Julie looked at me kind of sideways, an expression of happy puzzlement on her face. "January," she said, as she opened the first page. I watched as her eyes moved over the squares marking the first month of the new year. She started smiling. "Coffee with Claire," she read aloud. "Coffee with Claire. Coffee with Claire." She looked over at me. "Once a week all month?"

"Look at the other pages," I prompted.

She paged through the months. "Coffee with Claire. Coffee with Claire. Once a week all *year?*"

"Okay," I said moving my head from side to side. "Maybe we'll miss a week here and there. You might get sick of me by August. Maybe February!" I dug in my coat pocket and pulled out the rest of my offering. "Here." I held out the gift card.

"What's this?" Julie took the small plastic card from my hand.

"It's our coffee card for all of next year. Paid up. All we have to do is show up and drink it. And talk, of course."

Julie threw back her head and laughed. Long. Loud. And oh-so-sweet. A sound I'd missed much too much this past year.

She pulled me into her arms, holding the calendar around my back, as if sealing the promise of time together between us. "A year's worth of coffee *and* my best friend back," she said. "This is too much."

More tears pushed their way into my eyes. My heart felt as if it might break from happiness. Jim and Drew had made peace. I had my husband back. And now my best friend. Too much happiness. *Thank You.*

I held my friend close. "You're right. It is too much. But it feels so good."

EPILOGUE: TWO YEARS LATER...

Claire

"Gama!" My grandson came barreling through one of the store checkout lanes and threw his arms around my legs, nearly tripping me in his excitement.

Untangling myself from his enthusiastic embrace, I scooted us out of the way of the shopping cart being pushed our direction and knelt down in front of Will. "Hey, there." I smiled and pushed his tousled hair into some semblance of order.

In a flash, he ran his hand through his hair and undid the little bit of a style I'd tried to create. Oh, well. In the past two years, I'd learned my grandson had a personality all his own.

A gray-haired shopper, who seemed to recognize Will, stopped near us. She had a paper sack of groceries in her arms. "Is this your grandma?" she asked Will.

Will nodded, seemingly proud as punch to have me there to show off. "She's *old*," he said.

The woman caught my eye and laughed. "If he thinks you're old, I don't even want him guessing my age." She turned to Will again. "How old are *you?*"

"Three," he said, holding up four fingers.

I helped him bend his little finger down and catch it with his thumb. "He'll be four in a couple months," I explained.

"Ah," the woman said, lifting her chin in understanding, "a couple months when you're three can feel like years, I suppose." She reached out and patted Will's head. "I've seen you here. You're a good helper."

Will stuck out his little chest. "I work here."

"I know," the woman said. "I saw you helping your dad over there." She gestured to her left.

That seemed to remind Will of something. He pulled at my hand. "Gama, come watch me!" Will practically dragged me to the detergent aisle, where his dad was busy stocking merchandise.

"Hey, Mom." Drew stopped what he was doing and gave me a quick hug. "You ready to take this little guy for the rest of the day?" He ruffled his hand against Will's already unruly hair.

"I not little." Will was struggling to pick up one of the heavy Tide detergent bottles. He was staggering like a sailor with sea legs, but somehow he managed to push the container onto the bottom shelf.

"Good effort, Buddy." Drew passed on the compliment, then added, "But we've got to move the container up here." He pointed to a shelf higher than Will's head. "See?" Drew asked. "We've got to keep the ones that match together."

"Match," repeated Will. His eyes darted from the red-orange bottle he'd just shelved to the several identical bottles on the higher shelf. Squatting a bit and using both hands, Will pulled his detergent container from the shelf. "Dad, help me," he said. "Watch, Gama."

In a well-practiced move, Drew whisked little Will off the floor and lifted him third-shelf high. Will pushed the bottle into place, and as Drew set him on the floor, Will dusted his hands together as if he'd been stocking shelves his whole life. When it came right down to it, he pretty much had been. Half of it, anyway.

Déjà vu. Watching Drew and Will work together was akin to stepping back in time, back to the days when Jim started taking over the store from *his* dad. Back to when I was busy at home with Reed and Kaylee, and Jim would bring Drew to work to give me a break. Fast-forward thirty-some years, and Trisha was home with one-year-old Sophie, and I, *Grandma,* was on the docket to watch Will for the remainder of today. We were going to have lunch together at McDonald's . . . our not-quite-every-week treat, and then I'd take him back to the house for a couple hours before bringing him home. Between preschool, his short stints at the store with Drew, and his often-as-possible afternoons with me, my grandson was one busy little guy.

"Ready to go?" I held out my hand.

Will raised one finger. "Minute." He picked up one more detergent bottle and gave a *lift me* look to his dad. In one more swoop, the father-son duo had completed their maneuver.

"Can I help you, ma'am?" My husband, Jim, snuck up from behind and gave me a peck on the cheek.

"My," I said, rubbing the spot where his lips had been, "this is the friendliest store in town."

Jim pretended to doff a hat my way. "Westin Foods. At your service."

I still marveled at the many ways Jim had changed since his heart attack and surgery. After the initial bout of depression he'd gone through, his attitude had done a one-eighty once he'd made up his mind to sell the store to Drew.

Even now, as they briefly compared notes on some sale-related products that were out of stock, I could see a kind of zeal in Jim that hadn't been there a couple years ago. It was as if helping his son succeed in this business meant more to him than any success he'd had on his own.

Jim bent down and picked up Will. "How about if I walk you two to your car? And then I need to hit the road."

Will's eyebrows furrowed. "Grandpas don't hit roads."

Jim wiggled a finger against Will's tummy. "This one does."

"Got a full load?" Drew asked.

"Yup," Jim confirmed. "Got my route all mapped out."

I'd have had to be blind to miss the proud glint in Jim's eye as he referred to the online grocery order and delivery service Westin Foods implemented once Drew got his hands on the business. An idea that had overwhelmed Jim two years ago had put Westin Foods on the map around town. Working couples, stay-at-home-moms, and senior citizens didn't mind paying a small delivery fee to have their weekly groceries delivered to their doorsteps. A service the big-box stores didn't offer. Jim loved driving the customized Westin Foods van as often as it worked into his semiretirement schedule. Between serving on the bank board, his community volunteer work, and helping Drew, my husband was almost as busy as he'd been before he sold his business.

I buckled Will into his car seat in the backseat of my car and gave Jim a wave as we each climbed behind the wheel of our vehicles and drove away. I marveled at the fact that Jim seemed to find new purpose in getting up each day, now that he was helping Drew rather than running the whole grocery operation himself. The only area where father and son clashed was when it came to money. Drew offered to pay Jim a salary, hourly wage, or whatever Jim would accept. Every time Drew offered, Jim waved him off.

"Dad," Drew protested one evening after dinner at our house, "you can't work for nothing."

"I'm not," Jim said, leaving Drew to wonder how, exactly, Jim did his calculating.

I knew. Jim told me he was getting more—

"Gama! Gama!" Will was yelling at me from the backseat.

I'd been so lost in thought I'd almost forgotten my not-quite-four-year-old grandson, who was a big part of my plans these days. I caught his glance in the rearview mirror. "What?"

"McDonald's!" He swung a hand across his face and pointed somewhere behind us.

"Oh, good grief." I checked my mirror and switched lanes. I'd driven right past Will's favorite hangout. "You should be driving," I told him.

"I can'ts drive."

I took a quick right and swung around the block. "Apparently, neither can your grandma."

In short order we pulled into the parking lot. Will ran ahead of me, propelled by the tug of chicken nuggets and a prize.

"Do you remember Grandma is going to be gone for two weeks?" I reached across the table and helped Will pull the foil from the dipping sauce packet.

"Yup." He'd already stuffed two fries into his mouth.

It was hard to understand how a once-a-week date for lunch and playtime with an almost-four-year old could leave me feeling so bereft at the idea of leaving for fourteen days. It was a feeling I was ready to accept as the price for being attached at the heart to my grandson. "Grandpa will be gone, too."

There went a chicken nugget down the hatch. "Okay."

Okay? Oh, to be so accepting of what life had in store.

Trust.

A familiar tingle ran up my spine. There was that word again. The word that had been guiding me through the past two years. My book contracts had been fulfilled. And I was living life without the *homework* of a contract hanging over my head. Wesley was pleased with the residual sales of my books, and the additional sales that came from the book table at the fewer Friendship Factor seminars I was now leading.

Speaking of which . . . "I'll miss you," I told Will, trying to swallow a bite of my burger through a tightened throat.

"How many sleeps?"

In spite of my emotion, I managed a smile. If I hadn't spent so much time with Will, I wouldn't have a clue what his question meant. But, the good news was . . . I knew exactly what he was asking.

"Fourteen sleeps until Gama and Grandpa get back to Carlton. Can you count that high?" I knew he was good up to ten, but—

"Yup."

"You can?" When had he learned this trick?

Will dipped a fry in ketchup and held it in the air. "One, two, three, fourteen."

"Well, there you go." If only the time apart would pass that quickly. Then again, the time I'd spend with Jim on this Friendship Factor speaking swing, would be just as precious. Time we wouldn't have had if his heart had quit beating for good. Come to think of it, I wasn't going to wish away any of our time together.

I dug in my purse and pulled out a small, colorful makeup case I'd gotten free with a cosmetic purchase. Unzipping it, I held it open so Will could peek inside. "Gama has a way for you to count how long until she gets back."

It took Will only a nanosecond to recognize his favorite chewy candies. "Starbursts!"

"There's fourteen," I said. "You can have *one* every day, and when they are all gone, Grandma and Grandpa will be back."

"I'll eat fast," Will said, completely missing my math puzzle.

I'd give the bag to Trisha when I dropped Will at home. She could dole out my treats, a sugary substitute marking the days.

"Can I have one now?" Will asked.

"I brought an extra one. You can have it when you're finished with lunch. But you can't eat the ones in the bag until Grandma and Grandpa leave in two days."

He broke a french fry in half. "Gotcha."

Gotcha? This kid was changing before my very eyes. What might I have missed if I hadn't listened to the voice that had told me to *trust?*

"No," I said, reaching across the table and tweaking Will's cheek between my thumb and forefinger. "I've got you."

Will's eyes followed my hand as I tucked the imaginary piece of him I'd plucked off into my purse.

Will smiled, clearly onto my little trick. "I go along," he said.

"You bet," I replied, patting my purse. "You'll be right here." But I knew where he'd really be was somewhere much closer to my heart.

"I'm going to heat this up a little." Julie pushed herself away from my kitchen table and popped her coffee mug into the microwave. We'd been gabbing for over an hour, our conversation dancing around everything but the two weeks I'd be gone. As Julie waited for her coffee to heat, she picked up a stack of travel brochures from the table. "You're leaving tomorrow?"

"Crack of dawn," I said. "Since this is our maiden voyage, Jim wants to allow extra time in case we have to stop and figure things out."

I glanced out the window at the long, gleaming recreational vehicle in our driveway. It had taken Jim and me almost two years to talk ourselves into buying a motor home, but now that we had it, Jim was itching to get out on the road. The fact that I had a Friendship Factor seminar in Memphis, Tennessee was a good excuse for us to test out what Jim was calling our "RV"—our retirement vehicle. The two-day seminar was our only agenda. The time on either side of the conference was all ours.

"You're going to be gone two weeks?" Julie asked. "Who am I going to vent to?"

"I'll have my cell phone." I pointed to my purse on the kitchen counter. "And, believe me, if Jim and I are together twenty-four-seven I might need to vent a lot more than you."

Julie took her mug from the microwave and walked back to the table. She sat down, and then reached to the side and pulled the fancy, pink gift bag she'd brought along with her this afternoon onto the table. "I brought you some . . . things you might need on your trip." She pushed the gift bag my way.

When I'd seen her walk in with the pretty bag, I'd figured she had something up her sweater sleeve, but I waited until she was ready to reveal her surprise.

"You didn't have to do this," I said, pulling a sheet of pale pink tissue paper from the top of the bag. "But," I grinned at my friend, "I'm glad you did."

In quick succession I extracted Julie's treats—make that *my* treats. A bag of Crunchy Cheetos, a favorite only my best friend knew I loved. A yellow bag of Peanut M&M's. Strawberry licorice sticks.

"I'm going to weigh a ton by the time I get back," I protested, even though I was tempted to open the Cheetos right then.

"I have an ulterior motive," Julie admitted. "By the time you get back, you're going to need our walks together to get back in shape."

I reached out and put my hand on hers. "I don't need any excuse to get together with you."

"I know." Julie looked down at our hands, and then at me. "You haven't left yet, and I already can't wait until you come back. You're going to have all kinds of adventures to tell me about."

I squeezed her hand. "Hey, don't forget, we've got an adventure of our own planned."

"May twentieth," we said in unison.

We laughed together, too. I was going to be speaking at a mother-daughter tea in Grand Forks and Julie was going to be my sidekick, helping with my book table, and more importantly, helping all the miles I'd have to drive to get there to pass so much faster.

As I started to put the treats Julie had given me back into the bag, she said, "Wait, there's one more thing in there."

I lifted the bag. It felt completely empty. I peeked inside. Except for another piece of tissue paper, it looked empty, too. Pulling out the pink paper, I peered into the bag. Sure enough, there was a small plastic card lying on the bottom of the bag. I pulled it out, then laughed. "A coffee card to the Book Nook."

Julie gave me a silly smile. "The way I see it, I still owe you about a year's worth of coffee."

"That's right," I teased, "you do."

My friend looked out the kitchen window at the RV in my driveway and then back to me. "I wanted you to have something to look forward to when you get back."

I wiggled the gift card between my fingers. "Coffee's good," I said, "but knowing it's with *you* . . ."

I didn't have to say the rest. I knew that Julie knew exactly what I meant.

"Bon voyage." Jim leaned forward and started the engine of our RV. The engine of the monstrous vehicle caught and roared to life.

I turned and looked toward our house. Had I unplugged the coffee pot? Yes, I had. It still felt as though I was forgetting something. *Pesto.* Ah, our faithful companion would have loved this trip. He'd died of old age six months ago. There was nothing more I needed to tend to . . . except the miles ahead.

A strange sort of excitement trilled through me, as if I was headed off to summer camp for the first time . . . with my husband, no less. I shifted in the plush passenger's seat, settling in. "I feel like I should run outside and crack a bottle of champagne against the fender."

"Don't," Jim said. "With my luck we'd drive over a piece of glass and get a flat before we even leave our street."

"Okay, I won't." I smoothed my hands over the atlas in my lap.

"Here we go." Jim put the vehicle into gear and smoothly pulled us away from the curb, our car towing easily behind.

At least I hoped it was behind us. There were so many bells and whistles on this fancy contraption, we were going to have to trust we'd get the hang of things as we tooled down the road.

I was glad our first hundred miles would be on less traveled highways. It took some getting used to, sitting so high up off the road in our buslike vehicle. Two hours later, as we pulled onto the interstate, I found myself relaxing a bit

. . . and then ducking as we went beneath our first underpass.

"Sheesh!" My heart flipped like a fish out of water. I looked over at Jim. He was grinning—a big boy with his big toy. "You're loving this, aren't you?"

He didn't take his eyes off the road. "Yup."

I settled back into my seat. As long as Jim had things under control, I was going to page through a magazine. I pulled a copy of *Midwest Living* onto my lap, but instead of reading, I found myself mesmerized by the scenery passing by outside. Rolling hills. Flat prairie. A horizon that seemed to go on forever. Jim and I had talked about a variety of things we could do after this maiden voyage of ours. Volunteering with Habitat for Humanity. Serving as greeters in one of the national parks. The world was our oyster . . . or at least, with this RV, the United States was. Anticipation thrummed in my chest, down my arms. *Here we come. Here we come.* There was a whole new world waiting for us to discover in the days ahead.

"Ready for lunch?" Jim asked. We'd driven for hours since our light breakfast at home.

"I guess," I said, hoping the things I'd packed in the fridge had ridden along as smoothly as everything else seemed to.

Jim slowed down and turned off at the next exit,

parking our RV at the far end of a truck stop parking area.

An hour later, all that was left of our turkey and Swiss cheese sandwiches were crumbs. I downed the last of my skim milk while Jim finished chomping on a carrot stick. A handful of travel brochures sat between us. I started sifting through the possibilities.

"Oh!" I said, holding a pamphlet Jim's way. "I've heard the Biltmore Mansion is fabulous."

He took the colorful leaflet and opened it. As he studied the photos and the map on the back, I continued to rifle through the travel guides on the table top. Branson, Missouri. Nashville and the Grand Ole Opry. They all were on our way . . . or could be. After my seminar in Memphis, we could tour Elvis's mansion, then head to Nashville. From there, we could cut over to Asheville, North Carolina and take in the Biltmore. And from there, the Atlantic Ocean wasn't that many more miles away. The potential adventures in my hands suddenly seemed too much to take in. I rested my palms on top of all the places we could go.

"Jim?" I waited until he looked my way. "Did you ever think we'd have the chance to—" At a loss for words, I gestured to the travel guides on the table.

Shaking his head and chuckling softly, he put down the brochure he was holding. "Honestly? I was always so busy trying to stay one step ahead of things in the grocery business, or following the kids and their school activities, if I ever thought about taking a trip, it was more of a fantasy. Someplace I could go that would take me away from all the worries I had. I guess I never had a *place* in mind. Just . . . *somewhere* and . . . *someday.*"

I smiled at my husband. "And now it's *someday.*"

"And we get to pick the somewhere." He shuffled through the pamphlets, as if they were a deck of cards. No matter which one ended up on top, we'd be the winners.

He set down the brochures and again shook his head, as if he couldn't quite believe how he'd—we'd—gotten to this place in life.

"You know what's funny?" Absently, Jim rubbed the spot on his chest where his heart surgery had started us on this path toward retirement. "I look forward to going to work more now than I ever did before Drew took over." He squinted at me. "Does that make any sense?"

"It does if you're not trying to wheedle out of any of this trip." I raised my eyebrows, questioning.

Jim laughed. "No, I'm not trying to wheedle out of anything. I want to go on this trip. With you."

A comfortable silence surrounded us in our new home-away-from-home. The kind of quiet that made asking certain kinds of questions easier.

"Are you happy with the way things turned out?"

Jim paused while he traced a finger along the edge of the tabletop. Lifting his eyes, he captured my gaze. "Very. I'm very happy."

"Me, too," I said. "Although sometimes I wonder if there isn't something more I'm supposed to do. Do you ever feel like that?"

My husband worked the side of his cheek with his tongue. "There was a time when I thought the point was to work as hard as I could and make as much money as I could. Working with Drew, I've discovered what I've been doing is not one bit about money." He paused. "It's about *meaning*. I can't tell you what it means to me to have Drew—"

Jim gave a small cough and started blinking fast. The operation on Jim's heart had left him with a soft spot when it came to his family. A tender spot that touched me every time it nudged him.

I blinked right back at my husband. "Look at us. Two old softies."

"Be careful who you're calling *old*."

I smiled. "You don't care about the softy part?"

One side of his mouth turned up. "Nah, not so much."

Reaching across the table, I squeezed his hand. He squeezed back and then tapped the table with his fingers. "Ready to hit the road?"

"Ready," I said.

Jim did a quick walk outside around the RV. I

put the lunch dishes away. Then we both climbed into our seats and buckled up. Jim started up the engine and pulled back onto the highway.

As the miles slipped beneath our wheels, I found my thoughts drifting through the past. Raising the kids. Running the grocery store. My teaching. Writing. Jim's heart attack. Somehow, all that was behind us. But it didn't seem as if we were driving away from anything. Instead, it felt as though we were driving *toward* something.

Toward the rest of our lives. And suddenly, I couldn't wait to see what lay ahead.

A note from Roxy:

Thank you for reading *On a Someday*. I couldn't have written this book without help. I want to thank Darren and Shelly Deile (of Stan's Super Valu) for giving me a behind-the-scenes look at the grocery business. When I needed details concerning some of the medical issues in this book, Sarah Carlyle, cardiac nurse extraordinaire, appeared out of cyberspace to assist. Thank you! A special thanks to my sister, Kim. When the challenges of writing this book seemed too hard and high for me to conquer, she listened (and sometimes laughed) until I was ready to get back at it.

While I'm not quite over the hill, I'm not exactly a "spring chicken" any longer. The subject of retirement, and what to do with the rest of our lives, seems to crop up more and more in the conversations I have with my husband (and my friends). In *On a Someday*, my intent was to explore the time frame leading up to retirement. How does a person decide they've worked long enough? Are we ever completely "done" with work? Is there a time to turn over the reins to someone younger? While I don't have the definitive answers to these questions, I have given some thought to a myriad of possibilities. I've concluded there is a "second act" waiting. I'm excited to see what the future holds!

Conversation Questions

1. What is the difference between being so adept at your job that you no longer need to give it your all, and realizing you've grown complacent and need to do something to shake things up a bit?

2. If you are growing tired of your job, what are some things you could do to challenge yourself?

3. Is there a job you sometimes dream of doing? What is keeping you from pursuing that dream? Money? Education? Fear?

4. Have you ever felt too old to stay in your current profession? Is there a time to step away from certain occupations? How do you decide when it's time to retire?

5. Is there a certain *age* when you think it should be mandatory to retire?

6. Young people need opportunities to learn a profession. Talk about mentoring. How is this beneficial to both the younger person, as well as the more experienced worker?

7. Are we ever "done" with work?

8. What would you like to do "someday"?

About Roxanne Henke . . .

ROXANNE SAYLER HENKE lives in rural North Dakota with her husband, Lorren, and their dog, Gunner. They have two, very cool, adult daughters, Rachael and Tegan, and two equally-cool sons-in-law, Cory and Dave. As a family, they enjoy spending time at their lake cabin in northern Minnesota. Roxanne has a degree in Behavioral and Social Science from the University of Mary and for many years was a newspaper humor columnist. She has also written and recorded radio commercials; written for, and performed in, a comedy duo; and co-written school lyceums. She is the author of seven previous novels.

You can reach Roxy through her website at: *www.roxannehenke.com*

Center Point Publishing

600 Brooks Road ● PO Box 1
Thorndike ME 04986-0001 USA

(207) 568-3717

US & Canada:
1 800 929-9108
www.centerpointlargeprint.com